MW00574367

# A THOUSAND TIMES BEFORE

# A
# THOUSAND
# TIMES
# BEFORE

## Asha Thanki

VIKING

VIKING
An imprint of Penguin Random House LLC
penguinrandomhouse.com

ISBN 9780593654644

Printed in the United States of America

*Designed by Meighan Cavanaugh*

*for my nanima and nanabapu—*

*in acknowledgment and honor*

# Part One

# DAUGHTER

N adya, the first time you told me you wanted to be a mother, I froze.

It was after our third date, do you remember? I'd invited you to the art gallery. When you arrived, I played coy, picking up glasses of champagne, greeting guests. I might have even avoided your eyes. You felt important; you reminded me of something I'd witnessed but not yet experienced. Maybe this feeling was superficial—a lust for your hair, your smile, the way you moved in that burgundy dress. Maybe it was the way the light caught your arms and danced shadows along your skin. But that sense of your importance deepened with every sentence you spoke, every thought you shared. I wanted to hear every word in every language in your voice. I think I knew, even then, that I could spend lifetimes listening to you.

When I finally mustered the confidence to say something, I overexplained each of my sculptures, nervous. You kept prompting me: "What's the story behind this one?" and I kept answering.

Afterward, in your apartment, we shared secrets over wine. *Tell me something you've never told anyone else.* You went first. You told me you wanted children so casually and with such certainty, as though you could see them fully realized. You made no mention of your partner in that vision, and I didn't ask if you thought it could be me. And though you meant no obligation or pressure by this description of your future—I balked.

Something in my expression made you laugh and shrug it off, say, "I'm skipping too far ahead." You pressed your glass to your lips, and while I lifted mine, I didn't drink. In that moment, I wanted to say so much to you about my future—*our* potential future. It wasn't the right time, though I didn't know when the right time would be.

And then seven years passed, just like that, and I kept waiting to not be scared of how much you meant to me. Instead I grew frightened of you not believing me—of losing you. I thought, time and again, that I should tell you all of this plainly, with no overtures or introductions, but it felt too raw, too risky.

So maybe I'd spit it out, a strange sentence weighted with generations of expectation. You'd run; I'd memorize your back, curls bouncing as you left. Maybe I'd hedge forever until we landed, unhappily together, at the end of our lines, you still wondering why I kept secrets from you, what they were that could be so important.

Or maybe—maybe I'd tell you first about the stories my mother told me when I was a kid. Stories about her mother, and her mother's mother, and hers before her. She never ran out of them, always ready with a new one when I asked about a woman whose name I'd never heard before. When I was old enough to ask her if the stories were gifts or curses, my mother had shaken her head.

*They are an inheritance*, she'd told me.

I still haven't understood how to tell you, love, that there is—was— something literal in my mother's words. That the choice I made on our third date was to bide time until I figured out how to share this history and have you peer into it with me.

I have spent so long considering *how*.

See, Nadya, all of this has happened before. All these choices—to bite one's tongue or not—have already been weighed by other women before me. Each made the choice to have a family, to pass her story along through them. I know some of them doubted—I can remember this doubt, I dream of this doubt—but every single one of them found circumstances that made them answer *Yes. This is what must be done. I will have a child, and I will give her my secrets.*

I want to lie in bed with you and kiss the tip of your nose and explain to you that there are moments when it's no longer me in my body but the memory of someone else. To explain to you that it's been this way for a very long time. I might be meditating or in that liminal space between waking and sleeping, but mostly, this happens when I'm at work, my hands covered in drying, cracking clay, when I've hit a particular rhythm with a sculpture. Then I feel the memory of one woman, or them, or us, all together—it's hard to discern where I begin or end sometimes, Nadya—and my body and my art are no longer my own. The memories of all the women who came before me have control of my hands, my ears, my tensed neck. I hole up somewhere in the background of my own mind. I feel small in these moments, minuscule compared to the lineage taking control of me.

I have wondered if you can tell when it's me, and when it's me, accompanied. Maybe you know where I begin and end. I can barely remember myself—not sure if I am me or a sum of lives. What am I but the calcium in my bones, strings of genetic material from my mother, and hers, and hers before her? All of this has been asked before.

The last time we had dinner with your parents, joking about future grandchildren and cooing over your cousin's baby, you covered your mother's hand with your own. "Children probably aren't in the cards for Ayukta and me, but it's okay," you told her. "We're so excited for Amar and Zainab, aren't we?"

You looked at me reassuringly.

My heart sank.

You'd given up on me. When had that happened? Had you said these words to your mother before, running interference in the privacy of phone calls and solo visits? I never meant for my lack of answer to turn you away from the one thing you'd envisioned so clearly. You, who have always been so certain. Who shared, on that third date, on our fourth glasses of wine, the silhouette of your future. Whose eyes fill as we watch your nieces for your brother, when our friends announce their pregnancies.

In that moment, my fear transformed: no longer that my withholding would make you leave, but that you would *stay*, and it would break you. It had already begun to. Seeing you make room for what you thought I desired, this quiet sacrifice—I could no longer be a coward.

I thought of nothing else on the subway home from dinner, and then I booked that flight to my father's house. I left abruptly, I know; I'm sorry for that, for so much. These underwhelming explanations, my silences, end after today.

The *how* is not important, I know that now. It is only the telling that matters.

So here we are: You've come home with a brown bag of takeout in your hands. You kiss me hello and undo the bag's staples with punctuated movements. The air fills with the scent of coconut and peanut sauce as you remove the plastic containers. When every dish is displayed on our coffee table, you finally look over and read me; your eyebrows furrow with concern. I tell you I have something—a long and overdue story—to share. I must appear as anxious as I feel, twist-ing the rings on my fingers, knee jittering. Because you nod to me, I nod back.

"I'm worried you won't believe me," I say, pulling a folded tapes-try from its place beside the couch into my lap. It sits heavy on my thigh—scratchy, the fabric a near-black charcoal.

We sit frozen in silence—your eyes confused and my breathing too loud and too quick—until you break it.

"A story?" you ask, voice masked in a deliberate steadiness.

I nod.

"Then tell it to me like one," you say, "and maybe I'll understand."

# ONE

I tell you about Amla's childhood first—Karachi, 1946.

The sun beats down heavy this morning, air so thick you can choke on it. Everyone is lethargic: market vendors stretching out the prices of their goods, women beating clean laundry to a slow metronome. Even the autos groan at a glacial pace.

Amla watches from her perch on the balcony ledge, one leg hanging outside and the other placed firmly on the floor. She wraps her tongue around a thick cone of pistachio kulfi. The melting cream drips down her small hands, collecting in the nook between her index finger and thumb. Every few moments, she pauses to suck absentmindedly at the puddle, teeth biting down on the small flap of skin.

She likes to watch the bustle of the street, likes to imagine that she is weaving and bobbing among the crowd. There's something about the safety of one heel touching the rough concrete of the balcony that helps her daydream about outside.

This is how life goes for ten-year-old Amla. She eats breakfast with her mother every morning, just the two of them, her father already having eaten and left their home for the shop downstairs. She used to wake up at dawn to the smell of ghee as her mother made rotli, lingering in those moments that define an early goodbye, but dawn feels earlier and earlier in that way that days do as one gets older. So now she eats later in the morning, a simple meal of chaash and chickpea-batter snacks—her father already in one of the three mithai shops they own, mixing warm milk and sugar and saffron with a wooden spoon—and then she and her mother head together to the market, canvas bags tucked under their arms, and they return in the sun's midday heat to their home, bags full.

Amla likes this pattern; she likes how nothing changes, each day with Ba and Bapu feeling like the day that came before. The consistency comforts her, as well as the knowledge that her world is not so tumultuous, that she can spend the afternoon sucking on kulfi and everyone she cares for will continue to live their lives around her. The banal, this unfazed tempo, the days that pass you by as you blink— they are things she will never stop loving, especially once they cease. Then—and this stays in the blood, too, burns into the memory, *our* memory, the feeling lingering for generations—it will become a craving, a drug to yearn for: the sleepy haze of a life full of nothings. Breakfast with Ba. *Blink.* Pots of water on the stovetop, bags of fresh vegetables looped over their shoulders. *Blink.* Afternoons of tutelage spent doodling on her slate, nights of thin cotton blankets tucked up to her chin. *Blink, blink, blink.*

"Amla, come help," her mother calls from inside.

Amla swings her leg back over and onto the balcony, hurrying to wash the melted sugar off the palms of her hands. In the living room, Ba is taking down a heavy length of fabric that's been hung from two rusting nails embedded in the wall. As Amla inches closer, she realizes the cloth is not a sari or a blanket but a tapestry, so heavy with

10

embroidery and mirrors that it sags between her mother's hands. Small stitches etch scenes into the black cloth's surface, familiar reds and greens emphasizing row after row of women marching, their faces all in profile, some with the hands of young babes in their own and others linking arms with the women before or after them. She squints; the images dance, creating black spots across her vision.

The tapestry has hung on the wall for all of Amla's short life thus far, and still, she barely remembers it. She reaches up to touch the stitching, but Ba tsks. "Grab the ends for me," she says. "Help me fold it."

Amla takes the edges nearest her, holding her arms up high to keep the tapestry from collecting dust off the floor. She studies the images more carefully now, up close—oh, these women, parading behind one another, the colors of one skirt fading into the edges of the next. Bay leaf green melds into mustard yellow melds into purple, red. She finds herself losing focus, her head rushing, as though her blood were suddenly coursing warmer through her veins. *Ba*, she thinks. *Dadima. Mama. Ma.* A mother. Her mother, and hers, and hers before hers before—

"Focus on the corners," her mother directs, and the moment is broken. Amla shakes her head, scratching at her neck.

"What's—"

"Just focus on the edges, and I promise it won't be so distracting."

They stand across from each other, folding the tapestry like a sari. The cloth is halved lengthwise, then adjusted at its corners, and then halved again and again until it is a small square. Already, Amla feels herself forgetting the design stitched onto the tapestry's surface.

She turns toward her mother, ready to ask for answers, but instead her gaze catches on her mother's angles. The lines of her nose, her chin. Her long fingers, the now-useless iron nails she's rolling between her index finger and thumb. Her shoulders, their sharp edges. Ba leans forward and Amla realizes her mother is totally enraptured; Amla might as well not be there anymore. Amla is in awe of her awe, wanting to know the connection to this square of fabric, to name this feeling her mother already seems to understand.

"What are you looking at?" she asks.

"These are the people who came before us, Amu," her mother says. "They're all here."

"Are you there?"

"Yes," she says.

"Will I be on there?"

"One day."

Amla doesn't know what this means. But Ba takes Amla's hands in her own, intertwining their fingers, and they sit in silence with the folded tapestry between them.


**Ba packs the tapestry** into her valise alongside new saris, gold earrings, and leather flats, all in preparation for a wedding in Delhi. In turn—and this is the nature of the tapestry, not the fault of a forgetful child—Amla's memory of the fabric blurs, the naked wall becoming part of her reality once again.

Outside, the shouts in the street are shifting in tone. Amla isn't sure exactly why, and while I want to tell you what words are used, and in what way, and who is standing on the soapbox on the corner of the street, Amla doesn't recognize them, and that's not what matters to her.

It's not the *who*, anyway, so much as the *how*. The tension, the urgency. The pleading.

I wish she'd paid more attention, but it isn't necessary. You and I both know how this history goes, Nadya. There is less than a year before the partition. If Amla had listened, she might have understood that heaviness in the air outside the window. She would recognize the repeated words, if not the implications of them. Outside, vendors cluster together over copies of the *Sind Observer*, knuckles rapping against crisp newspaper; inside, the hushed exchanges extend late into the night, framed in her parents' familiar Gujarati. Amla peeks through her closed eyes, a single lamp at the kitchen table illuminating Ba's and Bapu's faces from underneath. She's not good enough at pretending; Bapu always halts once she's awake, no matter how hard she tries to breathe deeply and evenly.

"Let her be young," he will say. "Ten is a hard age already."

She feels safe at home despite the words stirring outside, the ideas some call dangerous. Amla doesn't know that she should be scared; she just knows the way her father asks her mother if she really wants to go to the wedding in Delhi, if this is the right time, if they should wait for the younger niece's marriage instead and give an extra elaborate gift with their apologies.

"But it's fine here," she hears Ba protest, "and it's fine there, too. If we're not worried here, why would we be worried about there? Why tell me not to go? What logic should we follow, never travel anywhere again?"

Bapu doesn't answer.

Their home is going to have new syllables; this is the only real information Amla knows. She cradles the word at night like a doll. *Pakistan*. She practices the way it sounds in her mouth. *Pakistan. Pakistan.*


**Bapu's sister visits the apartment,** delicately wrapped gifts under her arms and in her hands. She tumbles over her twin toddlers as they cross the doorway. Amla grabs the handles of the gift bags over the children's heads as Meenafai apologizes. "I didn't want to bring them, but Monty is sick and I thought, if I leave them with him, they'll also—"

"It's nothing, please." Ba, ever the embodiment of grace. She disappears into the kitchen. "Have you eaten? Your brother should be up any minute now—"

"Oh, I stopped by the store on my way up. He said he's closing, but I didn't want to wait with these hooligans around." Meenafai flops onto the daybed, leaning back against the wall. She closes her eyes; her children poke each other, the continuation of a squabble that began on their way over. "Please, don't feed me."

Ba emerges with a plate of mithai. "Amu, bring us chaash?"

Amla nods and retreats to the quiet space. She pours the mix of yogurt and water from its cooled clay pot into cups, mixing in cumin and salt and asafetida. The front door clangs open and shut just as she strips two leaves from Ba's mint plant.

"Meena!" Bapu calls in greeting.

There's something intoxicating about these siblings when they are together—Meenafai, the wife of a priest, her seven children always underfoot; Bapu, his crinkled eyes and gentle smile with one missing tooth on each side. Ba smiles, becoming a fly on the wall in their presence, soaking in the nature of a family constructed within the safety of its community.

Meenafai has done everything proper and reaped the benefits: she has given her husband sons; she has managed their home and the temple, overseen their staff, guided her husband through business investments. In return, she has some hold on freedom: her husband is twenty years her senior and uninterested in her social appointments, needing only her energy, her propriety, to maintain his respectability. This is how Meenafai ends up on the daybed, slouched and sighing, guard let down in front of her brother and his wife.

When Amla returns with the tray, she catches her mother's eye.

Ba shakes her head almost imperceptibly—*Don't make your presence too known*—and Amla knows to sit still after everyone has taken their cups, to just listen.

"There is a lot of talk, bhai, and I don't know how much of it is true." One of the toddlers is on Meenafai's knee, and she runs her fingers through his hair as she speaks. "My husband has been meeting with the maulana to make sure there are no tensions here."

Amla perks up at the mention of her friend Fiza's father as Bapu leans back in his chair, nodding gravely. "That's good."

Meenafai turns to Ba. "I hear they're still protesting at Red Fort. You're going to leave tomorrow?"

Ba looks from her husband to her sister-in-law. "I— Yes?"

"I mean, it's an impossible choice." Meenafai takes the child off her lap, and he scurries to find his twin on the other side of the room. "How can anyone know what's best?"

Ba looks down at her hands. "It's the same thing every few months. Stay here, and Karachi might erupt like it did with the navy mutiny. Go there, and Delhi might erupt because of protests." She closes her eyes. "If it's impossible to know one way or the other, am I going to miss the first wedding of my sister's children? I don't know. I don't know."

Amla doesn't know what her mother means by this—*the same thing every few months*—but you know the history as well as I do, Nadya. At the height of that year's monsoon season, in July 1946, Jawaharlal Nehru had given a speech determining that Hindustan would be partitioned. When Amla listens to the men in the street, when they wave their newspapers, she hears the consequences of that announcement rippling out, further and further.

Bapu pulls his gold case of cigarettes from his breast pocket, his sister beckoning for one. He nods slowly, twisting the home-rolled cigarettes between his fingers. He opens his mouth to speak.

Does he tell her to go? To stay? Amla is distracted by the way the light plays off of the steel sugar tin and reflects on her mother's hands. Does he tell her that the wedding is worth it, that they cannot put their lives on pause when they don't know which tinder might catch, when the fire might end? Amla will grow old never knowing. Does the answer matter? What Amla will carry forward from this moment is the image of her father's eyes trained on her mother. There is something pure in the way he looks at Ba, as though she is haloed. Amla recognizes this as love.

In the evening, after Meenafai has left and the kitchen's been cleaned, Fiza knocks on the apartment door, asking if Amla is free. Amla is relieved Bapu doesn't question whether or not she has completed her tuition homework; he simply lets her go. The two girls walk toward the Muslim gymkhana, the evening air brushing off the water and raising goosebumps along their arms. Amla tugs at the wrist of her kurti with her fingers, having ignored her mother's reminder to grab a shawl on her way out; it is November, and she always forgets how the cooler weather sneaks up.

The building is lit up, large lanterns in its cupolas refracting across the property. Autos arrive and women in fancy saris disembark, their partially pinned pleats draping off into the crooks of their arms, clutches held at their sides. Fiza's father officiated the nikah earlier that day—a small family affair, largely paperwork—but now the guests are abundant and radiant.

The two girls lean on the back of a bench, pretending not to look but taking stock of the guests. "This auntie," Fiza finally whispers. Amla looks over, eyes focusing on the mole high on her friend's right cheek as the game begins. "She just found out her son wants a love marriage now that he's returned from the war."

Amla hides a giggle behind her knuckles. "How about that one?"

"Oh, he's unhappy but he can't show his parents. His cousin just got into the medical college, but he couldn't pass the exam."

"And them?"

Fiza pauses. The group Amla's noticed has stopped a yard away from them, one of the men bending down to help a woman back into her heel. It feels intimate to watch, this type of touch.

"He's Muslim and she's Hindu, and they're going to break up in a few months if Karachi becomes a part of Pakistan. She'll have to move. Like your family probably will."

"And not yours?"

Fiza kicks at the ground, dirt encasing the toe of her shoe. "Baba says we are supposed to stay."

Amla watches her friend's legs swing through the air. Something between them seems to sit heavily.

I think I should slow down how I tell you this part. Fiza—she matters more than I realized. It is impossible to tell you what I need to tell you, without her.

There is no friendship for Amla like this one. She doesn't know exactly what it is, but her connection with Fiza feels deeper—more important. Maybe it's that they have so much of their lives in common: the same favorite dessert (kulfi), the same dislikes (okra and the boy two apartments down from Amla's). They share a love for imaginative play: In the evenings, Fiza and Amla meet on the roof of Amla's apartment building, where clothes dry on lines stretched from one side to the other. They play hide-and-seek, or Fiza reads aloud while Amla listens (Fiza's further ahead, her brain better at holding all the required scripts in one place). Sometimes they drape themselves in the drying saris and pretend they're both someone else, somewhere else: queens with palaces overlooking the water, with servants to fan them and bring them fruit, with young men draped in white arriving to recite ghazals to them. Amla will feed Fiza pistachios and they will pretend they are eating something more exotic, something they've never seen before, brought by ship from a place far away, and worth pounds of gold.

Their lives are also both framed by minarets and spires: Fiza's father is a maulana at one of the larger mosques in the city, while Amla's uncle is a priest, a pandit, at the mandir in her neighborhood. Amla doesn't know what the inside of the mosque looks like, but when she spends mornings with Meenafai—stringing marigolds and jasmine blooms together in preparation for different pujas, placing ghee-dipped cotton balls into bronze lightholders—she imagines Fiza and her mother doing the same.

There are days when Fiza feels like Amla's opposite, though. Fiza speaks up more; she's stubborn. She always has a plan for their days together. Amla can feel Fiza coaxing her out of her shell, beckoning her to participate in the world. When she returns to the apartment after an evening together, Amla wraps herself in her covers and wishes she could be more like the person Fiza believes her to be. Sometimes, in the dark, she thinks she is only real because Fiza sees her. She hopes she returns the favor; she hopes Fiza feels more like herself in Amla's presence simply because Amla sees her.

**When Amla returns to** the apartment after the gymkhana, the sky already dark, she is shaken. The thought of separation from Fiza scares her. "Pakistan," she whispers to herself, back against the closed door. "Pakistan."

Ba waits for her in the living room, the gas lamp casting a warm glow around the room. She is taking a night train, and her packed valise is on the floor by her feet. The space feels empty already. Amla feels childish, but she wraps her arms around her mother's waist and squeezes. "Wait," she says. "Don't go."

"I'll be back before you know it," Ba says, tousling Amla's hair. "And I'll bring you something special." But Amla's face reveals her concern, and Ba adds, "It's going to be okay."

"Are we supposed to leave?" She tries to remember what Fiza had said. "Are we on the Hindu side? Do we go where the Hindus go?"

"These lines seem clear but they're not, really," Ba says, leading them into Amla's room, beginning to tuck Amla into bed.

Amla squeezes her mother's hand. "Tell me, then. Bapu doesn't tell me anything."

"Your Bapu will never say this, but he's scared." Ba's voice quiets. "So am I. These are big questions with no easy answers. You want to know our side?"

Amla nods.

"Your Bapu's people have always been from this place, from the villages outside Karachi. This is the land of your Bapu's people, of Sindhis, and some are Hindu and some are Muslim, but they all speak Sindhi. Same topis. His family is here. Our family—your family."

"Not your family?"

"My family is Gujarati, not Sindhi, Amu." She tucks Amla's hair behind her ear. "But we're not so different, your Bapu and me, even if his family is here and mine is somewhere else."

They sit in silence for a minute and then a few minutes more. Amla imagines where her mother's family is, in that place she has never seen. These people who are apparently on her side, too, whatever that may be.

I shift my focus to Ba. She is remembering something far more specific: her hasty wedding ceremony, the sister who attended, the father who did not.

"There are so many things in this world that can pull us apart," Ba says, kissing her daughter's forehead. "Sometimes the people we call our own are worse than the ones we point our fingers at."

Amla still wishes she could go with her mother, not understanding what compromises her parents have made around safety. She thinks of the month ahead of her: making rotli daily, delivering the tiffin to her father at the shop downstairs, both of them pretending her attempts are as good as Ba's. She'll meet Fiza after her lessons, their hair in mirrored twin plaits, and then sketch her mother, over and over, on the charcoal slab. Ba's lines, her angles. They burrowed into Amla's mind at a moment she can no longer recall.

"Can I go with you?" Amla's voice is soft.

"Oh, Amu," her mother says. "We talked about this. You know you can't."

Amla sniffles. She wants to be strong for Ba, but she ducks her head, hiding fresh tears.

Ba kneels on the floor and takes Amla's small hands into her own. She squeezes Amla's palms, her thumbs. "Amu," she says. "You want something to make it easier?"

She leaves the room briefly, returning with a wooden box that she places onto the bed. "I was going to give this to you when I returned from the wedding, but maybe you should have it now."

The box is an unstained teak, with splinters at its lower edges and a brassy lock. Amla looks at her mother hesitantly, asking permission, and then traces her fingers over the grooves along the lid's perimeter.

"Hari uncle told me you were drawing instead of doing your maths homework." Ba laughs. "If you're going to do it, you might as well do it right." She presses a finger to the lock, and the box pops open. Amla cranes her neck, folding her hands underneath her thighs, knees bopping with nervous energy.

First, an open compartment filled with small pencils and pans of color; next, two brushes, one thin and one thicker; and then papers, at least twenty, full stacks that have been drawn upon. Amla squints. Is it the same image, repeated, on each page?

"Last year, I saw this man's paintings in the street," Ba says, her voice burning softly with excitement. "The way the goras stopped and stared at his work. To think, one of us, showing his own paintings so openly and to such attention. I thought of you."

She hands the papers over to Amla, who squints at the fading pencil lines in the dark. Amla was right: Each has the same image four times on the page. Each time, the image is interpreted slightly differently. The scenes feel incredibly ordinary—a woman readjusting her hair, or filling a basket with water, or leaning over a child. They don't feel like what Amla understands a painting to be: those elaborate images of noblemen, a world foreign to her own family. No, the people in these drawings are familiar. They might as well depict a neighbor or the woman selling dried dates on the street.

"These are copies of real paintings," Ba explains eagerly. "He sketched each one out before he put the paint down. You see how he mapped out angles? You see the light he's playing with?"

Amla nods. She feels like she might throw up.

Ba sighs. "I wish I had more for you, Amu—wish I could have brought him here and made him teach you. Will this do, for now?" Her voice is tentative. "Do you think you can try to understand how he learned?"

Amla cannot say a word. It isn't that she doesn't understand; in fact, she feels the opposite, that it is easy to understand how the artist had taken down the world around him. No, what she cannot express is how much this gift means to her. At ten, Amla is at a precipice—old enough to understand that her mother wishes she could do more, too young to have felt that heartache for herself. Too young to carry the burden of knowing you cannot give your child what they desire, but trying to provide it anyway. To ask a man selling his paintings for his scraps, his drafts, because you know you will never be able to afford to take your child into an archive, will never be able to purchase a photograph or a copy of one of the paintings.

"This is perfect, Ba," she says, and she hopes her mother will understand.

Ba's shoulders relax; Amla hadn't noticed the tightness in her body. Ba points to the box. "Once you get the drafts right, these are watercolors. Be careful with them. Don't pack them without drying them, okay?"

"Yes, Ba."

"Clean the brushes when you use them, don't stain anything, and keep it out of your father's way."

"Yes, Ba."

"And if you think something's really good, sign and date the piece. You'll look back and see how you've grown." She smiles. "Okay?"

"Okay."

Ba takes the pages back, tapping them down on her knee into a neat pile before placing them into the box again. "Take care of you and your Bapu, Amu. I love you, jaan."

Amla's blood rushes warm. She wraps her arms tightly around her mother's narrow shoulders, feels Ba's heart beat as fast as her own. "I love you," she whispers, committing this moment to memory. Even when Bapu and Amla wave goodbye to Ba at the train station, even when he coaxes her to stop crying with five jalebi—even then, she can only think of the watercolors, how she wants her first painting to be of the gas lamp on the windowsill and the splinters extending outward from the teakwood box.

**The next morning,** the apartment feels empty. Bapu doesn't wake Amla before heading downstairs to the mithai shop, and she stirs only when the sunlight warms her back so much she is sweating. She stretches lethargically, pulling on one of her favorite kurtis, and braids her hair haphazardly in the mirror.

*Not as good as Ba would do it*, she thinks.

She meets Fiza and the neighborhood girls on the rooftop. Watching these friends play clapping games, she thinks that none of this compares to what she shares with Fiza when it is just the two of them. She wouldn't ever bring their imagined palace into this public space.

Fiza calls Amla over to where she and some of the older girls are sitting in a circle, huddled in the rooftop's corner. Amla takes the long way, cutting under and between bedsheets strung across the roof, breathing in the smell of damp cotton. As she gets closer, the scent turns earthy. In the center of their circle is a bowl of ink, a combination of ash and bark, and one of the girls has a hand-poke needle tight between her fingers.

Amla raises her brows, and Fiza stands and takes her elbow, steering them away from the group to walk the perimeter of the rooftop.

"What if you told your father you could live with me? With my family?" Fiza asks softly.

A breeze rustles the clotheslines, bringing with it the taste of ocean salt. Amla opens her mouth to speak but pauses. She wishes she had a pencil and sketchbook in front of her, anything to avoid this question sitting heavy in the air.

"Your parents could live with us, too," Fiza continues after a minute. They round the first corner of the rooftop. "We'd make it work. My mother wouldn't mind."

"That's not true," Amla mumbles, picking at her shirtsleeves.

"I don't want you to leave, Amla."

She looks up at Fiza's eyes, the quiet pleading. "I don't know what Bapu wants to do."

"He doesn't talk about it with you?"

Amla shrugs. They round the second corner and cut between clotheslines, back toward the group. "We spend most of our time talking about Ba's sister and the wedding, or what's going on at Red Fort. Bapu says there are protests where Ba's going."

"Don't you think about it?" Fiza's hands have been outstretched, her fingers touching the laundry to both sides. Now they slash through the air, punctuating her words. "Don't you think about what leaving will mean?"

"Not being in Karachi?"

"We won't see each other."

"Maybe, by staying, you're the one who's deciding. To not see each other."

Fiza huffs. "That's not fair."

"I don't even know if we're leaving," Amla says, but she is thinking about the aunties who cycled through the living room when Ba was home, the way they whispered about steamboat tickets and whose were already purchased.

Amla's palms are clammy. She feels the nape of her neck grow moist. What could she say that might hurt the most—something is tender in her belly, reacting to Fiza's misconception that Amla has *chosen* anything at all—and she suddenly is running through the list of possible retorts: *You're not a true Hindustani if you stay*, like a man in her father's shop suggested to another; *Your father is putting you in danger*, like the man with the bhutta told the boy-customer in front of her; *Maybe you're the one who isn't in charge of her own life*. That one is all her own.

They turn back toward the group without saying any more, and Amla tries not to view Fiza's silence as judgment.

"I want one," Fiza says suddenly, stopping by the older girls. She looks at Amla. "Will you do it for me?"

"I . . . I don't know how." Amla squints, watching one girl squirm while her arm is tattooed.

"Leila can guide you, it's not that hard," Fiza says. "She learned last week. Something simple. Like . . . like your mother's trajva."

Amla thinks of the geometric pattern at the base of her mother's throat—four solid dots, the corners of a diamond. She imagines this on Fiza's throat, or the inside of her wrist. She imagines holding Fiza's hand closely in order to complete the hand poke herself, and she blushes.

"Where would you do it?" she asks.

Fiza steps one foot forward. "Don't you think?"

Leila, who had moved over after hearing her name, hands Amla a pencil and a piece of paper. "Draw it out," she says, and Amla does, and Leila shows Amla how she lights a match to sterilize the needle, long and silver with a rubber band wrapped around its center. "Makes it easier to hold," she explains. "So you go at an angle, and about *this* deep—"

Amla holds the needle between her fingers, the older girl coaching her through loosening her grip, and she looks up at Fiza. "I don't know," she starts to say, but Fiza shakes her head.

"I want you to do it," Fiza repeats. "That way, if you leave—" and Amla understands.

Leila squeezes Amla's shoulder. "I'll coach you," she says, and Amla nods. Fiza scoots closer, holding her leg by her knee, and Amla tries to keep her hand from shaking. With a deep breath, she dips the needle into the ink and begins to pattern the trajva across Fiza's skin.

# TWO

Amla's memories of Karachi will always be tinged with a sentimentality, an irreplaceability, so mine are, too. I describe Karachi to you with my eyes closed, as if I were not me but her. Let Amla tell you about how much she loves this place, how much it feels like home. How unaffected she is by change here; so young, she hadn't believed the voices outside might lead to a fundamental shift in her own life. She has never before had to worry about such things. What can Amla understand of separation, of nation-states and religious difference, of Hindustan, when she is surrounded by Hindus who eat halal and Muslims who light fireworks with her on Diwali? When she lives in a place that textbooks will acknowledge as almost peaceful during the coming summer of Partition, even if that peace is only relative, doesn't last—eventually succumbing to the bloody history you and I have heard about our entire lives.

Her comforts are in their means: the sweet shops her father owns, one inherited from his father and then grown into three locations.

Their spacious apartment, the neighboring aunties and Meenafai who serve as a second tier of guardians whenever needed. Years before she was born, Bapu had spent a summer apprenticing in the princely state called Porbandar, had considered settling along that coastline. But Meenafai had written many letters to convince him otherwise: She found the port in Sindh more beautiful every day; she saw more opportunity for him here; their people are Sindhi, and why would a Sindhi ever want to leave Sindh?

In the end, when Bapu was not yet Bapu, just a teenager named Anurag, he mostly considered staying in Gujarat for a girl who lived on the very outskirts of the city, so far it might as well have been the start of the next village. He had taken a job clerking for an uncle who was slowly losing money, all just to linger in those extended months. He wanted time to make this happen.

Chandini, the young girl who walked into the uncle's shop those afternoons, trajva at the base of her throat and along the backs of her hands—she dreamt of a life with Anurag, too. But when Anurag visited her home in an attempt to win over her parents, that dream seemed to fall apart. Though Anurag promised that he came from a moneyed and respectable Sindhi family; tried to translate Sindhi castes into more rigid Gujarati ones; tried to incorporate local slang into his Gujarati; brought chocolates, the expensive kind—still, Chandini's father looked at her, gesturing to their obviously Kutchi home, the embroidery adorning every cot and seat. He asked her quietly, tersely, "Have you no pride?"

That night, Chandini made a choice. In the bedroom she shared with her sister, that familiar tapestry draped on her cot like any other blanket, Chandini drew herself in Karachi with Anurag, charcoal staining her fingertips. As she drew, her hands began to move of their own accord. She was no longer alone in her body. In this dreamlike state, she drew a pathway to the man she was convinced was the love of her life. The next morning, when she saw the drawing, she couldn't remember making it.

This was how she knew it would come true.

The next day, on a midday walk along the chowpatty, when Bapu-before-he-was-Bapu asked Ba-before-she-was-Ba if she really wanted him to leave for Karachi without her, she said no. She described to him the route they would take: a quick ceremony, a journey by steamboat to Karachi, Meena there to meet them and help them settle into their own apartment. She had seen the drawing. She had faith.

**"Wait," you say,** the bowl of takeout still uneaten in your hands. "What do you mean, she painted it and knew it would come true?"

I try to find the right words. "I'll get there, I promise."

You sigh. "Look," you say, setting the bowl down on the coffee table. It clatters, the steel chopsticks rolling away. "I know I said you could tell it to me like a story, and I appreciate everything you have shared so far, but . . . Can't you just tell me? Do you have to start so far back?"

"This matters," I say.

You grimace. "Don't be facetious."

"I'm not." I pinch my throat. "I swear."

Stay with me, Nadya.

"What could be so important you have to go back generations?"

I shift in my seat. For the first time in years, I am being completely honest with you. It's a relief; it's the most difficult thing I've ever done. "Everything has to do with these generations," I say. "It *all* goes this far back. It goes even further—before Amla, before Chandini."

"What all?" you ask. "What everything?"

I think of a hundred ways to phrase it—the heaviness I carry, the generations on my back. "Please, if you can bear with me, Nadya," I say instead, "I promise I will not let you down."

**Meenafai has been teaching Amla** to make athanu in the two weeks since Ba's departure to Delhi. Together, they cut mangoes into cubes, mixing in turmeric, salt, and crushed jaggery. The sweet syrup sticks to their hands and Meenafai directs Amla to pour mustard oil on top, to wrap the cheesecloth around the bowl and tie a thick thread around the rim to seal it. After, they clear the potted methi plants to one side of the balcony ledge, making enough room for the big bowl to sit in the sun.

"Seven days," Meenafai directs, "and use one of these big spoons to stir it every night."

By the time the telegram arrives, the athanu has been sitting out on the balcony for two days too long.

CHANDINI KILLED IN RIOTS SIXTH OF DECEMBER *stop* ANTIMA SANSKAR COMPLETE *stop* VALISE BY COURIER

I am grateful that you don't ask me how Ba died. I can find the scene in my blood if I have to, and the suspicion that comes with her death remains with the daughters after: a hesitance to walk into large crowds, a wariness of white men in uniforms. A desire to hold a dupatta closer and closer to the body. The pain lingers. In these times, there is something dark in my ability to dream up alternative scenarios: that Ba was instead caught in the trajectory of a stray Molotov cocktail thrown by young boys wanting to get in on the action; that Ba was hit by a flying rock in a melee; that on a regular, quiet Friday, a cricket ball hit the back of her head as she walked by the grounds one late afternoon.

These help me sleep.

The telegram arrives for Bapu nine days after Ba passes. He doesn't show Amla the card, spares her from having to read the words. He sits her down to share the news. He lets her yell, screams that leave her own ears vibrating. She hides for the rest of the day among the mess of his and Ba's shared closet, where dupattas remain scattered across its floor.

She knows he holds the telegram close. Sometimes she sees his fingers touch his breast pocket, brushing aside his folded spectacles to hear the soft compression of hard paper. She will see the telegram only years later, when she knows enough about the world to know that this message would have cost one rupee—a single rupee, the smallest cent—for sixteen words, and that the uncle dictating the message at the telegraph office had determined the death of her mother to only be worth this much.

Bapu's eyes stay red rimmed; he has his head shaved. Amla forgets what he looked like before. He seems smaller, his kerchief almost always in hand. He loses weight; she sees his cheekbones as he puffs his cigarettes. She rolls her rotli over and over again until they are perfect rounds. Bapu makes excessive amounts of chaash, already spiced in a glass for her when she wakes. They do all they can do.

And in the meantime, there it is—the moment when that dull ache begins. The ache will stay with Amla—will stay with her daughter, and hers after her. I feel it even now.

**When her mother's suitcase arrives,** Bapu tells Amla it is hers to sort through. "Your Ba would want you to decide what to keep," he says, voice caught in his throat, kerchief wiping roughly at the bags beneath his eyes.

She unzips the valise in front of her parents' bed, breath held. Her

small arm arcs over it in one fluid motion. First there are her mother's shoes: flat mojari with a small tongue licking upward at the front.
Then there are the kurta pyjamas for household and night wear, made
of thin single-color cotton. There are the jewelry boxes, necklaces resting on cheap red velvet; there are the new saris, never worn and still
perfectly packed. Amla carefully pulls each heavy sari out of the valise and onto the bed. She unfolds the meters of embroidered cloth—
once, then twice, each motion stretching the fabric across the place
her mother used to sleep.

When two saris lie across the bed—one peacock blue and the
other a royal purple—Amla reaches her hand back into the suitcase.
But the cloth is heavier than she expected; not as bright as the others, either.

The small mirrors in the black fabric catch light from the window,
make it dance across the ceiling. Amla hesitates, remembering a feeling of unease when looking directly at the tapestry. But this time her
heartbeat stays steady. Her breathing, slow. She glances down: she
can see the stitching in its every detail.

The tapestry's design is startlingly clear.

Amla traces the women marching across the cloth, each woman
leading into the next. She tries to count, but it seems impossible; there
are so many, more than forty, as though the fabric is never-ending.
When she arrives at the final figure, Amla balks. It's newer than the
others, the embroidery fresher against the black tapestry. The hand
of the last woman has been adjusted, and the brighter colors of this
woman's hand hold that of a child, a girl older than a toddler and
younger than a bride.

This is how she knows, without understanding why she is privy to
this knowledge, that her mother died slowly, that she spent enough
time in a bed to finish this last segment of the tapestry. Memory, grief,

truths—all knock at a door Amla doesn't yet know how to open. She only knows intuitively that this child-figure on the tapestry is Amla herself.

Bapu's house slippers scratch along the floor when he trudges into the room. "Bapu," she says quietly, fabric clutched in her small arms. If she says too much, she knows she will cry. So when he stands before her, she only asks if he remembers the tapestry, if he knows when Ba had placed it on their living room wall. If he knows what it means.

"It seems familiar," he says, and he sounds confused. "But maybe she bought it on the way to Delhi. Your mother, she loves—loved—these Gujarati folk colors."

"That's not true," she says.

Bapu's eyebrows furrow. "What?"

"It was on our wall before she left."

Bapu shakes his head. "Are you playing pretend?"

Amla stares at him, wondering why he would lie to her, if he is. She remembers the tapestry so clearly now, the way that it had hung on the wall. She knows she'd helped Ba take it down before the trip. She remembers wanting to draw Ba's figure, all her straight lines and strict angles, during those moments when Ba's awe felt tangible. She runs her fingers over the embroidery, and there it is again, memory knocking at that door. Her mother's hands running along that same stretch of thread. So many hands—weathered and wrinkled, slender and taut.

This is how she learns Bapu cannot provide her with the answers she desires.

Amla folds the fabric around herself that night and the next, imagines Ba holding her close. She can hear her father shuffling around the kitchen, aimless, unwilling to be alone in the bluish dark. Does he remember the time when he would not risk waking her up, would not risk Amla overhearing the next bit of news? When Bapu returns to his room, he closes the door, but she still hears him cough, sob. Some nights, she hears him retch. When he does this, she pretends she is asleep, knowing he would recoil from her if she mentioned this nightly routine. Instead she settles deeper into her cot, replacing the caress of her mother's bones against her back with the tightness of a cloth that refuses, no matter how much she tugs it closer, to hold her in return.

**Once, the summer before,** Amla asked her mother if all the stories they taught in the Hindu girls' school were true. She had already checked with Fiza: these stories did not appear in the Muslim girls' school curriculum. Sure, she knew that the ones with animals talking and convincing one another to hold higher ethics were fables—but what of the ones with gods, with avatars sent down to earth? Some of the teachers referenced these the way they referenced recent history; others, like the fables. She asked her mother who was right.

Ba was folding clothes that had hung all day in the sun. "Well, no one," she said, "and also everyone."

"What do you mean?"

Ba cocked her head to the side. "If I told you there was a jalebi stand outside our window right now, and Bapu told you there wasn't, and I said you couldn't go check, who's right?"

Amla's knees trembled with energy. "Can I smell it?"

"No."

"Can I ask someone else to look?"

"No."

Amla leaned back on her hands. "I don't know."

Ba motioned for her to stand up, holding out one edge of a large lungi drape. Amla held it as high as she could, trying to keep the bottom from scraping the floor. "If I told you that you might get to have a jalebi tomorrow if you're really good today, what would you do?"

Amla narrowed her eyes as her mother came closer, folding the cloth in half. "Might? Like I maybe still wouldn't get to have it?"

Ba took the edge Amla had been holding high, trading the newly folded corner. "I mean, nobody knows for certain. You might not be good enough today. The jalebi stand might not be outside. But either way, you have to be good if you want one."

"How good?"

Ba continued taking the edge from Amla and handing her the corner until all that was left was an arm's length of cloth. She took the whole piece, folding it in half into a neat, thin square, and pulled the next drape off the clothesline. "I can't tell you that either. If you're really, really bad, though, you'll never get a jalebi. Are you going to spend this entire day focused on the jalebi?"

"I don't know. Maybe?"

"And tomorrow, if you're not good enough? And the day after?"

Amla's eyebrows furrowed with the puzzle. "No, I think? Maybe I just hope I get it?"

Ba nodded. She handed Amla the edge of the lungi. "This is why we don't worry about sides. Everyone wants the jalebi, but there's no way to know if you're going to get it, because it might not exist. So you just keep being you, and don't do anything to have the option of jalebi taken away forever, and be as good as you can be regardless of whether the stand is outside or not. Make sense?"

Amla switched the cloth's edge to her other arm, her left bicep aching. "What about Bapu? He goes to the mandir every day."

Ba paused for the first time in the conversation. "Your Bapu, he wants someone to tell him he's made good decisions. That he's lived a truly good life and deserves that jalebi. He wants a guarantee, even if no one can really give that to him."

"Is that a side?"

Ba shrugged. "Maybe. But Bapu being good should still be more important than him being right. Sometimes, people think they're right and they do things because they think other people are wrong, and then they stop being good."

Amla nodded like she understood.

"Here, do this for me," Ba said. "Promise me you'll be good, no matter what."

Amla pinched at her throat like she'd seen her mother do.

"Don't do that," Ba said, swatting away Amla's hand. "Not on your life. Here. Promise on mine."

Amla nodded, her hand covering Ba's as they pinched Ba's skin together, and Ba laughed and continued to fold the cloth, her elbow bending in and out as she traded edges for new folds in the salty summer breeze.

**During Ba's wake,** aunties rotate through their living room. Their condolences sound like sad bird songs, punctuated by chatter Amla tries her best to ignore.

"—motherless. What will happen to her—"

"—karma, I heard her father had cursed them—"

"—shouldn't have gone there, Chandini knew better—"

Amla picks at the embroidery on her kurti. White threads snake across the white tunic, teardrops and vines and peacock beaks. Meenafai brought it to the house that morning. Amla had never owned white clothing before.

"You'll never have to wear it again," Meenafai had promised, buttoning the back of the neck. She scrunched up the leggings and Amla stepped through them. "You can give it away. Cut it into cloth. You could burn it." She brushed invisible lint off the shoulders. "I'm so sorry, jaan."

The twins squeal amid the aunties' chatter, impervious to the weight in the air. Amla bites the insides of her cheeks to restrain herself from grabbing their chubby forearms, demanding they sit in the corner of the room and keep quiet. She forces herself to sit statuesque.

It is part of a bargain she has struck, in the time since Ba's passing. She can't understand why Ba is gone, why her mother has been taken from her. Once, she had promised on her mother's life to be good—and hadn't she been? Had she done something wrong? No one seems to have the answer Amla yearns for, and so she must ensure no one else can be taken from her so abruptly. No more surprises, no more grief. Whether or not there is a god, she has to try to be good.

*I can make it right*, she promises herself. *If I can be good, everyone I love will be okay.*

From her frozen position, Amla surveys the room. Amla used to imagine she would grow up to be like these aunties: hair pulled tightly in a braid down her back or in a clean bun at the nape of her neck. It wasn't the dream—the dream would be to rub elbows with the British women in their lovely coats and long skirts, to have a table at the Hindu gymkhana reserved for herself and her family, to watch cricket games from *inside* the pavilion each night—but to end up like the aunties had always been the more realistic possibility. Now, looking at their rouged faces, her mother's name mangled in their mouths, she cannot imagine it. She wants none of it.

Amla taps her nails on her tea saucer, anxiety building in her chest. She wants Ba to ask her to go make chaash. She wants Ba to praise her athanu. She wants Ba to walk in through the door and see the bustle and say, *Go, Amu, do your schoolwork*, knowing full well that Amla can't wait to finish school and tuition, and wants only to trace her mother's hands onto her slate in chalk.

Then, suddenly, there is Fiza. For a moment, when she enters the apartment, Fiza looks uncomfortable, registering her own dark clothes compared to those of the aunties milling about in white. But when she catches Amla' eyes, Fiza sweeps into the seat beside her, presses her shoulder into Amla's. She doesn't say anything, and Amla is grateful. Instead they weave their fingers together, Fiza's hand pulsing every few moments, a reminder that she is there.

**They escape to Amla's room,** a reprieve from the aunties. Amla sits cross-legged on the floor in front of her closet, Fiza on the bed, resting her elbows on her knees. The tapestry is draped next to her, fully unfolded, across the bed.

"Do you know anything about what it means?" Fiza asks. "Do you know why it was so important to her?"

Amla shakes her head. "But there's something different about it," she says. "It feels more familiar than it did before."

Fiza doesn't look at the tapestry directly, and Amla is reminded of how unsettling the fabric had been, just weeks ago. How she'd forgotten about it so quickly. She wonders if Fiza will forget about it, too, tomorrow or the day after. But Amla tries to explain it anyway: "This figure, this girl, I think she's me. And this is Ba. And this is Ba's grandmother."

Fiza squints. "What do you mean, that's you?"

Amla can't explain it, so she doesn't. She keeps pointing: "This is my great-grandmother, who was a painter. And her sister, who made small dioramas. And their mother, who sculpted . . ."

"How do you know this?" The skepticism in Fiza's voice—doubt and confusion, all together—forces Amla to stop. She remembers how Bapu had reacted to her questions about the tapestry.

I can hear your voice in theirs. I told you: all of this has happened, before.

"I can barely see them," Fiza continues.

Amla falters. "I look at them," she says, "and I can . . . remember."

"And they all were artists? The way you draw?"

"It's all connected somehow," Amla insists, though it sounds strange even to her own ears. She doesn't know how she has this knowledge either, only that she does. "This tapestry, the art. My mother." She struggles for words, but in her mind the memories connect so clearly: her mother making the charcoal sketch of herself with Bapu in Karachi, the way the tapestry enables her to do this. Other women, taking their futures into their own hands throughout this family history, making choices that shape lives beyond their own—and all of these women's images stitched into the tapestry's fabric.

*From one to the next*, she thinks, but the words almost feel like they are being told to her, not thought by her. The voice is not hers alone. *This is how we carry forward.*

She grabs her sketchbook from its place beside her bed and flips to its middle. "Look at these," she says, pointing to the pages split in four quadrants, just like Ba had taught her to do. It's the same scene over and again, of a crowd of women in her apartment, all but one wearing white. "I don't remember drawing these."

"It's been a lot, lately," Fiza says softly.

"No, you don't . . ." Amla falters. How can she name to Fiza what she feels—that she drew this wake before it ever happened? That she doesn't remember any of it; that she fears she manifested it? "I don't know how to explain it," she says instead. "I just need you to believe me."

Fiza takes her hand. Holds it closely, kisses her knuckles. "Of course I do," Fiza says. Amla wants so badly to believe her, in turn. "It must be so hard, not having your mother here right now."

Amla stares at the tapestry, at this embroidered woman holding her daughter's hand. It is the final time her mother will ever hold her hand, she realizes, and begins to worry about the tapestry. The fragile threads at the edges of it, what would happen if they began to loosen. She folds the fabric up wordlessly, tucking the weighted square into a stack of churidar. She thinks of the voice—not quite hers, but not unlike her own—and worries what might happen if the whole thing came undone before her eyes.

Because Ba died in Delhi, and because the antima sanskar was held there, Bapu does not have the relief of having seen his wife cremated. He has never collected her ashes. When he holds his hands out to the sun to pray in the morning, Amla imagines he feels as empty as she does.

Amla suggests they create a pyre of their own. She has seen the place by the water where pandits, bare-chested, recite rites in a foreign and formal Sanskrit. She does not get close enough to smell charred flesh, but sometimes, when the beach is empty, she walks near the black rectangles in the sand and wonders how strange it would be if, when you were cremated, the wood would burn and dissolve away to leave just a black dust silhouette.

Bapu agrees readily, and together they fill a crate with mementos of Ba. As much as he dreads going through Ba's half of their drawers, he cannot ask Amla to do it alone. So they sit together with the drapes closed, as though the lack of light adds a layer of sanctity, and they choose items endowed with Ba's memory.

Bapu's items:

—a red bandhani-print sari, the one she wore to their wedding;

—a pista-colored sari with blush-pink lotus petals embroidered across its full length, which she wore the first time she met Meenafai and the rest of Bapu's family;

—a pair of mojaris scuffed on the edges and wearing away at the toes, the ones she wore every day to the market and back; and

—a set of three single-color shawls—blue, cream, and purplish-black—that seem insignificant to Amla.

Amla's items take more work. Bapu asks her what she would like to contribute and she promises that she'll have them for him when he comes home from the mithai shop. At the end of the day, when the door closes behind him and he pats his sweating face down with his kerchief, he is greeted by the sight of Amla, three items neatly organized in front of her.

Amla's items:

—the white kurti Meenafai had given her for the wake;

—little bits of precious pigment from each dry chunk of watercolor, held in a triangle of folded paper; and

—pickled gooseberry—amla athanu—the oil leaking through layers of cloth.

They wrap the items in a large red cloth. Tell a pandit at the coastline what has happened. The sunbaked man, with a long graying beard and smelling of sea salt, looks at them and sighs. "It's wrong to do the ritual twice," he tells them.

Bapu has the wrapped items cradled against his chest. He looks like he will burst.

"Panditji," Amla says quietly, "I didn't get to say goodbye."

The priest's eyes soften. He tells them to wait.

The stack of wood is small, and to onlookers it must seem like a child's pyre. They place the wrapped bundle on top, toss rice onto it, toss sesame and mustard seeds. Pour ghee. Bapu leads Amla around the fire once.

The pandit motions toward the still-burning pyre. "What do you want to do with the ashes?"

Bapu shakes his head. "It does not matter."

Amla wonders what type of silhouette will be left in the sand. It cannot be that of a person, no, because her mother's body was never here. Will it be something from the sari—a lotus left behind? She squints her eyes as the flames crackle. The pyre doesn't smell the way she thought it would. As the wood resettles, collapsing onto itself, Amla thinks of the pigment burning under all that cloth and imagines her mother streaked in color.

A week later and Bapu and Amla don't speak over dinner anymore, realizing slowly how integral Ba was to bringing them both out of their shells. They had tried, in the beginning, to hold stilted conversation, but it's easier to focus on mixing the rice and vegetables in front of them.

One day, while Amla is sitting at Bapu's mithai shop counter, a customer tells him that a group of young boys have been killed in a village not far from Karachi's outer limits, their heads displayed on stakes. No one seems clear on whether the boys were Hindu or Muslim. Bapu glances over to where Amla is seated and says, in a sharp, formal tone unlike anything he's ever used with her, "We'll discuss that later." Amla wishes Ba were upstairs so she could ask her mother what this really means.

Meenafai comes by in the evening, and Bapu sends Amla to complete her studies. "You have a lot to catch up on, after that break."

*That break*, she wants to repeat after him, bitterness spiking within her. *You mean when Ba died.* But she leaves him and Meenafai at the entryway to the apartment, the feeling gone as quickly as it appeared. Her entire body tires.

She settles into her usual spot on the balcony, her book for writing practice balanced in her lap. She practices the consonant phonemes of an alphabet over and over. She doesn't ache for her drawing pad; doesn't sketch any angles of any mother.

". . . take a couple of months now, but might take four or five later." Meenafai's voice drifts over from the parlor room.

". . . you don't feel any need to leave?"

Tobacco smoke wafts over. Amla imagines the two of them leaning back in their seats, the gold cigarette case open on the table, Meenafai fanning herself with one free hand.

"We wouldn't. He wouldn't. There's . . . leave this temple without knowing . . ."

". . . should I?"

"If you go and get . . . we could always join after. Easier for . . . with one child, and not seven."

Amla traces over the phonemes. The sharp graphite of the pencil leaves dust trailing behind. She presses the pencil down, down, until a gentle crack reverberates up to her index finger and thumb. She isn't sure if she is angry at Ba for leaving her, at Bapu for not being able to bring her back. At Meenafai, because she knows this conversation will lead to their departure from Karachi. At Fiza, for thinking that holding her hand, saying sweet words, could make anything feel the same ever again. That ache that has settled into her bones, this rising wave of anger . . . She doesn't know where to put it all.

Amla begins to measure the days. One day, two days, three of

Bapu not raising the topic with her. Of keeping her in the dark. She reads it as deception. A full week, another. When Fiza asks why Amla seems different, why she isn't as talkative, Amla grumbles. If she breathes the words, she worries, she will be the reason they come true. But holding this in is so tiring; she finds herself exhausted from seething.

When Bapu finally tells Amla they are leaving, that he will put in for steamboat tickets, that they have only a few weeks, she has no more emotion to give. Her rage dissipates into resentment—a child's cruelty.

"It's because of the Muslims, isn't it?" She throws the words at him, her voice tinged with a pathetic toxicity.

Bapu stares at her like he has never seen her before. He blinks. He removes his glasses. "Why would you—"

"They said so at the mithai shop. Is that why we're leaving? Did the Muslims kill Ba?"

She doesn't feel the tears on her cheeks or the wobble in her knees. But when Bapu rests on his haunches, his face at her level, and places his hands on her shoulders, she feels steadier. "Quiet," he says, voice soft, filled with something Amla can't identify. She goes silent. "You think your Ba would ever stand for you talking like that?"

She grits her teeth.

"Never forget that our people have taken more Muslim lives than they have taken ours. We're not leaving because we're scared of what happened to those boys, whoever they were," he says, his voice return-ing to its normal timbre. "We're leaving because I am scared without your mother by my side."

There are so many questions—*What of Meenafai, Bapu? Why does she get to stay—aren't you scared for her, too?*—that Amla doesn't know to ask.

*Why would a Sindhi ever leave Sindh?*

43

"Are you scared, too?" Bapu asks, and there it is, that emotion Amla couldn't place: sorrow. His voice, tinged with it alongside warmth, forgiveness. "Are you scared without your mother by your side?"

She looks into the depth of her father's eyes. When he points his finger at her face, she can feel the heat buzzing off his skin. "I don't know how to protect you and I don't know what's left for us here. I won't risk staying, now that it's just me and you. You are not alone, whatever you are feeling—but we also do not speak that way in this house. Do you understand?"

She does not move.

"Do you understand?" he repeats, his voice stronger than it has been in weeks. This time, she nods quickly.

"Start thinking of what you'd want to pack with you, in case we get a steamboat ticket sooner than later," he says, releasing her shoulders abruptly. "Take what you need, and Meenafai will keep an eye on the rest." He pauses as he turns away, his voice gentler. "Think of it as a new journey, Amu: to know the place your mother came from."

When he closes the door to the bedroom, Amla begins to sob. She takes the tapestry back out from its place between the folded churidar, and holds it tightly against her chest until her suffocating lungs find air again.


**In early January,** Bapu is able to pull himself away from work long enough for him and Amla to take lunch together. Amla doesn't know it at the time, but this is the ritual's final recurrence—their last meal shared in the shop's back room, right hands mixing rice and ghee and dal together in the center of their plates. Amla breaks their silence. "I wish Ba were here."

Bapu sips water from a steel cup slowly. "Me, too." He pauses. "Did you know your mother hadn't seen her sister in ten—eleven years?"

"That's a long time."

"Yes. When people move away from their cities, it's not un-common."

Amla mixes her rice absently. "Is that what will happen with me and Fiza?"

Bapu stops eating, the excess dal dripping down his hand. He reaches for a napkin. "Amla, I don't know exactly when we're going to leave. The steamboat tickets—"

"But that's not what I asked."

He sighs. For a moment, he rearranges the items on the table in front of him: the steel bowl with dal, the smaller steel bowl with pickled mango, the steel plate with rice, the steel cup of water.

"We grow up and leave things behind, but we don't lose them in our minds," he says slowly. "Fiza and her parents will stay, but you are lucky to remember the name of their mosque. You will always be able to come back to Karachi and ask a man at that mosque where to find Fiza's father, and then you will always find Fiza's family."

*Ten years*, Amla thinks. She cannot imagine what Fiza will look like then. How do you age a person in your mind when you've barely seen who they'll grow up to become? She thinks of Fiza in a bejew-eled anarkali at her wedding and tries to age Fiza's face, the wrinkles that might appear by her eyes, next to her mole. She thinks of them in a large, trimmed courtyard, like the ones that would have been in raja's palaces. Children playing princess.

Maybe Bapu is thinking of this future, too, in the silence punctu-ated by chews and swallows. Maybe Bapu is thinking of how impos-sible it will be to send a letter from Karachi to wherever they end up if the institutions break down, if mail carrying becomes a dangerous job. If the ports close. If the streets are checkpoints that keep some in, keep others out.

When I tell you about this memory, those questions have long been answered. I try to describe to you, instead, how the sunlight glints off the steel plates and cups—off Bapu's full name, etched in Sindhi. The alphabet that the next generation of daughters will never learn to read.

The shop bell rings as two women enter the shop, and Bapu cranes his neck to see if his employees are on their feet. He must know his answer to Amla was insufficient because he takes out his wallet and says to her, "Why don't you go and grab two cups of jeera seltzer from the stand outside, and we can have some of this new mithai? Might make you feel a little better?"

If Ba were upstairs, Bapu would have suggested chaash from home, the buttermilk spiced exactly the way he prefers. Amla is certain of this—sees the way he amends his sentences, replacing a drink that will never taste exactly the same way again with another less laden with grief. Amla takes the paise from him. She wants to go back on all her anger with him, to take care of him the way he takes care of her. After all, this is Bapu, a father who would wake at dawn to boil milk and sugar until they are sweets that neighbors gift at weddings, who laughs off the idea of cooking at home—*Isn't that the entire job downstairs, jaan? Is it not enough?*—but who did still fry koftas for Ba on mornings he didn't have to go to the shops early. She thinks of the weekends when she and Bapu loitered outside the gymkhana grounds clutching sweet drinks bought from the nearby vendor. They'd cheer on the players alongside the men from Bapu's shop and the local boys who practiced in the open field by Frere Hall, dreaming of becoming one of the gymkhana players themselves. If they leave, there will be no more of these memories—not like this, not in Karachi.

So easy, wasn't it, this life.

*Blink.*

# THREE

How to begin describing this feeling to you, Nadya? When your feet touch land you've been told belongs to your people but you wouldn't know it. When what it holds is as familiar as it is foreign, when it beckons you as much as it escapes you. I feel a kinship with Amla here. I know what this is like; I know you do, too.

The feeling, for Amla, begins long before the steamboat docks in Porbandar. That banal life Amla held close turned on its axis, and by the end of January, their suitcases are packed. The violence has only just begun in Karachi, and they are among the first to leave. Meenafai's husband had negotiated with a ticket seller for their spots, and she presses the tickets into Bapu's hands, eyes welling with tears, teeth gritted. "I hope I am panicking," she says to her brother quietly. "I hope I am making you leave for no reason at all."

The door to their Karachi apartment is locked, the key left with Meenafai. Bapu's employees think he is being presumptuous; Sindhi Hindus are not yet fleeing from Karachi. But Ba's death is still fresh, the grief hanging over both Bapu and Amla, making the possibility of spontaneous riots uniquely tangible to them. Only later will they realize how good their timing was, how lucky. They are only six short months from partition.

And now Amla's feet are walking on Gujarati land, her mother's land. She watches her father's back as they disembark at Porbandar's port, Bapu's gait uneven from the weight of valises. He searches through the crowd ahead of them, hailing a porter, and Amla considers how unlike the people around them they are—Bapu draped in a thick shawl covered in block-printed designs, free of embroidery, while others in the crowd wear scarves reminiscent of Ba's tapestry, with mirrors and bright embroidered colors.

*We don't fit in here*, Amla thinks, breathless from trying to keep pace with Bapu. *There is no one like us here.*

She tries to come up with words to say to Bapu but fails over and again. She hasn't spoken to him for the entirety of the steamboat voyage—not when they left Karachi, only two suitcases with them; not when they passed Dwarka, with its temple on an island that only smaller boats can reach; not when the other passengers told Amla stories of a god who once governed that town and entertained his lover on that island; not when they finally docked and a conch shell played as the sun rose, and she wondered if this was the sound of her mother's people.

Amla hadn't meant to do this to him. She didn't mean to create a punishment out of her silence. She understood on some level that this, their departure, was his response to their shared loss, their shared grief, and so she kept her suitcase packed. When Bapu told her over breakfast one day that the tickets had finally been issued, she nodded and swallowed the instructions without argument.

*But.*

But when she said goodbye to Fiza, the words didn't feel like enough. This is the only thing Amla is angry about with Bapu, and she is not sure when or how she will stop being angry; she worries the feeling will never completely leave her, resting always somewhere within her. She wonders what will come of this festering, this resentment.

When the news reached Fiza, she had asked Amla if they could meet again later that night. Amla jumped at the chance.

On the roof, a plate of chili mango between them, Fiza made Amla promise to stay in touch even though they both knew this was subject to parental whims. Fiza held out her hand, and Amla placed her own on top, and Fiza asked, "Do you trust me?" A bowl of ash and tannin pigment sat behind her, the needle and rod next to it.

Amla did not hesitate to say yes.

In the immediate physical discomfort, Amla focused on the look of concentration on Fiza's face, her teeth biting her tongue until it turned more red than pink, the needle, the smell of soot and bark, the feeling of coconut oil and turmeric paste spread on top of the stick-and-poke. Amla tried to commit Fiza's face to memory, to age it into the woman Amla is certain Fiza will become. Her cheeks warmed.

"Now I have one and you have the other," Fiza said. "You have a way to think of me until the next time we see each other."

Amla tried to memorize their limbs next to each other—her right hand, Fiza's left foot—the matching geometries of their bodies. She wanted—wants—this to stay forever.

She holds those words close now—*the next time we see each other*—as she clutches her wrist, trailing behind Bapu. It feels like a promise. A reassurance that even as her life is unrecognizable, there is the possibility of returning to normal one day. It is the one thing she hopes for.

· · ·

**I pause as you reach** for me, taking my hand in yours, turning it over. With one finger you trace the tattoos on my wrist that I've had as long as we've known each other. "Trajva," you say.

"Yes."

Something is shifting in this moment; we can both feel it. Maybe I am telling you all of this exactly the right way.

"Go on," you say, and I do.

**Their new home is** outside of Sodhana, another stop from the port of Porbandar. There, Amla begins to dream of the women on the tapestry. She flies winged over Karachi, tracing her mother's journey over Sindhu Sagar; there is the memory of a grandmother who came to Gujarat from some landlocked place, where she'd known marshes and rivers but not this unending horizon; a sister who settled in Maharashtra so long ago that her family doesn't remember any place before it, not anymore; a daughter who married a man whose family brought her farther south, where the language sits sweet in her ears. Amla is slowly learning to tap into this knowledge, unintended and foggy as it may be.

But more often than not, her frustration overwhelms. She doesn't have the patience to sift through memories, to learn from them. Too much has changed; she aches for the familiarity of her life in Karachi. She continues feeling unsettled, shuffling around their tiny home, where the dust settles on everything and it feels like inside and outside have no boundary.

There's always time here, and nothing to break it up. No aunties circulating through the living room; no shouts from the street. She only knows the time of day by the goods train that goes to and from Porbandar, its sleepy whistle.

"I miss the sound of Karachi," she says to Bapu over a plate of chikoo. "Horns and hooves."

"We're lucky to have this roof, for me to have work," Bapu says. "We're lucky to have this place at all, Amu."

She roams the groves, identifying the saplings for mangoes, for sitaphal, for papaya. Bapu gasped when he saw the thriving line of kesar mango trees that had belonged to Ba's grandmother Kasturiben, his hands cupped as though praying to god, thanking her old and ailing spirit. He must know that, when the season comes, they will have more than enough to pack into carts and send along for sale, accounting the profit as his jaw hangs. Amla practices the name over and over to herself—*Kasturiben, Kasturiben, Kasturiben*—and traces the figure on the tapestry that immediately precedes her mother's, the woman whom she knows is her mother's grandmother.

She knows he's right; they are lucky. And it's not all that bad, no—she has spent the last few days leaning on a sitaphal tree, leaves crowning her face, the tapestry sitting in her lap. She isn't sure what it means yet. She retraces her figure, her mother's figure, but mostly their two intertwined hands.


**The night before they took** the train out to Sodhana, one of Bapu's old friends—the elderly uncle who had once run that failing shop when Bapu was still Bapu-before-he-was-Bapu—had hosted them in Porbandar. She'd slept heavily and brutally that night, tossing and turning on the blankets put down by Haresh uncle, and hadn't paid much attention to him. She'd been too overwhelmed with all the ways Porbandar differed so slightly—and yet so much—from Karachi, but snippets of Bapu and Haresh uncle's conversation keep coming back to her now.

"We'll stay at one of Chandini's grandmothers' homes while I find something that'll work for the whole family, my sister's as well."

"They're still in Karachi?"

"It's quiet there, nothing like what it's been in the other cities."

"This place is its own beast," Haresh uncle had said, the scraping of plates underscoring his words. "The Gandhi house is just down a ways."

"How hard do you think, Haresh, to find a house? Work?"

"People migrating—it's caused discomfort." A pause. "Be careful. People coming from Sindh—it's not like with Punjab, with the massacres. You've heard. Or Calcutta, back in August. People know Sindh is quiet. They may not be the most sympathetic to housing you, feeding you."

"Ah, so Karachi needs violence for me to find work here, is that it? Not just Jinnah announcing Pakistan is for Muslims."

"Anurag, you know it's more than that. People are—well, you locked up that beautiful apartment of yours, with all that nice tile, right? You put a padlock on the door. Sister and her husband keeping an eye on your business. And you're going to a place your wife's family owns? You're not coming here like the others are. It's always one Sindhi, with all his wealth left behind."

"But I might still have to come here, right?" There was the sound of footsteps circling the kitchen. "Anyone leaving any place has a whole life left behind."

"I'm just saying, you want open arms? You come here after you lose the business, after your home is set on fire. When you've got no backup place to stay. Then you get open arms."

**Amla and Bapu's new home** is one of many scattered across kilometers of tended land, all adjacent to the large estate owned by a man named Mahesh Shankar Sharma. He is referenced always with reverence: a former test match player whose son went into government service with the British, their money then reinvested into the land to build their agricultural empire. He has the largest, cleanest well on his land and has built an agriculture-adjacent business out of the nearby farmers' need for fresh water in the desert. The villagers, Bapu now one among them, must pay Sharma a rent for this. In action, it's a clever if corrupt workaround of a tax system built to disincentivize the zamindari and mahalwari systems dominating nearby regions.

And yet Mahesh Shankar Sharma is respected for having cultivated so much land and provided dowries and elaborate weddings for the children of the adjacent farmers. He hosts musicians on Thursday nights, sometimes visitors traversing villages to perform, and other times local artists themselves, flattered to have the invitation. Sharma calls himself a connoisseur of fine art, strumming on his tanpura after all the other artists have performed and refusing accompaniment; he will nod knowingly as young children call him *ustad* and *guru*. He tells everyone and anyone that he and his son have both been to London many times, bringing back portraits of pale white women with ruffled collars, their eyes blank, their gowns boring and heavy with wide hems. He employs the nearby women in his kitchen, the young boys on his land. *What a generous man*, the community says. *What a good soul.*

Bapu is now one of those people employed by the sahib, his time split between accounting for the man's estate and tending the land they have purchased from Ba's great-aunt. Sometimes it feels like he is never home. Without Ba, his absence is more startling, more painful, to Amla.

"Why you?" Amla asks Bapu. "Why not someone else?"

Bapu clears his throat. "He needs an accountant, and someone who can write."

"And no one else can?"

"Not many people, no. See, I continued my tuition until I started apprenticing, and that's why it's so important for you to work on your lessons, okay? At home, with your tuition books, or in school when you're ready. Your Ba would want that, for you to do more than she could."

It's the first time those words have appeared so casually—*your Ba*—and Amla doesn't know how to reply. How easily Bapu said them. Amla's chest tightens. "Oh," she manages.

"Her family's name, Sthanakiya, is strong in Porbandar," Bapu continues, and that moment of Ba, *your Ba*, is gone, glided over. She wonders if he even knows that it is the first time they have mentioned her without the context of her death, the pyre, her family in Porbandar.

Bapu's uniforms are split into two kinds now: the clothes he used to wear to the mithai shops repurposed for his days tagging the flow of goods through Mahesh Shankar Sharma's house; and dull-colored linen and cotton sets for when he oversees young boys tilling the field behind their house. He always returns in the evening, sweating through his shirt. *If you won't do the work with them*, he recites like clockwork, *you won't earn their respect.* She greets him with cold chaash, watches as he wipes his face with his sleeve and leans back in his chair.

Amla misses her father's smile, his relaxed slouch on a love seat, the way he looked at her mother every evening of every day. She tries to replace those memories of him with new ones—buttermilk clinging to his newly grown mustache, their games of chess on a dusty set left by Kasturiben's husband—but even as they settle into the old house, everything still feels too different. When she sketches like she used to, she closes her eyes and pretends she is on a balcony above a city street, imagines the routine she was so used to. *Blink and you'll be home*, she wills the universe. *Blink and it's there.*

. . .

**In this new home,** there is no Hari uncle to teach her maths while Ba cooks in the kitchen, no new books to trace letters in. Here there is a boys' school and a girls' school, and the nearest university is not at the edge of the city like it was in Karachi, but an entire train ride away. She doesn't know much about the boys' school, but the girls' classes seem like more of an unenthusiastic guise to force the older children to watch after the younger ones in an auntie's courtyard than an educational endeavor.

It takes her time to decide that she should go; Bapu doesn't require it of her, trusting that she'd eventually grow bored without school and inevitably find herself in the classroom. At first, she is busy exploring every nook and cranny of her great-grandmother's old house; then she is busy exploring the field, the places she can hide among the growing bajri plants, the best trees in the grove to sit and lean upon. There is her drawing project; there are the hours she spends checking on the tapestry, taking it out from its safe place between her churidar in the dresser and unfolding it, trying to see if any new image has found itself embroidered upon it.

So it is two months before the first day she sits in the auntie's courtyard. She feels eyes on her, the goosebumps at the nape of her neck standing up. When she glances around, no one appears to be exactly her age. The session ends with the students pairing off for the walk home, and Amla trails behind them, alone, trying not to be upset in public. The next week, she attempts to help a toddler identify the right conjugation for *I am hungry you are hungry*, and accidentally gives the answer aloud in Sindhi instead of Gujarati. The third week, a girl named Bahaar sits next to her.

That day, the auntie in charge is showing the older girls how to stitch a dart on a blouse. "For yourself, or to sell," she says, handing out a set of modern patterns traced on paper.

Bahaar writes her name on the paper blouse pattern in Hindi, leans it at an angle for Amla to see. In simple Gujarati, Amla whispers, "I'm not good at reading Hindi."

"What do you read?"

"Sindhi."

"Like Kutchi?"

"I don't know."

"How do you know Sindhi?"

Amla shrugs. She doesn't understand the question.

"Do you read Gujarati?"

"Some. My Ba taught me some."

Bahaar nods quickly, erases the first phoneme and the lines above the rest. When she turns the slate back, first phoneme rewritten, the name is legibly Gujarati.

"Bahaar. Like, seasonally?"

Bahaar nods. Amla writes her own name next to Bahaar's.

"Like, the fruit?" Bahaar whispers.

Amla nods. Bahaar rewrites Amla's name, changing the phoneme at its beginning and adding a horizontal bar to indicate Hindi. She points at the girl sitting in front of them. "That's Padma." She writes the name twice, once in Hindi, once in Gujarati. Amla feels her cheeks blush with the delight of newfound friendship, even when the auntie glares at them for their conspiratorial whispers and they don't speak for the rest of the sewing session.

The fourth week, Bahaar invites Amla to meet the other kids after class by the orchards, where the sitaphal trees sit low to the ground, leaves crisp and green. The trees are out of season, and her classmates savor this time to sit on the dirt and share stories, swap secrets, without fruit meat sticking to their clothes.

Amla hesitates. She wants to say yes—wants to feel like she belongs here as much as all the other children do. Instead she shrugs, *Maybe*, and does not go. She is thinking of Fiza, of a friendship she did not have to maneuver. A companion who made her feel like she belonged, all the time. She wraps her arms across her chest and walks alone to the empty house, tracing the trajva on her right wrist with one finger.

**In the late afternoon,** the sun beating down and Bapu not yet home, Amla sits with her watercolors against the mango trees by their house. No fruit hangs from the branches, the leaves deep parrot and evergreen. She traces the outer edges of the splintering box with the soft tips of her fingers. She wants to make art, like all those women on the tapestry made art. She wonders how she knows them—how she can remember them.

She starts in pencil with the moon, her mother's namesake, liking the way everything in a scene can be illuminated in a quiet glow. She knows, without really having learned it, that the whiteness of the paper will determine how much light comes through the image. She thinks of folding her paper in four, but doesn't.

With her eyes closed, she forces herself back to those moments she cherished; she imagines the way the balcony railing pressed against her thighs and buttocks, how it hurt her bones if she sat too long; the way her left heel rested on the ground. Something takes ahold of her muscles. Her hands move without conscious thought, pulling a few of the lighter pigments from the box, and dipping her brush in a steel water bowl she had brought from the house.

Her brush streaks across the paper, a landscape forming on its pages. She loves the way the moist pigment spreads, veinlike and hungry. Her eyes grow narrow, honing in on the smaller details. She returns to the dried patches to add layers of shadow. How do her hands know what to do? When did her eyes begin to see the world this way?

By evening, paper drying in the setting sun, a lavender gooseberry bush emerges, its shadows descending in violets and bluish-blacks, a gibbous moon dancing in the upper-right corner. The thin limbs of the bush reach upward toward the light, large parsley-like leaves bent as though in prayer. The sky is starless, the single bush alone, aglow.

Amla wipes the sweat from her forehead, her kurti sticky at her folds. The sides of her small hands are streaked with color, purples and blues turning black on her skin—color under her nails, under her chin. She hopes her kurti isn't also streaked this way. She scrawls her name and the date on the back side of the paper, like her mother had told her to do.

Amla doesn't bother to dust off her clothes before heading back to the house, the dirt perpetually clinging to everything. She rolls up the dried painting, her hunger quenched. She is filled with a calm that has escaped her for months.

Still, her stomach twists slightly. She can barely remember what she had meant to draw, cannot remember the act of painting itself. If she made any choices about this image, she did not do so consciously— she had been driven solely by some strange, deep-buried desire.

You remember what I told you about Amla's mother, Chandini? About that painting she made of her life in Karachi? There is truth to Amla's suspicion—that there had been something there, beyond herself, just as there had been when she painted the aunties at Ba's wake.

But how harmful can it be, a hand reaching out for her mother?

At first the change is small and unnoticed: when Amla hears about the gooseberry bush beginning to grow by the sitaphal grove, the way it breaks the gridded planting of the trees, she will smile to herself and think there is something magical in the air. Look, a bush that shares her name, in this village so far from the city in which she was named. How strange and beautiful for this bush to take root in the place that belonged to the mother who named her.

Only when the bush grows large, disrupting the field's water consumption to the point that the sitaphal trees near it seem to grow weaker and drier, when the gooseberry bush dwarfs them as it claims the soil for itself, as it starves its companions, makes them thirst—only then will Amla think of the painting, stacked among the others behind her closed closet doors, and begin to wonder. Years later, an older Amla will look back at this moment of a child's innocent plea, of a girl reaching out for her mother, and understand how seductive this power was, how alluring. She will think of all the mistakes she has ever made, and then she will think not of Ba, as she so often had at that age, but of Bapu, and all the ways in which she failed him.

On the fifth week of class at the auntie's house, after the girls practice sewing their darts, Amla follows Bahaar and Padma to the sitaphal grove. She lags a few steps behind them, unsure of what makes her feel deferential: if it is her age—both the other girls are thirteen, nearly fourteen, on the other side of girlhood compared to Amla's newly eleven years—or her foreignness to the community. Maybe it is the way they walk, as though the knowledge of every shortcut straightens their spines. Maybe it is how they share small bits of information about the boys who are old enough to be useful tilling land, stories of stolen glances when vegetables are traded or milk is delivered.

"Amla?"

She looks up, startled. "Yes?"

"I asked, how long have you been here now?"

"Oh, I guess . . ." She trails off, trying to measure the passing days.

"When did you leave Karachi?" Padma prompts.

"Oh," and this is easier, the day they left imprinted indelibly in her mind. She counts. "We left Karachi at the end of January, and then we were in Porbandar in February and then I started coming to class in April."

Padma, the tender one of the two, nods slowly. "You've had a lot in the last six months."

Amla nods back.

Last week, the British had announced their plan to leave India. Though it was what all the adults seemed to be talking about at the market, Amla couldn't find it in herself to care. It had been her birthday, the first without Ba. The day passed otherwise uneventfully: she spent the evening with the other children at the estate's groves, watching the younger boys play cricket, the windows of the houses lit up with candles in the evening such that the distance between them felt a little smaller. Bapu tried to make everything feel normal, bringing her a chocolate cake sent by Mahesh Shankar Sharma. They ate it and smiled at each other and said nice things about its composition, but secretly Amla wanted jalebi from her favorite stand in Karachi, and she had a feeling Bapu did, too.

She looks up at Padma, still waiting in front of her. The sitaphal grove widens beyond them. "I miss home," Amla says.

Padma takes her hand and squeezes it before letting go. "I bet it's overwhelming here, with a lot of new people."

"Sometimes," Amla says, "and sometimes not. Karachi has more people."

"I'm sure it's so much larger."

"More people that I know," Amla amends quickly, trying to say this neutrally—she doesn't want the older girls to feel like she is ungrateful or to know that she wishes she were on the other side of a steamboat voyage.

Padma nods. "I'd miss my friends, too," she says, and she takes Amla's hand once more, leading them toward the line of sitaphal trees.

Amla is thankful for this, the way Padma seems to know when to stop prying, when Amla feels like she could burst. They follow the laughter echoing toward them until they are with the others, mostly girls and a few young boys. Amla watches them tell one another stories and gossip and she imagines she is one of them, always has been, and in some ways it feels as though she could be.

**For months,** Amla has been writing Fiza a letter in her mind. Bapu had offered time and again to send Fiza a telegram for her, but Amla doesn't know how to boil it all down. She has never had to do this, has always been able to share everything at the moment it happens. To have to choose now, the what, the which, the why—it overwhelms her. So, in between chores, while watching Bahaar and Padma laugh at each other's chatter, she adds sentences to the letter she will not write. Time passes faster than she thinks it does, and as the letter grows longer, it begins to take on an intimate quality, so much so that Amla knows she wouldn't ask Bapu to transcribe it for her.

*I miss you,* the letter begins. *I look at my trajva and think of you every day. Do you do that, too?*

*Bapu wants to hire people to make this house bigger. He says we are used to having more space, and that we'll want it if family stays with us—if Meenafai and all join. I don't think it's too big or too small. I just wish it was in the city.*

*Remember that time we stole the slippers from the gymkhana during Nooran's wedding reception? I saw a girl who had a pair of mojari just like those. I nearly took them.*

*I'm sorry it's been so long. I keep imagining conversations with you to fill the time. It's almost like you're here. I almost forgot you weren't.*

When she finally asks Bapu if they can send Fiza a telegram when he next goes into town, like they do every week to Meenafai, he nods eagerly. "Tell me what you'd like it to say," he says, "and I'll do it."

"Hello," Amla dictates. And then she stops. *I miss you. I'm sorry for being angry when I left. When will I see you next?* But Bapu will ask what she is sorry about and she's not sure she can explain—not sure she even remembers. "Gujarat is different from home. I miss sitting with you on the rooftop. I miss you."

"That's what you want to say?" Bapu laughs as he notes the words down. Amla nods. "Fine, I'll have that sent right away."

By the time Bapu hands her Fiza's reply, two weeks have passed. "I would've gone to town sooner if I'd known she had already sent a reply," he says apologetically. "Next time, I'll take you with me and show you how to do it yourself."

Amla nods, watching Bapu take the crisp yellow paper from his breast pocket. She likes the idea of sending a telegram to Fiza, un-filtered.

HELLO GOOD TO HEAR FROM YOU *stop* I THINK OF YOU WHEN YOUR MEENAFAI AND PANDITJI COME BY *stop* I HOPE YOU ARE WELL

It doesn't even sound like Fiza. Amla swallows her excitement.

She wonders if Fiza, too, had balked at the idea of having to voice the desired message to her own father, who in turn would deliver the message to the telegram boy. She imagines what Fiza might have said if she'd had total control: *I miss you* stop *my days are not the same* stop *I see my trajva and think of you too* stop *when will you come back?*

Even if she had asked that last question, Amla is certain Fiza's father would have removed it, knowing it would be cruel, just as Bapu would crumple at the question if Amla asked it.

The next time Bapu asks if she wants to send a telegram, she writes even less, unsure how to bridge the distance: "Hello. I hope you are well." When Fiza's reply returns, just as formal, as untrue to their friendship, the desire to write telegrams fades. In that moment, Amla decides the imagined Fiza is better than the limitations of father-dictated telegrams.

In these next months, Amla begins to dream about her mother, and her mother's mother, and hers before her. I tell you about them, because what she wakes up feeling from these dreams makes them as real as any memory.

In one dream, Amla and Ba sit on the ledge of the Karachi apartment balcony, their legs swinging in the breeze, people and autos like ants beneath them. Ba reaches behind Amla's ears and pulls her hands back to her own temples—a knowing gesture, a blessing. *May I take all your sorrows as my own.* As Ba pulls her hands away from Amla's face, Amla closes her eyes. Sometimes, when she reopens them, her mother is being pulled away by young men, and other times, she is the one being pulled away, unable to see the face of the person grabbing her. The dream is always like one of those movies at the cinema she and Fiza used to sneak into: all gray and scratchy.

In another, Ba kisses her cheeks, sings her favorite lullaby. As Amla feels her body grow slack, all the women from the tapestry join in, too—these abstract, profiled bodies singing beside her mother, humming sweetly, vibrations rocking Amla's body as they call her one of their own.

And then one night, she dreams of the painting that had made her feel foreign even inside her own body—oh, now she remembers the act of it, too, her hands moving without a single thought, the blood coursing through her veins with a new and frenetic energy. It forms on the page, the emerging gooseberry bush, pushing its way upward from the earth. She wakes with a start, sweating. She has changed something; *she* is responsible for the bush's appearance, its rapid growth. It is connected to her own image sewn upon that strange tapestry. Even if she doesn't understand how, in the recesses of her mind she knows this to be true.

# FOUR

I don't envy Amla her childhood, Nadya. No matter when we are alive, we are always leaving people we love behind. Sometimes it's by choice—a new job in a new city, nothing so intense that it removes the possibility of return—but other times it is this, the choice that Bapu made for Amla: to forfeit everything you know in the hopes that this sacrifice will help you protect the people you love.

We pray that our new lives will feel worthy, that they'll match what came before. I have seen that they can, that they do. Still, too often they are but poor imitations—comforting, maybe, eventually, but still not quite what we ache for.

If I were Amla, Nadya, I too would hold on to whatever made sense.

Here, her promise to be good—that one ask Ba had made all those years ago and which she'd renewed at Ba's wake—she directs it now toward Bapu. Small tasks begin to define Amla's efforts: be nicer to her father, smile at him more. Keep secrets for Bahaar and Padma. Be a good friend. Don't let go of dream-Ba.

Her hands are always clutching at something, chasing smoke in the dark. If only she could catch what she is looking for. Could understand what she'd done with her painting.

When she finds herself alone in the afternoons, sewing aluminum mirrors into a new skirt she had begun under Padma's careful guidance—*Don't crinkle, there you go, embroider around, beautiful, you've got it*—Amla sits on the floor by her cot and closes her eyes. She leans her back into the wood, lets the dirt on the ground cake under her fingernails. The tapestry sits heavy beside her. She tries to still her fingers and knees. Breathes, in and out and in again.

Oh, the first time Amla tries to tap into the memories. It's almost painful—I know this, practiced this when I first received the gift. I know that want, when it feels like you are right there, your hand reaching out toward this unknowable abyss, like you are swimming toward this entire history but so slowly, your legs held back by some gentle force.

When it was my turn, I stroked confidently against that current. My mother had told me what to expect, and so I called forth these women by name.

But Amla doesn't know what she's looking for. She will nearly have a hold on it, of them, and then her fear, her hesitance, will pull her away. She doesn't understand: she cannot force this. The women she feels on the other side of this veil, they are not shadows. Not silhouettes. They can be made tangible in her mind. If she could take the risk of that final leap, grasp for their hands, they would reach back for her. She ends that first attempt crying, aching for Ba, not knowing that her mother, her mother's dadima, their mothers before them, are so close.

If only she could calm herself. Could pull back from that instinct to fear the unknown, to call out for her mother. This is why it comes to us in our art, I think—when we are thoughtless. All body and energy. But Amla—she is so young. A child.

This memory, this pain. If I could live in the past forever . . . Sometimes, I'm scared I would. I could live days rewriting this memory, daydreaming how I would lace my fingers through hers and tell her what she doesn't know yet: we live in each other's bones. She does not need to go searching. Everyone who came before her will be there to hold her when she is ready.


That summer, Mahesh Shankar Sharma announces he will host both Jethwa representatives and British officials in June, and all are invited. The estate comes alive at this news. Bahaar is ecstatic, coaxing Padma to teach her more complex darts and hems and embroidery, and her energy is contagious: Amla decides to sew herself a chaniya choli on the off chance that she needs to look a little nicer, that she might be seen.

When she tells Bapu about the project, he laughs. He must hear the voices of the older girls in the words she uses. "You're sure you don't want to make yourself a nice kurti? You already have so many pants for them."

But Amla is insistent; she knows Bahaar and Padma and their classmates are taking this opportunity to look regal and she wants to evoke something of these friends, too. When they discuss their patterns and the fabrics brought in from town by the teacher auntie, Amla drips with envy. She wants to carry herself like these older girls; she wants to be them. She is intoxicated by a mixture of deep love and jealousy, as though the solution would be to wake up one morning and look in the mirror and see, there, Bahaar.

"You'll probably be standing in the corner of the dining hall, waiting for someone to finish their water just so you can roll up delicately and refill it," Bahaar complains when they are sifting through fabrics at the auntie's. "I don't know if I'll even be in the house."

Padma shakes her head. "You can take my job. I don't want it."

"The sahib always wants you there, though." Bahaar holds up a bandhani pattern. "Is it too folk? I don't want to look plain, you know?"

As though Bahaar could pass for a city girl. Amla tries to picture Bahaar in Karachi—with her skin dark from both sun and genetics, kohl sweating into the creases around her eyes throughout the day. Her arms are shaped by labor on the estate, her shoulders broad. She talks loudly. Amla isn't sure if propriety has to do more with personality or appearance, but she knows Bahaar—with her belly laugh, her pining over the estate boys, her hair always frizzing out of her plait through a combination of carelessness and humidity—would have been deemed improper by the aunties she remembers, who would have turned up their nose at the mention of her caste.

Padma, on the other hand, would be adored. She has that look that could pass for proper anywhere; it's likely why she is always invited to Mahesh Shankar Sharma's house. She reminds Amla of Fiza: quiet, like Amla, but funnier than Amla, kinder than her, too. She doesn't have that confidence that Bahaar wraps around herself so tightly, but maybe that would make the aunties in Karachi like her more, anyway. They would dream of making a good match for her.

"It's not too folk," Padma tells Bahaar. "The colors are quiet. You'll look nice in that, orange and green."

"Do I want to be quiet, though? I'm trying to be matchmade here." Bahaar sifts through the fabrics collected in Padma's arms, eyebrows furrowing. "Why are you trying to look like an auntie's auntie? These are the plainest things I've ever seen."

"These blends are easier to work with," Padma says. "Now let's talk about your—"

"You're so beautiful," Bahaar says, tone almost whining, "and it's like you don't even realize your potential when the rest of us are—"

"I like the colors," Amla says, partly to Padma and partly to herself, but mostly to halt the sense of discomfort she can feel rising in Padma. Amla's hands skim through the fabric options until she lands on a mustard yellow and unwraps it. At the edge is a row of embroidered peacocks in sets of two, beaks turned in toward each other. Rows of circles border the peacocks, stacked above and below them. Amla imagines herself as one peacock, her mother the other, and clutches the light cotton to her cheek.

Bahaar takes the fabric from Padma's arms, wrapping it around her head like a dupatta, unfazed by Amla's interruption. "Oh, I'm Padma, I know I'll end up okay because all the outside men compliment me and give me attention when I play sitar."

"It's not funny," Padma says quietly. "I don't like it there."

"Why not?" Amla asks, louder this time, and it's as though the girls finally remember she is present.

Bahaar jumps on her words like an animal. She turns to Padma, hands on her hips. "Yes, why not, exactly?"

Padma looks so uncomfortable that Amla almost regrets asking, especially now that she's been ganged up on. "I don't . . . It's just . . . The way people look at you, there."

Bahaar scoffs. "The way they show you off? So shy."

Padma shakes her head. "No, not that. It's different. It's the way they stare. It's like you're on the menu."

"The people who do that, you mean the guests? Or the sahib?"

"Let's not talk about this—"

Bahaar presses. "Padma, what are you—"

"The guests, of course," she rushes to say. "Of course not the sahib, I would never say something like that."

"Of course," Bahaar says quietly. She nudges Amla with her elbow.

"Of course," Amla parrots.

For a moment, the three stand silent in their circle.

"Don't say anything to my mother? I know she feels flattered when I get asked about sitar." Padma pulls the fabric closer, eyes cast downward.

"I would never," Bahaar says. She gestures to Amla.

"I won't say anything." Amla doesn't know how to assure them of how little she understands of what has just been shared, how few people she has to gossip to.

"I mean it," Padma says, and she looks Amla directly in the eyes. "I wouldn't want to offend him. He does so much for our families."

"I won't say anything." Amla pinches the skin at her neck like her mother did when making promises that mattered. "I would never. I swear."

After another morning of blouse stitching with Bahaar and Padma, Amla hugs a pot of well water to her chest and trudges home. She has seen the other girls balance pots atop cloth rings on their heads, but after breaking one too many she is embarrassed to try again. Compared to her schoolmates, Amla feels severely less-than.

The feeling is only amplified when she arrives in the courtyard. Three well-dressed men stand sentry-like outside the door, watching her carry the pot against her chest, spilling water in snakelike threads. She knows she should avert her eyes as she walks past them but finds herself curious, looking up to memorize their waxed mustaches and elaborate jewelry. She nearly walks into the outer wall, distracted by their presence.

"May she live long! This is Amla herself," Bapu says loudly as she enters the doorway. He widens his eyes at her—a signal.

"Ah, what a lovely daughter you have." The gravelly, sickly sweet voice belongs to a man unlike any other Amla has seen in Gujarat. "Hello, young lady. I'm Mahesh Shankar Sharma. Mahesh uncle. I don't think we've met."

Amla sets down the pot carefully and tries to understand how the person before her fits into Bahaar's and Padma's stories. This uncle feels so other to her, carries an atmosphere that makes her feel like she should be honored to be addressed by him at all.

Sharma is dressed in a long black blazer over a crisp white button-up shirt, one so starched and fresh that she wonders how he possibly got from his estate to their home without dirtying it. On the bottom, he wears an equally spotless white dhotiyu. If he has been sweating, Amla can't tell; an embroidered shawl is draped over his left arm, perfectly perpendicular to the ground. His eyes follow her movements, meet her own too curiously. She catches on the details—the thick gold hoops in his ears, the clean shave of his beard, the clean nail beds of his toes. The tobacco tinge of his teeth, the tongue that flicks out to wet his lips. She has to stop herself from glancing over to the doorway to see what his shoes might look like. Instead, she catches Bapu's still-wide eyes. He tilts his head to the side.

"Oh," she says, and her body registers what Bapu is trying to tell her to do before her mind does. She bends down and reaches for Sharma's feet, asking for blessings.

"That's a good girl," Sharma says. He touches the back of her head as she begins to stand up, palm pressing down, and for a moment she's confused, wonders if he's telling her to keep crouching. "Bless you, child."

She breaks away from his palm and smiles in a grimace. "Thank you, ji."

"Amla, why don't you get some water boiled outside?" Bapu gestures to the back, and Amla seizes her exit. She bear-hugs the pot of water once more. "And, sahib, if you'll be staying?"

"No, no, I shouldn't impose . . ." she hears Sharma say. Amla turns to the chulha without a moment's hesitation. Behind her, accompanying the feeling of Sharma's gaze on her back, she hears, "She's growing up to be such a beautiful girl," and she feels dirty somehow. Remembers his eyes, his tongue. Remembers Padma's words: *It's like you're on the menu.* She thinks of how some of the other village girls whisper—how they warn.

She wants to retch.

She stays outside at the chulha, sprinkling whole cumin into the water, watching it boil and boil and boil until Bapu himself comes to her. "You can stay out here," he whispers, handing her a fresh pot to cool the water in. "I brought your sketchbook."

Amla imagines Bapu is not himself but Ba, handing her a sketchbook and a teakwood box, and that Amla is suddenly on the balcony in Karachi. She blinks, and the image is gone.

"Thank you," she says, trying to stay quiet. She takes the book from him and presses it against her torso, as though to push what little breast she has back into her body. As Bapu starts to walk away, she tries to think of the right words. *Thank you. I love you. I see how you protect me.* Maybe Bapu knows the missing words in her silence, one quiet man to his quiet daughter. He ruffles her hair, his hand erasing the specter of the sahib's touch, and winks before retreating into the house.

That evening, their empty plates stacked between them, she tells Bapu her plans for her outfit have changed.

"I switched to a kurti," she says.

Bapu furrows his brow. "After all this time?" He pauses. "Is it because you want to ride a camel? You can still do that in a long skirt. Don't let go of all your hard—"

"No, you were right," she says, and somehow she feels like she has a secret to keep, something that makes her stomach turn with a shame she can't place. "I have a lot of pants for a kurti." She looks toward the front door, where the sahib's men had stood, willing Bapu to remember alongside her.

But Bapu doesn't turn. "Whatever you want, jaan. This dinner is extravagant for no reason," he says, pulling out a cigarette. "You making your own clothes, this man finding ways to make it as expensive as possible. And, can you believe, he wants me to find the money for it? His dreams, and I have to see where I can cut other expenses of his?"

Amla looks at her father blankly.

"It's not your problem, Amu." He sighs. He touches her nose and cocks his head to the side. "If there are indeed camels at the party, I promise we'll sort out getting you a ride. Go, sleep. You can leave the dishes for me."


**The mental letters to** Fiza continue. Amla crafts them while watching these new friends interact, jealous that Padma and Bahaar have each other.

*The heat is picking back up,* the letter now reads. *I miss the breeze coming off the water in Karachi.*

*I pretend here, all the time.*
  *I thought this would be easier by now. Bapu said so.*
  *I have friends. I think you'd like them. But don't worry, you're still my best friend. No one can replace you.*

*I thought this place would feel like home because Bapu said it was once home to Ba.*

*I don't know why it doesn't feel that way.*

"I think I want to make this into a salwar kameez instead," Amla announces to Bahaar and Padma when they are next sitting in their small circle, handiwork draped over their crossed legs. "Do you think it would work?"

Bahaar nods slowly. "I think you can keep the hemming from the chaniya and turn that into the ankles, or the hem of the kameez . . ."

Padma waves her hand to quiet Bahaar. "Why, Amla? You've put so much into this."

Amla shrugs. She doesn't know how to say aloud the feeling she is having difficulty naming even in her head. The look on Mahesh Shankar Sharma's face, the feel of his palm against the back of her head, her relief when Bapu let her stay outside and draw. Something creeps along her neck when her mind settles on the details. It makes her want to protect herself, to have more layers. Pants, a shirt longer than a blouse.

*I don't think anyone understands me the way you do*, she adds to the letter to Fiza.

"I miss wearing churidar," she tells Padma. "We always wore kurtis back home. In Karachi."

"Okay." The concern on Padma's face slowly disappears, the wrinkles filling back into perfect skin. "I can show you how we might salvage the material and have enough for that. We might have to have a plain dupatta now, okay? But I think yellow will be easy to find. I'll draw you the pattern."

Amla flushes, grateful. She feels cared for by these new friends—and relieved, too, by the idea of pants at this party.

*It's not the same as us,* she adds to the letter, *but I'd be so alone without them.*

**Amla wakes up late** the next morning. For a moment, she doesn't understand where she is, disoriented by the sun already high in the sky. She curls her fists around the thick bedding of her cot, the blankets that always dressed her parents' bed in Karachi. When she wanders through the house to the kitchen for a cup of water, she realizes the pot is empty. There is no sign that Bapu has slept, just a full ashtray at the kitchen table, the candle burnt down to its wick.

Amla takes out the salwar kameez, barely formed, and removes the few stitches she has made. They seem hasty, and she pretends Padma is there watching her, instructing her to have patience.

*Do you ever try, really try, to be good?* she asks her imagined Fiza. *Do you know how to be?*

Amla is trying to decide if bad stitchwork counts as not being good.

*Ba would know,* she thinks. *Ba always knew.*

She guides the needle through the cloth, slower motions, rhythmic ones. Her brain begins connecting ideas in ways she hadn't before: Her mother gave her the tapestry; her mother gave her the box of watercolor pigments. Ba taught her about being good. Had her mother always known she would find herself here, clawing at memories, confused by paint stains she can't remember making?

Maybe Ba had made paintings and not just sketches. Maybe she'd tested if she could make something come true, like Amla's watercolors could. Somewhere, in the recesses of her unconscious mind, clarity fights its way to the tip of her tongue: *Ba used charcoal, not paints.*

*How do I know this?*

Amla needs answers. To tap into the memories, to finally know her story is not hers alone: it belongs to every person on that tapestry before her. She is accompanied, carried. If only she could close her eyes and imagine herself alongside all those women, marching in profile, just as she is on that dark, heavy fabric.

Amla feels this need. It makes her try again.

She sits on the ground outside this time, the chulha's warmth dissipating into the early afternoon. She lets herself sweat. She licks the salt from the groove above her upper lip.

At first her mind wanders; she thinks of the walk to the gooseberry bush, the sitaphal trees growing around this new inhabitant of their space. The goats and cows that roam around town, the camels when visitors come to sell cloth.

Amla shakes her head. This is not what clearing her mind means.

She cleans the grime out from beneath her left-hand nails with her right-hand ones, and then switches. She breathes slowly. What are these stories she has access to now?

*Ba*, she thinks, unprompted. She asks for her mother without fear. *What can you show me?*

It's the first time she does it right.

The memories come to her in bursts. She sees her mother's neck, the trajva diamond tattooed upon it. Ba bites at her lip, her hands stained in charcoal, while she sits with a sketchbook on the chowpatty. The ocean breeze cools her skin, smells of salt and sweat.

*Blink.*

She feels, in the body of a child, the soft wrinkled hands of a grandmother, Ba's grandmother, a woman Amla has never seen. She caresses these hands in her own—no, in Ba's own—the woman's fingers long and delicate like Ba's. Beside them, a stack of papers covered in charcoal drawings, as though Kasturiben had been instructing Ba.

76

*Blink.*

A woman Amla can only name as a grandmother's grandmother's grandmother, great-greats to such a degree that she can barely recognize the world this woman is living in, with thick, silvering hair parted straight down the middle, her eyes accentuated by heavy kohl and crow's-feet at their edges. In the sun, in a desert that reminds Amla of this one she lives in now, the woman looks at her with a clay figurine in her hand, seems to say, *On that tapestry, I am there, too. I am also the mother you are looking for.*

Amla thinks of the watercolor box, and suddenly she is seeing memories tied to a thousand different teakwood boxes just like hers. A painting of mango trees thriving in the middle of a drought; here, a woman at her wedding, her face and hands scarred with burns, but no one cares, no one cares; an aging couple embracing a newborn; an oasis, water found in a desert; too many mothers for Amla to account for, and each one guiding another, a child:

*Act with care.*

*Do not overdo what cannot be undone.*

*Do not ask for excess.*

*Do not take risks you might regret.*

She can see all those moments she never had before. It makes her cheeks blush, her heartbeat accelerate. Amla has found an inroad.


**The next time the girls** meet for a sewing session, Bahaar has an announcement to make. "Padma, you're relieved from duty," she begins. "You don't have to go to the sahib's party if you don't want to."

Padma looks at her quizzically. "I don't have to . . . what?"

Bahaar's voice picks up with excitement. "They're scrapping the entire sitar segment. Sharma sahib came by my parents' house and asked me to play harmonium. It's just going to be me and dholak players, and then the fancy musical guests later. Can you believe it?"

Amla forces herself to smile, her gut twisting. She doesn't like the fact that the changes have been made by the sahib. Something feels wrong about him, about the way he moves through their village. She knows Padma feels it, too. Wordless, Amla surveys the materials in front of them: her chaniya choli turned kameez nearly finished, lying in a clump in her corner; Padma's two chaniya choli already complete and neatly folded. Bahaar follows her eyes and folds Amla's fabric for her.

"That's exciting." Amla pauses before continuing, not sure how to voice her hesitations without ruining this new friend's happiness. "You'll do great."

Padma leans over to squeeze Bahaar's shoulder, and Amla isn't sure if she's reading Padma's body language correctly, but she's certain she sees relief.

They work in a punctuated silence, Padma leaving early to help her mother with the younger children. When Bahaar suggests they take a break, Amla forces her nodding to look eager.

They meander toward Bahaar's house. Amla is surprised to see that it matches the size of hers and Bapu's, despite Bahaar's larger family. Bahaar waves to them as the two girls walk past—her mother, her oldest brother, and his wife, noting, "The other brother's somewhere around here"—and they go to lie among the burgeoning bajri plants, looming like wild grass over them, the heavier millet heads stirring with the breeze. The sun begins to set over the desert—*their* desert, the way Amla thinks of this place now—and she closes her eyes, pressing her spine into the ground.

"Tell me something you've never told anyone," Bahaar says, breaking their silence.

Amla mourns the quiet, the comfort of not speaking. The question turns her stomach. "I don't know."

"You can think for a moment," Bahaar adds quickly.

Amla hasn't told secrets to anyone since leaving Karachi—since leaving Fiza. She wants nothing more than to re-create that feeling, to confide in someone the way she would confide in her best friend and feel the acceptance that comes with it.

"Sometimes I draw things and they come true," she says in a rush, pretending Bahaar is Fiza, as though the girls are in any way interchangeable. It feels like a betrayal.

"Oh, that's not fair." Bahaar laughs. "You can't invent the secret. Share a real one."

"I'm being serious," Amla says before she can contain herself.

"Amla, come on," Bahaar says. "I won't share if you make jokes. You have to share, too."

Amla's blood heats in frustration. She wanted to feel comforted, believed. Not this. Even if Fiza hadn't fully understood what Amla had tried to tell her about the tapestry, she had still tried. Fiza would have taken her seriously because she always took Amla seriously. But Amla also feels the extreme of her reaction—that's the age, every friendship a make or break—and so she knows if she continues down this road, if she stakes her claim on this argument, she won't ever be taken seriously. She wouldn't have lived up to the pact of secret-sharing.

The only other secret that comes to her mind is her dislike of the sahib, but she isn't sure that's the kind of secret Bahaar is seeking. Isn't sure she's supposed to share that one out loud.

"Let me think," Amla says. "I promise I'll come up with one."

"I'll go," Bahaar says with a sigh, "but you owe me, then."

"Okay."

"What we say stays here, okay?"

"I promise."

Bahaar inhales. "Sometimes, I'm really jealous of Padma." Her words tumble out like they've been waiting to escape. "Everyone treats her like she's meant for some better life than this one, like she's supposed to marry some guy who lives in town and comes from more than us, and you know what? She doesn't even want it. She doesn't want the way people look at her, the things they want for her. We joke about her marrying one of my brothers and it's like she's okay wanting my family, this home, this life. And I should be flattered."

Amla forces herself to stay still. She feels caught in between.

"And all I want is for people to see me the way they see her," Bahaar says, her tone lowering. "I want everything she has, everything she doesn't want. So getting to play the harmonium at this dinner next week, I mean, it's like the tables have turned. What I would give . . ."

What can she tell this friend to make her feel better? This fourteen-year-old looking up at a girl three years her junior. Amla wants to act like someone Bahaar can share her secrets with, but she has nothing to offer, no advice or wisdom. What does she know?

"It doesn't matter," Bahaar says eventually. "If Padma doesn't show up, you'll at least be there, right?"

"Of course," Amla says. She pinches the skin at the base of her throat. "I promise."

Bahaar smiles. "Do you have your secret?"

Amla turns to lie on her stomach. She searches for anything in her memory that might live up to Bahaar's expectations. "I can tell you about the time my best friend, Fiza, and I stole slippers from a wedding reception at the Muslim gymkhana. Is that a good one?"

Bahaar laughs like an older sibling entertaining the younger one, and Amla glows with the feeling of almost-sisterhood. "Of course."

"Okay," she says, sitting up cross-legged. "So my friend Fiza's father is a maulana at the biggest mosque I've ever seen . . ."

She leaves out that she is constantly aching for Fiza's company, that she wants her hands held by her best friend's. How she feels like she is grasping at something intangible, all the time, like she will forget Fiza just as she fears she is forgetting her mother. How sometimes it feels like Fiza is dead, too, just as absent as Ba. It's strange, but sometimes it is easier to think of Fiza this way—the knowledge of the alternative, that Fiza could be out there and slowly forgetting her, too much to bear.

When she returns home that night, Amla keeps contemplating Bahaar's disbelief. The lack of faith. She heads straight to where her churidar are folded and pulls the tapestry out from its safe spot beneath the pile. As she holds it in her hands, Amla tries to figure out how to explain that what she experienced the other night was true. That her mind isn't just playing pretend. She traces the women with her index finger. Could it be possible that all these women were able to will realities into existence through their creations—a child, a lovers' reunion, the end of a drought? When she sits beside the chulha, Amla can see the line of sitaphal trees, the gooseberry bush just beyond them. Sometimes she is certain it was her; other times, she falters at the impossibility. Can it be true, that she really did this?

That doubt—I had it, too. I look at you sitting across from me, Nadya, and I feel that same worry Amla felt with Bahaar. That I can't be believed—that what I'm saying is too unfathomable. You see why, don't you? I am sure I would doubt you, too, if these roles were reversed.

But stay with me, Nadya: Amla runs inside, grabbing the teakwood box from its place underneath her cot. Fuming, she starts to draw lightly in pencil. She breathes deeply; she wants to return to that physical space she'd occupied when she had yearned for her mother, painting the moon and the gooseberry bush. Her eyes close.

But her mother is not at the forefront of her desire today, no; in her gut, she feels a different, still desperate hunger. She wants, more than anything, to be with Fiza on their Karachi rooftop, to share a secret with a friend.

The women, the lineage, their many lives—they rise like tides through her veins, and Amla navigates the current, finding little pools of memory that hold lessons. That caution. *Act with care*, they tell her. *Ask for what you need. Do not take risks you might regret.* But she is not doing anything dangerous, no; she scans through the memories like flipping the pages of her sketchbook.

Amla takes to these rivers like they are her birthright—and they are. This is. Pencil meets page meets movement, her whole body now their puppet. No turning back.

*Advice taken*, she says to those memories. *I know this is what I need.*

She focuses only on her breath, this expansion and contraction of lungs. Just a body, just muscles—her tendons should feel sore from how quickly the paintbrush moves across the thick page. There are moments when her skin stings, the pointed edges of the page leaving paper cuts along her dry wrist. Still, her mind feels removed from her body. She pushes forward.

The front door opens and closes; Amla doesn't hear it. Her father peeks into her room; her eyes don't even acknowledge him. Even after Bapu begins to snore, and later, when the sun begins to peek out from behind the heavy drapes, she continues feverishly.

At some point she stops to sleep, pushed to exhaustion. The painting sits at the bottom of her cot, where her feet don't yet reach. It'll dry by the time she wakes, and then she'll see something she can't understand: A crinkled page, two women in a gray tiled space, valises in hand. Blurred figures mill all about them. She doesn't know what an airport looks like, but you or me, we'd know this place immediately. We've flown through it so many times. But Amla, she just knows that the paint leaves purple stains on her bedding.

That night, Amla doesn't dream her mother is leaving her. For the first time in a long time, she dreams of an entirely normal day in Karachi, the sweat sticking to the cloth at the nape of her neck, the smell of bhutta rising from the corner stand. Playing pretend with Fiza on the apartment rooftop. Ba's and Bapu's laughter when he comes home, a plate of jalebi waiting for them on the table.

Before she knows it, the week of the dinner celebration has arrived. Bapu makes and pours his own version of chaash for the first time since the month after Ba's death. It tastes a little too much of cumin and could afford less asafetida, but Amla is impressed that he took the effort to cool the buttermilk in the clay pot, that the consistency is just thin enough.

"You think so little of me." Bapu laughs when she says this out loud, clinking her cup with his. "As though your Bapu wasn't breaking his back making mithai every morning. Where did you and Ba think the sweets came from, hmm?"

"Not made at home, though," Amla points out.

"No, nothing like the work your Ba did every day," he says, shaking his head. "Your mother carried the world on her back, you know that?"

Amla sips her chaash, a smile blooming against the cup's rim. She would trade any number of birthday gifts for the sound of Bapu's laughter, for this moment over and over.

When their cups are empty, Bapu readies for the sahib's house, his week devoted to paying vendors and preparing taxes in case the British officials ask about land value. "A new letter from your Meenafai came in yesterday, but you were already asleep," he says on his way out the door. "Everyone is doing well."

He says it so casually, so quickly, that Amla doesn't have a chance to ask her usual questions: how the twin cousins are growing up, if they've seen Fiza and her father lately. The door is already closing behind Bapu.

*No matter*, she thinks. She knows where Bapu leaves the letters, always watches him tuck them away into his bedside drawer while she pesters him for answers. Now she goes through his neat stack slowly and systematically, like it is a tuition assignment.

*February 1947*

*I worry I made you move to a new place for no reason, that there was no reason to leave here at all. I hope your journey is unnecessary. I like to think you'll come back and fight with me, angry with me for pushing you to leave Karachi. I'm glad to hear you made it safely to the house. Chandini would love the idea of you raising her daughter in her grandmother's old home, that it's not just sitting empty any longer. I hope the mango trees are everything you wanted them to be.*

*I'm sorry to hear Amla is not ready for school, though I'm sure she doesn't miss tuition. Fiza stops by every now and then to ask about her. I hope Amla makes new friends quickly there. My children are restless and wearing me down—do you want me to send one along to you? You'd be doing me a favor.*

*March*

*Considered sending you a telegram but there's no rush now. I'm sure you heard about the violence in Rawalpindi? If not, just know Harneetben and her family are fine in Karachi but they haven't received news of her sister and children who were in Pindi. You remember when we were kids and we'd get free food from her gurudwara? I keep thinking about that and praying, more than I ever have in my life.*

*April*

*Bhai, don't worry about us. The children and I are fine, and my husband and the maulana are doing their best to keep everyone calm. There have been a few incidents but mostly just young boys stirring things up; they don't know what they're saying. There's nothing serious for you to worry about; I'd send a telegram if it were that important.*

*Harneetben and her family are the last Sikhs left in our building. They're thinking of taking a train eastward but don't know where to go. Lahore is a whole different matter than Karachi, I hear. Harneetben is scared to go on a train but also too scared to stay here much longer.*

And then there's the letter from May, and this letter Amla will only understand many years later, when there's nothing she can do anymore. When everything has already transpired. She strings phonemes together, traces the curlicues of the script with her fingers. She reads the note over and over and still she cannot imagine the scene that Meenafai's words describe, as though the words refract reality, twisting it into a kaleidoscope.

*Your last letter made me worry about Amla,* Meenafai writes, *but I'm taking you at your word that she is fine.*

> *I don't know that I have good advice for this child you helped,*
> *but just remember there is so much at stake for a young girl like*
> *that, who's been through what she has. No one will believe her*
> *enough to take on a powerful person. I pray this is a small thing*
> *and that I'm reading into your words—and still I advise you to*
> *do nothing. This is a private matter for the girl's family, and*
> *your involvement might only make them more ashamed. You're*
> *an outsider, Anurag. You're not from this place, even if you live*
> *there. You're not one of this community—and even then, your*
> *intruding wouldn't be welcome.*
>
> *Sometimes I think violence is all around us. Harneetben's*
> *family is confirmed dead. The murmurs of what happened*
> *there . . . I keep wondering where a girl can go to be safe. I tell*
> *my husband every day, we must keep our doors and the temple*
> *doors open no matter what happens outside. Take care, bhai.*

All those years later, when Amla fully comprehends every part of this letter, every implication, she will be a grown woman, married and in a new city she's begun to call her home. She will reach for the phone to call an old friend, will hold it pressed to her ear, her heart thumping, the bill increasing with every passing minute. Padma, who she has not seen in years, will tell her that one of the musician girls from the village had been practicing for the party at the sahib's house, a session so long that her calloused fingers ached with deep black grooves. Her mother couldn't stay and wait for her, the younger children needing watching. And then, after the session, Mahesh Shankar Sharma had asked the girl to stay a little longer so he could critique her technique.

Amla will learn that the sahib had led the girl into his study, where he kept the other instruments, and that the hungry look in his eyes had translated into ravenous hands, that when the girl had finally been able to get away, her neckline was torn and her eye was swelling. That as she held her broken wrist up to her bleeding nose, she was able to trip Mahesh Shankar Sharma over his own tanpura and race down the stairs leading from the entryway. She made it to the door.

Amla will learn that Bapu must have heard the commotion from the office farther down in the bungalow, where he was crunching the numbers of a camel procurement earlier that day. The sahib had come out in a fury, yelling, presumably at Bapu or anyone else around, to *take care of this problem. I want it gone.* And Bapu had come running outside and told the girl to *get up, walk fast* and held out his hand. She pointed at her limp wrist and grabbed his arm with her other, and he must have thought for a moment, considered her, before saying, *Let's get you home.*

When Amla learns all of this, she will beg Padma, this girl she once saw as an almost-sister, to tell the story again—just the part about her father, please, one more time, and one more time after that, even if it is unfair. Even if she knows it makes Padma feel shame for never having said anything, for not having shared this sooner. Padma will not complain, will answer every question in tribute to a long-ago friendship. Amla will imagine every moment of it, a movie reel behind her eyelids, a memory that doesn't belong to her but that she will take to the grave: a memory of her father, who will forever feel to her like the definition of goodness. She will wish she had known then what she does now. She will wonder if it would have changed anything.

But in this moment, Amla is still a child. She has no concept of the story behind this letter, of men's power, and yet it lingers with her. She folds the letter as it had been before and then gathers all of the papers carefully, trying not to wrinkle them even as the desert heat makes the edges curl. Though she doesn't know who the girl Meenafai mentions is, she keeps thinking of the relief in Padma's shoulders, of Bahaar, and wonders how to protect more of the people she loves.

# FIVE

How do I choose which bits to tell you?

You sit beside me wondering if I started this story too many generations ago. I wonder if it was long ago enough.

Imagine this is only my story. What could I tell you about motherhood? I'd sit next to you imagining what it would be like, only knowing it from one side. What if I began with my mother—would one type of motherhood be enough to explain?

Imagine what you would gain if you had the entire history, if you could see every time, the same scenario presenting itself, the same questions of what to do, what to ask for, who to tell. Who to pass it on to. How each of us have grappled with these questions.

Should this story have begun ten years before all of this, with Ba and Bapu's arrival in Karachi? I could have spent my time describing to you that walk along the chowpatty, the way Ba-before-she-was-Ba had to shield her eyes from the brightness of sunlight on ocean. I could walk you through the moment when she knew she would leave

Gujarat and go to Sindh with this man, when she knew she wanted to begin a family with him. When she drew it.

Maybe the story for Ba begins before this, when she was just Chandini. We could read the letters that she and the sister in Delhi had dictated to send to each other, laugh at their giddiness when they rushed for a neighbor who could help them read the letter aloud whenever a new one arrived in the mail. The excitement of sisters who had made their bond last despite the space between them. A distinct type of sisterhood.

Or even a decade before: Chandini as a girl, forever loved by her grandmother, the one who grew up in that house that Amla and Bapu will occupy. The two sisters compete for their grandmother's love; they both want to be the daughter who this grandmother calls the most beautiful, want to get the rarest gifts, their favorite gold jewelry, all gifted by this woman—but Kasturiben dotes only on Chandini. The girls dare each other to pull pranks on their grandmother without being found out: Chandini, graceful, can pluck earrings from the woman's lobes while she sleeps; the Delhi sister, not so graceful, has her ear pulled by her grandmother in punishment. A motherhood.

And isn't it true that the story begins before then: with this grandmother, from the moment she is stitched onto that tapestry to the moment she stitches Chandini onto it, her favorite granddaughter, the one she knew wasn't as sweet as she seemed but who was clever instead, so clever that she felt she could trust Chandini with a gift like this one.

And doesn't it go back further, then, to each profiled figure on that tapestry; doesn't the story begin so long before everything, aren't we made entirely of people who precede us; is there anything original in the calcium in our bones? Even now, sitting here, all my feelings are mirrors of what others before me have felt—some emotions my own, some I carry from ghosts. I begin where another ends; does that mean I have no beginning of my own? Look, the compounding of motherhood upon motherhood. If we raise children to be like our parents, or to be unlike them, and our parents did the same, then how far back must the dominoes go?

I try to trace the memories I have. The further in the past they are, the more they blur together. I cling to my grandmother because she remains clear to me; meanwhile, Chandini's memories fade. Always, though, the memories that stand out the most are the extremes—the best ones, the worst ones. I place a fingernail on a line of ancestral traumas like the ridges of a spine. See, there's one, now another, a third, so many. Here, this one, this vertebra belongs to Amla. I scoop the bone from flesh, hold it up, investigate: *Let me understand what you have passed along. I could not be who I am without that which you have given me.*

The day of the dinner, Amla presents her finished salwar kameez to her father. She has kept her project in her room, hoping to feel his pride the way she can imagine Ba's. But when she twirls it around, offering to wear it so he can see how detailed she was with her measurements, Bapu sips his lemon water in a serious silence.

When he finally speaks, he leaves little room for argument. "Absolutely not."

Amla stares. "What do you mean?"

"You're not going to that party."

Amla's eyes widen. "But Bahaar's performing, and—"

"Bahaar is older than you," Bapu says sternly. "We are not interacting any more with the sahib than we have to, okay? No, the best thing you can do is stay home. You understand?"

It has been an unspoken agreement, ever since that afternoon the sahib came to greet them, that Amla was supposed to keep her dis-

tance from the sahib's house. But Bapu had not asked her to forgo
the party, not explicitly, and so Amla doesn't understand when things
changed. Doesn't know his reasoning. All she can think of is the promise she made to her friend, and how promises are supposed to be kept.
"If I have to stay away from the sahib, shouldn't Bahaar have to,
too?" Amla asks now.

Bapu looks at her like he's scrutinizing her, like her phrasing and
tone reveal that she's grown up faster than he expected. "What Bahaar does is up to her parents. You have to follow my rules, Amla.
How often do I ask something of you?"

Bapu knows her well. Amla kicks at the floor; following Bapu's
rules is the best way she knows to be a good daughter. "But . . . but
my salwar kameez, I've been working so—"

"I know you have, jaan," he says, and two fingers pinch his nose.
"I want you to get to show it off, but—"

"And you?" Amla scuffs her foot on the floor. She feels petulant,
childlike. She is. "Are you staying home?"

"No, he wants me there to talk about estate taxes and the crop
yield this past year."

"What if I stay with you? I promise, Bapu, I promise if you let me
go I'll stay next to you the whole time. I won't leave your side. I
promise."

"Amla—"

"I'll even hold your hand in the crowd," she offers, words tumbling over one another. "*Please*, Bapu, I told Bahaar I'd be there. I
*promised* her."

"Enough, Amla." Bapu's raised voice forces the wind from Amla.
He sighs, and his posture softens with his tone. "There is nothing
that will sway me. I've been thinking about this for days, and I don't
feel good about you being in that house or among that crowd."

"But"—and Amla lapses, unsure what she can say—"I won't run off anywhere. I'll stay with you. I just want to listen to Bahaar. Please, Bapu."

"I can't, jaan," he says, and he pulls out his gold cigarette case with one hand, resting the other on her shoulder as though to steady her. As he taps out a cigarette, he says softly, "My word is final. It's done."

Amla kicks the table, so much energy and anger coursing through her muscles, but she stubs her toe and bites her lip to keep from crying out. She huffs all that evening as Bapu combs oil into his mustache, changing into a clean white button-up and a gold-lined dhotiyu. She hides in her room until he leaves, and then, adamant, she slips into her completed salwar kameez.

If only she were older. She hadn't understood what happened to the girl from Meenafai's letter, and there is no one to explain it to her. If only Meenafai were there. If only Ba. Maybe part of her frustration is Bapu's avoidance of saying it directly—but how does one say such things directly to an eleven-year-old child? He's never heard someone use words like *consent, assault,* never mind explained those concepts to a girl so young. He's probably never thought he would have to, leaving it in the realm of topics meant for Ba to cover.

Amla twirls in her room, pleased with the fit, with the way the mirrors send light dancing along the walls, and tries to shake off the conversation with Bapu. When she slides her small pair of mojari onto her feet, she's thinking not of the girl in the letter, not even of the sahib, but of what it means to be a good friend. To be there for Bahaar when Padma can't. To be there the way Fiza would be there for her, if she could be.

*Being a good friend is a way to be good,* she thinks. Ba would be proud of her.

. . .

A thirteen-gun salute announces that the Jethwa guests have already arrived at Mahesh Shankar Sharma's estate. The crowd is large enough for Amla to hide among. She weaves through the parade of people, searching for any familiar faces so she can avoid them: there are the teenagers who farm their land; the young boy whose mother once taught Amla how to make ghee; and, kept at a distance by the other adults, two of the young laborers Amla recognizes from the time one of Bapu's bulls died. They had dragged its carcass onto a cart, taken it to the farthest corner of the estate for burning, maybe, or leather making. Amla keeps her head down, increasing her pace to match that of the adults nearest her, letting the crowd propel her forward and hide her from their sight.

The closer she gets to the estate, the brighter the lights around her and the better dressed the people. The entrance through the outer courtyard walls is packed; Amla recognizes the teacher auntie, the inhabitants of the largest houses in the village. The epicenter is a sight of luxury; regal princes of Porbandar enter in finely embroidered sherwanis, crisp pants, slicked hair. The crowd acknowledges their standing with hands clasped behind backs, bowing.

Amla keeps her eyes trained for Bapu, but he must already be inside; even now, as the last of the Jethwa party are ushered through the gates, the crowd begins to dissipate. Men her father's age or older—it's impossible to distinguish age with sun-weathered skin—tap their children on their shoulders, ushering them back onto the paths that lead to the well or to their homes. They are dressed in their best wear, but even that does not compare to Bapu's. Amla is shocked, having imagined everyone dressed like the businessmen in Karachi, just as her father had dressed; she had assumed there were secret blazers in the closets of every farmer. It is in this moment she realizes how out of place she and Bapu are.

Amla, whose hands are as smooth as Padma's if not smoother, who has never wanted for a meal. Who has never been asked to help Bapu tend their land. Her most frightening moment was leaving one city for another; her greatest tragedy the same as millions of children across her country who lost their mothers, never mind those left orphaned. How do you even understand what you have at that age?

How naive she is.

The differences between her family and the others in the village make it easy for her to enter the estate. She only has to voice who she—and her father—is to the guards at the gate to get inside. When she says "I'm the accountant's daughter" and "He came early to meet with the sahib," they inch to the sides so Amla can join.

When she is past the men, she nearly gasps. The courtyard is lavish, a tiled pond at its center with candles floating among lily pads and lotus flowers. Some servants line the perimeter with steel serving plates in their hands; others weave among the crowd to wait on the men and women scattered across the yard. It is almost like the gymkhana on a wedding day.

*No,* Amla thinks, *better than.*

She smiles shyly at one of the stone-faced servants and reaches for a small steel bowl of khaman dhokla. The sound of Bahaar's presence travels to Amla before she can even begin to look for her; a harmonium begins to play, the beat of a dholak alongside it, and Amla strains to make out the elevated stage near the house entrance. When she finds a place where she can stand with an uninterrupted view of Bahaar at the harmonium, she bites into the dhokla, relishing the spongelike texture, the coating of lemon and coconut and coriander and mustard seeds.

Bahaar is almost unrecognizable, her hair pulled back in a sleek and tight plait, clearly oiled down against the humidity. In her tailoring, she had positioned the cloth so that the chaniya hem and choli sleeves are evergreen, the large middle portions of both a bright orange. Her eyes are kohl lined, her lips tinged red. She looks bridelike to Amla. Angelic.

Amla glances over the crowd nearest the stage, imagines being able to sit up front, head propped up in her hands. She doesn't know how she'd manage her way through the cluster of people without calling attention to herself. If Bapu were anywhere nearby, he'd notice her immediately. She perches on her tiptoes, trying to catch sight of her father, and instead spots the sahib, watching the musicians from where he lounges in the corner, his eyes focused on Bahaar, a piece of paan folded in his mouth.

"—*how to say it*, the plan is being drafted right now. Mountbatten will announce it tomorrow."

A new song starts, Bahaar leading with new chords on the harmonium, and the conversation behind Amla grows louder. Distracted by their voices, she loses the beat of the dholak. The speaker's Gujarati is mangled, a British accent defining its corners. Amla almost chokes on her dhokla, wanting to laugh at how garbled the voice sounds. She tries to avoid swinging around to see its owner.

The intended audience is a woman, one who speaks much more naturally, but formally. "If the princely states get to decide—"

"Oh, they will."

"—Porbandar will certainly choose India. Maharaj Rana Sahib wouldn't do it any other way."

"No, he wouldn't," the British voice agrees.

Amla turns as though to grab more dhokla, the British officer and Gujarati woman now in her sights.

"I'm surprised at how soon the decision is being made," the woman continues. She looks older than Ba, her gray-streaked hair pulled tightly in a bun. Her sari—styled so the pallu drapes over her left shoulder to hang down her back instead of draping to the front over the right shoulder in Gujarati style—is as elegant as the outfits of the Jethwas. "I thought you were leaving it until next year."

"The violence across the country—*how to say it*—it's not like here." He chews a handful of sautéed peanuts loudly. "For all this place's simplicity, I'd rather be in a village like this one than caught in Delhi or Calcutta. This is an easy assignment."

The woman smiles curtly, the candlelight making her pink sari appear orange. "No, you wouldn't be caught dead there."

It's a conversation Amla recognizes—even the teacher auntie has whispered about it, the British announcing they are leaving India. In another world—in Karachi—Amla would have relayed these tidbits to Ba and Bapu, staying up late to hear their whispers.

The past always crops up in unexpected ways like these; she finds herself thinking of her old banal routine, yes, but also of Ba's passing, of the steamboat, of Fiza—everything, everything, always everything at once. She finishes her second piece of dhokla just as the musicians announce a quick break to quench their thirst in the overbearing heat. Abandoning her eavesdropping, Amla navigates her way to the stage.

"Bahaar!"

Up close, Bahaar looks familiar again, and she envelops Amla in an embrace. Holding her friend tightly, her neck turns at the perfect angle to watch Sharma sahib retreat from the stage to the private dinner. For a moment, Amla thinks he makes eye contact with her, watching her watching him, and she burrows her face into Bahaar's collarbone.

"Amla! You're here, I was looking for you before."

"I'm sorry I'm late," she rushes. "But I'm here now—just like I promised."

Bahaar fiddles with the large silver earrings tugging her earlobes downward. "Making the most of my chance today." She laughs before putting on a formal accent. "How do I look?"

"Like a princess," Amla says, and she means it.

The dholak player calls that their break is over, and Bahaar takes a deep breath. "Are my eyes smeared?"

Amla shakes her head. "You look perfect."

"The heat always makes them smear." Bahaar wipes at her eyes with an aggressive swipe of her hand. She looks around anxiously. "Go, enjoy yourself. When they're done with the dinner inside, they're supposed to have dancers and more musicians and everything else out here. Don't leave before then, okay? That's when I'll get to relax."

"Okay."

"I promise I'll have dessert with you after. I hear there's pistachio kulfi—didn't you say that's your favorite?" Bahaar says, and Amla grins tightly, trying her hardest not to think of her Karachi balcony, of kulfi dripping down her hands in the heat.

Amla means to stay nearby, to spend her night listening to Bahaar play the harmonium, to hear her voice accompany that of the older ghazal singer who is encouraged to join from the crowd. But as the clock tolls double digits and the moon glows brightly, the entryway to the house swings open to announce the conclusion of the private dinner, and Amla is distracted by the crowd, by the glimpses she sees of what grandeur is hidden behind those carved wooden doors. She peeks inside before another set of servants comes pouring out: all dark mahogany and beige tiles, higher ceilings than Amla could dream of.

"Get out of the way," barks one of the men with a serving platter on his shoulder as he rushes past, and she startles, stumbling backward. She catches herself on a large flower pot.

"I'm sorry," she says to no one. She turns to check the plant, to confirm its huge petals and leaves are unscathed, its soil neat and pressed down.

"You have some on your kameez," a woman says, and Amla quickly wipes at her lower back and buttocks.

"Thank—" She recognizes the woman immediately. "You're Padma's mother."

The woman nods, eyes flashing with recognition. Her hair is netted, her makeup quiet except for lipstick. She wears a white uniform with two sets of buttons down the front. "Amla, right? Look at those hands—let's get those cleaned up, shall we?"

Amla glances down. Her fingers are stained rusty from the plant's anthers, soil bits gathered beneath her nails. She lets Padma's mother take her by the wrist and lead her inside, past the lounge area with the large wooden swing hanging from the ceiling and the library lining the walls, to a door at the far side that leads to the kitchen, where everyone is dressed in that same double-breasted white uniform. She motions Amla toward an elaborate bronze waterspout and drain. "The soap is in the corner."

She wets the bar and then scrubs at her hands, thinking of how much she would give for her house to have a spout like this, too. To not need the regular trips to the well. When she's older, she'll realize how much more manufactured the sahib's power is, how it goes beyond a simple bronze waterspout: She'll wish for Bapu not to have had to pay rents to Sharma for irrigation, for the flow of water from Sharma's controlled reservoir to Bapu's fields. She'll understand the communities' performative gratitude, the threat they had lived under all their lives by a man who touted himself as pious and altruistic.

"Where's Padma?" she asks as she dries off her hands. "Bahaar's performing, and I thought Padma would be here, too, but—"

Padma's mother shakes her head, dismissive. "Padma wasn't feeling up to it. The crowd here doesn't suit her."

"She's performed here before, though, right?" Amla asks. "Isn't she used to this crowd?"

The woman eyes Amla. "I wouldn't force my daughter to be anywhere," she says firmly, already turning away. "Challo. Best get out of the kitchen before someone sees you where you shouldn't be, beti."

Amla is disoriented, though, and does not know which way is out. She eyes the magnificence around her, feeling like she's in a dream. She tries to piece it all together—Padma's mother and the way Padma had seemed nearly relieved at the news of her and Bahaar's lineup switch, how odd it is that she isn't here now—thinking about all this so intensely that when she swings open another door, eyes glazing over the colorful spines of books along the walls, Amla nearly walks right into her father.

**I have no other way** to tell you this story than through every moment Amla revisits five, ten, twenty years later. She will be rocking her daughters in their swinging cribs, thinking not of how she can thank the gods for their health but rather of where she was, every second of this evening all those years prior, the choices she could have made to be by Bahaar's side all night.

There is the moment she sees Bahaar playing harmonium, when she could have chosen to sit at the very front by the stage, gazing up at this sister-friend.

There is the moment she peeks inside Mahesh Shankar Sharma's house, when she could have found her way to another plate of food rather than inside, seduced by the lavish interior of a bungalow owned by a man whose wealth stems from charging his neighbors for fresh water.

There is the moment she runs into Bapu, when she could have simply apologized, could have admitted that she had disobeyed him, could have told him that she promised Bahaar and that the promise was the only thing that mattered, and maybe then he would have let her sit at the very front of the stage.

Instead, when Bapu looks sorely disappointed in her, and after he says so, Amla's response is to stomp her foot on the ground, to say he is unfair, to say she wishes Ba were there to be on her side. He tells her to be quiet, and she says *no*, and he says if she won't behave herself *then I have no choice but to take you home*, and Amla says, cruelly, *Ba would never have done that. You're nothing like her.* And the truth is simply that Amla is overwhelmed and a child, and there are so many secrets and so many places she's supposed to call home and she doesn't seem to have found home anywhere except with Bapu— and yet.

And yet, here he is, disappointed in her. She had tried so hard to be a good friend, but those same actions had made her a bad daughter. She wishes more than anything to have found a way to be both. If only she could turn back time, make a different decision.

Bapu tells her she has to stay with the women in the kitchen, that he has just one meeting left with someone important because of something related to *Mountbatten* and *violence everywhere* and *making sure your Meenafai and her family get a steamboat ticket as soon as possible, so stay here until I've asked and then we'll both go home together.*

"It's not home!" she shrieks at him, and before he can respond, she turns on her heels, her chest feeling like it will burst with all the emotions she cannot contain. She is in the crowd, now; she is in the pavilion, scouring for Bahaar and a harmonium that won't appear. Her chest feels heavier. She is retreating into the house, now, watching

Bapu as he alternatively rises on his tiptoes and bends down, trying to find a daughter who doesn't want to be found.

Because she thinks about this evening every day until the day she dies, I think about it endlessly, too. It is the spine of her story. It is my inheritance—this complicated, twisted gift she has given me.

**Amla is drowning** in the unbearable heaviness in her chest—wants, desperately, to be alone. She slips through the house, past colorful dupattas tucked into skirts and men's hands shoved into pockets, and into the kitchen, and then into the hallway outside of it. From one of the windows facing the courtyard, she can make out the raised stage, where an older man and a younger one sit at the farthest edge, angled ever so slightly toward each other, sitars resting against the outer sides of their right thighs, the instruments' long necks and pegs angling upward to their left. The dholak player at the adjacent edge watches their movements, palms and fingers a constant flurry against the leathery heads of the drums. No Bahaar.

She scans for Bapu's figure again in the crowd, but the lamplight is sparse and the people stand too closely together for her to make out where any single person might begin. Shame gathers in her stomach for the way she yelled at him, and she steps away from the window, lest he see her. She cannot let him find her.

As she turns, she can hear the sitars complete their set, the dholak rounding out the end of the piece. The crowd applauds gently as Amla searches for where to go, where to hide. There is a brief silence as the applause dissipates and Amla stops; she is convinced she heard, close by, a screech, a shriek. She glances around for someone, anyone, to confirm the sound, but she is alone in a tiled hallway where everything echoes.

Maybe just another cawing bird. Maybe a peacock brought for

show, just as the camels were. She hurries deeper into the house, past the wooden swing hanging from the ceiling, the lines of books on mahogany shelves.

Does she hear it again? She turns up the stairs, where the bungalow's hallways are dimly lit by gas lamps. It's quiet here; the sound of her own breath drowns whatever remains of the crowd outside. She counts each room she walks past, searching.

A small yelp, and Amla realizes she has passed the sound. She steps backward to the third door and holds her ear against the heavy wood.

She pushes it open, gently at first and then much faster when she recognizes the crumpled figure in the study. The hinges let out a squeak that resounds in the hallway; Amla's heart thumps in her ears. The girl on the floor reaches out a hand.

Amla wraps her arms around Bahaar's body, her forehead pressed against the blood crusting down from Bahaar's nose. Tears drip into Amla's hair. Bahaar tries to speak through hiccups but falters into silence.

They sit like this, entangled, until Bahaar is no longer taking three or four short breaths for each of Amla's deep ones. "We have to go," Amla whispers to the older girl. "Let's get out of here."

They take the stairs slowly, one at a time. Bahaar props herself up with one arm around Amla's shoulders. Past the kitchen whose door is closed; now past the porch, devoid of any person. They stop at the water garden to pat some of the blood off Bahaar's face.

As they make their way toward Amla and Bapu's house, the music behind them fading, Amla wonders how this could have happened. *When* it could have happened—and she regrets immediately those moments when Bahaar was out of her sight, when she'd gone to the kitchen, when she'd fought with Bapu. When she'd been such a child.

I know what you're thinking. Maybe if Bapu had told her what happened to the nameless girl in May—she wasn't too young, not if all of this could have happened so close to her—maybe, if she had known, Amla could've done something.

Amla had assumed that keeping her promise would be enough, that it would keep Bahaar away from whatever it was that this man made her feel in her gut. Keep her friend safe. Every promise she has kept is a trade, for her: do this right and she will not have to find another place to call home; keep this secret and no one she loves will be hurt or harmed; be good and she will make the lives of the people she loves better, easier, *more.*

*And yet*, she thinks. *And yet.*

**Bapu enters their home furious, yelling.** "How many times," he says, tossing his shoes into the corner of the entryway. Amla watches him shut the double doors into the house so loudly they shudder. When he sees the two girls, though, his expression falls apart. "My god," he whispers now, and he looks past Amla to Bahaar asleep on his daughter's cot, a bruise flowering across the older girl's neck, and his jaw ticks angrily.

"Bapu, I'm sorry."

"I know."

"Bahaar—"

"Yes. I know."

He must be wondering how their lives have become punctuated this way. He must be wondering how it is possible to shield Amla from this. He must be wondering whether somehow this is his fault, for having chosen for both of them to come to a place like this one. Bapu inhales and exhales slowly, again and again.

"We have to do something," Amla says, because she, too, is wondering about those questions, those hows. "We have to—"

"Right now, all we have to do is take care of Bahaar," he says softly, and he takes to his knees, holds Amla's hands in his own. "Are you okay? What did you—"

"I found her in the study, with the instruments," Amla says. "I'm okay."

"Lay out some fresh clothes."

"Yes, Bapu."

"Do you know if she has talked to her parents? Has she gone home at all?"

"No, Bapu."

"We'll figure that out in the morning, I guess." He runs his hands through his hair and then pulls his cigarette case from his breast pocket. "My god."

"Bapu, the sahib—"

"Don't say anything, Amu," Bapu says quickly. He shakes his head. "Don't say anything at all."

She doesn't need to understand to follow Bapu's instructions— she is to sleep in Bapu's cot, Bahaar in Amla's, Bapu watching the candle melt. Amla's stomach turns. Her every cell buzzes with the need to do something—to go out onto their land and yell at the moon, to light bajri plants on fire. To stomp the ground until it breaks in two and swallows her and Bahaar and Bapu whole, their house collapsing into itself, the earth folding over them, the moon caught in their gravitational pull, bathing them in sweet, sweet light, escorting them anyplace away from here.

There is nothing to do but open the teakwood box.

Here, a memory of justice.

Here, a memory of revenge.

Here, a memory, and a memory, and a memory. Ridges along a spine.

But Amla, breathing deep, pushes them all aside. She doesn't want to be told how others navigated this in the past. Those stories already live deep in the recesses of her own body. Now she is thinking only of the way the paan stained Sharma's teeth as he watched Bahaar at the harmonium. His hungry eyes. The placement of girl onto menu.

She doesn't have to understand exactly what happened. She doesn't have to have words for it to know it. She knows. She knows.

Amla considers every secret, every promise, and begins to paint—until it is no longer night and she remembers only the blur of her trajva across the page. She paints even as Bapu peeks into the room to check whether she has slept. She waves him away, back to his vigil. There is no need for a chaperone. She has already made a decision.

Is this the gift that the tapestry gives her? The ability to do something when she can do nothing else, to channel this energy somewhere? I hold myself still, memory coursing through blood. This is a history I want to change and cannot.

When I'm alone, when I'm wondering what all of this means, I sit with these memories first. Who holds the blame—Amla, for her impulsivity, or her mother for never explaining to her how this all works? How does anyone ever learn the rules of this ancestry? But no matter what questions I ask, what is already being done cannot be undone, the images she sets in motion with every frustrated gesture of an eleven-year-old's hand.

The perimeter of the painting is a deep mahogany, framing a formal head-on image of Mahesh Shankar Sharma. A wreath of marigolds droops down from the upper-left corner of the frame and curves to the upper right. It is a tradition reserved only for the already-dead.

As the painting dries on the floor, beside Bapu's cot, the newspapers announce the Mountbatten plan—the partitioning of Hindustan into two independent dominions. Cities, in the morning, will begin to trickle, then to flow and erupt, red. Weren't they already, you might wonder. But this entire night is the door that locks behind us. You must understand: this is the terror my mother woke from, crying; that I will wake from, crying, and that my daughter will wake from, crying, and my granddaughter, too, will remember it, crying, she will; and oh, I will carry it from one to the next to the other, this earth I bear upon my back.

# SIX

One morning in July, Amla waits impatiently for the postmaster to hand them the telegram Bapu expects from Meenafai. She shifts from one foot to the other, her heart caught in her throat. But the feeling isn't unique, no; every night for the past month has been shaped by this frenetic energy: She watches Bapu carefully when he returns from work, wondering if it will be the day that the news comes. She eavesdrops on the older children, trying to hear of any rumors that might betray what she has done. She tags along with Bapu on his errands, eager to move her body, to tire herself out.

The postmaster's office is next to the train station, and Amla hates the platform when it is empty. The wind whistles through the saplings, and Amla is filled with the eerie sense that this station is a liminal space, an in-between space. She doesn't know it, but many stations that look like this one are already brimming with ghosts.

The postmaster announces Anurag Sthanakiya's name—the surname Bapu has taken ever since Kasturiben and her husband signed the house title over to Chandini and her immediate family—as a young boy returns from the back of the office, a yellow paper in his hand. The postmaster nods, handing them the telegram.

Bapu points at something on the other side of the window that's too high up for Amla to peek over. "That headline," he says, shaking his head. "This world."

"You can take it," the postmaster replies, sucking at a pipe between his words. "I have another."

Bapu hands Amla the telegram as he takes out his wallet. "How far west do the trains here go?"

"Not to Pakistan," the postmaster says, passing Bapu the newspaper. Amla traces the lines of the man's wrinkles with her eyes, how his skin flaps, soft and loose, at his neck when he moves. With a glance toward Amla, he lowers his voice to a whisper. "Those trains that go through Punjab, back and forth with those bodies? The closest ones to us go from Bombay through Surat through Ahmedabad and then north to Firozpur. That's as close to us as it gets."

Bapu scratches at his mustache, nodding slowly. When he raises one hand in a goodbye, the postmaster mirrors him. "Come, Amu."

Amla follows him out, trying to peek at the newspaper headline under Bapu's arm. She offers to carry it for him, but he only shakes his head. Soon she gives up, fanning herself with both hands instead. The summer has felt warmer than any prior, sweat clinging to Amla's skin like another layer of thin cotton, but still Bapu insists they walk back to their house instead of trying for a bull cart. She feels the sweat drip down her neck even though their pace is slow, Bapu reading the telegram over and again.

"Your Meenafai has a steamboat ticket," he finally says. He takes a kerchief from his pocket, wipes the sweat from his forehead, underneath his eyes. His shoulders loosen. "The panditji is sending her and the girls first."

"They're coming here already?" Amla tries to picture Meenafai in the house, her raucous children sprinting through its rooms.

Bapu smiles, offering her his kerchief. "Can you imagine us, all together again?"

"What does it say, Bapu?" Amla asks, pointing with one hand at the newspaper still folded under his arm. "The postmaster, what was he saying about stations?"

"He did mention those, didn't he." Bapu folds the telegram and tucks it into his breast pocket. "I can't seem to keep the world from you, Amu. No matter how hard I try."

She remembers the hushed conversations in Karachi, how she had to plead with Ba for more information. Now there's this tired man in front of her, worn down, and there's a flood outside that she can't see, a bloodbath, and no dam can contain it.

"Britain approved the partition of Hindustan," Bapu says. He taps at the headline, at the date in the corner: July 18, 1947. "In a month, everything will change."

"Pakistan," Amla whispers, remembering that new identity of her home.

"Karachi will be its capital," Bapu says as they turn a corner, their house coming into view. "Meenafai is coming here, but not a lot of Sindhi Hindus have left. We'll see. If things settle, we'll go back and have our stores and apartment again. Doesn't that sound nice? We don't have to stay here if you don't want to."

"Do you want to?"

Bapu shrugs. "Sometimes . . . sometimes I think there's no looking back for me." He sniffs, eyes focused on something far away from Amla, and adds, "I don't know what Karachi would be like without your mother."

Amla thinks of the tapestry in her room. "Ba's always with us."

Bapu turns to Amla, placing one hand on her shoulder. "Yes," he says, his voice soft and broken, wishful.

Ever since that night at the Sharma estate, Bapu has held Amla close. Her movement around the village is more limited than ever, Bapu implementing a strict companion rule. During the days he goes to account at Sharma's house, Amla must have another person with her to fill water from the well, to go to the market, to attend classes—or she can opt to stay on their land, cleaning the debris left behind by the construction boys, preparing vegetables for that night.

Amla doesn't resist her new restrictions. For a month, she has woken up with nightmares of her friends' faces patterned with bruises, of their hands reaching toward her. Even if she could roam the village freely, she isn't sure where she would go. The thought of the estate, with its mahogany shelves and courtyard pond, the memory of two ghostly sitars strumming in the air, enough sound to cover a girl's quiet pleas, makes Amla's stomach turn.

**The crinkled painting** of Mahesh Shankar Sharma with a frame around the perimeter of the page—the marigolds, closest to the viewer, draped like a half wreath—collects dust beneath Amla's cot.

She's supposed to keep the space clean, but sometimes when Amla is alone in the room she should feel comfortable calling her own, she sees the silhouette of Bahaar underneath the blankets and feels unsafe. In the days after the party, she asked one of the girls from school to detour with her by Bahaar's house, rapping her knuckles on the front door until someone answered. Bahaar was never home; Bahaar was always busy. But when Amla asked where her friend had gone or where Amla might find her, Bahaar's mother wouldn't concede any information. Padma does the same, only more kindly, telling Amla to be patient, that some things take their own time. So now, when those nightmares come calling, Amla awaits Bapu's return in the main room, where the tapestry hangs on one wall. When he is too long in coming home, the insects chirping outside and the dusk breeze moving through the bajri stalks like a wave, Amla leans into the nightmare, nudging an uneven stack of sketched pages out from beneath the bed. With one finger, she fans them out across the floor, surveying each one. She keeps them in order. Here, Amla's attempt to pin down the color of her mother's skin, the watercolor too thick and crackly. Here, roughly drawn, Bapu in the morning with chaash and chickpea-batter snacks. Here, aunties gathered in the Karachi apartment, as they had during Ba's wake. Here, pencil sketches of gooseberry bushes and mango trees and sitaphal crushed and rotting in the dirt; the watercolor of two women with suitcases; the watercolor gooseberry bush that became real.

Amla lifts the painting of Sharma, the final page in the stack. She sits with this one for hours, tracing her own brushstrokes. She knew from the moment she painted it what it depicts—her own mother's image hangs in their house, flowers strung from the upper-left corner, through a valley, and then to the upper right. She knew it was the painting of a dead man.

She rocks back and forth on the floor of her room, the painting shaky in her hands. She wonders again, this painting, is it good? When she made it, did she choose right? If only Bahaar would open the door. If only Bahaar's mom would let her inside. She wants to hug her friend's waist, holding on tight. Until then, Amla can only keep pulling the painting out from beneath her cot, her skin flush with a mix of shame, discomfort, and excitement, and pray that she has looked out for Bahaar the right way.

. . .

**In the late afternoon,** the sun dances along the mirrors sewn into the tapestry. The cloth looms above Amla as she pores over her tuition books, a convenient source of distraction, procrastination. She'll soon need another book; Bapu has promised to pick up the next level when he goes into the city later this month. He's been on a hunt for furniture that reminds him of Karachi; most of the local items are sculpted wood—"Which is fine," Bapu says hurriedly to the shopkeepers in Sodhana, "absolutely beautiful and fine, but not quite what I'm looking for"—and Bapu wants colors that will remind Meenafai of the foamy blue of Sindhu Sagar, the sandstone of the Merewether Clock Tower, the dull green of Frere Hall's roof. In Porbandar, Bapu has a better chance of walking into stores and finding velvet seat covers, running his hands along newly stocked cloths—all a far cry from this village with its small market, its every face instantly recognizable, its rows and rows of carved wooden chairs with minute variations.

"The construction boys are here," Bapu says, tossing a handful of almonds into his mouth. He raps his knuckles on the newspaper he took from the postmaster. "I'll be outside."

Amla nods and points to her book. "I'll be here."

She waits until the doors creak closed behind him and then quickly slips off the chair and onto the floor, her palms pressing downward. She faces the tapestry, remembering the time she had first attempted to observe it: the images tricking her, mocking her, blurring together. Now, as she carefully traces the outlines of each woman on the cloth, the experience couldn't be more different—every image crystallized, every profile stark.

She stares at the last two figures on the lowest rung, the woman

ASHA THANKI

holding the young girl's hand in her own. The space below this row feels infinite, and Amla can't guess how many more women might fit onto the cloth. She focuses on the hands, the feeling of being held, like she has so many times before.

*Ba*, she thinks, *remember that time*—and then she is there, reliving the night Ba left, the first time she had ever placed her hands on the teakwood box, watching her mother pack a suitcase she'll never unpack, the smell of ghee and the orange rust of the gas lamps in the window;

and then she sees herself through Ba's eyes, sees her own hands trace the edges of the teakwood box, her own eyes widen as she touches the dried watercolors for the first time, and she feels the emotions her mother feels, that overwhelming fountain of maternal love, and she bestows it upon herself, both mother and daughter in this moment and this memory, all of it happening in the present and the past at once—

A shout outside forces Amla from her reverie.

The evening sky is painted in pastel hues, expansive across the horizon when Amla pushes against the front doors, peering across the small stretch of dirt where they hang the clothesline, where the construction boys have left wheelbarrows filled with brick. She calls out to the back of the house over the clanking of hammers and stone. "Bapu? Did you hear that?"

The bustle is at the house across from them, the one that belongs to an Ayurvedic doctor. In the lamplight, against the setting sun, two silhouettes are framed in conversation. Amla recognizes the hunching frame of the doctor. The other she isn't able to name, but as he comes back down the path from the house to the road, she sees his uniform, his jewelry, and remembers the visit from Mahesh Shankar Sharma just a couple months ago. Was it only so recently? She takes a step back, stomach twisting.

"Hey!" Bapu calls to him. "Everything all right?"

The servant looks around furtively as he walks up to Bapu. "The sahib," he says, voice low, almost embarrassed, "they found him dead."

Amla watches Bapu's face—the registration of shock, the furrowed brow. If she weren't watching so carefully, so closely, she might have missed the small twitch at his lips, almost as though Bapu wants to smile. He shuts this down, jaw visibly clenching. "How?"

The servant shakes his head. "I don't know. We sent a runner two towns over since they have a Western doctor, but our doctor says it's too late."

"My god," Bapu says. He pulls on his chin. "My god."

"God indeed," the servant says. "Whoever did this is bold, trying to start something local today."

Amla's breath hitches.

Bapu frowns. "You think someone did this?"

"He was perfectly fine yesterday, no?" The servant spits a chewed clump of tobacco and takes a deep breath. "Today, the news, and then something happens to Sharma sahib? Some people are saying someone must want to start something." He glances at Amla, eyes softening. "Be careful, bhai."

"Of course," Bapu says, and he steps back, too. "You as well. Take care."

Amla stays rooted for an extra moment, watching the back of the servant as he jogs toward the Sharma estate, and Bapu takes her by the shoulders as though steering her into the house. She blinks as they cross the doorway, trying to register the servant's words. "The sahib is dead, Bapu?"

She tries to picture Sharma sahib dead—tries to think of what a dead body would look like. She imagines him asleep, unanswering, white sheets tight around him in the bed, chest unmoving.

Bapu looks down at her and swallows, as though buying time to frame his words. "Amu, I'll go to the sahib's house now and pay my respects. Why don't you go see your friends?" He is thinking, she realizes, of Bahaar. Amla nods, eager to try again. This time, it will be different. She finally has good news.

He crosses the kitchen quickly, reaching for a matchbox along the way. At the far window, the only one facing east, he lights the tall candle that sits on the sill. Amla can't remember the last time he lit this candle in the evening; she is accustomed to waking up in the morning with the candle recently snuffed, the smell of burning in the air, Bapu having whispered a prayer toward the sun.

Maybe he is thanking the gods Sharma is dead, a grateful prayer for this twisted justice. Maybe it's not a prayer for Bahaar's sake at all, but for Amla—that she has been kept safe. "Someone's looking out," Bapu mumbles as he combs down his mustache, readying to go to the sahib's house. Amla watches him silently, biting at her cuticles.


**The rumors pick up** like the humidity, dripping and undeniable, constant. As often as there are updates about massacres and migrations, there are new details to add to the circumstances of Sharma's death. The young men who take bundles of cotton for ginning in the next town are convinced Sharma died of overdrinking and oversmoking, his liver unable to handle any more, the road in front of his courtyard always reeking of that hookah and tobacco—*No*, say the women who manage the carts of painted jewelry, their own arms covered in silver cuffs, *this is what happens when you show off and entertain, when you take too many girls; hasn't everyone seen the young girls and their aunts brought in, maybe Muslim, maybe Christian, some lower-caste, all to entertain the sahib in his courtyard? Were we to*

*think he was just a connoisseur of good music, that it had nothing to do
with who was singing and playing?*

The local children gather at the sitaphal grove to discuss what
they've heard. Amla wouldn't normally join, but she is hopeful Padma
will be there, that she can ask about Bahaar. The day they received
the news had been like any other, Bahaar's mother turning Amla away
at the door. But today she sees Bahaar's older brother walking toward
the grove, too, and Amla wants to tug at his sleeve, ask how his sister
is doing. He jogs half-heartedly with his lanky teenager strides and
Amla can't reach him before he is surrounded by others. Instead she
lurks at the group's farthest edge, hoping to catch him alone when he
leaves.

The young girl who sells dried red peppers in bunches with her
mother wants the cause of death to be poison, for police officers to
come investigate. It would be exciting, the girl says. Their village has
no drama.

One of the shorter boys shrugs. "Maybe the Jethwas didn't like
how much he showed off at that party," he says. "Maybe they thought
he was too powerful."

"Maybe it's just karma," says teacher auntie's daughter. "Plain and
simple."

"No, I bet his son wanted the estate to himself," someone else
says. "It's so much land."

"Maybe he wants to convert the estate into a factory."

"No, a school—"

"I bet his son wanted all the money."

"No, the jewelry—"

"No," Bahaar's brother says forcefully. The group falls silent. "The
taxes from the well. Someone stood up for us."

Hums of agreement spread slowly, and Amla considers pretending
to hum along with them, as though the well has anything to do with

the man's death. If only she could be lost in imagination with them—but she *knows*. The painting flashes in her mind—no, the *act* of painting: the image of her own hands—the stains of dried marigold pigment lining the length of her thumb, the underside of her wrist.

She remembers, too, the first time that phrase had been used—*on the menu.* Padma begging Amla and Bahaar not to say anything, her eyes wide as she insisted, *never the sahib*—a way of telling Amla that there was too much at stake.

*Do something good,* she thinks now. *Listen to one thing your friend told you. Don't say anything to anyone.*

Amla waits another ten minutes, but Padma doesn't show and there is no way to speak to Bahaar's brother alone. She sneaks off from the group, following the quiet pathway home.

At dinner, she asks Bapu what he thinks, what would happen if someone had caused Mahesh Shankar Sharma's death.

Bapu brushes this off. "Keep your head down," he says. "Everybody wants to think there's an explanation. Sometimes people die. Maybe it's karma. Maybe it's not. I'm just glad—I mean, I'm glad he was at home with family."

She nods, unsure how to ask more questions without betraying her secret. *Besides,* she thinks, *it's been nearly two months since the painting. The gooseberry bush showed up the next day. Maybe this . . . maybe this* was *someone else.* Or maybe her father was right—sometimes people just die.

But the words feel empty even as she thinks them. After their plates are scraped clean and Bapu has looked over her lessons, Amla takes the painting out from beneath her bed for the third time that day. She holds it in her hands, tracing Sharma's chin, neck, right shoulder. She stares until the image blurs, until her dry eyes are forced to tears.

. . .

**The telegram from Meenafai** arrives the next week.

ARRIVING 4 AUGUST EVENING WITH THE GIRLS *stop* THANKFUL TO HAVE
A STEAMBOAT TICKET *stop* PRAISE GOD BHAI SEE YOU SOON

Amla traces the words with the tip of her index finger, her lips
moving soundlessly as she repeats the words over and over.

"Can you get the place ready for their arrival?" Bapu asks before
leaving for work, gulping down the rest of his lemon water. He hands
Amla the steel cup as he bends over, slipping his feet into sandals.
"It'll be good to have family around again, don't you think?"

Amla nods, watching him leave. It would be nice to have Meenafai around, even the children. It would be better than being alone,
better than waiting for Bahaar to speak to her. Having other beating
hearts in the rooms around her, other warm bodies in her room at
night, other voices, has to make all of this better.

After a day of trying to do the work alone, Amla asks Padma to
help her, even though her first instinct is to walk to Bahaar's house
and try once more to see her. Padma offers to bring water from the
well before meeting at Amla's house, and Amla has to keep herself
from crying when Padma arrives. She is relieved. They haven't had
time together like this, away from large groups or parents' ears, in
weeks.

"Have you heard what people are saying?" Amla asks feverishly as
they prepare the chulha. "About Sharma sahib?"

Padma slowly sets one full pot of water onto the ground before
lifting the other from the cloth ring atop her head. She musses the
younger girl's hair with her now-free hands. "A bit. Are you captivated by the promise of drama?"

Amla tosses the ring into the air and catches it as Padma grabs ingredients—a bag of flour, jaggery, spices—from inside the house. "I wonder what you think," she calls. "What Bahaar thinks."

"You should ask her yourself." Padma emerges from the kitchen with full arms.

"I went last week, but her mother . . ."

"I know it's hard to hear she's not ready yet, but keep trying," Padma says, leaning down to the chulha. "It'll help. She avoided me, too, for weeks."

Amla releases a long breath, the knot in her chest loosening. Maybe Bahaar isn't as upset with Amla as she's assumed. "Maybe I'll go tomorrow?" she says. "After we get everything ready for Meenafai?"

Padma smiles. "I think that's a great idea," she says. "Maybe after your Meenafai gets here. I'll help you move the cots after I finish cooking. Are the sheets ready?"

"Oh, no," Amla says, and she stops tossing the cloth ring. She places it gently by the stack of vegetables Padma's collected before hurrying inside, calling back behind her, "I'll hang everything now!"

Padma's laugh follows her through the house, to the clothesline outside the entryway. The basket is already outside, Amla having forgotten about it as soon as Padma arrived. She tosses a damp kurti over the clothesline, spreading its sleeves wide. From her perch on a tall step stool, she stretches the fabric at the waist like she'd seen Ba do hundreds of times. *Keeps away wrinkles*, Ba would remind her. *Don't want it all bunchy at your tummy.* She does the same with the leggings, then the sheets.

Amla wonders what will make Meenafai happy when she arrives. It's not as easy as running downstairs to a mithai shop anymore. Maybe Bapu could bring home sugarcane. Would that be special enough?

*Maybe you don't know what will make Meenafai happy*, a small voice in Amla's head says. *Maybe you don't know what will make anyone happy, what anyone wants.*

*If it were any other time of year*, Amla retorts, imagining the taste of sitaphal, of mangoes, of gooseberries. Nothing luxuriously sweet feels native to August. Any other month, she would know exactly what to do for a visitor, Meenafai included.

"Beti?" Amla doesn't notice the well-dressed man setting his bicycle down at their courtyard entrance until he repeats the word again.

She jumps up. "Yes?"

"Do you live here?"

Amla nods, wondering if she should call Padma from the back. But the man's voice is kind, and he keeps his distance from her. "Yes."

"Are your parents home?"

She shakes her head. "No, it's me and my friend."

"This house is Anurag"—he glances down at a note in his hand— "Sthanakiya's? This is the house, no? Belonged to Kasturiben Sthanakiya before?"

"He's not here right now."

"Do you know when he'll be back?"

Amla nods. "This evening, after work." She pauses, trying to remember how Ba spoke to strangers. "I can tell him you came by?"

"No worries, beti," the man says, swinging one leg back over his bicycle. "Thank you. I'll come back another time."

Amla nods, already moving on. There is a pile of laundry that needs to be hung, makeshift beds that need to be set up. Padma is making dinner for Bapu; Amla must find the perfect welcome gift for Meenafai. And soon, she will try again to see Bahaar. Amla will bring something for her—maybe Padma's food, maybe the new embroidery she's been trying—and she will finally get to see her friend.

The kind man with the questions doesn't matter to her. She watches him bike away, his figure growing smaller in the distance, as she hangs pillowcase after pillowcase on the line.

. . .

**When Meenafai arrives,** her entrance is like a fresh breeze, like the evening air coming off Sindhu Sagar. She calls for Amla before she's even set down her bags. "My lovely child," she says, setting her knees to the ground so she and Amla are face-to-face. "My darling, my beautiful, my sweet, sweet moon."

Amla wraps her arms tightly around her aunt. "It's so good to see you," she says softly. *You smell the same*, she thinks. *Like Karachi.*

"I'm so happy to see you," Meenafai says, pinching the tip of Amla's nose lightly. She takes Amla's hands, flips them, the trajva from Fiza facing upward. "Ah, your father wrote me about this. Tell me, how do you feel about this choice?"

"The trajva?" Amla smiles. "I feel like Fiza is with me."

"You can't undo this one," Meenafai says. Her tone is matter-of-fact, not accusatory. "Are you happy with it? You're okay living with this forever?"

Amla nods. "Fiza did it for me. And it's in Ba's pattern. I won't regret that, ever."

Meenafai follows the pattern with her index finger, lightly tapping in the middle of each diamond. "You certainly are your mother's daughter," she says, and she kisses the back of both of Amla's hands before standing up and surveying the house. "I'm sorry we're about to take over so much space. This house—my god, bhai, this is lucky."

"Chandini's grandmother's house," Bapu says, lugging in Meenafai's bags with his right arm, one of the younger girls asleep on his left shoulder. "Praise Kasturiben."

"Praise indeed," Meenafai says, and her long strides take her away from Amla to the bedroom doorway. "I see someone already set up beds? A good host at your age already. Thank you, Amla. The little one's been sleeping ever since we got on the train."

Amla nodded. "I thought you'd like it. You can have the cot and I'll take the floor."

"I would never." She waves Amla's words away, taking the sleeping child from Bapu. "I'll sleep next to this one. She's been fussy since she had to leave her twin behind."

"I'll get the rest of the bags," Bapu says, pausing by Amla. "Did you spend the day at Bahaar's?"

"I tried," she says.

Bapu's lips form a line. "Don't lose heart."

"I won't." Amla is earnest, remembering Padma's advice. "I'm going to keep trying."

Bapu tousles Amla's hair and turns toward the front door, where the other cousins wear various measures of exhaustion across their faces. Meenafai points them to Amla's room. "It's the heat, isn't it?" she asks Amla. "There's no reprieve."

"I miss the ocean," Amla says. "I miss the port."

"You wouldn't miss it right now." Meenafai places the sleeping toddler on the sitting bench, tucking her dupatta under the girl's head. "It's so full, it's stifling."

"People leaving?"

"People coming," Meenafai says. Bapu walks into the room with a tray of chaash, places it on the table. Meenafai lifts her fingers to him in a small *V* shape and he laughs, wordlessly pulling out his cigarette case. She passes one of the steel cups to Amla before taking her own. "That place won't be the same, bhai."

"Isn't your husband still saying it'll all phase out?"

"He's a different generation," Meenafai insists. Bapu lights her cigarette and she breathes in slow, breathes out. "He thinks it's all going to be the same. He doesn't think things can change any more than they already have. You know what's ridiculous? He thinks he can ignore all of this. You and I—we know better. I think of you, just before you met Chandini, following along the Dandi March. We were basically kids then. It was the only time I ever wished I wasn't in Karachi—that I was where you were, in Gujarat. You remember the look on our mother's face when she found out you went?"

Bapu shakes his head at the memory. "I feel so far from then, now."

"Seventeen years. A lot has changed."

"Not just Chandini," he says, watching Amla sip from her steel cup. "I thought I was marching for labor, for self-rule. Sovereignty. Marching with thousands across class, caste, creed. I never thought, then, that I was marching to divide us in two."

The room falls quiet as Bapu smokes his cigarette. The date of the partition had been announced alongside its approval, that day Amla and Bapu had gone to the postmaster's. August 14. It lurks around the corner, ten days away.

When Amla places her empty cup on the table, Bapu cocks his head at her, a gesture that she can leave. Her bedtime is nearly past, but Amla is reluctant, slow to go into the other room, trying to memorize this moment that rings so familiar to their old home.

"The panditji thinks the world will keep spinning," Meenafai's voice continues as Amla changes into her nightgown. "You and I, bhai, we're *people* people, you know? We have seen it, how easily the ground can shift, open beneath us. You can feel the energy, no? It's different. In what, just over a week . . . by god, it will be a new world."

Amla closes the bedroom door softly. Bapu's murmured agreement disappears as she nestles into her blankets, and Amla imagines the siblings sitting in quiet, smoke from the cigarettes twisting in the air.

**The week they spend together** as a family, construction on the house addition still ongoing, leaves a taste like dessert on Amla's tongue. Like kulfi, best had on a balcony in Karachi. As Amla is put to work, making meals and watching Meenafai's children, it is easy for her to forget all else that has happened—that is happening still. She is happier than she's been in a long time.

The oldest of Meenafai's daughters, Rohini, is about Padma's age, and Amla invites Padma over, introducing them nervously. She wishes she could invite Bahaar, but still she has not been allowed into the house. *Give it time*, she reminds herself, *be patient.*

Meenafai compliments Padma's kurti at dinner, fingertips tracing the fine stitching. Padma blushes, offering to teach Rohini and the younger girls. "It's amazing how much Amla's improved already." She laughs.

Amla wonders what it would be like if Bahaar were here with them, how Meenafai would respond to such a spirited personality. She might have found it kindred, might have taken Bahaar under her wing. Might have given her advice on using arrangements for your own good, how to gauge what sacrifices you're willing to make in order to get the opportunities you want.

Meenafai brings news of Fiza, or rather of her family: the maulana has been trying to help manage the flow of Muslims leaving India. The family spends most of the days preparing for dinners at the mosque, the rows and rows of cross-legged people guaranteed at least one good meal. They're not called refugees yet, with full independence and the partition just days away. They're preemptive migrants, like Bapu and Amla were and Meenafai is now.

But alongside the news, Meenafai does not bring a letter, a telegram, a photo. Amla wonders if Fiza made the same decision she had, all those months ago—to savor the memory of each other, not forcefully bridging this distance.

As the week comes to a close, Bapu's trips to the market return more news of the trains in Punjab, the villages just stations down. In some ways, they are lucky this village is so segregated, *that the Hindus and the Muslims live such separate lives,* he says in the evenings when he trades news with his sister. He parrots the postmaster's words. *They are lucky to have found a place without outside violence.*

Meenafai looks at him and rolls her eyes. "Meena Thakur becomes Meena Sthanakiya," she drawls. "Only you would think that we could belong here, taking on Chandini's grandmother's name."

Amla hands the pair steel cups of lemon water, Bapu already passing Meenafai one of his cigarettes. They will spend the evening just as they have spent the others, trading news commentary and old stories until the candles have puddles of wax beneath them. Amla tugs on Bapu's sleeve and gestures toward the clean kitchen, as she has done every few days for weeks now. "Can I go see Bahaar?"

Bapu nods at her quickly, his brow furrowed at his sister. "Meena, it's the blood in my daughter's veins," he replies to her, and Amla takes the cue. "That makes it our family blood."

She slips on her sandals at the doorway, the open windows carrying her father's and aunt's voices outside. Metal scrapes as someone moves the ashtray.

"No, that makes it Amla's blood," Meenafai says as Amla leaves. "It makes this land hers and hers alone. You and I will die begging for a Sindh that only exists in our memories."

**Bahaar's mother takes an extra** moment to open the door, but when she does, to Amla's relief and surprise, she gestures for Amla to come inside. "Bahaar is in the back," she says, and Amla remembers that Bahaar shares her room, shares most things. Outside is possibly the most private space Bahaar has.

Bahaar greets her with a hug—not as tight as what Amla is used to receiving from her, but it is touch. It is the opposite of avoidance.

Amla grins at her friend with her whole face, giddy. "I missed you," she says. "I've been coming by . . ."

"I know," Bahaar says. She motions for them to sit on the backyard swing, wrapping a cotton quilt around herself so that she is fully cocooned. "Sorry."

"It's okay."

"I wasn't really ready to see you," Bahaar says. She nestles into the corner of the swing, facing both Amla and the fields beyond them. Even though it doesn't seem like Bahaar is looking at her, Amla follows suit, turning diagonally to face Bahaar and the back of the house.

"It's been busy at my place, too," Amla says, even though that isn't what Bahaar is saying. "My aunt came in from Karachi. She's going to stay with us."

"That's exciting."

There is a long pause.

"I wanted . . ." Amla trails off. "I wanted to be here for you."

"I know you did."

"I wanted to make it better."

Bahaar grimaces. She reaches over to touch Amla's hand. "I know," she says, "but you can't. You know that, right?"

Amla doesn't know what to say, and the two swing back and forth, the wood creaking with every oscillation. The chulha, four feet away and still with red embers, sends heat their direction. Amla reaches her free hand toward it.

"Did you hear about the sahib?" Bahaar asks suddenly, and Amla is surprised to hear the question she'd wanted to ask emerge from Bahaar's lips. She looks at Bahaar, trying to keep her breath and voice steady.

"Yes."

"I keep hearing rumors about how and why."

The neutral statement makes Amla nervous. She bites at a finger-nail, speaking around her teeth. "A lot of the others talk about it. No one really agrees."

"Hm."

Amla waits for Bahaar to say more, but she doesn't.

Finally, Amla asks the question she's wanted to for weeks. "Does it . . . Does it help you?"

Bahaar looks directly at her then. "What do you mean?"

Amla falters. "That he's gone—does it make anything better?"

"Nothing makes it better," Bahaar says, and for the first time her voice is cold. She retracts her hand from Amla's. "The hurt stays."

"I thought—"

"Then you were wrong," Bahaar says.

"But . . ." Amla tries. "Didn't he deserve it?"

Amla bites the inside of her cheek as Bahaar pushes herself off the swing. The wood creaks louder. She turns to face Amla, and she sounds less angry than before, yes, but also speaks to Amla as though she could not understand.

She is right in that; Amla does not.

"Maybe. Yes." Bahaar swipes at her eyes rapidly, no kohl on her eyelids to smear. In that moment she returns to the Bahaar that Amla recognizes—standing still, shoulders taut. Tall. "And yet it fixes nothing."

Amla doesn't know what to do. She cannot apologize. She cannot argue.

"Yes, it's good that he can't hurt people the way he hurt me, the way he hurt lots of other girls, too," Bahaar says, voice soft enough that it can't carry into the house. "But him being gone can't make what happened . . . un-happen." She stops. When she speaks again, the words tumble out fierce and fast. "Everyone has reactions to what happened, you know? My parents think I should leave, but the only way to do that is to be married. This is the problem with people like that man—the power they have determines the course of our lives. He decided for me what comes next. And he didn't even think, he—" Her voice falters. "Do you get that?"

"I don't . . . I don't know," Amla says, but her hand twitches at her own lie, the specter of her watercolor brush between her fingers and thumb emerging from the fog of memory.

Bahaar pulls the quilt more tightly around her shoulders. "You're too young." She sighs. "I don't mean to be upset with you. Nothing is your fault."

There is a painting beneath Amla's bed that begs to differ. She blinks, tears collecting with shame. "Even though he's dead," she says slowly, processing, "it's not better for you."

"You know, if someone had killed him for me, I wish they'd have come to me and asked what I wanted," Bahaar says, mouth tightening. "I wouldn't say I wanted him dead. My brothers even offered, you know? Not that Chotu could."

"What . . . what would you have wanted?"

Bahaar takes a deep breath. "I wouldn't have wanted it to happen in the first place."

Amla pulls her knees to her chest, tears soaking into her salwar. These are not the words she wanted to hear.

Eventually Bahaar sits beside her again, and eventually they speak of Padma and Bapu—but there is a distance between them now, and Amla isn't sure if it can be bridged. Bahaar does not comfort her, but Amla understands that it is not Bahaar's fault she feels this way— that it is not Bahaar's responsibility, even if Amla doesn't have the words to explain this understanding.

As the sun starts to set, Amla says her goodbyes. She squeezes Bahaar's hand, but they don't hug, and she ends up leaving from the backyard to avoid Bahaar's mother's eyes. She walks at first, but then she is sprinting home, the taste of bile in her mouth. She stops in the dark to sob. She is ashamed to think of who she is going home to—Bapu, who she has disappointed so many times; Meenafai, who loves her so dearly, who does not know what she has done.

Amla bites at her knuckles. She did something horrible and it didn't even help the one person it should have, and now she can't take it back. She is not good, she thinks. She cannot be, no matter how hard she tries.

She should never have made that painting.

When she reaches the house, Amla retreats into her room. Even with her girl-cousins surrounding her, Amla tucks herself into fetal position on her cot. She can hear Meenafai ask what is wrong, hear Bapu explaining what Bahaar has been through, how seeing Bahaar must have affected Amla. She hates that he must defend her, even when she doesn't deserve it.

Amla pulls the sheet farther over her shoulders and sobs.

# SEVEN

D o you understand how impossible it is now, Nadya?

All of this has already happened. I cannot change how this story ends. I only tell you this history because how better to demonstrate it, this gift and this curse, than when it is in the hands of a child? Amla must live with the consequences of these choices. So must her daughter, and the next, and the next. It doesn't matter if you or I promise that we will not let the same happen to our child— we don't know, do we, how they'll make mistakes. Our children are bound to make them—like all children, like all people.

What will be the painting that undoes our child? My nightmares are sometimes of this question. Are you prepared, Nadya, for this possibility? Am I?

**The man on the bicycle** returns for Bapu on August 10.

He is flanked by two officers in khaki as he cuts across the court-yard, where the youngest girls are playing, to the entryway where the doors are open wide—was it foolish to have thought they were so safe from everything outside?—and stops, his silhouette blocking the light.

"Anurag Sthanakiya," he says, his voice so much firmer, sterner than it had been last week when he asked Amla for all those details. "We're taking you in for questioning."

Bapu, sitting beside Amla in the main room, his pencil placing check marks next to the lessons she has completed correctly, stiffens. He blinks at the man in the doorway, getting up slowly, and Amla starts, recognizing him. She tries to stand alongside Bapu, confused and scared at the command in his voice, which before had sounded so kind.

Only Bapu's hand holds Amla's shoulder down. "Meenaben," he calls.

"Are you Anurag Sthanakiya?"

"I am," he says, and he wipes his hands on his linen pants and takes a sip from his cup of water. His movements feel deliberately slow. "Meenaben, could you—"

"We just want to ask you some questions," the investigator says, "about the death of Mahesh Shankar Sharma."

Amla gapes as Meenafai appears in the back doorway, bringing with her the smell of chulha fire.

All this time, Amla has been so focused on Bahaar. This one attempt to be good—its consequences are visible now, like extended and intertwining paths of dominoes. All this time, helping Bahaar has been only one of those paths. Amla takes Bapu's hand and pulses it, wanting to pause time, to explain. He pulses her small hand back.

"We can do that here," Bapu says. "I'm happy to answer anything you have to ask."

"It wouldn't be appropriate, sir," the investigator says. He glances over at Amla as the laughter from outside echoes in. "These are . . . delicate questions."

Bapu closes his eyes. He must know, in that moment, the questions they have.

The puzzle only becomes clear to Amla later: that the first question you might ask when a man dies is if anyone had incentive to hurt him; that someone could point toward the girl he raped; that, after turning over Bahaar's house and questioning her brothers, the terrified girl might reveal who helped her get home, the only other person who knows what really happened that night.

Or maybe the investigator had heard the name *Anurag* mentioned with suspicion before—the new outsider, the man with his hands in the sahib's accounting books. He might have asked around, heard that the daughter of this man speaks Sindhi better than she speaks Gujarati, that they are strangers laying dubious claim to the Sthanakiya name. That last week, Anurag had been at the train station, picking up a woman who came in from Karachi—Sindhi people, then, not local. Not one of them.

"Search the house," the investigator tells the officers. They separate into the two bedrooms and the investigator looks pointedly at Bapu. "To support the investigation, of course."

"Of course." Bapu's voice is cold. He turns to Meenafai, and she nods back at him quickly, her hands holding her elbows so tightly that her veins jut out. Bapu leans over to kiss Amla on the forehead. "I'll be back soon, Amu."

Amla looks up at Bapu frantically. "Wait," she says. She can hear the scrape of her cot moving. "Bapu," she says, "there's something I need to do before they—"

"Stay right here," he says, even as she scrambles to her feet. "It's going to be okay." He takes her hand and squeezes it again, this time more tightly. Even when he takes his hand back, hers still echoes with his touch.

Fists opening and closing anxiously, Amla watches the uniformed investigator standing outside her room, but it's too late. She cannot run in and grab that horrible painting from beneath her cot. "Promise, Bapu."

He pinches the skin at the bottom of his throat. "With all my life."

**Meenafai spends the next days** going back and forth from the house to the jail—a dark and humid building, just a desk and two cells, near the rail station. In the morning, as she walks out the door with a dupatta over her head, her jaw jutting out in an angry underbite, she sends Rohini and Amla to the market with an outline of exactly what she wants them to purchase and how she'd like it prepared by the time she returns. After making lunch, she goes back to the jail, this time instructing the two girls on her tuition expectations of them and on basic care for the youngest.

"Don't talk to a single soul who comes to the door," she says, aggressively smoking one of Bapu's cigarettes. "Stay inside, stay silent. Be proper."

Amla has never seen this version of Meenafai, the one who has taken complete control of the situation—fearsome and commanding. Amla looks at Rohini, and she looks back at Amla, and with a huff they stay inside the house where the breeze cannot rush over them, stripped down to the thinnest of their kurtis. The sweat gathers on their necks and backs beneath their plaits. They alternate heating water on the chulha and cooling it in the clay pots inside; they drink an excess of chaash to stay cool.

When the youngest ones wail, Rohini tells Amla not to worry. "I've always handled them," she says. "I know what to do."

Amla sits in front of the tapestry, her tuition book in her lap. All the lessons are complete, have been for a few days. She closes her eyes and clenches her hands into fists. *When will Bapu come home, Ba?* she asks the tapestry. *What should I do?*

But the tapestry doesn't answer her.

She throws the tuition book across the room, feels her neck and cheeks tighten, tears welling in her eyes. She rocks back and forth, back and forth, sobs escaping her chest. "I just wanted to make things right," she says to the tapestry, pleading. "No one ever taught me how to do this."

She imagines the tapestry escaping the walls, its corners coming toward her. An embrace, a chokehold.

When the officers had left, everything was overturned in the bedrooms. Amla's cot lay on its side, the makeshift beds heaped in piles. She had shuffled through them in a rush, her eyes wide, her hands shaking. Her pile of watercolors, the ones she went through at night, had been in the corner with her tuition books. Only one painting was missing.

Amla pulls at her hair, crumples onto the floor almost in prayer—her knees folded, her back hunched over, her arms and head touching the ground. "Why didn't you stop me from painting it?" she begs. "Why did you let me do it?"

She hears the voices of the women then, and she isn't sure if it is the tapestry or her frustrated, wailing mind.

*We all must choose for ourselves.*

*We have all been so young as you.*

*It is impossible to be a child in this world*, the tapestry says, its voices a chorus, soothing.

*This world will always try to take from us, to quiet us, over and again. And yet, and yet, and yet . . .*

When Rohini returns to the room, Amla's cries have subsided, her body on its side as though sleeping. Rohini sits beside her, runs her hands through Amla's hair. "It's all going to be okay," she says. Amla ignores her. "It's all going to be okay."

**When Meenafai returns** from the jail that day, she downs three glasses of water before saying anything. She sits at the table with her head in her hands, and in that moment she looks exactly like Bapu after a long day of accounting.

"Amu," she says, and her voice is strained, "I need to ask you something."

Amla's throat goes dry. She moves at a glacial pace to stand across from her aunt, avoiding eye contact. "Yes, Meenafai?"

"You should know, the investigator was hired by Sharma's son," she says. "They're paying the police. Your father is being held for questioning. They don't have much, but they have two things: They know Anurag helped your friend Bahaar and . . ." She takes a breath. "They have a painting."

Amla's heart stops.

"The fact that your father helped Bahaar—that probably won't be an issue. They questioned her brothers, too, and they're already back home. But the painting—it has your name on it, and it is dated from June." Meenafai looks at her searchingly. "That is more than a month before he died. They found it beneath your bed."

This moment feels inevitable to Amla now.

"Did your father try to kill him, Amla? Did he tell you?"

Amla looks up at Meenafai, shocked. She must have seen this painting at the jail earlier that day, knows Amla painted it, and yet her questions are not about Amla's actions but instead about Bapu, about whether or not he is as good of a man as they all think he is.

"He didn't do this," she says quickly, her words tumbling onto one another. *Bapu is good.* "You have to believe him. You're his sister, you have to . . ."

"I want to," Meenafai says. She softens her tone, bending at her knees to match Amla's height. "But, Amu, you have to be honest. How did you paint this man dead before he was? How did you know he was going to die?"

Amla bursts into tears, her words trapped inside her throat. If she could throw up right then, she would, but her stomach is empty. She feels herself redden, her hands tightening into fists at her sides. Where are the tapestry's corners now; where is their embrace, the warmth, the feeling of Ba's arms around her? She wants only to know the right answer, to have the words that won't frighten away this woman sitting in front of her, the sole mother she has left.

"I will fight for Anurag until the day I die," Meenafai says, taking Amla into her arms, "but I need to know. Do you know who did it?"

"It was me, Meenafai," Amla sobs through hiccups. "It was me."

Meenafai laughs even as she is crying, too, Amla's fear contagious. She wipes Amla's cheeks with her open palms. "Sweet child," she says, "loving child. Of course it wasn't you."

"But I—"

"You cannot blame yourself."

Amla stomps her foot. Now that she has said it, she needs Meena-fai to understand. She needs to be believed. "I did it," she says. "I painted it, and then it happened, Meenafai." She pinches the skin at her throat.

Meenafai frowns at Amla in confusion, just for a moment, and then she does what any adult would do in her situation. She pulls Amla's fingers from her throat and hugs her closely. "You must be so tired," she says, with a patience and a kindness that Amla does not deserve. "Let's get you some water and some sleep before your imagination runs wild."

**Amla misses his presence** in the house, misses the way he would tell her to study, the way he would check that the chulha was no longer burning. She sits and waits for Meenafai to come home from the jail, for news of when Bapu will be released.

Meanwhile, the village refuses to match Amla's sulking, despite her desire for every day to be dreary, rainy. She aches to see outside what she feels within. With two days until the partition, there are fireworks in the streets, yelps of delight through the windows, mithai delivered to doorsteps from the only shop in town.

"It's one thing to be excited about the goras leaving," Meenafai mutters as she enters the house. "It's another to do it knowing thousands of people are dying as they go to made-up countries."

Amla doesn't know what to say. Tens of millions of people are moving from one place to another; she's shielded from the violence taking place in Punjab, in Jammu and Kashmir, in Delhi. She's just a child, excited that Meenafai has offered to take her to the jail to see Bapu today. He continues to be held until there are *adequate answers*, the investigator has told Meenafai. Then he'll be free to come home.

Meenafai prepares a basket of fruit and clay pots with still-warm vegetables for her brother. She doesn't know what exactly has changed, she tells Amla, but Bapu seems more confident he'll be out any day now. Maybe the police have stopped caring, knowing that Bapu's incarceration is temporary, that there isn't any evidence to go on but the painting of a young girl, and you could not lock up a man on the basis of a child's imagination, however dark.

At the doors, Meenafai bends down and fixes the way Amla's kurti sits on her shoulders, licks her thumb and wipes at a dirt stain near the bottom of her pants. She adjusts her own sari after, its familiar eggplant color masking sweat stains. "Only talk to your Bapu, okay?" She pats down the hair escaping Amla's braid and frizzing by her ears. "Don't look at anyone else, don't talk to anyone else. Understood?"

Amla nods. "Understood."

Inside, the desk officer waves Meenafai toward Bapu's cell. Meenafai pivots Amla toward the cell on the right, away from a drunk man babbling on the left.

Bapu's face cracks open like it hasn't seen light in days. "Amu," he says, standing up from where he had been sitting cross-legged, reading a newspaper. "How are you, jaan?"

"How are *you*?" she asks back, running forward to the cell. She grasps at Bapu's hands. "I'm sorry you're here."

"Oh, I'll be out in a heartbeat, won't I, Officer?"

The officer grins. "This is bakwaas, bhai," he says. "Give it another day or two."

"See?" Bapu laughs, and Amla can't tell if it's real or fake, so she chooses to believe it. "I just have to wait for the new Sharma sahib to get on board. But then I'll be home and we can drink chaash and I'll teach you all the cricket rules. We'll pretend we're with those boys who played by Frere Hall and it's not so hot and everything's green."

Amla can't help but smile. "I can't wait, Bapu."

"Me neither," he says. He reaches a hand through the bars, pinches her nose. "How are things at home? The girls?"

"They're good," Meenafai says. She starts handing Bapu fruit through the bars, and he places them on a kerchief on the floor. "The village feels excited, though."

"Lots of change in two days' time," Bapu says. "No more British, two separate countries."

"Do you think it'll be—"

"The town is so separated. I'm sure it'll be fine."

"The news always makes me nervous," Meenafai admits, and she tears off a piece of rotli and pops it in her mouth before handing the rest to Bapu. "Some of the women are talking about what's happening in other towns along the railroad. I've been eavesdropping at the well."

Bapu's eyes dart to Amla before returning to his sister. "It's going to be okay."

Even Amla picks up on the hint: the conversation turns away from the upcoming Independence Day toward gossip about other villagers, updates on the children's tuition. Amla stays quiet, watching her father's hands as he tears his rotli, the way his hands shake a little. He feels older than he was a few days ago, more wrinkled, more gray. She wants to think it's just the way the light hits him, but she can't shake the feeling that the jailhouse is claiming him.

"This is going to get better, right, Bapu?" she asks before they leave. "You're going to come home, everything's going to be better?"

"Not even a question," he says. "I promised you, right?"

Amla nods. She thinks of the tapestry, the way she is certain it spoke to her. *You have learned from this mistake. You won't ever overdo it again.* "I believe you," she says.

**In those final nights** before independence is official, violence peaks.

The Pakistan Special train from Delhi to Karachi is derailed. Its passengers are stabbed; the train is set on fire. There are wires strung above the train's path to sweep the passengers from where they sit on top of train cars. When they fall, if they survive the impact, there are people waiting for them. The same thing in Lahore; the same thing in Rawalpindi.

The violence continues into the next day. The auntie across the street, the wife of the Ayurvedic doctor, fills Meenafai in on the details when they meet at the well. Meenafai returns with three pots of water, forbids anyone from leaving the house. "I'm in charge now," she says firmly, "and I will be the only person going to the well, going to market. I will be the only person to leave the house. Do you hear me?" She looks each of the children in the eyes, even the toddler blubbering away. She pulls her dupatta over her head, tucks a little pouch of chili pepper into her pantline. "I'm going to get a newspaper and talk to Amla's father. If anyone comes to the house, you stay in the back room."

When she returns, out of breath from jogging, Meenafai tracks the news like it is an obituary. She motions for Amla and Rohini to sit with her, and she starts reciting mantras that Amla cannot keep up with, more mantras than Amla has heard in her lifetime. Amla thinks of Bapu, waiting in that cell, his handkerchief full of fruit, and wishes he were here, lighting his windowsill candle.

In the evening, the village grows agitated. From Sodhana to Porbandar, there are fireworks as often as there are torches. There's talk of armed men raiding isolated villages, leaving no one alive. The doctor's wife crosses the street with updates; Meenafai hurries to the next house over to pass these along. A town two stops over found some of its young men dead; was it a personal fight or a political one? The stories are all twisted. It becomes impossible to tell what is happening to Hindu towns and what to Muslim ones. Does it matter which happened first? Does it matter which it is if the village feels awake when it should be sleepy, when the visits from the doctor's wife stop because hushed threats haunt the streets? Nothing eases their fear; Meenafai gathers all of the children into the main room.

Amla wishes she could take down the tapestry, wrap herself up in it, as they wait. They sit and listen for sounds in the distance—at the outskirts of the village where the Muslim and Christian sections begin—to cease.

There are shouts; a fire is lit at the rail station. By morning, the postmaster's office will no longer stand. At the edge of the village, someone burns row after row of nascent bajri stalks. The blaze stops at one of the irrigation canals, the next field already barren—nothing to catch flame. Each action has an equal and opposite—a field for a field, Hindu store for a Muslim one—and no one knows if men are coming into the village from the trains or if the people outside with torches are all their own.

Rohini and Amla stay awake through the night with Meenafai, the three taking turns pacifying the younger children. When dawn creeps over the horizon, the doctor's wife comes back and beckons Meenafai outside. Half asleep, Amla feels Meenafai's arm leave her clutches, watches her aunt walk away from her. She remembers it in slow motion: the doctor's wife takes Meenafai's hands in her own, leaning in and whispering to her in the entryway. Meenafai looks frozen for one second, two. Her face is oddly blank. And then she wails and her body gives way as though boneless; Amla, still sitting in the main room, can hear Meenafai's knees hit the ground.

Rohini rushes to her mother and Amla blinks. "Anurag," Meenafai is shouting. "No, get out! No, no. Not this, not now."

The doctor's wife is still talking, now to the children. The men who lit the rail station and the postmaster's office on fire, she repeats, had also killed the officers in the station. She meets Amla's eyes briefly.

No more grinning desk officer, Amla understands. No more drunkard in the left cell. No more accountant, the Sindhi, the outsider—no more Bapu—on the right.

She blinks, her brain wrapping itself around the words. The rail station, the postmaster's office, the jail—

Amla runs to her room, to her sketchbook and the watercolors, and tries to draw Bapu alive. Bapu free from bars. Bapu in the room with her and Meenafai. Even as she inhales through her flaring nostrils, exhaling through her tightly wound mouth—even as she presses her hands to the floor like she'd done every time before, the state of semiconsciousness escapes her. She needs to be in that dreamlike haze in order to paint something that will come true—in her bones, she knows this; she needs to let go of herself, needs to not remember. She needs to hand her body off to the women marching across the tapestry.

*Take from me*, she begs. *Inhabit me.*

She forces herself to draw, acutely aware of every movement of her brush across the page. She concentrates on Bapu's shoulders, on the ground beneath his feet. Is this angle right? She second-guesses herself. She presses her brush down too hard, lingering on spots on the page where she shouldn't. The brushstrokes are heavier than they need to be; she hasn't crafted any shadows, isn't sure what should be in the background—has she ever really decided, before?—and so eventually she gives up and leaves the background blank, a light lavender gray.

*Don't abandon me, Ba*, she says to the tapestry, hands shaking. *Help me undo what I've done. Help me bring him back to life.*

But she knows even before the watercolors dry, before her brush has made its last stroke, that this painting does not have the magic in it that the others had. Some things, still, are impossible.

Hours later, the sun high in the sky, Meenafai hiccups through her tears and gulps down water, directing the children to that same makeshift puja she'd created the night before. This time she doesn't say the names of the towns, just *Anurag Anurag Anurag* over and over, and she lights the small candles in front of statues of gods Amla doesn't know all the names of, and she sticks incense into the outer shell of fruits, and she cries, and Rohini places her hand on her mother's back, and even though Meenafai reaches for Amla, she just watches—she doesn't know what to do—she just waits for something to change, for a god to appear and Meenafai to be comforted. It doesn't happen; of course nothing happens. Amla thinks of the painting that didn't take. She stares at the flames, rocking back and forth, hugging her legs to her body.

# EIGHT

I hug my legs close to my chest, a position as familiar to my body as it is to my memory. My vision has long gone soft, absorbing nothing, but I focus now on you, Nadya. You wipe your tears with your sleeve, leaning over to grab a napkin from the coffee table. I don't realize I'm crying until you hand a second one to me.

When I shift my body, my spine aches. My feet have gone numb. One of us gestures to the other and we move to the bedroom, where you stretch, bones cracking, and lie belly-down on the mattress.

"How do you remember this and still . . ." You are shaking your head slowly, your voice soft. "My heart would break over and over."

I sit beside you. "Mine does."

I told you, I don't know how to tell this story. Or maybe I've storied it so many times I've lost perspective on where to focus. This is why I wanted to linger in Karachi—it matters to me that Amla was safe somewhere, once, that she had a fulfilling childhood and a best friend who loved her and whom she loved. That there were days with Ba and Bapu that melded into the next one. Ten years of life like that. Ten years of beautiful monotony—a life that was static, its energy contained and perfectly distributed every single day.

Amla remembers her life like that, at least, and so in her memory it feels like there is this place that is truly home. A place that kept her safe, its trisyllabic name a mantra in her mouth. *Karachi, Karachi, Karachi.* And it was hers—her memory, her home.

When I say the name, when it's just me speaking, Karachi remains the home of another person. On my own, I associate no sounds or smells or colors with Karachi—without Amla, there is no sea breeze, no bhuttawala, no minarets in the skyline. I only call it home in someone else's voice, in someone else's memory.

There are so many other women, so many other places that could be home. We follow Ba's line, her grandmother. Your questions all live in this space: Were the others better at this, managing this gift, containing its curse, than Amla? Were their mistakes this large? Or were the stakes just lower, the times somehow easier—did they know, in the face of their circumstances, that the gift shouldn't be used so carelessly? Were they so good at managing their emotions? And if they did use this gift to navigate their circumstances, to circumvent their trauma—how, then, do you separate what is your own trauma and what is everyone else's? How do you comprehend the trauma you've unconsciously caused?

(Do you try to call the trauma home?)

I worry I do that, when I story this lineage. I'm worried I'm calling the worst of it my identity. We only have hints, don't we? Without this lineage, the memories it gives me, I only have the trajva I've seen on my grandmother's wrist, the stories deemed good enough to pass down. With that tapestry in my own hands, its cloth seventy years older but no more weathered than when Amla held it in front of her, I find myself looking for answers as she did, and which none of these women have.

Maybe you can't see, yet, why I am so torn. I know where I come from; can you imagine what it's like, to be able to live every life that came before yours? All this pain, and somehow I understand it as the deepest luxury. It is the greatest gift I could have, and the greatest burden, and my mother offered me the choice to carry it. Any child could have that, too. What more could I want than the ability to remember all of my mothers, to feel them inside me, to continue this lineage onward?

This world is impossible. And yet, we survive. And yet, this pain. And yet, and yet, and yet . . .

**Is the rest a fog?** Amla feels she is walking in an upside-down, colorless world.

The younger Sharma sahib comes by to express his condolences, two servants standing a meter behind him. Meenafai does not let them inside, does not offer water or a spot in the shade in which to speak.

"The investigation—no matter how many people we've spoken to, it doesn't seem killing my father would've been in Anurag's nature," he says. "The Western doctor says there's just no explanation for how my father died."

"I knew that all along." Meenafai crosses her arms. "It's too bad you are the reason he was in that jail."

"Sister, I—"

"Thank you for your condolences," she says curtly. "You may go now. So long as I live in this house, I expect you will leave me alone. My daughter will bring over the taxes for the well later this month."

The young sahib hesitates. "The community knows how reliable a man Anurag was, how kind—"

"Don't speak of his reputation," Meenafai interrupts. "Don't ever let his name escape your mouth."

147

The man nods and turns to leave, the servants half bowing to Meenafai before following their employer. Meenafai watches them leave, and Amla watches Meenafai. The woman's profile looks like a mother to Amla.

**There are more nights** like that one—more fireworks and more torches. None of them scare Amla the way the first had. With Meenafai holding her tightly, all the children gathered together, she has everything she can call her own in front of her eyes.

*You lose people when you can't see them*, she thinks. If she has learned anything, isn't it this?

Karachi is tense but nothing like Punjab, the panditji says in a telegram sent to the next town over while the postmaster's office is being rebuilt. The panditji still has hope. The mandir still has so much good work to do.

"When you send him an answer, will you also send something to Fiza for me?" Amla asks Meenafai as they sit in the open area between Kasturiben's house and the new addition.

They have begun spending every morning here together, sitting mostly in silence shoulder to shoulder with lemon water and the waking sunlight. In the beginning, Amla used the time to draw both of her parents in pencil on two of the largest pages out of her treasured sketchpad, the one she has kept since Karachi. Meenafai would bring her water every hour, cooled in the clay pot, and sit with her, tracing with one fingernail her brother's name carved into the steel cup. When Amla finished the drawings, Meenafai had come back from the village center with two perfectly sized frames, two garlands of marigolds and jasmine. *We'll trade these out every week*, she said, *if not sooner. It will be both of our jobs*, and Amla had cried for the first time for all that she had lost, and Meenafai held her close and didn't promise anything, didn't say everything would be okay—just let her cry, just let the tears leave wet spots at the breast of her kurti. The space between them is negligible, Amla has realized. They each need the other now.

"What do you want the note to say?" Meenafai asks.

"Tell her . . ." Amla thinks of the letters she had written in her mind, all the words she never sent. "Tell her I hope she is safe and her parents are safe. Tell her I think of her when I look at my trajva." She lifts her arm, pointing at her tattoo, and Meenafai smiles. "And also I'm sorry, and I'll do better at sending telegrams if she does, too."

"I'll send it tomorrow," Meenafai says. A bird squawks; a train whistles in the distance. "What are your plans today?"

"Padma said she'd come by," Amla says, tracing over her trajva absentmindedly. "Bahaar was going to come, too, but . . ."

Meenafai reaches over and squeezes Amla's left shoulder. "It's not your friend's fault."

"I know." Amla isn't sure how to describe it, those conflicting emotions collected in her stomach, but Meenafai understands anyway. More likely, she feels them, too.

"It's okay to take your time," Meenafai says. "In a few days, I think we should go to Porbandar. You need lesson books, and Anurag had some furniture on reserve. We should pick it up."

"Together?"

"Is that all right?" Meenafai breathes in and out, closes her eyes. "I also . . . I also think we should take your Bapu's ashes to the sea."

"Sindhu Sagar," Amla whispers.

"It's where he belongs," Meenafai says, voice trembling. "It's the closest thing to home."

. . .

In Porbandar, Meenafai squashes a cigarette beneath her sandal and grips Amla's hand tightly. "Stay near," she says, adjusting the burlap bag on her shoulder. Amla couldn't imagine doing anything else, with the crowd near the port so frantic and bustling.

"This way to Kirti Mandir!" a guide yells. "Come see Mahatmaji's birthplace!"

"—to the station! Rajasthan, Bombay, Ahmedabad? A train in the next hour to Rajasthan, Bombay, Ahmedabad!"

"I can take you by bull cart anywhere in the city, sir, where are you—"

Meenafai scours the boats anchored at the port, nearly all disembarking passengers with bundles of cloth balanced on their hands or soft suitcases hugged close to their bodies. Amla gapes at the steamboats; had they always been so large? Had the passengers on their boat had as many belongings, seemed as tired? With their topis, their fabrics, so many of them look the way she and Bapu had. Sindhi styles, she recognizes now. She kicks at a rock in her path, watching it dance along the road in front of her.

Meenafai leads Amla along the chowpatty, away from the ports. She hands the copper pot she's been carrying to Amla, telling her to wait while she goes to the row of fishing boats pulled onto the beach. She asks a dark man emptying nets from his boat if he has a moment. *Could they possibly come out on the water with him?* She can pay well.

The man surveys Meenafai, the paisa she holds out in her hand. His expression barely changes as he looks at Amla, the copper pot in her hands. "I'll take you out and back quickly," he says. Meenafai hands him the money, and he motions them onto the fishing boat.

After Meenafai and Amla have rolled up their pant legs and

waded into the ocean, the water only reaching their calves, the man pushes the boat into the sea and helps them in. Amla hands off the pot as she grips the edges of the boat. Meenafai, smiling at Amla's nerves, pulls her dupatta over her hair and motions for Amla to do the same. "Keeps your head from getting too hot," she explains.

Amla does so, but needn't have; the salty spray keeps her cheeks cool. The boat rides out on the quiet water, the voices of the chowpatty crowd growing farther and farther away. When the boat is rocking quietly, Meenafai begins mumbling mantras under her breath.

"Should I join you?" Amla asks. "I don't know these ones."

Meenafai shakes her head at Amla but doesn't stop her Sanskrit recitation. From the burlap bag she takes out a pinch of rice and tosses it into the ocean. Sesame seeds, mustard seeds. Amla's heart tightens. She recognizes the mantras now.

"I didn't know you could do this," Amla whispers. "I thought all panditjis were men."

Meenafai smiles and nods but keeps reciting. Amla thinks of how many of these death rites Meenafai must have heard as a pandit's wife, how she would have learned some of the verses from hearing them over and again even if she could never perform them in public.

"The urn," Meenafai says in Sindhi. Amla hands it over obediently. Meenafai begins the mantras again and takes off the cloth tied like a lid around the pot. She beckons for Amla to hold on to her arm, the one carrying the urn, as a substitute for holding the vessel itself. When Amla does so, Meenafai pours out the ashes slowly, the breeze blowing the sandy bits toward the beach, the ash turning dark in the water.

*May you live a thousand years*, Amla thinks, and she feels her mother's voice singing the words to her. *May each year have fifty thousand days. May I take all your sorrows as my own.*

. . .

**If Amla follows the coastline** from the fishing boat with her eyes, she might make out the land continuing north. The sky is a bright blue with sparse clouds, the glare of the sun straining her eyes. If she could follow it for sixty-five miles, if she could suddenly land herself on the tip of Dwarka, she would see, if she squinted just right, the coastline of Pakistan.

Sometimes I wonder if I should take a boat to that spot off the coast of Porbandar. Would I be able to close my eyes, feel Amla connected to me, know if the boat I am on is in the exact spot hers was in? Would the salty spray of the sea beckon me home?—and if it did, would it name that home Porbandar or Karachi?

This is all part of that same story. Amla dreams of a home that her children won't think twice about. Ba dreamt of her family house at the edge of Porbandar. Her grandmother, a village thirty miles east. And on and on. Even if the ocean could tell me the answer, if that memory could inhabit me and offer one, the practical world might still deny me. The officer at the border asks what country my passport is from, which type of visa, who is my father's father and my mother's mother and were they of Indian origin or Pakistani.

*What are your reasons for coming here?* To trace the calcium in my bones, I want to answer. To know the place that calls me one of its own.

Amla and Meenafai return to the shore, watch children play in the water along the chowpatty. They take the train back to their village, where the construction is nearly complete on the second house behind Kasturiben's. The coming harvest means the air is beginning to smell of sitaphal and mangoes.

They will hire young men to work the fields behind the house, the same boys who had worked alongside Bapu the prior year. Meenafai will take on work as a schoolteacher, her religious knowledge impressive to the older members of the community. *How much you know*, they say. *You're nearly a pandit yourself.* Amla will smile, thinking of the gift Meenafai gave her, to know her father was laid to rest by family.

Meenafai's husband keeps writing that he means to follow but he is convinced everything will work out in Karachi. When he does finally write that he will come to Gujarat, that his mind has been changed, it is because January 6, 1948, has passed. The violence that had been so present everywhere else has finally materialized in Karachi. Someone lit a fire in the mandir on that day, the same day Bapu's businesses were looted and lost like most Hindu businesses in the city. A week later, after huddling in a neighbor's apartment with his sons, the panditji takes every last rupee they have and purchases steamboat tickets, enough for him and the four boys. He tells Amla when she is older that he can't escape the memory of the white dome of the mosque, the red kalash of the temple, the smoke rising and the blood dripping and the shouts—my god, he wakes from nightmares because of the shouts—that filled the streets that night.

"We can build a life here," Meenafai tells him, late at night in the kitchen, Amla overhearing from the next room. "We are somehow all together, all safe. We can return to a simple life."

"I never thought it would happen like this," the panditji says.

"I know."

"All I want is for us to go back. To Karachi. To a different time."

"I know."

The sound of spit, of gurgling. "I keep looking for god," the panditji finally says, and Amla suddenly feels guilty for eavesdropping. "I keep reciting, and I keep looking, and I cannot seem to find god."

. . .

**If only she, too,** could go back in time, to a different place. Undo all the mistakes she has made.

There is something broken between Amla and Bahaar that cannot be remade. Even if Bahaar had never told the officers about who helped her that night, Amla is certain she will never surmount the shame at making the decision for Bahaar in the first place.

And now the sympathy of Meenafai and her cousins and the villagers for the loss of Bapu. Amla wants to yell at them, to force their kindness away. Amla hasn't been good. She hasn't kept any of her promises, hasn't saved any of the people she loves.

What would Fiza think of her?

At least Fiza had pretended to believe her, and Amla keeps remembering this. That moment, Fiza kissing her knuckles. Maybe there could be a way to help Fiza understand—to show one person how and why this had all transpired.

Amla takes her sewing needle and thread from the table in the corner of her room, tiptoeing over Meenafai's sleeping children there and back to her cot. She had created an entire chaniya choli from scratch; certainly she is capable of sewing the silhouette of a girl like Fiza onto the tapestry.

"How do I do it?" she whispers. "How did Ba do it?"

The tapestry feels warm beneath Amla's hands. *Only to one of our blood. Of our family.*

"But she is like my blood," Amla says. "She is like family."

The tapestry's answer only echoes in Amla's mind: *One of our blood. One of our family.*

Amla threads the needle anyway, a bright marigold that feels like Fiza, and begins to sew. She tries to copy the style of the other women, profiles with colorful clothing. She's halfway through when she realizes the thread is broken, and not just once but over and again, falling out like hair.

Frustrated, she hits the cot with her fist. Rethreads. Retries. The threads keep slipping out of the tapestry. Even when she tries again and takes care to check every few seconds, she finds herself unable to continue—her needle too blunt, suddenly, to penetrate the tapestry's fibers.

"Stop it," she says, louder than intended. "*Stop!* Let me!"

Meenafai comes running, and then Rohini, but by the time they reach Amla, she is crying on her cot, draped in the tapestry. No one asks why, because aren't there enough reasons now? And Amla is thankful they make this assumption, because she knows she can give them no satisfactory answer.

The way the years pass—the way decisions must be made, the way life becomes something almost routine again, almost banal—should ease Amla's heart. Meenafai becomes their mother bird, aggressive and clever and loving, her nest of children now including Amla. She maneuvers Amla's wedding with a Porbandar family when she is seventeen. Amla leaves almost everything she owns in that house; she likes to imagine her father haunts it, that he gets to walk among their belongings. She takes only a few of her kurtis, two dupattas embroidered by Padma, and the tapestry. Always the tapestry.

In Porbandar, she speaks only Gujarati to her husband; he barely knows of her past in Karachi, her Sindhi story. He doesn't really ask, but then again, he doesn't really know how to speak to her and he's rarely home. He is a man devoted to his work, his status: He works in partnership with the government; all of his friends seem well-connected. He buys oil for his hair and has Amla massage it into his scalp; he pays for a barber, for nice trousers, for salty snacks from the namkeenwala because he doesn't know how to make any for himself.

He touts her last name when he introduces her at the few parties they attend together, relishing how it presents her caste. Sometimes she thinks it's all he knows about her. She wants to tell him it's fake: that she never met Kasturiben Sthanakiya, that Meenafai's last name is actually Thakur, that her parents were Anurag and Chandini Prakash. She is all of these people—Amla Prakash, Amla Thakur, Amla Sthanakiya—those surnames all streaming through her blood, all these people who raised her, but Suresh Dave only cares for how Sthanakiya reveals her Bardai Brahminness. So she says nothing, and for him she slowly becomes Amla Dave. Every day she wears the costume, she sheds something that used to belong to her.

She has babies—three of them, a boy and two daughters. Each one is born while her husband is traveling for work, and his parents don't live in the city, so she goes to the hospital entirely alone. She doesn't mind this, no—this way, she gets to dictate the children's names on their birth certificates without argument:

—Anurag for the boy, never a doubt in her mind that she would name him after her father;

—Vibha for the first daughter two years later; a name to summon the moon, to recall the meaning of Chandini's name; and

—Arni for the second daughter another four years later, named to pair the sisters, for the balancing brightness of the sun.

She feels the women on the tapestry coursing through her blood as she labors, and almost always after, when she looks down at the children in their cribs. When they cry, she feels every mother who has come before respond by instinct. This can make her smile; it mostly makes her cry. She feels her mother among those mothers, too.

Amla dreams of babies—of children begged for, of children denied, of children lost. She sees her mother sketching her in charcoal,
swaddled tightly, mewing as she sleeps.

Like this, days turn to years: perfectly round rotli fluffing up on
the stove, three children constantly underfoot. Sometimes, while they
nap or study, Amla writes letters—long ones in Sindhi to Meenafai and Rohini, sharing her children's heights and preferences; shorter
ones in Gujarati to Padma. For a while, she tries to write to Bahaar,
their conversations always superficial despite all that they once shared.
It reminds her of those early telegrams she had sent to Fiza: some
things, Amla realizes, remain too large, too complicated, to put in writing. When she married, those telegrams had faltered, too. She had
been so tired, so empty.

And then, one day, Meenafai sends a photo of a couple outside
Sind Club, an address written on the back. *Write to Fiza*, Meenafai
has scrawled beneath the address. Nothing else—no name for this
man who must be Fiza's husband; no background. Amla spends hours
staring at the black-and-white photograph. She studies the husband's
face, wonders if Fiza finds him attractive. Mostly, though, she looks
at Fiza, her face grown from child to woman, her posture dignified
and cheekbones strong, and tries to imagine how she looked on her
wedding day, a princess in an anarkali, light bouncing off silver
threading.


**Those days by the Karachi seaport** with Fiza, making up stories
about wedding guests, feel an entire lifetime away. Even the day
Bapu died feels distant. She wonders how accurate her memory is;
she wonders if a daughter would be able to tap into her blood, verify
how real it all was, tell her own stories back to Amla one day. She
marks the years: In 1947, she was eleven years old; in 1953, she was

seventeen and married, her son born that first year. And then it is 1965, and her oldest daughter is nearly the age Amla was when she lost her father. There is more news of liberation, and with liberation comes more violence, and Amla grits her teeth while her husband mutters under his breath about *those Muslim bastards at our borders*, and she thinks again of Fiza, of their letters now consistent, back and forth, and the next time her husband leaves for work, she sits Vibha down and tells her about her own childhood in Karachi, a city that belonged to her as much as it belonged to Fiza, and of everything she has learned about the tapestry, and Vibha nods—Vibha, whose head is always calm, who is cautious and delicate and would rather do the work herself than paint something into being—and then Amla sews Vibha onto the tapestry. It takes this thread as readily as it had once fought her. It is the most effortless embroidery she has ever done.

She believes, because Vibha is more mature than she was at that age, that she can do for Vibha what her mother was unable to do for her. What Chandini would have done, had she been alive. *It is the right age, under the right circumstances*, she tells herself. *I understand most what it is like to receive this gift at ten years old, so I can help her most when she is ten years old, too. It must be right.*

She kisses her daughter's knuckles. She thanks Vibha for placing this heritage onto her own shoulders.

Slowly, the chorus begins to leave Amla. They leave like a lullaby, like sleep settling in. They take root in Vibha.

Amla is amazed by the quiet; her mind hasn't been this still since she was ten years old.

Some moments in our lives never leave us; some of them get carved into our bones. They become fundamental to our understandings of ourselves. This is what it's like to trace Vibha's figure on the tapestry— to know what is coming, to know what will happen to her and this family, to want to stop time right here, at this figure's final stitch.

# Part Two

# SISTER

F uck," you say, hands on your stomach, eyes following the ceiling
fan. The mauve comforter swaddles all of you except for your
left leg, which has managed to snake its way free at the edge of
the bed. I lie in the opposite direction, my elbow at your shaking right
foot. I've crumpled the matching sheets beneath my neck for support.

"Yes," I say, glancing past you to the alarm clock. It is nearly 4 a.m.
"Fuck."

I'm ashamed of how closely I watch you. I am prepared for your
rejection, your doubt. My lungs constrain with anticipation.

"It's a lot, Ayukta," you say. "I'm not sure if I understand how any
of it works. Am I supposed to?"

"I don't, always."

"But you know it's true, still?"

"People believe in a lot of things without understanding how they
work," I say, tracing the patterns printed onto the comforter, one of
two we bought in Jaipur.

You sit up slowly, chewing on the inside of your bottom lip. "I need a break," you say. You look over at me, my expression pained enough that you reach over, squeezing my hand. When you kiss my forehead, when you tuck my hair away from my face, I turn your hand over in mine. Your nails match the comforter. I wipe one clammy palm after the other on the cotton, and you smile.

"I want to know the rest," you assure me. "Just a pause, before."

A soft light has begun to peek through the bedroom window. As you grab your robe and pad into the kitchen, I force deep breaths. You aren't running yet.

Look at this, the life we've built together all around us. I sit up on the mattress slowly, tracing our history together with my eyes. At the end of the hall: our velvet evergreen couch that we splurged too much on when we first moved in together, draped with white blankets from your parents. The posters that line the walls—concerts, mostly, but also the protest signs from when we marched together, advocating to keep *Sindh* in the Indian national anthem. You'd insisted we save the posters and frame them. *It means something to you*, you'd said. *Your history belongs in our home.*

It's hard to point at anything in this apartment and name what is only yours and what is only mine. Over the years, it's all blended together.

Outside the kitchen window, the restaurant across the street is already alight with cooks preparing for the day. We could live anywhere in the city, but you've always loved it here, where the aroma of red sauce sometimes drifts its way upward to the window. At our stovetop, with one solitary bulb on, you stand frying eggs, your hands rotating through jars of garlic powder and onion powder and paprika. The eggs sizzle in their browning butter, the toaster glows red, but you watch me, the rubber spatula upright in your hand.

"So," you say, "you can remember all of that?"

I nod.

"I'm only going to ask this once, and then never again." I wait, forcing myself not to bite my nails. "Are you sure these memories are all true?"

I nod again, and you inhale deeply. You're processing my answer, not questioning it, and Nadya, when you take me at my word, I feel my lungs loosen. I can breathe again with this, your doubt followed immediately by your trust in an ancestry that feels as fantastic as it is inescapable.

You flip the eggs and set them on the ceramic plates we got from my mother that Christmas when you met her for the first time. I huddle in my corner of our couch, still swaddled in the bedroom comforter. You rest the plate on my knees, finding one of my arms through the blankets to hand me a fork. Two steel cups of water sit on the coffee table.

"I haven't had breakfast this early in years," I say.

"I want to know everything," you say. "And at this pace, you're going to need some energy to get me to the end. Eat."

"Don't you work today?"

You shake your head. "I sent an email about feeling sick some-where between two and three a.m."

I take a bite of egg, yolk runny and surprisingly orange. "It feels weird to talk about this," I say.

"With me?"

"At all." Another bite, another two. "Everyone's kept it a secret."

"Your mother, too? Your dad doesn't know?"

"Not as far as I know."

"I wonder what it would be like to know my mother's memories," you say. Your curls bounce around you as you say this. For such a small person, you always speak with your entire body.

"I've tried not to," I admit. "Too strange, you know, to live in her memories when she was still alive, next to me. For years I only accessed the memories from her childhood, before I was born. I've only just started to peer into her life after she became my mother. It feels . . . weird, seeing myself through her eyes. To have memories of me that are not mine. I've been going slowly."

"Tell me about how it's passed along," you say, pulling one of the blankets onto your legs. You brush toast crumbs off the couch and onto the floor.

My feet find yours in the middle of the couch. "Well, the tapestry is responsible for that. When your image is sewn onto it, you gain access to the memories, the power."

"But you can access Amla's memories from before she was sewn on," you say. I can see the gears turning.

"I can access them, but it's because of how Amla remembered that time." I try to find the words for you. "It's similar to how you might tell a story to someone else, leaving out the details that didn't seem important to remember."

"That seems faulty."

"I guess all memories kind of are." I pause. "A lot of my mother's are like this."

Your eyebrows furrow, doing the math. "Is she next? On the tapestry, is your mother next?"

"No, actually," I say, gripping the steel cup tightly between my hands. "Do you remember . . ."

"Oh my god," you say, eyes widening. "Her sister."

"Yes." I nestle deeper into the couch, preparing myself for this next chapter. "My grandmother passed it to her eldest first."

Her name was Vibha.

# NINE

In these memories, the mornings are brightest. The sunlight hits Vibha's bed, the middle cot of three. In those moments between sleeping and waking, the sky so bright her closed eyelids paint it red, Vibha can slow time. There are only her breaths, only the gentle snores of two sleeping siblings beside her. She scours her mind for the thoughts she'd been thinking before she fell asleep the night before, pulls them into the morning with her, organizing and revising and planning before she's even acknowledged the waking day.

She is eight years old, now ten, now thirteen. For years, every morning has been like this, the slow and steady pace of waking before anyone else. She collects these moments. When she finally tiptoes out of bed, she steps into the sunny rectangles of the apartment floor. A light-footed hopscotch from the bedroom to the washroom. A twirling dance in the living room, her nightgown brushing against the love seat as birds fly in and out of her sunlight, wings flapping shadows across her path. A resigned half-leap into the kitchen, where the windows are too high and westward-facing for this morning game.

She sets water to boil, reaching into the cupboard for cardamom and Ma's chai masala without having to look. Some mornings she takes down a steel tin so filled with fresh methi leaves that they burst upward as she pops off the lid. She slices the methi into long, slim strands before mixing in chickpea and whole wheat flours, sometimes bajri flour, too, on a high-rimmed plate. This is her favorite part: she sprinkles in the chili powder, the turmeric, the cumin and coriander, the yellow oil, a few sliced chilies. The colors spill across the yellow-beige flour like dried pigments on fresh paper. She almost doesn't want to mix them together, wishing she could pause the process, the day.

And then, always the moment that cuts the enchantment of the morning: the push forward, the mixing of the colors on the plate with her hands, the oil clinging to her fingernails and in the curves between her fingers. The morphing, the cæsura, of a beautiful image.

Their housekeeper, Shantaben, comes in the afternoon, cleaning the powders from the kitchen counters, preparing the next meal. Vibha watches from the next room, always curious about how a morning enjoyed must be erased in its aftermath.

On her own, Vibha recalls those colors. Tries to catch the glint of the steel plate, the reds and yellows and greens scattered atop off-white flour. The bowls of onions and potatoes at the edge of the frame. Ma squeezes her shoulder, and she smiles. The sketch always feels off, a second-rate copy. Nothing compares to the memory, to those colors in the morning light. Mostly, nothing compares to the feeling of that moment: the warmth, the impending loss, the liminal space between decision and action.

It is mundane, yes, and yet this is the only image, the only moment, Vibha feels she needs to capture. It is the only painting that gives her energy.

**When Baba travels for work,** Ma leads Vibha to the rooftop. They have been spending Vibha's eighth year there, Ma teaching Vibha to draw like she can. Vibha likes to go most when her brother isn't home; when he joins, he spends the entire time huffing and sighing. He doesn't understand the value of this secret Ma has given them—a peek into something she so clearly loves, the life she could have had. This is why Vibha likes to paint, for the look it puts on her mother's face when she does it well.

Today, Anurag doesn't join, but Arni does. The three of them look out from the roof, Ma keeping Arni from getting too close to the edge, until Vibha points at a building farther down the winding path. "That one," she says, and Ma lingers by the roof edge while Vibha starts to sketch.

They are working on shadows this month. Ma has a large second-hand book—more like thirdhand or fourthhand, the way it is worn and tearing—that they use as a lesson guide. Draw first like this. Add in complexity here. They started using the book when Vibha turned six. Nearly two years of Baba's travel have passed since, and Vibha is halfway through the book.

Next to Vibha, Arni crawls around, sometimes picking up her pencil and other times picking at the roof floor. Four years younger than Vibha, she isn't coordinated enough to angle the pencil lightly, designating shadows on the street the way Ma asks Vibha to. Or maybe distraction is in her nature. Even now, Arni reaches over to trace the edge of Vibha's sketch paper, and then to trace the drawing of the building itself.

"Stop," Vibha hisses at her sister. "Sit still."

Arni giggles. "Make light go up," she says, continuing to reach over and brush her fingers across the work Vibha has already done.

"Sunlight goes *down*." Vibha pushes her sister's hands away. "Stop it."

But Vibha's annoyance only makes Arni more earnest in her efforts to blend the pencil. She taps on Arni's hands, but her sister is now grabbing at the paper. Vibha calls for Ma and, as though on cue, Arni slices her finger on the heavy-stock paper. She wails and Ma bounds from the rooftop's edge to its center, where the girls are sitting. Vibha sighs.

"I didn't do anything," she says. "Arni was being—"

"Arni is just a child," Ma says. Vibha wants to retort that she's a child, too, but she understands what her mother means: Arni doesn't go to school yet. She can't walk the city alone or even in a pair. She is the baby, and Vibha is supposed to always be taking care of her, watching her—protecting her.

Ma coos at Arni, and Vibha pushes her sketchbook aside. "I'll take her downstairs to wash her hand," she says.

"No." Ma hoists Arni onto her hip, the four-year-old child making Ma's figure look so small. She leans over to look at the work Vibha has completed in the first few minutes. "This is good," she says, "but you can do even better. Is the sunlight coming down or at an angle?"

Vibha squints at the sky. "At an angle?"

"There it is." Ma turns back to Arni. "Pay attention to the details. I'll take Arni down, and when I come up . . ."

"It'll be what you want," Vibha promises. She pulls the sketchbook back into her lap. "I'll be more careful this time."

Ma smiles at her. "Good," she says. "You're going to be better than me. I know it." The words make Vibha feel warm inside. At eight years old, this is all that she wants: to make Ma—who is sometimes sad, sometimes delicate, sometimes silent and absent—proud.

. . .

**When she is ten,** nearly eleven, Vibha's mother tells her a secret. "When I was your age, I started learning how to change the world," her mother says. "Would you like to learn, too?"

Is it her mother's way of asking consent? Vibha almost hesitates; she likes her world exactly as it is. She doesn't want to change any of it. In this way, she is so much more like her mother at that age than she knows. "Do I have to?" she asks.

"Think of it like a gift," her mother says, tucking Vibha's hair behind her ear. They are in the kitchen, the only ones awake. "This has to be our secret, though."

"Can Anurag do it?"

"No," her mother says. "This secret isn't for boys."

"Arni?"

"Only my oldest girl."

Vibha smiles at this; she feels special. Ten is a good age for secrets that belong to no other siblings, a good age for undivided maternal attention.

"Learning to do this is a commitment," Ma says, "a promise," and Vibha nods though she doesn't know about commitments yet. There is nothing more serious in her life than tracking the comings and goings of the neighborhood dogs in hopes of sneaking food to them. So she sits next to her mother on the parlor chairs later in the evening, when Anurag is helping Arni with her homework and Baba is reading his book in the bedroom, and Ma begins to stitch the silhouette of a young girl onto a large tapestry Vibha has never seen before.

**Sometimes, in the nights** after that one, she sees her mother in her nightmares. Or, more correctly, she becomes her mother, sees memories like dreams. Feels anguish and regret and loss—such loss that she wakes up even before the sun begins to creep over the horizon, her hands wet with tears. She has never dreamt something real before, but she knows somewhere in her bones that these dreams are history. Something tells her that everything she has seen and felt in those dark hours is true. She wakes with the ache of familiarity, of nostalgia—and the weariness of a long, long life.

She knows, from the dreams, that what is happening to her is unlike what happened to her mother. That this is not science, but instinct, and that she is better at tapping into the lineage than her mother was. She is better at meditating, at sitting still and calm, and she begins to see, within this gift her mother has given her, a warning. *We can't always control what we create*, she understands. *Do you feel the regret in your mother's memories?*

While she wants to know what her mother did, she is cautious in her curiosity. If her mother has secrets to hide, her mother should hide them, Vibha thinks, and maybe Vibha should help her do that hiding.

I took my cue from Vibha here. I think she knew, innately and innocently, that love isn't about unearthing that which was hidden from you. And just as loving your parent doesn't mean excavating all that they've tried to bury, for Vibha, loving her mother meant not revisiting Amla's history until she was explicitly told that she could.

She won't mess this up, she tells herself. She will show her mother that she is right to carry this gift, this burden.


**Vibha's brother is taking** her to the chowpatty on his bike; she balances on the back of his seat, hugging him close. They weave through the narrow roads, past colorful posters of new movies playing at the theater, and she hums the songs to herself with her cheek pressed against her brother's back, the vibrations tickling all the way to her ears.

It is two years later, January 30, 1968, the twentieth anniversary of Gandhi's death. There is a long line of visitors at the entrance to Kirti Mandir, Gandhi's childhood home, and Anurag weaves around them as they get closer to the beach. Even there, ten boys are putting on a play near the edge of the water, and Vibha watches closely: the boy with a simple white dhotiyu covering him; the boy next to him with a dupatta over his head, Gandhi's wife, Kasturba. They play out the Dandi March with the coastline of the Arabian Sea, holding water in their hands and exclaiming about how they've found a way to make salt without the British. They shout about swaraj, independent rule, and then one boy makes his hand into a pretend gun and squints his left eye, and shoots the boy playing Gandhi.

When Anurag gestures for Vibha to hop off the bike, she keeps her eyes trained on the group of boys as they collect paisa from passersby. She wonders if the story could have gone any other way.

"What are you thinking about? You want to join that natak?" Anurag asks, teasing, and she shakes her head quickly. "You're growing up so fast," he says after a pause. "I feel like it was just yesterday you were four years old and Arni was born. Now you're twelve? You're a whole person."

"And Arni's not a whole person?"

"She's the baby," Anurag says, laughing. "She'll always be the baby."

Vibha is irked when he says this, but not enough to defend her sister. "Baba says I'm going to have to grow up once you go to university," she says, scuffing the sand with her sandal. "He says I have to be better friends with Arni. Since you'll be gone." *Only a few more years left like this*, she thinks.

Vibha has always been doted on by her brother. The allure of being his confidant still outweighs the sisterly bond. Sometimes she feels guilty for it, seeing the way Arni tags along only to be left out. When Ma sits all three of them down for creative time, Anurag writing silly stories in his notebook and Vibha learning her mother's style of watercolor paintings, Arni seems to retreat. She isn't good at following Ma's rules—*if she would just try harder*, Vibha always thinks, *if she could just do what is asked of her*. But maybe—and she doesn't have the words for this feeling yet, but soon, when she's older, Vibha will—this is the burden of the older daughter to bear. And Vibha has never seen any older daughter break the rules, has never seen an older daughter defy her parents. When she sees Arni painting impulsively when their mother has asked them to sketch carefully, when Ma tells Vibha that this gift requires caution, Vibha understands: the gift, the curse, is her responsibility to bear.

**Vibha uses the gift** only three times.

There is one week when her mother makes all the children stay inside. They sit in the living room, Ma leaning in to the radio as she listens to its words. *Urs festival. Violence. Curfew imposed. Army called in.* Vibha does not know the details of what has transpired, but we do: Over five days, more than five hundred people were killed. More than six thousand shops were damaged—largely Muslim shops, largely damaged by Hindus. It was the most deadly week since Partition.

Thirteen-year-old Vibha experiences the 1969 riots as the roar of motorbikes past their building, the flash of saffron-colored cloth that I recognize as the uniform of Hindu nationalists. She climbs onto the parlor seat to peer over the windowsill, and through the sound of the engines and the cries in the street, she hears the yelp of an animal in the gully between their building and the next.

"Ma!" The alarm in her voice leaves no room for argument. She streaks across the room and she can feel Ma's silhouette gliding behind her. A rush of words as Ma tells Anurag to stay with Arni, to open the door only for them, and then they are down the stairs and in the emptied street. Vibha finds the injured dog immediately, her white fur printed with motorbike treads. Her whines are catlike.

"We can't leave her," Vibha says, Ma already reaching toward the dog. The street animal bites in Ma's direction just once, and then can only pant and whine, has no energy to carry through on the threat. She allows Ma to cradle her in her arms—this life, this bloody, broken body—and they escape the eerie silence of the street.

Baba says nothing when he arrives home, only "If the dog should die, let it die in a Brahmin's house." Ma, rubbing turmeric into the dog's wounds, doesn't answer. The green trajva on Ma's wrist darts through the dog's yellowing fur.

"She'll be okay, won't she?" Vibha asks, one hand on the dog's jowl.

"I can't promise you anything," Ma says softly, and Vibha takes a scoop of turmeric powder into her own palm, speckling the floor yellow as she does so. "We're powerless in this."

And there's something about that word, *powerless*, that rings hollow for Vibha. Some whisper of memory, some ancient voice. She nods slowly to her mother, and then, as soon as she can, she retreats to the watercolor room.

She slows her breathing. She feels for the threads somewhere in the dark of her mind, grasps at them—mothers, grandmothers, ancestors. Her pencil moves across her sketchbook while her mind escapes. The graphite dog takes shape on the page, sitting tall, snout turned upward to bark, this wound healed.

It is not that she doesn't think of Ma's fear, her caution—she simply has no reason of her own to think of this power as anything but a gift. And isn't saving a life what this gift should be for, if it is meant for anything?

*Let us do something good,* she pleads. *Let me show Ma something good.*

**The second time** she uses the gift, it is to kiss the boy who lives in the apartment directly below theirs.

He had gone to the boys' school a few blocks away with Anurag and stayed to attend university in Porbandar, and Vibha has liked him for a while—since the afternoon he cracked a window of the neighboring building when his friends dared him to conduct cricket batting practice off the apartment's rooftop. Ever since she saw him get dragged away by the ear while she stifled her laughter behind hanging laundry, she has thought she loves him.

Vibha is cusping womanhood: at fifteen, she's only two years younger than her mother had been when she married. Vibha has another year of school, and then she isn't quite certain what comes next. But for now, she feels unwatched. She misses her brother, off at university, but has grown into the space he left behind. The apartment is incapable of containing her: she dances around Shantaben in the kitchen, learning from her the basics of cooking; tutors her little sister on the rooftop, always surprised by Arni growing more and more into a person; even takes the dog with her to walk kilometers along the chowpatty. But there's an ephemerality to this autonomy, a certainty of it fading once she finishes her final year in school. Baba has hinted once, twice at the possibility of meeting marriage suitors; she knows there is no world in which she will experience an abundance of choice, just one in which she picks according to the options she has been dealt.

Sometimes she detours from the shoreline with the dog to listen outside the cinema, mouthing the words to Lata Mangeshkar's songs in *Dushmun.* Even as she imagines herself as Mumtaz, she knows this world of a woman falling in love with an attractive, alcoholic stranger is a romantic storyline not meant for her. Never mind the impossibility of a man who could sing like Kishore Kumar, whose smile makes her and the other girls in her class swoon—never mind the impossibility of an alcoholic stranger in Gujarat, the state that has banned alcohol; or in Porbandar, where every Bardai Brahmin knows every other, ready to report on transgression.

Longing nestles into her gut.

Vibha is surrounded by constrictions. Ma relies on hypotheticals to teach Vibha about carefulness. "What would happen if you drew *this*?" Ma asks. "What consequences could come from *that*?" Ma is always looking for Vibha to give her extreme answers, but as Vibha grows she wonders more and more about the likelihood of those outcomes Ma fears so much. Ma can dream up hyperbolic consequences to any painting, wanting Vibha to harness the gift for its memories and not its power. But every warning about carelessness pushes Vibha to brainstorm how she might prove to her mother that small changes can still be meaningful, even if only to one person. Even if only to herself. She hasn't opened the door to her mother's memories, but she knows what her mother has told her: a gooseberry bush her mother drew into existence—a small change, Vibha thinks, harmful to no one—still rests in the orchards by her great-aunt's village home. Vibha wonders, what if that's all the gift is meant to be? Small treasures.

One morning, as she is working on the sketch of the still life that has evaded her—the spices on the kitchen counter, the jaggery tin and vegetables resting beside it—with the dog curled into a circle at her feet, she closes her eyes and is overtaken by yearning. Maybe the lineage agrees with her, about this smallest of changes—the desire to feel desired, just once, without something coming of it. She is not asking for a proposal, a marriage. She stops humming the *Dushmun* songs, finds her arms moving of their own accord to take a new sheet of thick paper, to switch brushes and pigments. Without thinking, she draws the boy downstairs, paints the pink of his lips on hers, outlining her arms on his torso, his shoulders. She paints herself with flowers in her hair, Mumtaz as Phoolmati.

The kiss doesn't happen until months later, over Navratri, when Anurag and the other apartment boys are drinking homemade hooch on the roof. Vibha goes to collect her family's laundry from where it hangs, the wilted flowers from a puja earlier that week scattering across the rooftop. She takes a few flowers in her hands, the thick marigolds still damp with life. The boy from downstairs is on the staircase when she returns to it, on his way to rejoin the older boys. In the tightness of the stairway, she can smell the moonshine on his breath, the crumpled flowers in her sweaty palms. *What luck*, she thinks, and she steps closer to him and he pauses before taking her lead. When he kisses her, it feels like a dare, as quick as the loud crack of wooden ball on cricket bat, and when he steps away, it's as though he doesn't know what has transpired—only that in the darkness someone found a drunken courage, and that someone may not have been him.

Vibha walks away from the moment as soon as it is over, leaving the boy in the stairwell behind her. She tucks the stem of a half-alive flower behind her ear and holds the dry linens tight against her chest.

**The boy in the stairwell** isn't the type of boy Baba wants Vibha to marry. He makes this much clear to her at dinner the next week, treating it like a strategy session.

"A respectable family," he says between bites. "A Brahmin family, of course. Gujarati. Bardai, ideally. That's where a daughter of mine belongs. The Labadiya boy, he's going into a government job. Or Yuvraj Mehta's nephew, who's in Ahmedabad now."

Vibha chews her lip. She has watched Anurag argue with her father, their tempers so like each other's, but she herself has managed to step delicately through conversations with Baba. She treats his words like the shadows that used to be cast along the floor—dancing light-footed around them as she had as a child.

Ma catches her eye. "Suresh," she says, "aren't we a respectable family already?"

"That's why she should marry someone of the same standard."

"Didn't we get married so that our daughter wouldn't have to make the same decisions we did?"

Baba stops eating. "What decisions, Amla?"

Ma pauses. The question is cutting. Maybe Ma thought she had been mediating the conversation, but Baba's ire now has a target.

"We got married," Ma says slowly, "because it made sense."

"Because we came from the same standards."

Ma glances at Vibha across the dinner table. "We came from different places."

"And still?" Baba makes their coded language explicit. "We match caste. We match culture." He scoots his chair out and it squeaks against the floor. When he stands, he looms over Ma. "Why would you question this? And in front of her?"

Vibha looks at his accusatory finger pointing at her. From Ma's rooftop sessions on the gift and their family's past, Vibha knows about the surnames that camouflage Ma into this community. She knows that Ma has hidden the Sindhi part of herself that Bapu gave her, that same part that runs through Vibha's blood. There is an entire history buried, if not erased, in this household.

"I think Ma is trying to say that it might be nice to have a choice,"

Vibha says, because even if Baba doesn't agree with this, it is a better explanation than Ma's history. "She's just trying—"

"Don't talk back to me," Baba snaps.

"She wasn't, Suresh, don't listen to—"

"You either!" His hand slamming on the table makes the glasses topple, water spilling over the table. Vibha goes utterly still. "I will decide who she marries, and the two of you will stop inserting yourself into things you clearly don't know enough about." Baba's cheeks are red; his forehead, too. His hand curls into a fist. "Use your brain. What type of people do you think we are?"

He storms away, his meal half-eaten on the dining table, and Vibha and Ma sit quiet for a moment, their food still untouched.

Ma taps her fingers on the table. The bags under her eyes are dark, and she looks so exhausted. Not crying, not in shock. The weariness resounds in her voice when she speaks.

"I thought if I married him . . ." Ma inhales deeply, her voice soft. "You wouldn't have to marry someone like him."

"I know."

"You and Arni, I wanted you girls to have your own path."

"I know. And Arni will have that," Vibha says, reaching across the table to Ma's hand. "I promise you. Arni will have everything: university if she wants it, choices for her husband. I don't mind taking this responsibility, truly, if it's off her."

Ma smiles tightly. "I know, Vibhu." Her voice catches, and she removes her hand from Vibha's. "I'm going to do the dishes."

"Shantaben will be here tomorrow."

"I need something to do with my hands," Ma says, and that's when Vibha gets the idea.

It is the third time, the final time, that Vibha uses the gift.

She paints her baby sister all grown up.

Vibha pours her heart into the painting. All those moments she

178

chose Anurag over Arni, all those times she shunned her sister for acting out of line. Every push and pull of their relationship, every apology she's never said aloud. Every time she prioritized herself over the person she viewed as a child.

The lineage, they call on her, caution her. You cannot pour your heart into an act like that and not feel the weight of every love, every sacrifice, of the sisters who came before you. *Who is this gift for, if not for one you love?* Vibha is halfway through the painting before her hands are not hers alone, and then the portrait is so much more than this—no longer Arni at the edge of girlhood and womanhood, but instead Arni aged, older, standing beside a seated Ma. The older woman's silver mane foreshadows the daughter's steady graying.

Here is the problem: she does not insert herself into the painting.

It is the problem with such a specific gift as this one. It leaves room for error, for quiet mistakes. And there's no correcting a painting that you don't even know you're making. Something driven so much by emotion that your eyes glaze over, your hands move of their own accord.

Vibha does not notice, or does not remember, or cannot. In her fugue state, she is focused on the ways shadows dance across her sister's face—*Here, let me give you smile lines, crinkles at the edges of your eyes, signs of a life that has been laughed through. Let me make you unhardened. Let me give you this gift.*

**And this is the outcome** her mother had tried to avoid, isn't it, because of course Amla, too, had wanted only to do good things with this gift, and of course she would have made a boy love her if she could have, would have wished for dogs that were alive and good futures for her loved ones. *If she could have, if she could have.* Instead she'd made choices within the confines of what was available to her, made decisions that no adult seemed to. And yet here is Amla's daughter—Amla's careful daughter, the hesitant one, the one who is supposed to avoid what Amla could not—painting a future that does not include herself.

In a few months, this future will begin to lay roots. Vibha's life will wane, her future fading, the one of her mother and sister alone taking shape. You cannot undo what has been done—isn't that what the tapestry told Amla when she was young? Nothing Vibha can paint after this will bring back the future she's called into being. There is no crawling back from here.

Part Three

MOTHER

ll this time," you say, and your voice changes in a way that makes my stomach fall. "All this time, you just said you didn't really see yourself having kids. That you were open to it, but *don't count on it, Nadya.*"

I hug a pillow against my chest, speaking low into it. "I know."

Your coffee mug is clutched so tightly in your hands that the tension is apparent in every muscle. "It's barely a half-truth," you say. "Being uncertain about having children is really different from being concerned your child will hurt themself—erase themself—because of this inheritance."

"I have a difficult time imagining something worse for a child," I say, measured. These are the stakes of this inheritance. I shift to kneel on the couch, begging you to look back at me. "Nadya, what I said to you was true then and still is now. You have to know that, aside from the consequences of Vibha's decisions."

"I just . . . I never even asked any follow-ups," you say, tugging the comforter more closely around your shoulders. "I wonder what I would have asked, if I'd known it wasn't just about you."

"Nadya, I'm not telling you this history as a way of saying no to having children," I say slowly, and now you look up at me. I lean back on my ankles, leveling our heights. "I just—I didn't want to make this decision, to have a child, without you. And this history is about all of it—the good and the bad. There's so much to it."

"Ayukta, love," you say, hand covering mine. "What good have you told me so far?"

My heart sinks. Oh, how terribly have I shared this story, that you can't see: it is not only pain that these memories, these lives, carry. I keep making promises to you that this story gets better. And I make another one to you now: "You'll see how gray this all is, by the end— at the very least, how it's been a gift to me."

Through the window facing the couch, the city begins to wake. Our prayer plant on the sill is already drinking in the morning sun. I gently pull you close, breathing in the scent of your hair. Coconut oil masks yesterday's shampoo. Familiar, like incense guiding me home.

I regret that I have not given you time to sit with all of this history. Haven't I had years to understand, decades to call my mother with another question? Don't you deserve the same? And here you are, only hours in. I'm a coward. I can't even admit that you would have been better prepared if I'd shared this all more slowly, since the time we began seriously planning our lives together. I should say all of this to you, but all I say is, "I'm sorry."

With a squeeze of my waist, you pull away from me. I search your eyes—for what, I don't know. At first, I was scared you wouldn't be-lieve me; now, I'm scared I've taken so long to tell you, that withhold-ing this has been a betrayal. Until this story is done, until we are on the other side, I will fear losing you.

You stretch, ribs cracking as your heart opens. You down the rest of the now-cold coffee and take my mug from its place on the coffee table.

"Let's get out of this apartment," you say. The mugs clatter in the kitchen sink as you fill two thermoses from our cabinet. The decanter is still half-full. "We need fresh air."

I twist my spine, watching as you grab your coat and slip ratty sandals over your socks. You gesture for me to hurry up, and I slip quickly into boots and a cardigan missing two buttons. I follow you out the door, down our three flights of stairs, and toward Fort Greene Park.

Outside, the coffee steam moistens my chin and nose. It's going to be bright today, the kind of winter sun we both love. I want to take your hand, but I don't. I wouldn't want to be touched if I were you, and it's enough for me that, after what you've heard, you're still willing to walk our usual route alongside me.

"What if someone doesn't have daughters?"

I exhale, relieved you've chosen the subject. "Nieces. Cousins. People you share blood with."

"But what if there's no one?"

I feel a heat in my neck, around my shoulders—like there's a story I could close my eyes and watch on the backs of my eyelids, like a movie, like I could reach out and hold it if I wanted. *All of this has happened before.* I pull myself away. I need to stay here.

See, I can always escape into another life, another person's silhouette. If we don't have a child, I will still remember the feeling of motherhood in someone else's skin. I will be okay. But I also don't know how to tell you that I can't really live my own life for myself so long as this gift sits within me; I don't feel like my feet are grounded. Am I me, or am I me accompanied? Am I the person I would have grown into without the gift? I don't know. I don't know.

Sometimes I wonder, if we have a child, will I feel some relief as the lineage slips away from me? What if I only want a child to remove this burden of memory from myself, to make it no longer mine to bear? Better not to have a child, maybe. Better not to have such a selfish reason for becoming a parent.

"There are people who have used the gift to have children," I finally say to you. "Paint them, sculpt them, draw them. But also . . . it could be any child, not just a direct one, so long as they carry this blood. It could skip a generation and wait. You could pass it to a faraway branch on the family tree, to a cousin however removed."

"So why are there no men? Do you remember any men?"

I shake my head. "I think they worried about what it means to give someone who's always had the most power even more of it."

You nod and sip your drink, and we both watch a dog run across our path, our heads turning in unison.

Would a child raised by us be okay? A child you carry wouldn't have my blood; do we choose this for them, leave them unable to access these memories or change their circumstance, their life? A child I carry has my blood—has these options. Possible access to memory. Possible art that changes the world, even if it is only their own small one.

I could carry our child and still we could decide not to sew their image onto the tapestry. Is it worse for our child to never have had the option, or is it worse to have the option but never receive the gift? Do we hide it from them, this part of me? And if you carried our child and we told them about this history, they might ask why we chose for this gift to end with me. Why we took the choice away from them. What do we say, then—that I'm scared? That we cut off their access to a gift that most direct ancestors on this side of their lineage have had—a gift that has served as a road map for me to understand my existence? That has given me a path back home?

What an amazing and beautiful thing, to know where I've come from. What a frightening, ground-shifting, incomprehensible thing.

# TEN

When Vibha dies, it is morning. The emerging light patch-works across the apartment floors. Pigeons coo on the next roof over. The silence is eerie; Arni is accustomed to the sound of her sister's coughs, her sister's steps, heavier and heavier, across the floor. To have a peaceful morning, a quiet morning, is to know the inevitable has come to pass.

Arni reminds herself that she is supposed to be prepared for this: nearly two years ago, Vibha's lungs began collapsing into coughs, her weight slowly disappearing. Arni won't know exactly what her sister suffered until much later, when she has friends who are doctors and they explain Vibha's infection with a tsking sound, a pitying look in their eyes. "It's so common in the third world," they'll say, "so easily preventable." It *breaks their hearts.*

For now, Arni feels only emptiness. She remains statuesque. She will hold herself together, she thinks; for Vibha, for her memory, Arni will not bite at her mother today.

Ma begins to scrub the apartment almost immediately, filling the void with the back-and-forth swish of sponge and soapy water on floor tiles. Arni tries to stop her, tugging on her sleeve and reminding her that there is time. She pushes down her frustration—for Vibha. She begs Ma to stop, reminds her that there is grieving to do first. They need to sit and cry, not move, not make decisions. Arni needs time to still herself, to understand what it means.

Her mother shakes her off. The flat becomes spotless, from every tile in the closed kitchen to the windowpanes behind the living room love seat. Even Shantaben, who at first welcomed the help of Ma's obsession, opens her eyes wide as she sets plates on the pristine table. Ma wipes the dust from the bookshelves, filled with books on history and poetry that Anurag and Baba have collected. She takes out each of her children's old textbooks one by one, wiping down their hard covers, and then empties the kitchen cupboards of every steel dish and cup and wipes down those shelves, too. She gets on a chair to clean the lamps, moves the navy love seat to sweep beneath it. The only time she goes outside the flat, she buys five pairs of slippers and insists everyone in the house wear them, even Shantaben. Apartment turned sanatorium.

At first, Arni spends her time watching her mother clean or watching Vibha's body. Anurag takes the train in from Ahmedabad, and she keeps vigil on the parlor chairs until he arrives. When the pandit walks her parents through the rituals, she follows Anurag's lead, mumbling words she doesn't understand. Only after Baba and Anurag leave with Vibha's body does Arni get on her hands and knees alongside Ma, reaching for the corners of shelves Ma can't, toes squirming against the house slippers. Now it is right to clean the house; now it's all that's left to do.

In the following days, when Baba is at work, Anurag nudges his way in and they tackle the rooms like an assembly line of hands:

Arni's long-fingered, slender ones; Anurag's, calloused and adult; Ma's, with her right wrist tattooed in green geometries. On these days, Arni pauses to watch Anurag work. If she squints just right, she finds pieces of Vibha's face refracted back at her. Anurag's nose is Vibha's nose is her mother's nose. She tries to push away the feeling that the wrong sibling is standing before her, that she would trade Anurag for another day with her sister beside her. She wonders if it is the same for Anurag, if her own face causes him pain in its nearness to Vibha's, its *almost*ness. She wonders if, in those minutes with the pandit, Anurag thought Vibha's cold and hardened face looked vaguely like Arni's.

The loss of Vibha deepens the bags beneath Ma's eyes, makes her movements sluggish. Vibha—her firstborn daughter, the one who had picked up her mother's love of watercolors, who always knew how to charm their father into taking the family out for falooda. This gaping hole of a person. Arni can sense her mother processing this sudden change, unable to turn back time.

"You'll have to tell me if this keeps up," Baba says to Arni while Ma sweeps the apartment balcony for the second time that day, the fourth time that week. He pulls at his freshly shaved cheeks, shaking his head. His suitcase is already packed, his train ticket purchased for tomorrow morning. In a day, he'll begin a trip to farming regions, overseeing his subordinates as they go door-to-door convincing farmers they should invest in better irrigation and rust-resistant seeds: *Have you heard of these new fertilizers?* or *Would you be interested in your own tractor? You'd be amazed how much labor you can cut with one of these.*

"If what keeps up?" Arni clicks off the gas with one hand, the other lifting the boiling chai from the stovetop. She presses two fingers to her temple; how Vibha had done this three times a day, she doesn't know: her eyebrows hurt from concentrating on the pot, the liquid inside so thin it could burn at the pot's bottom. The milkwala keeps apologizing for the thinning fat content of his deliveries, bowing his head when he speaks to Ma. They are lucky to have milk delivered at all.

Baba remains in the kitchen doorway, watching Ma on the balcony. "Maybe we should have a pandit come. Have him cleanse this place, make your mother feel better. Do you think she'd like that?"

"You think Ma would want a pandit?" She hears her sarcasm and bites her lip, praying Baba doesn't.

She's lucky. Baba scratches at his mustache; it is his instinct, not Ma's, to seek answers in faith. "I'm not sure what she wants."

Arni pours his cup of chai silently. Baba hadn't been there to see Ma's sadness turn to anger after the men had left for the cremation, hadn't heard her tears turn into muffled shouts. *This is how things are*, Baba had said before leaving, *only men at the pyre*. Ma had begged, and Arni had watched from across the room as she fell to her knees, as she pleaded to simply join them, never mind asking to light the pyre herself. Baba was not one to relent on his decisions, and the longer Ma begged, the angrier he got, shoving her hands off his feet, slamming the door behind him: *This is how things are.*

Ma's footsteps recede from the balcony to the bedroom, the doors creaking shut behind her. Arni takes an extra minute at the table, her arms crossed, cream from the chai crusting onto the cups. When Baba takes his chai to the living room, Arni makes her way to the second bedroom, pausing in the hallway, which is measured by a set of watercolor portraits at eye level. The names of each face in the portraits are written in Gujarati in the lower-left corner of each frame, her mother's name in Sindhi—the only Sindhi words Arni can read—on the lower right. She touches her fingers lightly to the frames as she passes them: *Meena Thakur. Anurag Prakash. Chandini*

*Prakash.* She lingers on the watercolor of her parents on their wedding day—*Suresh and Amla Dave*—a simple painting capturing a simple wedding, the background pale and pinkish, her parents' faces separated by a hanging red dupatta. She wonders if Ma will paint Vibha now, will place her portrait on the wall with a half wreath of marigolds.

She pauses at the door to the small room at the end of the hall, the bedroom that Arni and Vibha had shared before Vibha's illness. Over the past couple years, when Anurag returned for his term breaks, they had crowded into the room, into the space by Ma's watercolor station—a large, stained table with pans of pigments and half sketches, a can of brushes on some uneven corner that rattled them all awake when Vibha kicked in her sleep.

This room was the first one cleaned, the one in which Vibha died.

Arni nestles into the clean pile of blankets near the painting station, tucking herself in the light comforter that was always her sister's. She lays her head on the pillow that no longer smells of Vibha and tries not to think of their last conversation. She sleeps remembering her sister's coughs, pretending the empty bed beside her is warmed by the bodies of siblings, that the edge of the blanket clutched in her hand is her sister's soft palm.


For a week, Arni doesn't leave the flat. When she finally does, she feels the hair on her arms and neck rise, her body having forgotten that the seasons would continue despite her mourning. She lugs her wooden crate of paint cans and brushes to the roof of their apartment building, fingers itching for the handle of a thick-bristled brush.

It's how she was raised. There was once a time when all the children crowded around Ma's painting station, and Ma would stress the

importance of using *existing scenes* as beginning points. Eventually
Anurag tired of the exercises, sitting with his tuition book while the
girls watched Ma attentively. Arni had felt so young, four years between herself and Vibha, six between her and Anurag, and the painting sessions felt like a secret club she'd joined late.

*Start with what you already see,* Ma directed them, pointing to the
street from the window or taking them up to the roof where laundry
hung from wires. *Imagining comes after you learn, once you're older.
Once you understand how this works.*

The girls would nod, not really understanding. Once, on a rare
occasion when Anurag joined them—still gentle, tender at that age—
Arni pushed him away. "You don't even like to paint," she remembers
insisting.

"I'll just be near," he said, holding up his little notebook, pencil
wedged between his clumsy fingers. "I won't interrupt."

Arni shook her head at him, bossy, wanting the extra time with
Ma. She wanted in on that intangible thread connecting her mother
and older sister—feared that her brother competed for that same attention. Each time, just as Arni thought she was close to creating
that shared connection for herself, she would get excited and paint
in thick strokes, bold and impulsive colors streaking the page, and
she'd watch her mother's face fall. Here was her imagined Porbandar
(but underwater, like Atlantis; no, with flying cars; no, with over-
grown vines snaking up the buildings; and on and on), and each
time, it wasn't what her mother wanted. When Arni glanced over at
Vibha's paper, she always saw her sister's hesitance. Pencil sketches
preceded any application of pigment, her first colors nearly transpar-
ent. It was no surprise that Ma took Vibha, and not either of the
other siblings, under her wing. They were painting together before
Arni was out of the womb; she never had a chance.

All the better for her, Arni had eventually told herself—she liked pressing into paints thicker than watercolors, harsher ones. She liked being unwatched, unable to disappoint. But already the seed of that resentment had begun to grow.

Over the years, the outer wall of the roof entryway became her canvas. She leaned into full-armed brushstrokes, into the idea of a mural hidden to most of the residents, viewed largely by children scurrying away from their mothers hanging laundry.

The building manager regularly complains and hoses down the roof. *The residents don't like it*, he says. *The women complain that their laundry smells chemical.* Arni has never heard any aunties complain, no, and she loves the cat and mouse of this—loves the way the colors rush off the tiles and down the sides of the building when the roof is watered down, all these cerulean and orange and rusty saffron shades puddling into a muddy brown in the street. She likes the chance to start anew. In the mornings after a roof cleaning, she leaves a basket of fresh fruit at the manager's door as she formulates the next design.

Now, the crate wedged between her arms, Arni claims the wall to the right of the rooftop door. She nods at the women draping damp laundry onto the wires, the sun bright in her eyes. As she sets down the crate, the muscles in her upper arms pulse; she hasn't carried out this ritual in weeks.

Arni knows to work through the physical pain—she craves it, the soreness she's sure to feel at the end of this. She pulls a folded bedsheet from the crate and places it beneath her knees. She unpacks her paint cans—all of them Vibha's most beloved colors. She makes small dots on the lower stretch of the wall, the bottom of her imagined canvas. She moves the bedsheet with her, scooting a foot or so at a time, careful that her dotted line is even. The paint drips down, little spots of color against the dusty white tiles of the roof floor. Her right side is doing all the work of bearing her weight as she stretches over—when she extends with her brush, her left leg counters backward. Her abdomen tightens. She licks the salt from her upper lip.

After an hour, she stretches her back, her spine cracking nearly all the way down. Her neck pangs from its downward concentration. The base layer has been set for the next mural—dark teal, Vibha's favorite. A warm breeze rattles the paint can lid, and Arni wipes her sleeve against her forehead. She dips the thick brush back into the paint can, reaches for the upper-left corner, and begins again.

That night, Arni dreams—as she already has countless times—of the night Vibha died. Of her sister's desperate, raspy voice.

"I have to tell you," Vibha repeats, "I have to tell you." And her hand grips Arni's too tightly, her milky eyes wide like saucers, and Arni wakes, her heart pounding in her chest.

*Not this*, she thinks. *Not now.*

She is not ready to face this memory.

Inside the flat, weariness settles into the vacuum. Arni tries to get extra wear out of her white kurtis, but they turn yellowish with dust too fast, the armpits translucent with sweat. The rooftop isn't kind to white. Ma buys two simple kurtas for Baba, but he doesn't even touch them. "I can't do government work looking like a mourner," he snaps at Ma, his grief having long given way to his customary temper. "You think they want me going door-to-door in white? It'll look like I'm asking for alms. Sell them back."

Arni watches Ma's face fall; of course she can't sell the white outfits, not with the stench of fresh death still on it. When Ma rubs oil into Arni's hair one evening, she sniffs at Arni's neckline and insists she change. The next day Ma rounds up all the white kurtas, soaks them in soap, and rubs at them until Arni thinks the fabric might tear, and they wear Baba's unwanted kurtas like nightgowns around the house for a week. The fabric flies around them, bird feathers, wings.

Outside the flat, the significance of Vibha's passing feels lost. In October 1973, Diwali comes and passes; the family does a small puja out of habit but doesn't celebrate, their year of mourning only just begun, as their street alights with fireworks and drums. Anurag returns for the long break, and Arni returns to the roof. She finds comfort in her usual role, the youngest child somewhere in the background. Nobody looks for her.

More and more, the world begins to feel foreign to Arni. It's not just the loss of Vibha. Essential commodities—milk, cooking oil, grains—have been growing scarce; the water to their building is regularly shut off early in the evening from overuse. On her way to hang laundry, Arni eavesdrops on the uncles next door, whose voices travel down the hall, their door propped open as friends and sons come and go.

"The politicians have their heads up their asses," one uncle usually says.

"No, it's the hawkers," another says. "They've created a black market and they're invested in keeping it open."

"No, the bus drivers—"

"No, the bus conductors—"

"It's the traders," someone says. "The marketwalas compete for the highest price now. When was the last time you bargained down?"

"The industrialists," another uncle says, and his tone is proud, like he's the first to nail the answer. "They're putting all the locals out of business, raising prices, bringing machines to do good, honest men's work."

"No, it's the politicians," the uncle who accused the hawkers says. "They're leaning back, smoking pipes, manipulating all of us and lining their friends' pockets."

These conversations are happening in apartments all across the city, even more so outside the bounds of Porbandar. It is not the fault of hawkers, of bus drivers and conductors, of traders and walas. Arni is only beginning to understand the puppet strings around her, the different ideologies and loyalties: the divides between her father, who looks up to Gandhi and the Congress Party in this hometown they share, who knows personally the fight for an independent country; and her own generation, Anurag's generation, who don't feel loyalties to men who died before they were born. Already, in Ahmedabad, a city so filled with universities it is owned more by the students than the politicians, teachers whisper of organizing, fearful of a crackdown or of losing their jobs.

Baba despises these conversations, is annoyed by the echo of voices down the hall. He complains about the way the uncles' voices are raised, met by the cheers of friends drunk on homemade hooch. "I want some peace and quiet in my evenings, is that too much?" he asks Arni, and she shrugs. "If I hear one more grown man whining while sitting on his hands all day . . ."

Anurag winks at Arni across the room, and she pats Baba's back and keeps gathering plates from the table. She knows Anurag has joined the men next door each day since he's been in town, smoking cigarettes with the uncle who lives there and his son; she keeps her mouth shut. When she goes to the roof to hang laundry and spots Anurag with a cigarette in hand, he nods at her and she nods back, their secret.

. . .

**A few days later,** Anurag lures Arni away from the rooftop with the promise of kulfi, his wallet in hand. "On me," he says as they unchain their bikes, and Arni rolls her eyes at the gesture. "Let's do something nice before I go back to school."

The navy paint on Arni's bike is chipping; Anurag's has been freshly coated in a deep green. She wonders when it was painted over—by whom. The doorman, the same one who was on duty the night they loaded Vibha's body into the car and to the pyre, nods at them and Anurag nods back. Arni meets the doorman's eyes blankly.

"I don't want you to go back to university," she admits when they're on the street, avoiding looking at her brother. She leans down to roll up her churidar so the bike chain can't catch on the thin material.

Anurag teeters from one tiptoe to the other, the bike moving in tandem. "Me neither," he says. "Let's go to the stand by the chowpatty, okay? No racing, it's still muddy."

Arni beckons for him to lead the way, easing into the rhythm slowly; she relishes feeling the downward push of the pedal in her shins more than her calves, the way she leans more weight on her arms than on the seat. She squints her eyes, wanting to focus on the breeze on her cheeks but unable to close her eyes on a bustling street.

They weave this way from their apartment building down to the ports, the bikes jostling over the rocks in the road. She can smell her whole city when they cycle, the scents of roasting chickpea flour, the charcoal, the peanut oil. Even the smell of shit is better this way, fleeting. A man leading two roped goats yells at them for taking the narrow pedestrian alleys instead of the larger roads, and Arni calls behind her, "Sorry, uncle!" and keeps bouncing along, Anurag's laughter just ahead.

They come to Kirti Mandir, the line of tourists extending into the street, and from here the pathway to the beach is a straight shot. She can just make out where the sky blends into the Arabian Sea—*Sindhu Sagar*, Ma sometimes calls it—when Anurag's cycle screeches to a halt inside one of the shaded walkways.

"Why did you do that?" she huffs, coming to a teetering stop beside him.

"They brought the play here." Anurag points at an announcement, hand-painted on a wooden easel propped in the corner: POLITICAL NATAK ARRIVES TO PORBANDAR! in bright red. He hops off his bike. "It has to be . . . Oh."

Through the walkway, a crowd has gathered in the open square. Arni follows her brother tentatively, sizing up the crowd that has gathered. Most of the audience is young, around her age, and male. A few older men at the very back shake their heads, tsking.

Arni pauses in front of them, next to one of the few young girls. Two men appear in a lively conversation on a stage at the center of the square, and though the men must be trying to project, she can't make out a word.

"What's this?" she asks, nudging the girl beside her with one elbow.

"Those are the teachers from the boys' school," the girl whispers back. She looks Arni's age, fifteen or sixteen, maybe. Runaway strands escape her once-neat plaits. "I only got here a few minutes ago."

"What's it about?"

The girl looks around, as though to gauge if anyone will find her opinion controversial. She leans in closer to Arni. "Chimanbhai and the rising price of food. Corruption."

Arni's eyebrows jump. She's torn between wanting to elbow her way to the front of the stage so she can listen and wanting to hop on her bike and ride away so she can see the look on her father's face when he hears about it. "Do you know where the play started?"

"My brother—he's somewhere closer up—said Morbi Engineering, but he's not sure. Maybe Gujarat University? I don't . . . I don't know anything about this." She shakes her head vigorously. "I'm not part of this."

Arni maneuvers her way to Anurag, a few bike lengths down. He looks captivated, mouth agape. "Can you believe?" he whispers when she pinches his arm. "They're really beginning to spread the message."

"What do you know about it?"

"I went with PK and a couple of the guys, earlier this year," he says. "It was the same, performed in the street by some of the teachers. See, they're trying to show the people blindly following the Congress Party politicians, the sheep and the chair . . ."

He doesn't take his eyes off the stage, but Arni hears grumbles behind them, hears footsteps crunching. Somewhere outside the square, a rickshaw beeps loudly. When she turns, her heart quickens; by each entryway are a handful of beige-uniformed policemen.

"Anurag, let's go," she says, pinching him again.

"No, wait, there's—"

"You can't even hear them," she says, more insistently, and something more biting comes out in her tone. He looks at her with a start, and she points over at the policemen and he follows her eyes.

"Fuck," he says, and they edge out their bikes, ducking into the walkway they'd entered from. Arni bows her head to the officers, Anurag placing his palms together. Arni considers briefly the notion that the officers might recognize them, might pause and place them as Suresh Dave's children. Report their presence to their father. She pushes the thought out of her mind, straddling her bike while Anurag readies himself ahead of her. As she presses on the pedal, as they push onward to the chowpatty, the policemen's calls to clear the area echo behind her.

. . .

**They sit in silence** on the beach, the breeze sending a salty spray every now and then that cools the sweat on Arni's forehead and neck. She rolls up her leggings; she digs her toes into the sand. Her fingers are sticky with cashew kulfi no matter how much she licks at them, and the breeze makes her fingertips taste salty, too.

"It's logic that flies in the face of a political stance you and I know too well," Anurag says. He's answering a question Arni hasn't asked. He squints into the ocean, the edges of his eyes wrinkled. Arni always thinks of his face as too expressive, too prone to creases, the lines of his smile or in his brows never far from the surface.

"It's an indictment of corrupt politicians," she says. She closes her eyes, soaks in the sunlight. "What does that have to do with you and me?"

"It doesn't, at least not yet, not directly. Not in terms of what we might believe," Anurag says slowly. "But Baba's opinion—well, you know how defensive he gets about the Congress Party and politics. He doesn't think there's a better way to craft the world than the way Gandhi and Nehru did; he doesn't think everyday people are good enough, you know? He won't even talk to Shantaben. Watch, when we go home, he'll know who got beaten at the play, but he'll still tell you about how the politicians are doing all they can right now. He's complicit. He's as bad as the corrupt politicians themselves."

Arni doesn't know what to say. She's always shrugged off her father's callousness, his reverence of politicians, as part of his personality. *It's how he is*, her mother has said before, and consequently Arni has considered his flaws innate, not chosen. Not able to be shed. But now she imagines him snakelike, remembers every time he has come home with more sugar to fill the bowl even as her school friends complain about the prices, every time he talks of restless lower-caste neighborhoods, of Muslims who should know better.

*Everyone is having as tough a time of it as the next person,* Baba says, even as Ma maneuvers to put ghee on the table, even as Baba's job remains steady. *But the people complaining have made their own karma. Not us, not us.*

"You're going to have to think for yourself," Anurag says. "You're taking university exams next year. You're going to start building your own world. And Baba's world is driven by what other people say, by how one should act because of their place in the natural order." He sighs. "Baba thinks everyone deserves what they get. That Shanta-ben was born to be a maid. That Vibha . . . You ever ask him if he believes it was Vibha's karma that killed her?" Anurag's tone turns icy. "I wouldn't recommend it."

The crux of the street play flashes in Arni's mind: a chair standing in for the corrupt seat of the politician, sheep for the people who blindly follow. "Head sheep, Baba," she says.

Her brother coughs out a laugh. "Don't ever let him hear you say that." After a moment, he adds, "You don't have to believe it just because I do."

"I never thought about it, I guess." She brushes her hands against her pant legs. "It's easy to be annoyed with him, but in context . . . Do you think Ma is like that also? Do you think Ma believes in karma? Or doesn't think people can be better?"

Anurag pauses. "I've never asked Ma about politics. But she's not out in the world, you know? What does a person who doesn't leave the home know about society?"

The tide comes closer to their feet, only a meter or two away from where they sit. A gull caws somewhere above them.

"She used to spend all this time focusing on painting and art,"

Anurag continues. "She could have been a great teacher, or a great artist, but she's so content just being at home. She doesn't have ambition."

"What do you know about ambition?" Is she irked? And why—why should she defend Ma when she's already frustrated with her? Doesn't her brother know her mother better, having had more years with Ma than her, being more an adult, more likely to think about these big questions Arni has never even considered? She runs her hands across the sand beside her. "And if you have so much issue with the politics, what are you doing about it?"

"I'm doing what I can. There have been protests in Ahmedabad. I'll join one as they get bigger," he says, shrugging. "You wouldn't understand. It's easier to grow up when you're not at home. You'll figure out right and wrong on your own time, when you go to university."

She bristles, caught between having this precious time with Anurag and the reminder that she's still the baby to him. His condescension. She thinks of all those evenings in her mother's painting room, her mother doting on Vibha's cautiousness, her hesitance; her mother admonishing Arni's brash strokes, her fantastical images and impulsivity.

She can't place her mother's eyes in those memories; was the look on her mother's face disappointment or frustration or sadness? Maybe there was the scent of nostalgia in Ma's eyes, too, and Arni couldn't tell if it was for Ma's past or for what Vibha had been like at Arni's age. She wonders what she missed—what Vibha seemed to grasp so quickly.

When Arni speaks, her voice is soft. "I know more than you think I do."

That night, Arni finally allows herself to remember—to open up the wound that is her and Vibha's last conversation.

Vibha asks for a glass of water; Arni gives it. Vibha asks about their parents, if they are home; Arni answers no. They sink into silence, a habit they formed early in childhood—a sinking that feels like being pillowed in a deep velvet chair, a feeling that even Anurag enjoys enough to take part in. Their mother never understood this habit. "What's wrong with you three?" Ma would say. "When I had friends at your age, I couldn't ever get them to shut up."

In this silence, Arni knows her sister is going to leave her soon. She feels her own palms vibrating like she's been rubbing them together, stagnant energy itching to get free.

"Do you want me to read to you?" Arni asks. She's almost insistent; she wants Vibha to say yes, wants her sister to pick the longest book in the house—maybe the untouched and still-dusty Bhagavad Gita that had belonged to their great-aunt Meenafai's husband—*Oh, a long book, please*, she thinks, *one that never ends.* She glances around the bedroom for a book, but there are no shelves here, only their mother's watercolor desk.

"I have to tell you," Vibha finally says. She motions toward her school chest, in the corner by the closet. "There's a cloth there, black. A tapestry."

Arni wants to cry, then: there is no extension to be granted. She follows Vibha's directions, finding the tapestry neatly packed in parchment, protected. "What is this?"

"I have to tell you," Vibha repeats, and the story comes out in halts and pauses, and then quickly like vomit, the lamp on the windowsill sending shadows across the room as Vibha describes an evening a very long time ago.

They unfold the tapestry over Vibha's bed like a quilt. Arni studies it as if it is a test she must pass. She feels a headache coming behind her eyes. She squints; her eyebrows furrow.

"Is it bright or is it—"

"Don't look for too long," Vibha says. "It won't let you, not yet."

Arni doesn't understand what her sister means, doesn't understand what she's supposed to see.

Arni tries to force it; she turns the tapestry around, looking only at the refracted half-images on its backside. The reverse stitches of women in horizontal rows, faces in profile. She can't concentrate long enough to count how many women are in each row, but she knows there are many rows and knows this must mean many women. She traces her fingers over the figures' outlines, only able to make out heights, the widths of skirts, and the points of noses.

Arni traces the final figure in the final row. "This is you?"

Vibha nods. "One day, Ma will talk to you about it. Be open, okay? Be willing to listen. You don't know what it means, not yet."

"And you can't give it to me."

Vibha seems to hesitate. Shakes her head. "It's not my place, I don't think. It's for Ma to give."

"But why you?" Arni blurts out, and she regrets it immediately—the exhaustion on Vibha's face, her sweat glistening in the candlelight. Her coughing fills the room, and even then, with no answer coming, Arni doesn't take the question back. *Why you? Why not me?*

"Promise me you'll be patient with Ma," Vibha says before Arni leaves the room that night. "Listen to her."

"Fine," Arni says, "I promise," even though she is not sure she can keep this one. A lie—her last words to Vibha, a lie.

But in her bed all these weeks later, back in the room she had shared before Vibha's health worsened, the moment leaves a sour taste in Arni's mouth. The thought of the heavy fabric, scratchy and soft and starchy all at once, brings that question back to the surface. It makes her angry. Every time she catches a dark corner of the tapestry peeking out from the bottom of her closet, she is reminded of her mother's decision, of Vibha's *first*ness. Of what it means to not have been considered for a lineage she didn't know existed.

She wonders what would happen if she set the tapestry on fire.

If she took a pair of scissors to it.

If she pulled out its threads one by one.

# ELEVEN

All this time—*all this time*—the lineage is seeping back into Amla's bloodstream. How light she'd felt when she had sewn her daughter onto the tapestry, when she had given Vibha this gift, shedding it like shorn hair. She feels weighted now. Had she given her daughter a gift, in the end—or yet another burden to bear?

*I am trying to be a good mother.* Amla repeats the words over and over in tempo as she scrubs the kitchen counters, the table. She waters the plants on the windowsill, the ferns soaking in the humidity, the burgeoning curry plant breaking from the soil. She dusts; she sweeps the floor until her body aches from being so bent over. Her spine, she thinks, has started to curve toward the earth from the marathon of chores. An offering, an attempt to return. *I am trying to be a good mother.*

She begins, slowly, to leave the house again. To edge back into a routine. At first, it's only to the apartment courtyard where she knows Anurag and Arni keep their bikes. She needs her purpose back, she thinks; she repaints Anurag's bike while he's home, a shade of green that falls somewhere between bay leaf and wet mehendi. There is not enough for her to fully paint Arni's, too. A part of her justifies this by thinking Arni wouldn't appreciate it, has never been careful with her things—the same part of Amla that knows there's a gulf between them that she has never tried, enough, to bridge. When Anurag notices, her son squeezes her shoulder, towering over her. *I'm a good mother*, she tells herself.

Later, she tells Shantaben not to worry about stopping by the market the next day. She'll do it herself. It's there, as she weighs two small brinjal in one hand, that she is caught by the first of Vibha's memories to return to her. The market stand disappears before Amla's eyes; she is transported back to the flat. The catalyst is the smell of brinjal roasting—in the memory, the aroma catches on fabric, in hair, the pillow cushions.

She sees through Vibha's eyes. Evenings with Arni at her side, a silly card game, Anurag showing tricks he's learned from friends at school. They sit on the floor of the living room, crowded around the coffee table. The old parlor chairs, before they bought the love seat. Amla feels her heart beat too loudly in her chest, her lungs trembling too much to hold their own. She gasps for air.

"Madam?" The brinjal seller waves a hand fan, motioning for her to take it. "Madam, are you okay?"

Amla blinks at him, one hand lifted to politely decline the object. "I'm fine." The street sounds come back to her, the grunting of animals, the hum of vehicles. She wipes the tears off her cheeks with the backs of her hands. "I'll take these two—and two more. These."

The man nods, and she doesn't bother to bargain down the price. She stares at the rows of vegetables without really seeing them—absorbs their colors more than their shapes. The red of heavy tomatoes, the grassy tones of bitter melon. "Do you have sitaphal?" she asks without registering the man's face, and in a moment she is called to the next table of fruit.

She hands over paisa without thinking, takes seven sitaphal and fills the canvas bag roped around her shoulder. She doesn't take enough onions, enough garlic. Even as her right side leans with the uneven distribution, she takes the longer way home, looping her route so she can keep the beach within her sight just a little longer.

At home, Amla empties her market bags onto the table and stares at the questionable haul. She had not thought this part through, had never considered that her daughter's memories would return to her own body. She tears open one of the sitaphal, not yet soft enough for her liking. Of course this makes sense; children on this tapestry have died before. Of course the lineage would find a way to continue. She plucks the fruit into its segmented bits, leaving them to dry on the table.

Amla tries to carve her way back into a routine. While Arni paints on the roof and Anurag is off with his friends who are home for the Diwali break, Amla returns to the market. She buys chikoo one day, sitaphal the next, papaya. She has a vendor slice a mango open, sprinkle chili powder and salt over it. "Enjoy, madam!" he calls after her, and she closes her eyes to take in the scent of ripening fruit and roasting vegetables, her feet leading her toward the chowpatty.

She stands on the side of the street, on the cusp of where the beach begins. A man leads a camel across a fifty-meter stretch; children yelp and tug at their mothers' skirts for money for a ride. If Anurag and Arni weren't home, she thinks, if they wouldn't question why their mother had detoured so far, she would roll up her leggings and step onto this sand, into this ocean. If Vibha were with her, they would sit on the stone edge and Amla would point out ways she learned to play with light when learning watercolors—here, start with the lightest color; here, plan it out—and as she considers these hypotheticals, there it is again: the silhouette where her oldest daughter should be.

Amla would have kept Vibha by her side until the day she died. Sometimes she looked at Vibha and felt like this was the girlhood she could have had, the young woman she could have grown into. Other times, in Vibha's hesitation when she sketched, in her passivity, Amla couldn't recognize a single genetic relation. *Who are you?* she would think, relieved. *Is it possible that this daughter doesn't have it in her to make the same mistakes I did?*

As a child, she'd resigned herself to never trying to use the gift of this lineage again. She swore it every night of her childhood as Meenafai kissed her forehead before bed; she considered burning her pigments before her marriage to Suresh. But as time passed, as she grew older, she felt the reminder of this lineage nestle into her stomach—heard its chorus in her dreams, heard it beg and plead. *Our one imperative, in this life and all lives,* Amla heard it whisper, *is to stay in this world. To survive. To do better.* And this appealed to Amla, this idea to do it over again—to have another chance. Hadn't each painting just been Amla trying, a little harder, to place the world into focus? She began to create her art again, but only slowly, cautiously. Most of the time, she kept the lineage at bay.

She knows that sometimes her lean toward the creative worries Suresh. "Every impassioned woman on my mother's side went mad when she got old," Suresh jokes. "You won't do that to me, will you?" She'd always smiled and laughed when she was young, but every year she ages she understands those women more. The trappings of four walls, of chores, of children, even, as much as she loves them.

At home, Amla mashes the ripe fruit, mixes in the thin milk. "Natural sugar's easier to come by," she announces, handing one glass off to Anurag, another to Arni, where they sit in the living room. They look up at her from their books with surprise the first day, and the next. Every day, a different drink in their hands.

"When did you get so inventive?" Anurag asks on the fifth day.

"When I was ten," Amla says, "I made a different athanu every week for a month. Tell me, how have you helped around this house lately?"

Arni laughs and Amla returns to the kitchen, wordlessly pouring the fourth glass—already served in its own cup, placed at the seat of the dining table Vibha always occupied—down the drain, just as she has each day.

Later, Amla cleans her daughters' closet, the only part of Vibha's room she hadn't touched in those early days. Arni had discouraged it, insisting they keep the closet door closed, that it wasn't necessary. Now Amla understands why: she finds the tapestry among Arni's things. Her hand freezes on the fabric, its texture intimately familiar to her.

The sisters had talked about it, she realizes. The secret of Amla's choice—of Vibha's right to this tapestry—is no longer something Amla can confine.

She sits in the creaky chair by the watercolor desk, its locked drawers holding her old paintings. She has held on to them: the wake after Ba's death, the gooseberry bush, the two women holding valises. Her attempt to redraw Bapu to life. Others that she's painted since. The only one she doesn't have is that of Mahesh Shankar Sharma. When the jail burned, so did the painting. At the time, this felt fated. Soon after, however, Amla began to wish she had it, if only to place her shame onto the physical object instead of carrying it herself.

She will have to teach these mistakes to Arni, she realizes that now, a weariness settling into her bones. She had thought Vibha didn't need such direct reminders; she was always so careful. She had promised Amla, even. "I'll only do the smallest things," Vibha had said, a child who spoke like an elder. "I promise not to do big things."

And Amla had believed her, because she knew that Vibha was better at speaking to the lineage than she'd been at that age. Vibha was primed for the best of the gift, the reason why Amla passed it forward.

Amla won't make the same mistake twice.

She will have to take a heavier hand with Arni, convince her to act against impulse. It seems like an impossible task. Amla has already considered the alternatives: of passing the gift along to Anurag, of asking the lineage to help her embroider the image of a faraway relative. But every time her son argues with Suresh, she is reminded of how similar they are; every time he puffs his chest, she wonders if he believes the stances he parrots. She cannot imagine giving him this gift. And for the faraway cousin, to wake up one morning and have this gift in their hands—Amla won't do it. Isn't that what happened to her, after all—waking up one morning, with no guidance and everything changed?

It has to be Arni—even if Amla doesn't trust her yet.

The only comfort is that Amla knows where she comes from. The blood in her blood, the marrow in her bones.

During that period when Amla had stopped painting even for pleasure, she spent her time visiting the older women on the tapestry. Sitting at the windows with the sun on her face, she lost herself in memories, watching the blur of a woman creating a sculpture of the baby she longed for; painting a field rich for harvest; drawing her parents old and alive. There were always going to be things the art couldn't solve for—fires, deaths, acts of god. But they could make little changes, to help them do better.

This is the only comfort: that the greatest gift she can give her children is the reassurance that their ancestors held them, cared for them. A thousand mothers who might be better at mothering than her. There is always something those stories can teach them. After Ba died, after Bapu died, memory was all Amla had ever wanted. How lucky she is to have it, housed in that little pile of black cloth. How lucky her children would be, to have it.

The world is changing quickly. Amla can feel it. *This is the one thing I can offer my daughter that ties her to this history*, Amla thinks. *It is one thing I can do, as her mother.*

**Sometimes, before Suresh comes home,** Amla closes her bedroom door and turns to the teakwood box that used to hold watercolors, retrieved from its dusty corner in the closet. Envelopes with fat letters stand near the front in a tight row; others are stacked lying on their backs so that the addresses of writer and recipient are visible. *Fiza Qureshi*, all the envelopes say. Some of the older ones are addressed to *Amla Prakash*, but most to *Amla Dave*. Each envelope was cleanly opened, no straggling paper bits in the way. They are ordered chronologically, and thus also ordered by shade, white to beige to yellow.

I had told you Fiza was important, that there could also be joy. Look how this love comes back.

This is the other reason why Amla has become grateful for the tapestry, for the gift it bestows. You remember how Meenafai sent that photo all those years ago, that reminder to reach out to Fiza? Well, Amla had.

She'd hesitated at first, but how could she go her whole life without knowing who Fiza had grown up to be? And then she found out that the man in the photo was Fiza's betrothed, that the wedding was scheduled for the next summer. 1961. That Amla, and therefore Suresh, was invited, and Fiza would love for her to be there.

This was how she found herself in London, her baby on her lap, watching her childhood best friend get married.

She'd been giddy the entire airplane trip. They'd asked neighbors to watch over the two older kids, but Arni was still breastfeeding, and Amla clutched her baby to her chest. In the window seat next to Suresh, she bounced Arni on her leg, making faces to prompt laughter, but her mind remained far away. Even when Amla turned to her crochet needles as her baby slept, she made nothing, twisting her fingers through the wool and undoing each loop of the scarf she'd copied from one of the neighbors' books. Before she'd gotten on the plane, Amla had thought she could spend those hours making something that would keep Fiza warm, hold her close. But on the plane, it seemed so silly. Every time Suresh began to snore, she pulled out that photo from Meenafai and traced the cheekbones of her best friend. This person was beautiful, she thought, but she didn't know if this person was Fiza.

Throughout the ceremony, she tried to watch Fiza's eyes. Fiza was draped in a silver-pink anarkali, just as Amla had imagined as a child, with a sheer dupatta pinned to her hair. Her makeup had been done for her; Amla couldn't imagine Fiza choosing to do herself up like this: pink lip, hair blow-dried or teased to poof out. Amla wanted to catch a glance of the trajva on Fiza's ankle. She wanted to hold up her own tattooed wrist and say, *Remember me?* Instead, she watched as the pair signed the marriage contract. She clapped politely alongside Fiza's extended family members she didn't recognize, shook the hand of Fiza's father even though he didn't recognize her and there wasn't any time, no, not enough to remind him, as the crowd of guests made their way through the familial greeting line and the sleepy baby in Amla's hands began to stir. As she rushed to the bathroom, undoing her front-hook blouse, Amla wondered why she'd come here in the first place.

Afterward, Suresh insisted on two days of sightseeing. All Amla wanted to do was leave the coldness and the strangeness, to weep in the comfort of a familiar place, but she couldn't tell him why and so could not tell him at all. As they walked thousands of steps, from the bridges to the towers to the shops on cobbled streets, Suresh spoke of how wonderful it was for them to be young and married in London, and Amla nodded wordlessly.

But the important part, really, comes next. Amla and Suresh were scheduled to fly to India the next morning, and Fiza and her now-husband were scheduled to visit family in Pakistan before beginning their honeymoon. Their gates were in the same terminal. Two women with valises in their hands, just like that painting from so long ago.

All this time, Amla had assumed it would not come true. For years she had thought the only thing she had done with her gift was evil. Suddenly, that wasn't true anymore. There she was, across the airport from her childhood friend, whose hands were bright red with mehendi as she walked toward the bathrooms, and something in Amla's gut pulled her away from Suresh, directing her to mumble half words about needing to refresh herself. She off-loaded their child into his arms, and though she sometimes felt empty without the baby close to her, she barely noticed the missing weight from her body. She went right up to Fiza and grabbed her hand; she turned her own wrist upward, showing her trajva that would always match Fiza's.

This memory—it is like time collapsing.

Amla barely remembers what they speak about for most of those thirty minutes they steal from their husbands in a bathroom in the international terminal of London Airport. But she does remember them sitting in two barely used parlor chairs, Fiza holding Amla's hands in her own. She lifts the skirt of her long dress to show Amla her foot, and Amla traces the trajva with her index finger.

"Do you love him?" she asks, her head pounding.

"Like a friend," Fiza says. Or maybe she says, "Like friends." Or maybe, "We were friends."

Amla is barely listening; her heart resounds through her body. She doesn't know where to set her gaze—on Fiza's collarbone, on her lips, on her eyes. She can see the girl who Fiza used to be, grown into this face, and she wonders if she looks like that to Fiza, familiar even if she is twenty-five years old and not nine. She wants to clutch at Fiza's hands.

Fiza must read her mind. "You look like home to me," she says, and Amla feels like crying.

"I didn't know what it would be like to see you get married."

Fiza's smile disappears, and her whole face seems to sadden altogether. "I didn't realize you were there."

"There were so many people, ones you know better, and I didn't know how to approach you," Amla confesses. "I wasn't sure what you'd want."

When Fiza leans over, Amla can smell her perfume—jasmine. She feels her entire body react with something between nostalgia and longing. Yearning. "But I know you," Fiza says, and Amla can't take her eyes away from Fiza's lips now, can only think of closing her eyes and breathing in deeply. She feels her neck, her cheeks, flush. "It's meant to be that we're here now, in the same place, don't you think?"

When Amla was a child, she had not known that the women in the painting were herself and Fiza. What would she have done had she known they would find each other again? She mourns those childhood telegrams, every letter she had written only in her head.

"Yes," she manages. She catches her breath, forces herself to meet Fiza's eyes. "You looked beautiful at your wedding."

Fiza's hand is on her cheek, then, the jasmine scent overtaken by earthy mehendi. "I wondered what it would be like to see you again," she says, and an announcement outside the bathroom begins to call for boarding. *Pakistan International Airlines, to Karachi International Airport.* "That's me."

Amla doesn't mean to, but she covers Fiza's hand with her own. "I've missed you," she says quickly. "It was my fault we didn't stay in touch, and I regret it. I will always regret it."

Fiza smiles. "I've missed you, too," she says, and she kisses Amla then, the surprise of her lips on Amla's, a moment Amla wants to linger in but which feels gone too soon, the heat spreading across her collarbones. Fiza and her valise are already turning the corner of the tiled bathroom when Amla has time to blink, when Amla touches her fingertips to her lips.

**Even as the years** tumbled into one another, Amla is surprised by the contrast of their childhood telegrams and their adulthood letters. There were times when she couldn't pick the right set of fifteen words to send from Gujarat to Karachi; now there are too many words, each begging to see the light. Her letters have always been written quickly—she is thankful that she doesn't have them in front of her, can't see how horrible her Sindhi handwriting has become—and haphazardly, in the mornings before her children and husband are awake. What letters she would write if she only had the time.

Amla pulls an envelope from the box at random, marking its spot with the newest letter from this morning's mail. She traces the date in the upper-right corner: May 15, 1962.

*My dearest, my oldest friend,* Fiza begins the letter.

*Ever since we've begun writing each other again, I've been
thinking about the games we played as children. Two queens
ruling our palace, imagining our servants and wild animals.
I always had tamed a tiger. Did you have a bird? I imagine
something elegant, with long feathers. Or was it a snake?*

Amla places the paper back, takes out another envelope. January 23, 1968.

*Don't apologize for how long it's been! I understand—I watch
my brother's children, help his wife out around the house. I live
an absurdly leisurely life—I mostly help with bookkeeping for
the shop downstairs—and sometimes I envy my friends who are
exhausted at the end of the day by their children. But then, I
think that would mean remarrying, and that would mean giving
up the freedom of my spinsterhood, and I think I don't envy you
at all. I remember the way my sister-in-law downed methi seeds
and ajwain and fennel just to support her breastfeeding. I gag at
the thought of eating seeds like a bird.*

Another one. June 18, 1971.

*Have you heard about or read the piece by the Goan Christian
journalist from Karachi? My sister-in-law has family in
Leicester and they write that it is the most damning indictment
they have seen yet. I won't say more—my brother, he thinks
these are things one only speaks of, does not record, does not
sign their name to—so here, let's speak in parallels: I keep
thinking about January 6, 1948. I know you weren't there, but,
Amla, you must have talked about it with the panditji when he
joined you and Meena auntie. I keep thinking about the young*

217

*boys then, and now I think of the young ones out east, and I wonder, what does it mean to call a country home? What does it mean when your country doesn't consider itself yours— doesn't claim you? I don't know how to sit with any of this. Do you understand this feeling? Do you look at this new India and think this, too? Sometimes I think I am glad I do not have children, or what would I tell my children of all this? How could I possibly tell it all, and tell it right?*

Amla inhales slowly, exhales through pursed lips. She unfolds the newest letter and sits on the edge of the bed. September 10, 1973.

*I ache at the news of your daughter's passing. Meena sent a telegram. What I would give to be next to you right now, to take your hand in mine. I feel the grief in my body; I can't begin to imagine what it must feel like for you. You are my family, and your loss echoes within me.*

*I wish we could go back to those evenings on the water and simply stop time there. To go back to before we were both married. We could freeze ourselves before everything changed. I wonder, if we'd had all the time in the world and none of the fear that came after, what life would we have? My queen, our palace. I would give the moon to see you again.*

**Do you see** what I see?

So many histories to trace. So many stories that tell me who my people are, who I am. I don't know Karachi's port the way Amla did—I don't know Kutch like Chandini—but here, this longing for Fiza, I know it. I take your hand in mine, my gaze lingering on my ring upon yours.

I worried at first when you asked me to marry you without knowing what our future family might, or might not, look like. I didn't say yes, not then, but I wanted to. I worried you were jumping in too quickly, making too big of a sacrifice. Oh, that fight afterward, that argument. I have never been as scared as I was when you said that you needed time.

I thought I'd done right by you—I was trying to protect what you wanted. But I'd only succeeded in hurting you by not saying, immediately and enthusiastically, yes.

Eight months passed, and I threw myself into my work; there was nothing but sculpture after sculpture. I considered following my instinct and handbuilding what I really wanted—you—but I wouldn't allow myself the comfort of this ancestry. I would not be able to live with myself if you came back because I had sculpted it. How would I know if you meant it? I would never know whether it was your decision or mine, and so I would not force you back even if I could.

But you came back, Nadya. We built this life, and you told me it would be enough.

"It's terrible," you say now, and my hand on yours grows clammy.

"What do you mean?"

"For Amla to receive those memories back from Vibha." You finish your thermos, the metal clanking on brick as you set it down. "I can't imagine anything worse."

You can't even see it, can you, beyond the grief? I angle myself toward you. "Vibha was still alive for her. For me. Those memories are always there."

"But there aren't any new ones."

"No, but—"

"If we had and lost a child, you would always experience their life," you say quickly. "Imagine grieving while sitting in their memories. You'd be losing them over and over again."

"I can imagine," I say. "Amla grieved exactly like that—and she kept *finding* Vibha, over and over again."

"And you'd want that?"

I could laugh. "Of course I'd want that. Those memories, they're what makes this a gift. If we lost our child, if I had to take the lineage back, I'd be able to find them. It would balance out the grief." I take your hands in mine more confidently. "My mother might be gone, but she's still here with me whenever I need her. I close my eyes and, Nadya, I can *feel* her. She's right there, when I miss her. Revisiting her—it's like finding home, in spite of everything."

"Your mother had a full life. You're not sitting in grief thinking about who she could've been and what she might've done if only she'd lived longer," you say, meeting my eyes. "But a child . . ." You shake your head. "It's the worst possible thing that could happen to a parent."

I take a long moment before I answer. "When my mother died, I felt like I couldn't breathe," I say quietly. You know this already; you were there. "I didn't want to eat, to speak. And you're right—I kept thinking of my last moments with her, of how I hadn't known they were last moments."

You squeeze my hand in yours.

"And then one day I was in bed and I was aching for my mother, for her to appear and be with me, and I was a child again, and she was telling me stories as she tucked me into bed." The words come out faster, louder. "She was singing the only lullaby I've ever heard her sing. I think it was the first time I slept through the night after she passed. And I didn't miss her, not really; I got to *have* her, to be in a memory where nothing was lost, not yet." I take a shaky breath. "You're right. I lost my mother; I am always losing her. There are always going to be memories where she is gone. But I will always be able to find her, to have her. Always."

You pull down your sleeve and reach up to my cheeks, wipe away tears. "Until you pass it on."

"Yes."

You hesitate for a moment. "And won't that feel like losing her all over again?"

I close my eyes for a moment, the wave of that future loss crashing over me. Threatening to tear me apart. But I have thought about this a thousand times. "I will be giving our child a gift," I say, and I take your hand, pressing my lips to your knuckles. "They will have every story of my mother. They will have her, and I will have her through them."

I think of sitting with my mother at our kitchen island, swapping stories as I discovered new memories. Every phone call I made to her with another question about another woman on that tapestry. She'd made this same decision. She knew what she was giving up, as well as what she was giving.

It would be enough, I think.

# TWELVE

The week Anurag returns to Ahmedabad in November, the Diwali break over, a cold drizzle descends on Porbandar. Arni feels her body echo the season, the tension in her shoulders relaxing, the painting she had begun on the rooftop washed away. She breathes deeply again.

At school, when she and the other girls sit along the covered steps of the single-story building, she nods along as Vruthi complains about the contents of her tiffin. "It's tough on us, too," Arni chimes in like she always has, but the words feel emptier than she expected. They don't fill the space they used to; even if the milk is thin, even if no staple feels abundant, Anurag's words sit in her gut. She wants to write off the natak they stumbled upon as a dream, to stop herself from questioning Baba any more than she already does.

She lingers outside with the pitter-patter of slowing rain on metal gutter. She wonders what Vibha would do.

Risha auntie—*Miss Risha*, they call her during class—calls Arni's name. "Not feeling like maths? Maybe we don't like it because we haven't done enough work to make it easier?"

"No, miss." Arni snaps the three compartments of her tiffin into place—one level of dal, one level khichdi, another with thin rotli, no ghee—and nods at Risha auntie as she passes her. The woman smells starchy, like baby powder.

Risha auntie nods back, following her into the classroom. "Great. Now then, Vruthi, solve the board since you've had all break to think about it."

Almost as soon as she takes her seat near the back of the classroom, Arni feels a tap on her shoulder, the crackle of the paper as it is tucked between her spine and her seat. She reaches around as Risha auntie turns to the chalkboard, unfolding the note beneath her desk.

*I'm so sorry about Vibha. I wanted to come by, but my mother said you'd probably had enough folks come by to bother you with condolences. I remember it being tough, when my brother passed away.*

The note is written in Gujarati, and Arni recognizes the handwriting, the same as the notes from building management about the smell of paint bothering the neighbor aunties. Sakshi, the manager's daughter, has the seat directly behind Arni. She takes her stubby pencil and checks that Risha auntie is facing the board.

*Thank you.* She bites at her lip, unsure what to write. *Not many people came by.*

The motion of returning the scrap paper awakens a familiar physical memory for Arni. She twists her arm back, an extended stretch, and she feels like she is eight, ten, twelve—all the years when Vibha wasn't so sick, when she was still in school with Arni. Years of passing notes back and forth, the two of them, no other confidants needed in their tight circle.

Another tap on her shoulder, another slip of paper down her chair.

*I saw you'd started something new on the roof,* the note says. *I think it must have washed away. What was it?*

Arni tries to contain her face, to look like she's still thinking about the algebra on the board, but she feels warm. Noticed.

"Turn to page 146 in the textbook," Risha auntie says. "You're going to take fifteen minutes and solve each of these practice problems. Don't make the same mistake your friend here did on the board, yes?"

"Yes, miss," the class echoes.

Arni opens her notebook to a new page, flips the textbook open. She doesn't copy over the arithmetic, no—she checks that Risha auntie is staying at the front of the classroom and she sketches as best as she can the mural she'd begun on the rooftop tiles.

**Amla can't help but smile** into the soapy dishes when Arni returns from school, when she is followed by Sakshi as she lopes through the door. There is something about the two girls' laughter when they close the door to the bedroom, ringing golden down the hallway— the way the hum of their voices reverberates to Amla in the kitchen.

Linger here in this moment—Amla brims with love she can't express; she rages, she fears. It is inevitable that everything will change. After all, for Amla to be convinced of Arni's readiness, Arni herself must change.

Amla isn't ready to make this decision for her daughter. She feels Arni is too young, even though she is older than Amla and Vibha had been when they received the gift. Arni is too unpredictable. Impulsive.

But maybe that is the test: that no one is ever ready enough, old enough, to receive this.

I want to take her hand, kiss the wrinkles on her knuckles. She is right in this. We are always children compared to what this tapestry demands.


**Sakshi doesn't ask before touching** the brushes and notebooks on Ma's watercolor desk. "Wow," she breathes. "This is yours?"

"My mother's."

"That's even more impressive," Sakshi says, and Arni tries to see the desk from that perspective: not old and rickety and taking up space, but rare. Space for a mother to define herself in some other way than by her children. "Does she still paint?"

Arni hasn't seen a new portrait by her mother in years, just the frames in the hallway. But Anurag had claimed there were others, that Ma could have been great. "Only when inspiration comes to her, I guess."

"She taught you?"

"She taught my sister, mostly." Arni sits on the edge of Vibha's old cot, Sakshi still standing over the desk. "I wanted to try my own style."

Sakshi leans over and takes the folded piece of paper, their note, from her bag. "This is your style?"

Arni takes the note from her, unfolds it slowly. It's in pencil, nothing like what she'd dreamt it would be—but the idea is there: an entire street scene, from the children begging to the woman hanging blouses in the window line. Instead of shades of graphite, Arni imagines the colors from the rooftop—the teals-to-white of the sky, the spread of sunset from the opposite corner. The colorful clothes of the students clutching books to their chests, hair in plaits and uniforms donned. The shopkeeper feeding an alley dog.

The scene is busy, yes, but the mural is not about what the people are doing. No, the secret Arni has woven into the image is that each person, from the dark-skinned man cleaning up after the cow in the corner to the child tiptoeing across their roof's edge like it's a tight-rope, shares the same face: Vibha's.

Maybe Sakshi can see it; maybe she can't. It only matters to Arni that *she* knows, that she sees her sister in each person.

"I like murals that make me think," she says. "Ma always draws what's happened, exactly as it happened, and Vibha did that, too. That's fine for them, but . . . I like something different."

"You like imagining something new," Sakshi says, and she sits next to Arni on the cot, looking over her shoulder at the pencil draft. "Full power. You get to create all of it. Control all of it."

*Think of the world you're going to build for yourself,* Anurag's voice echoes back to Arni. *Do you want that world to be Baba's world, all its hierarchies—or will you build your own?*

She glances toward the closet, where she has kept the tapestry since the night Vibha shared it with her.

"I like that idea," she says to Sakshi, who smiles back at her. "I'd like to paint a future I could control."

**That night, after Sakshi leaves,** Arni sorts through the mail, through all the chits of condolences. She wonders what it means to her father's coworkers, to these distant politicians and their wives, that his daughter is dead. She wonders what a card means, what it cost them.

One envelope is addressed to Arni, Anurag's name scrawled on the return address.

*Thought I'd share my world with you,* he's written on a scrap piece of paper. *A little peek at who I am outside of home.*

Arni unfolds the second, thinner piece of paper—a full page, "Arts," from the student newspaper.

Of course Anurag's name would appear in the center of this page. She has to reread the announcement twice, three times: Anurag has won a poetry prize at the university, one gifted to a final-year student showing promise in using art to honor the Gujarati legacy of liberation. The head of the English department is quoted, says he *expects great things from Anurag Dave.* The article names the papers his poetry has appeared in, and she remembers that old notebook from their childhood, the one clasped between his chubby, preadolescent fingers—had she even known he was still writing? In the margins of the paper, Anurag has left her a note:

*Attended a protest for the natak. The group is putting together a pamphlet. I'll bring it when I come home. Maybe you'll learn from it.*

Arni folds up the newspaper, places it between the pages of her sketchbook, the only place she knows Baba would never care to look. When had Anurag become a writer standing for something?

*You can never know a person*, she thinks, *not your brother, not any of your family.*

Arni has been thinking this a lot lately, usually with one hand jimmying a hairpin into the lower-left drawer of her mother's painting desk. She can hear the crisp paintings scratching against one another when she shakes the drawer, even as she knows this unlocking technique is futile. Her mother will carry her secrets, her father and brother will fight about politics, and Arni will hide in the shadows of the family like she always has, with no one to notice she's even missing.

Arni kicks at the desk with her slippered foot, toes flexed. Nearly two months since Vibha's passing, Arni's grief has soured to anger. Two months, and her mother has said nothing about the tapestry. Arni wonders if her mother means to keep it from her forever. She worries that Vibha was her mother's daughter; she worries she is her father's.

*Create your own world*, that's what Anurag had said—but what did he know, the oldest son with the luxury of being college educated?

Without Vibha ahead of her choosing not to go to college, without her mother giving her the tapestry, Arni can't figure out what her parents will ask of her. Why pay tuition for a daughter you're going to marry off?

She grits her teeth.

*Anurag's only sending this paper clipping because he wants to re-create the conversations he used to have with Vibha*, the doubt in Arni's head tells her. *You'll always be the baby girl—second-choice child of second-choice gender.*


**There is another letter, too.** One of the envelopes in the pile is more heavily packed than a standard card, a little more weathered than the local letters. Arni almost doesn't recognize the name, but she takes the envelope with her to the hallway, to the watercolor portraits hanging about eye level. Arni studies the Gujarati script in the lower-left corner of one of the portraits, and then she studies the name on the envelope. *Fiza Qureshi.* A woman's portrait framed in the hallway alongside her mother's other paintings, but of whom her mother never really speaks.

She wonders if Anurag, who seems to know all about her mother's paintings, knows who Fiza Qureshi is.

She should hesitate; she knows she should. She should leave the letter-opening for Ma. But Arni has a frustration she can't suppress, and so she leans against the wall, toes on cold tile, and slides one nail beneath the envelope's lip. When the glue doesn't give, she takes the envelope between her teeth and tears a straight line down the side.

The pages that unfold are soft. When she shakes the envelope, a dried jasmine bud falls into her palm. She wonders who this woman is that sends her mother flowers through the mail.

Mostly, she will remember this: when she holds up the first page to the light, she can't read the Sindhi script, can't tell the difference between consonant and vowel. She skims it anyway: she searches for the punctuation, follows the hand of this woman who writes to her mother in long and flowing sentences, with lists and asides riddled with commas, with underlines in the first paragraph, with parting words written over themselves so they're bolded, emphasized.

The woman who wrote these words overflowed with emotion. The woman who is supposed to read these words should, in turn, be overwhelmed with emotion.

Arni has not thought of her mother as this type of woman before. Whatever this is, it's another secret being hidden from Arni. Another truth denied to her. She wants to kick, to scream. There is so much she doesn't know.

She takes the dried jasmine flower and rolls it between her index finger and thumb until its scent is entirely released, its petals crumbling. Is this yet another thing that Vibha knew and Arni didn't?

Arni feels her chest collapse. Her breath is ragged. She closes her eyes and cries.

# THIRTEEN

Even if she'd prefer otherwise, Arni knows the rooftop doesn't belong to her, especially on these weekends in November when the humidity dies down and a cool ocean breeze rustles the hanging fabric around her. She bristles when a group of young men and women, about Anurag's age, take the corner closest to her painting wall. The smell of hash slowly wafts over as the group settles in, and Arni clamps her teeth down on the insides of her cheeks. This rooftop is the one place she gets to paint without interruption. She likes that her only usual company are the aunties hanging their husbands' ratty white tank tops on the clothesline, the people on other low rooftops of buildings nearby.

For the last week, these university students have invaded her territory, and their voices carry. "We should bring in a speaker."

"We should speak ourselves," a girl—a young woman, Arni corrects herself—says.

"Have the teachers talk."

The thick breeze carries over the scent of ash and mint. Arni forces herself to focus—on the brush in her hand, the new mural she is painting.

"No, I hear their trade union limits how much they can do."

"What if it's outside their capacity as university teachers, though? What if it's personal?"

Nearly each time the students have smoked on Arni's roof, their conversations have been punctuated by the same undercurrents: agitated ones, passionate ones.

"—do you blame? Going after the black market when it's just people trying to get by, to do what they can."

On the wall, Arni has finished penciling in a village scene, a memory from a childhood visit to Sodhana a very long time ago. But now she isn't sure if she remembers the color of the dirt in the Gujarati desert correctly. Would she know, once it's filled in with paint? Would her memory tell her if she'd done it wrong? She tries to remember if the dust clung to her like a second skin, the color it left beneath her nails.

If Ma would just talk to her about the tapestry, she thinks stubbornly, then maybe she could be certain.

Arni has two buckets of paint in front of her, one beige, one reddish like clay. She pours a few ounces of the red into the other, watching it puddle.

"People want to blame the milkwala for the price of milk," the first student says. Arni finds herself paying a little extra attention to his words—finds herself reeled in by the charismatic tone, the appeal, even if the stump speech is only to a handful of college friends. She has done her best these past few weeks to keep her eyes from lingering on him—on the way he leans against the roof ledge, lanky; the way he smiles at her and waves as she sets up her paint. "Someone out there boiling milk to make ghee has no choice but to sell it on the black market when politicians don't care enough to secure food quotas for their own state."

"Maybe there's no money—"

"Chimanbhai Patel can give money to the UP Congress Committee but not his own people? Can't subsidize basic commodities?"

"I'm just saying that Congress's whole platform was alleviating poverty."

"Oh, come on, yaar."

Arni smells the hash more strongly now, wonders if the charismatic boy exhaled in her direction.

"You want to talk about a platform of Garibi Hatao—you want to promise a world of no poverty—in the home of Mahatma Gandhi, while prices go up? Inflation? Unemployment? I mean, are you planning on staying in this state after you finish school? Can you even imagine having a family here? How are you going to buy ghee every week for your wife on a shopkeeper's salary, huh? Even young painter-girl's agreeing with me—right, painter-girl?"

Arni hadn't realized she was nodding—hadn't meant to be caught listening, had been focusing on stirring the bucket of paint with the flat stick. "Shit," she says, turning around, brush still in hand. A drop of the clay color lands between her sandals. "Sorry, I didn't mean to listen in."

"Don't apologize," the student says, and Arni furrows her brow as he motions for her to participate in the conversation, creating space for her in the group's circle. "You agree with what I'm saying?"

She chews the inside of her cheek and thinks of the play she and Anurag had stumbled upon, the corrupt politician's chair and the people following like sheep; she thinks of her father convincing farmers to buy machinery that will shift their fates. Of Anurag writing poetry honoring a legacy of liberation.

"I think . . ." The ideas are still forming, the words lost. She finds herself wondering what Vibha would say—the cooler, older daughter, the one who could hold her own with strangers, who was thoughtful, not impulsive, when she spoke. When Arni closes her eyes, she thinks of the mural she had tried to paint, each face her sister's, long rinsed away.

"Tell us." The student leans forward, either genuinely interested or equipped with sarcasm Arni can't read. She glances at his friends, at the way the other two men study her with curiosity, the way the woman's eyes squint slightly.

She inhales deeply. She wants to use her own words, not ones that evoke Vibha or Anurag. "I think we've been lulled into thinking the past makes up for the present," she finally says. "We asked politicians to serve us, but they're enjoying sitting on top. If we're willing to find a new faith when gods we pray to don't serve us anymore, shouldn't we do that with politicians, too?"

The charismatic man nods, smiling. "You sound like you're organizing with the students. She's got our lines down, doesn't she?" His friends nod.

"I'm learning," Arni says. "Slowly."

"You know"—and Arni is surprised that this is the woman speaking, the one who'd looked at her so skeptically before—"we all start somewhere. You ever paint for anyone besides the pigeons up here?"

Arni shakes her head.

"You might think about it," the woman says. "Even as you're learning the politics—you might find a way of your own to contribute to the campaign."

"Think like the Americans," the charismatic man says, and Arni watches the joint burn orange as he takes a long drag. "What if your art could win hearts and minds?"

. . .

**Maybe it's the excitement,** this feeling of being noticed just for doing what she always does. Arni hasn't felt so light in months.

In that lanterned room, all that time ago, Vibha had warned her of these emotions. "Like a kite flying too high," she had told Arni. "Ma will ask you to control yourself. Just because you see an opportunity to change something doesn't mean it's the right decision."

Arni was torn then. She has never wanted more than to prove herself as good as her sister. Equally worthy of her parents' pride. But years of being the one who was out of line—*and for what,* she thinks, *paintings that were too bold?*—had her wanting to dig her heels in further.

There are so many questions she wished she had followed up on with Vibha. *Why not take advantage of an opportunity? Why pull back from the world?*

She cringes at the memory of what she did ask. *Why you?* It echoes, as much as she wishes to erase it. Her sister on the bed, dying— *Why you?*

Sometimes Arni hates herself, her audacity, even as she tugs it close, the only identity she feels is her own. This same thing Ma will want to strip from her, the only thing that is true to herself.

"What would have made me be enough?" Arni had demanded of her sister. "If I'd been more like you?"

Vibha had paused. "Maybe you have to lose me first," she'd said. "Maybe you have to grow up without me."


**Arni careens into the flat,** the adrenaline from the rooftop still pulsing in her veins. Her mother stands at the arch of the hallway, arms tucked in by her stomach and palms cradling her elbows. One shoulder leans against the wall. Her eyes look so far away Arni wants

to reach out a hand and touch her, as though to remind her she's cor-
poreal.

But Arni doesn't do that; instead, she huffs out an incomplete
thought. "Ma, Vibha told me something and we have to talk about it."

They've been orbiting each other for the two months since Vibha's
passing. Arni has been too stubborn to bring it up, even as every day
without this conversation has made her angrier. She can see the surprise on Ma's face now, the slow blinks into realization. "Oh," Ma
says, and then with more energy, "Yes, let's."

Arni opens and closes her mouth. She thought she would have the
words—after all this time, hasn't she thought enough about this conversation to know what she needs to say?—and she grasps for them
and keeps grasping, keeps swallowing her spit until her mouth is too
dry. "Vibha told me about an embroidered blanket," she finally chokes
out. She should have thought through her approach before.

"A tapestry," Ma corrects. "What did Vibha say?"

"That you sewed her image onto it, and that you were on it, and
your mother, and the women before her." Arni pauses. "She said it
was our birthright. A gift in our ancestry."

She tries to keep her tone deliberately neutral. Ma's eyes study her,
as though she knows what's coming next.

"You didn't choose me," Arni says, eyes narrowing.

There it is, out in the open, the words that have sat on Arni's
tongue ever since Vibha first told her to take out that tapestry. She
finds herself thinking about this even when she doesn't mean to: How
did Ma choose which daughter was good enough to get a chance?
What did it mean, really, for Ma to make that choice?

"It wasn't about choosing you or not choosing you, Arni." Ma sighs.
"It was about Vibha and the timing. You were so much younger."

"But you hid this from me," Arni says. "A *birthright*. And I didn't
even get to *know*?"

"It's not that simple." Ma lifts her hands like she's exasperated, and this only makes Arni seethe.

"You could have told me," Arni says, and her voice nearly breaks, all this emotion finally spilling out of her. "But nothing, not even after losing Vibha—why couldn't you tell me after? *She* did." Arni grits her teeth to hold back tears. "It was the last thing she ever did, but Vibha told me everything. And still you didn't say a *whisper* about it."

"Arni—"

She shakes her head. "I was never going to be enough for it, for you."

"That's not it," Ma says, stepping closer. "I wasn't comparing you girls. I didn't . . . I didn't think you'd ever *have* to know."

"Great," Arni says flatly. She wants to walk back her tone, but she doesn't know how to or if she even can anymore. "Now that I do—what's stopping you? If I already know, why aren't we taking that tapestry out of my closet and moving forward with it?"

"Your birthright," Ma repeats, as though still thinking about Arni's phrasing.

It doesn't seem like she is considering at all, for a single moment, Arni's last question. This makes Arni want to throw everything to hell. To face her ancestry, this tapestry, and refuse it. But she cannot—and it breaks her to have to voice this aloud. "If I were on that tapestry, I would be able to be with Vibha. To remember her life." Arni's voice cracks. "And you won't give that to me. Why—why deny me my sister?"

Ma closes her eyes, as though she cannot look at Arni with those tears beginning to stream down her cheeks. "This is about so much more than . . . That tapestry is a way to connect to our people, to the blood that runs in our veins, yes, but it is also a power. One that demands that we be careful."

"And I'm not that," Arni says, her tone dulled.

"You can't know until you're in this position, and no one else will understand—they never do." Ma shakes her head slowly. What is she remembering in this moment, Arni wonders. "Oh, jaan. I want to give you this gift, but only when you are ready for it."

"Vibha was ready at *ten years old*," Arni says, tone biting, but she doesn't pull back. There is a part of her that wants to hurt her mother, to hurt whoever took Vibha away from her. "But I'm the one who's not ready?"

"Stop," Ma says, pleading, "listen to me," but Arni has momentum now.

"You have *never* wanted me to be on that tapestry," she accuses, "and you are being so *selfish* that you don't care if it's the one way I get to have my sister back. What did I ever do to deserve that, to be kept out of everything that you and Vibha shared?"

"Stop," Ma says again, and this time she bridges the distance between them, reaching across to clutch Arni's wrist. This time, Arni has no choice, can feel her own pulse trapped by her mother's spindly fingers, the desperation in this gesture. "Give me a chance to explain everything the best I can."

They lay out the tapestry on the floor of the living room and stand over it, as though surveying its stitches for a lost earring clasp. The love seat and parlor chairs are pushed against the walls, the coffee table heaved to the far corner. Arni squints at the fabric and glances away, the images dizzying, these profiled women, all in a row, dancing in her irises.

"This will wane," Ma says, answering Arni's question before it can be asked. "When you're sewn onto it, it stops being so . . . dazzling."

When her eyes land on her mother, Arni realizes Ma is watching the tapestry like a mother watches a baby, surveying its face for emotions. Arni expects her mother to laugh or reply to it.

Arni nods. "That's what Vibha said."

Ma points to the final stitched figure on the tapestry, a child in the middle of an incomplete row. "There she is."

Maybe just a few moments of silence; maybe minutes, five of them, ten. The setting sun bears down on the flat; a chorus of rickshaw horns echoes at the street corner. Ma leans down to touch Vibha's embroidered figure. "This is how you get a gift. The chance to change your world."

Arni follows the edges of the heavy fabric with her eyes, the length of one side to its corner, and then to another length. It helps her vision to have the tapestry in her periphery. She crosses her arms.

"It must happen all the time," Ma says softly.

Arni continues to trace the tapestry's outline. "Someone on the tapestry dying before they passed it forward?"

"Someone on the tapestry dying before they could really explain how it worked to their child."

This might be the first time Arni looks at her mother and sees more than the woman in her current context. Her mother was a daughter once; was a child bequeathed a gift once. Does that creature in Arni's gut soften? She tries to course correct, to be *open-minded*, like Vibha made her promise to be. "How old were you when you were sewn on?" she asks.

"I was ten years old when my Ba died."

"You had to teach yourself."

"I didn't do a good job on my own," Ma says. She hesitates. "It took me a while to figure out how to learn from the lineage. How to listen."

"Your mother never explained it to you? And your father—"

Ma was already shaking her head. "He never knew."

"Why did your mother keep it from him?"

Ma considers the question, staring down at her open palms. The backs of her hands are growing softer; Arni can already imagine the sun spots, the wrinkled fingertips, like Meenafai's. "My parents did their best. I was so young; it was all so unexpected. You can't understand—you can't know what it was like, then."

"But you don't think your mother should've told you before you were sewn onto it?"

Maybe Ma thinks, *There are a lot of things they should have told me.* Maybe she thinks, *There are a lot of things I was going to tell Vibha.* "I thought things could be different this time," Ma says instead, answering an unspoken question. "I would arm you with knowledge. Practice."

"But Vibha was ten when you sewed her onto the tapestry." The accusation is neither up-front nor completely absent. "Just a kid."

"I was just a kid, too."

"And you said you were too young."

"We had the luxury of time that I didn't get to have as a child," Ma says, angling her body toward Arni. "I was there for her, I could tell her what I knew. I thought it would be easier to teach Vibha the way I would've liked to have been taught at that age. I know the mistakes you make as a child. I know them personally."

Arni exhales slowly. She clasps her left hand in her right one. "All this time, Vibha could've done—what? Drawn herself alive as an adult? Painted herself healthy?" Arni's voice cracks. "Did you even tell Vibha that was an option? Did she know?"

"You can't undo what's been done." Amla's volume rises to match Arni's. "Vibha was being cautious. You don't understand how wrong it can go; this isn't maths or science. It's something in the blood, in your intuition. You have to be careful."

"So you gave it to her because she was cautious."

Ma glares at her. "This isn't something to toy around with."

Arni walks away from her mother, pacing the perimeter of the tapestry. "If you hadn't sewn her on . . . *You* would've had better control than a child, right?"

Ma closes her eyes. "Maybe," she says.

"And then, maybe this wouldn't have happened."

Ma inhales through her teeth. "Maybe I could have done something. I don't know. There's no way to know."

"Does Baba know that?"

"Your father could never understand," Ma says. "What it means for power to not feel like a right. For power to not be a solution." She exhales, and Arni wonders if her mother is thinking of that word she'd said earlier. *Birthright.* "He could never . . . Men, they never."

A breeze carries the scent of the street, of engines and sea salt, through the open window. In the silence, Arni feels time slow; the way her mother's hair lifts with the breeze, the vein pulsing in her mother's neck. She traces the tapestry once more, her eyes reaching from corner to corner, landing on her mother. "I want to be on it," Arni says. "I'm ready."

Ma studies her. "For Vibha?" Before Arni can answer, Ma shakes her head. "No," she says. "Not yet."

"Why?" An edge of desperation enters Arni's voice.

"You will understand one day, I promise that," Ma says, fingers pinching at her throat. Her speech quickens. "I want you to have it—I *do*—but when you are *truly* ready. Not before, not in anger or loss, not when you might make a mistake." Her mother's eyes are pleading, searching. "I am trying to *help* you. I don't want you to make the mistakes that Vibha did, that I did."

Arni wants to sob. She is exhausted, has rendered herself so vulnerable only to be denied. "I don't understand," she says softly, glancing at the dizzying designs.

"Let me teach you about the rules, about how to be careful," Ma offers.

An extended hand. Arni tries to swallow her anger, the betrayal of not being the chosen daughter, her frustration with her mother for continuing to put off this inheritance. Still, her hurt drives her to bargain. "I want to know what you're so scared of with this gift."

Ma leans down, grabbing the edges of the fabric to fold it. She keeps her lips tight; she doesn't look directly at Arni. "In time," she says.

"And I want"—and Arni's pushing her luck a little, can feel how much her mother wants her buy-in—"I want to know how you found out about the tapestry, and your paintings. What you've done with them."

Ma beckons for Arni to grab the opposite corners of the tapestry. "In time," she says again. "No more secrets."

And those words—they make Arni bolder, give her more ammunition. She thinks of a dried jasmine blossom twisting beneath her fingers. "Fiza," she says. "Who is she?"

This time, Ma pauses. "Fiza?" Her voice is distant.

They meet in the middle, the fabric folding over lengthwise. Arni takes the new edge, stretches it back out.

"She writes you letters and her portrait's on that wall. She sent another letter after Vibha passed. I—"

"Do you have that letter?" Ma asks quickly. She takes the next fold from Arni, draping the tapestry over her arm. Arni tries to meet her eyes but can't. "Where is it? I never saw—"

Arni falters, the hope that her mother would tell her everything shattered. "It's in the bedroom. In my closet. I'm sorry, I couldn't read it, but I didn't know, I wanted . . . Who is she?"

"That letter is *mine*, Arni."

"I'm sorry."

Ma hands her the heavy square of the tapestry forcefully, and Arni stares at it as her mother's footsteps recede. Down the hallway, she can make out the sound of Ma searching, the eventual rustle of paper being unfolded from an envelope. She hears Ma leave the room, walk to her own, and shut that door behind her.

**Amla is fuming.** She paces the length of her bedroom, Fiza's opened envelope still in her hand. What had she hoped for—that Arni would listen, maybe, that she would share how she had felt and give Amla the chance to explain what a massive undertaking the tapestry could be? For Arni to have an open mind? None of that—Arni had left room for none of it.

*Unfair,* Amla thinks, but also, *This is why.* Arni isn't ready; she's so quick to anger, her father's temper mixed with Amla's own rash childhood decision-making. She taps Fiza's envelope on one hand. To approach Amla so righteously, and then to reveal the letter— Amla walks back all the options she has considered these months. Is there any other child who would be more suited to the tapestry than Arni, even if they didn't have the benefit of Amla as a guide? She doesn't know.

*Arni will not get the answers to all of her questions,* she thinks, not now. Not until Amla has answered these new ones for herself, has practiced the words in her mouth. They each have their priorities: Arni wants to know more about the tapestry, fine; Amla must pro- tect Arni from herself.

And then there's the matter of Fiza. In the safety and quiet of her room, Amla runs one finger across the envelope's ripped-open edge. She aches for the violence of this rip, for the fact that she was not the one to have undone the envelope.

*I'm trying to be a good mother,* Amla says to herself. She takes the pages of the letter from their sheath. *But I don't have to share every secret.*

**Suresh sends Amla a telegram.** The protests in Rajkot on December 3, the result of police knocking down doors of marketwalas suspected of hoarding essentials, have cut his trip short. The government is concerned about his travel. He'll be home in two weeks, and he'd like nothing but to close his eyes and sit at the window with the paper, undisturbed.

Amla hands her daughter the telegram and, wordless, they spend the next weeks in an on-and-off cleaning frenzy. Regardless of their frustrations, their anger, with each other, they are aligned when it comes to Suresh. Amla hangs sheets, dishcloths, towels on the roof; she flicks the smaller fabrics before hanging them, the water ghostlike as it's carried away by the breeze. Arni, usually lethargic when it comes to house chores, carries her own weight, dusting the living room and tidying the kitchen. The air between the women buzzes, frantic; they always make the home look neat for Suresh's returns, but now there's a furtiveness to their routine. If they can clean the house, Amla thinks, if they can make it look like a perfectly normal set of days, Suresh will have no reason to think she has shared any secret, revealed any vulnerability, to her daughter. Amla feels the tension in her bones; she bites at her lips until, one day, she looks in a mirror and realizes they are reddish with scabs, and then she stresses about the way she looks, too, knowing Suresh will have a comment when he sees her.

The timing is jarring: ever since that conversation with Arni, Amla has felt herself further cocooning, hiding the most vulnerable parts of herself from her daughter. She doesn't tell Arni what she's learned about Vibha, now that the memories are settling into her body. She has dug into them with greed, found that moment when Vibha drew the painting of Arni, leaving herself out. Amla feels her heart crack open in that memory, feels her world shatter over and over again.

Amla does not yet see the gift Vibha has given Arni. Even I found it hard to see at first, until I understood.

See, even if Vibha had married the Labadiya boy, even if Vibha sacrificed everything, Arni was never guaranteed a choice. Not with a father like Suresh; not in their strict community, in their conservative city. Without this painting, Arni still might have withered. Vibha knew this—could foresee it. She would have made it all work if she could protect her sister, but Arni would have rather died than be forced to marry someone, to give her body over without love, to bear children and treat a stranger of a husband like he was a god.

Amla should be proud of Vibha. She painted her sister alive and happy—fulfilled, yearning for nothing. Vibha gifted my mother her entire life.

But Amla cannot see this yet. And so she sits in her sorrow, her disappointment in herself. She feels she has not been a good enough mother.

She imagines how Arni will look at her when she knows everything. Already there is so much silence shared between them—an alliance for the sake of Suresh, sure, but little otherwise. Amla knows she could coax her daughter back to her by revealing more about the power, about her regrets as a child, but she isn't ready to do so yet. She hadn't even voiced those things to Vibha. If she could only get Arni to see her side—if only Arni could slow down, could grow up like Vibha had. Then one day—she reminds herself—Arni would have the ability to discover everything without Amla having to tell her anyway. When her daughter received those memories, the past would provide its own explanation.

. . .

**Later, Arni will return** to certain days, trying to fit her understanding of events together with her mother's, analyzing the distance between their experiences.

Amla pays a rickshaw driver an exorbitant fare. Baba has not yet returned, but she makes Arni promise not to mention it to him. When Amla asks this of Arni, she pinches the skin at the base of her throat; when Arni nods her head, when she says "I promise" out loud, she pinches her own throat, a mirror image. Amla ushers her then into the rickshaw, and the auto's guttural engine carries them to a road Arni has never walked before.

"This is where Porbandar's Sindhis live," Amla says, soft enough that only Arni can hear. "Tell me if you see anything you like."

It is the first they have spoken of anything besides chores since their argument. "Why are we here?" she asks her mother as the rickshaw pulls away.

Ma is silent for a long moment. "My mother died in 1946, on the sixth of December," she says finally. Twenty-seven years ago, this day. It is explanation enough for their truce.

From a distance, the street vendors are like all the others Arni has seen. The shops extend into the street, the more appealing fruits and vegetables set near the front to lure in pedestrians. Amla and Arni walk past a home improvement store boasting hundreds of shades of smooth tile, another store stacked with carved wooden chairs. A young man calls out to a motorbike repairman, haggling prices over passersby. And though all of this could be found on the streets Arni bikes past when Anurag is in town, an unfamiliarity nags at her, and she realizes slowly that she can't understand the words being spoken around her, only the occasional phrase; she feels as though the world has morphed for a moment, reduced entirely to this street bookended on one side by a market stand with hand-stitched Sindhi topis and on the other by a stand with long, embroidered ajraks.

Even Amla is transformed when Arni looks back at her. Her shoulders have relaxed, a tension Arni hadn't noticed before now dissipated. Amla strolls slowly, her fingers dancing along the dupattas as she passes them; occasionally, even as she keeps walking, she says something kind to a vendor, who in turn beams with pride. Arni feels like her mother has grown more beautiful, her smile more charming. She might as well be dressed like a queen; she walks like this small road belongs to her.

Amla notices Arni's eyes on her as they pass a mithai shop. "Now here," she says, "this is where I have a story for you."

Inside, Amla orders them pistachio kulfi, the fan sending the wispy hair by her temples and ears in all directions. Again, Arni notices the entire conversation is held in Sindhi. She wonders if Amla has missed speaking Sindhi; she wonders if Amla escapes to this road often while Arni is in school, if she has come here for years to find some connection to home.

"Your grandfather spent a summer in this neighborhood," Amla says as they settle into two plastic seats outside the mithai shop. "He lived with one of his school friends in a flat where the lower floors always flooded each monsoon season. He ended up clerking for an uncle closer to the city outskirts—"

Arni watches her mother's lips closely. She will want to remember the stories word for word as her mother told them, but they'll escape her; she'll remember instead the distance in her mother's eyes, the forlornness, the sentimentality. She will remember and then will want to have hugged her mother close, to have taken her hand. She'll want to have erased that anger inside of herself. She'll come back to this over and over, to relive it, to slow it down. From what she can remember, there is some hidden treasure here.

. . .

**For Amla,** there is no daughter next to her, no kulfi in her hand. She is telling this story aloud as she listens to Chandini, who has taken over Amla's mouth. Amla is holding the hand of her own mother, willing forward a memory rooted deep in their past.

An hour later, Arni squints at the neighborhood. "I guess I don't understand," she says. "Do you think of yourself as Sindhi or Gujarati?"

"Sometimes life is more complicated than calling ourselves one thing."

"Are Sindhis Hindu? Or are Sindhi Hindus Brahmin?" You can almost see the equations in Arni's head, the attempt to apply categories she knows to categories she doesn't. "How is your maiden name a Gujarati Brahmin name?"

Amla laughs. "It's not that simple," she says.

"You're married to a Gujarati man, and we live in Gujarat, and Anurag and I are Gujarati. But you speak Sindhi, and that script is more like Urdu than Hindi, and you think Karachi is more home than Porbandar is, and yet . . ." She trails off.

"And yet I live here, and I gave birth to you here," Amla finishes. "And yet, I've stayed here."

Arni bites at her kulfi. "Do you miss it? I feel like I would miss this place all the time if I had to leave."

Amla's lips tighten into a flat line. "Come," she says. "We have more to do at the apartment." She pats down her kurti from picking up in the breeze, and the two walk toward a huddle of rickshaws. *Embrace all these complications*, she wants to say to Arni. *Nobody who left a home during Partition knows where they're from.*

They sit in silence. Amla's gut pangs as they turn away from the Sindhi neighborhood. She hopes her daughter never finds herself in a position where she cannot return home.

· · ·

**At the mention of Chandini,** of Amla telling her daughter the story of her parents' meeting, of what roots her—and therefore me, therefore us—you take my hand. Our walk around the park has long finished. You tug me up and off a bench, bones cracking. I shiver as the early winter breeze hits the backs of my thighs.

"Okay," you say to me.

"Okay?"

You lead us in the direction of our apartment. "I am beginning to understand."

# FOURTEEN

How quickly Arni is wrapped up in the possibilities, the conversation with the students on the rooftop advancing her political stance, while the potential to change her world resides in the tapestry. Sometimes she wonders how vigorously she believes what she had said to the students, about her own beliefs and the state's politics; sometimes she thinks she is playacting, trying to become the strongest, most adult version of herself. Here, the vacuum of space she can occupy—her brother at university, her sister . . . What does it mean for the tapestry to offer her a chance to claim her self, her life, when the opportunity only exists because Vibha is no longer alive? But Ma has not given her more, when it comes to that heritage. Arni spoiled everything with Fiza's letter; she knows it.

Arni only lets herself think this in the dark when she can't sleep, when she has no choice but to emerge from her room and stand at the kitchen counter, boiling water with mint and cardamom and tea. She learns to embrace the bitterness of this, to forget the luxuries of sugar and milk. She imagines Ma mimicking her patience during the daytime, crafting ghee from thin milk, rationing the sugar.

When they were young, Ma would mix ghee and jaggery until the two were a caramel-colored paste. Vibha and Anurag heeded Ma's requests to enjoy the treat slowly, to mix it into every other bite of their dinner. *Don't spend the good things too fast*, Ma would say. *Only as much as the bite needs.*

Arni would spread the paste onto her rotli like jam onto toast before rolling the rotli into a thin cylinder. She'd bite into it, the rotli—already lathered in ghee—mixing sweet and salty with the jaggery paste. When Ma noticed, she would flick Arni on the wrist, once tapped her twice on the nose. *This is why you're going to make trouble*, she said. *You don't know when to stop.*

Arni keeps coming back to this moment—*you don't know when to stop*—as she paints a line of mango groves and bajri stalks across the rooftop wall. The college students are conspicuously absent, their usual corner empty but for burnt cigarette butts slowly being blown in one direction or another by the breeze. Sakshi sits on a rickety metal chair beside her, maths notebook in hand.

"I just don't see the value in this calculus," Sakshi says, scuffing her shoe against the floor. "What do we think is going to happen, suddenly rents will be announced in the form of derivatives?"

Arni laughs, leaning back on her haunches. The December weather means her paintings last much longer on the rooftop, but the shift from the itchy, sweaty summer jars her. "Is that what you'll do next?" she asks. "Help your father out with the building?"

"I think so." Sakshi teeters backward on her chair, eyes on the clouds. "We don't really have money for university, and my father's always stressed with late rents now that it's gotten . . ."

Arni waits for Sakshi to finish the sentence, but she doesn't, and Arni nods. "Yeah," she says. "Makes sense, how it's gotten."

"And you? What do you do next? You're good at these maths, even physics. Even Risha auntie doesn't know what to do with you anymore. Do your parents want you to go to university, like your brother?"

Arni cocks her head to the side. "Huh," she says. "I don't know."

She hears Sakshi put her pencil down. "Because of Vibha?"

"I always hoped I'd go to college," Arni says, and she turns, cross-legged, to face Sakshi. "Vibha was the one with that family pressure on her to marry, you know? Not me. That was the one good thing about being so much younger. No one thought about me because they were busy thinking about her future. But now . . ."

She appreciates that Sakshi doesn't say anything, giving her the space to relax; she finds her worries pouring out of her. "Vibha never questioned our parents on marriage, or anything really, but I did. Even when I never said it aloud to them, I did. And now I feel like I'm supposed to fill this role that I never wanted, and it's just another thing I don't get to decide for myself." Arni motions to the mural forming on the wall. "I don't want to just do what they wanted Vibha to do. I want to choose for myself. Is that . . . is that so much to ask?"

Sakshi shakes her head. "No," she says, and Arni is thankful there's no pity in her voice, just understanding. "I don't think it's too much."

"I feel like I shouldn't say these things about Vibha, not with her gone."

"We get to think about our own lives, though," Sakshi says, and she opens the maths book again. "Speaking of family anxieties—come over for dinner next week. My mother wants to have you by. I think my parents feel better about your paintings now that those students are always smoking up here."

Arni smiles, excited. Her first instinct is to run home and tell Vibha that a friend has invited her to dinner. She's felt this way so many times in the past few months, every time she walks home with Sakshi, when they detour to a street food stand on the way or peek into the theater. She feels her cheeks slacken, the smile leaving her eyes. Always, the moment of realization.

"Of course," she says. "I would love to."

"I'll let her know," Sakshi says. "Maybe you come by early if you want to study for the Hindi final?"

"Yes, that sounds perfect."

Sakshi hums softly, pencil scratching against the maths book, and Arni wonders if it will always feel this way, the shadow of a sibling following her. Would she feel like this if she were on the tapestry? She wonders if it would be easier to agree with her mother, to learn to be a different kind of person. Would it be enough to place her feet in her sister's shoes; would her grief fade away? Would it be worth changing herself?

Arni dips her paintbrush into the blend of indigo and cerulean by her feet, the colors for a woman's sari, and traces over her pencil lines on the wall.

Looking back, Arni should have known it would all go sideways. There had been signs:

Anurag unexpectedly returns home. It was a surprise to Ma, to Baba—to Arni, too, who didn't have enough time to cancel dinner with Sakshi, whose mother was almost certainly cooking by the time Anurag showed up on the apartment doorstep. Arni knows Baba will be annoyed, but she cannot bring herself to cancel at the last minute. She closes the apartment door softly behind her as she leaves.

It is clear Sakshi's mother has been cooking all day. She hands

Arni a heaping plate—at least two servings of rotli and rice (no ghee in either, but plenty of cloves and cardamom in the latter to compensate), okra cooked with chickpea flour sweet enough that Arni can taste the specks of jaggery.

The flat is meager compared to Arni's, clearly designated for the building manager. A cot in the corner of the main room, Sakshi's textbooks stacked neatly beneath it, indicates how different the girls' lives are. There's no navy velvet love seat in Sakshi's apartment, nothing so trendy, but every piece of furniture looks sturdy, reliable, to Arni. Even as Sakshi's mother prepares a side dish of chicken—"I know your family doesn't eat meat, but I hope you don't mind. Sakshi's father always prefers . . ."—Arni is struck by such visible difference so close to home, the clarity of what it means to be in her own class, caste. She thinks of their housekeeper Shantaben's home, which she's never seen—will never see—and of Shantaben's gentle strike, her phone call that morning: "I won't be coming in today." How Sakshi's father is excited by the students organizing, how Shantaben has drawn her line—how Baba is on the other side.

As the girls sit across from each other at the table, Sakshi gushing about the new George Harrison album that the radio plays sometimes—"Zakir Hussain is on it, how have you not heard?"—Arni feels like this time is worth Baba's frustration. She wants to stretch dinner until the sky is dark, keep laughing and joking with a girl her age, who feels like a sister.

So she stays longer than she'd intended, aware of the generosity of this meal, of the strange deference between manager and resident. As late evening falls, Sakshi's mother turns on the few lamps around the kitchen. Arni glances at the ceiling lights, but she isn't as discreet as she thinks she is. "They've been out," Sakshi's mother says, and Arni sips her lemon water, embarrassed. Before she leaves, she tries to wipe down her seat at the table, asks what their system for rinsing dishes is. Sakshi shakes her head, and Sakshi's mother waves her away, but Arni keeps standing with her plate in her hand, unsure what to do if disallowed from helping.

"We make do," Sakshi's mother says, and the sentence answers a question Arni has been thinking but knows is inappropriate to ask. "Now go, your parents must be waiting. Say hello to them for us."

Arni starts at the mention of them—of Baba, who is waiting for her by now, irritated. She nearly mows down Sakshi's father as she leaves the flat, calves preparing to take the stairs two by two.

"Oh! Watch your feet," he says, laughing. "I hope dinner was good?"

"It was great," Arni says. "Thank you for having me."

"Of course," Sakshi's father says, and as he twists the doorknob, he pauses, turning back to Arni. "You're not going out tonight, yes? You and the family, you'll be home for the rest of the evening?"

Arni nods. Before she can ask, he is already explaining. The second sign: "The police have been out of line all day. Shutting down and searching shops, beating shopkeepers like in Rajkot. You and your mother, you should stay home."

Slowly, the words register. She steps backward, pressing her palms together. "Yes, sir. Thank you."

She pulls herself up the staircase by the handrails, her stomach full and cheeks tight from smiling. When she turns onto the fourth floor, cigar smoke and loud, argumentative voices fill the air. The third sign: the uncles in the neighboring flat have their door open, are unabashedly sipping moonshine. Her father must be beyond frustrated by the debate echoing down the hall. Arni catches every other phrase, like *protests in Saurashtra* and *Morbi Engineering* and *shutdowns in Jetpur*. She wonders if Anurag spent the afternoon in this flat, if he is sitting at dinner reeking of moonshine, too.

One of the uncles is monologuing as Arni opens the apartment door, and she shuts it as quickly as she can, trying to leave any variable that could upset Baba outside.

The final sign: no one notices her arrival. That would be normal, before Vibha passed, but not anymore.

"Sometimes you have to *make* people listen," Anurag is arguing loudly, he and Baba at the long ends of the kitchen table. Ma sits stone-faced between them, her hands folded in her lap.

"Those students were given such a privilege to attend that university," Baba says, shaking his head. "They've given up something so valuable, something that people would give their life for a chance at. They've disrespected the institution of education."

Arni steps into the doorway of the kitchen and makes eye contact with Ma, who shakes her head almost imperceptibly, as though begging Arni to stay there, out of her father's sight. To stay quiet.

"They are not protesting *education*—"

"Then they should not be vandalizing the home of education."

"It's not about the location!" Anurag yells, and the table teeters with how quickly he rises from his chair. He pounds his fist on top of the table. "We elect these men and then they take power away from the people who gave it to them. Our lives are never our own. How can you not understand that?"

Baba takes his dinner plate and slams it on the table in front of him, hard enough that the ceramic splinters. Arni gasps, but her mother looks like stone. "You don't speak to me like this," Baba says. He keeps sitting, but he straightens his posture, his hands on his kneecaps. "Not in private, not in front of anyone. This is not my son."

Anurag's cheeks puff out as he exhales, and in this moment he must register Arni because he seems to catch himself, realizing the wildness of the situation. He speaks softer: "You ever wonder, Baba, why you are taking the side of an institution instead of people just like us?"

"They are not like us," Baba says, and now he pushes out of his chair, walking to his bedroom, door swinging behind him. "They are not like me."

---

**"What happened?" Arni asks** her mother later, when they are scraping mostly unfinished plates into steel tiffins.

Amla shakes her head slowly. There are some things she will never know how to explain to her children. How lucky they are to have this life, no matter how it seems. How can she explain that the only reason she has kept her sanity all these years is that the smell of the ocean reminds her of the walk by the harbor in Karachi, even if the roasting meats are different?

A child born after Partition can never know what it was like, Amla decides. Those are words she has heard from Suresh's mouth so many times, and she's begun to believe them. How can she explain this, Suresh's understanding of the world, to a girl who has never known the violence that binds their generation? His politics are born of those years after Partition, when this city worshipped Gandhi and the Congress Party, the party synonymous with British opposition. One of the first things Amla learned about Suresh was that he had walked beside his father in the Dandi March when he was a child; he told her that he thought he saw a nation emerging before his eyes. He spoke of Gandhi like the man could do no harm. Hadn't he put Porbandar on the international map, after all? But her own father had been there, too. Amla remembers Bapu's disgust with Partition. He had marched, yes, but solely for independence—he hadn't believed that independence and partition were meant to go hand in hand.

Suresh believes in a project that Amla naturally cannot; it ripped her from her home, even as—and she knows this is what Suresh believes—his was taken back. Freed. He thought he saw his country reborn, better than before. But what does Suresh know of crossing a gulf, of leaving everything you have behind? He has never known or loved someone from outside his community. He has never been punished for pride, for wanting only to come home.

Sometimes Amla looks at Suresh and his anger and thinks, *Is that what happens when you believe you have control over this world?* It was easy, only natural, for Amla to hand her life over to him: she needed him, needs him still, to survive. But her children—she will shelter them from him. It is her job to protect them.

It's not the marriage she would have wanted for herself, Amla thinks, lying in bed beside her husband, their backs turned to each other. She faces the closet—faces her teakwood box filled with Fiza's letters. But maybe this marriage is enough. Or it's all she can ask for—a roof over her head, children who can go to school, an apartment that isn't at the whim of one landlord or another. After all, after Partition, she never thought she'd be able to have even a quarter of what her parents had. Not their things. Not their love, either: those memories, of a Chandini and Anurag who built a life together, who broke family bonds for each other—all of that belongs to the time when her days were predictable, when she was a child licking kulfi off her fingers. This is what Suresh clutches at as well—something familiar and steady. Whether he knows it or not, that era is long past.

**The next morning the news** will be widely available: Just like in Rajkot, the police assaulted shopkeepers in Porbandar and Jetpur, alleging some were hoarding food grains. They shut down the cities.

Curfews, closed shops. Shantaben sends notice, again, that she won't be coming by. Amla sits at the living room window and listens to the street while her children and Suresh sleep. The shouts, the horns. Nothing, she thinks, can scare her now.

Forty students at Morbi Engineering have also been suspended for vandalism. While protesting the rise of the mess bill days before, some students ransacked a laboratory, vandalized the furniture in the mechanical department. One of Anurag's friends, a student at Morbi, gets news that the college is facing indefinite closure. For Arni, it is the first time she has heard of anything like this; it will not be the last.

In a week, on January 3, L.D. Engineering College in Ahmedabad will follow suit. But the response won't be as clear-cut; the students won't face mere suspension. Anurag, returned to Ahmedabad by then, will send telegrams, will address them to his mother and sister only:

POLICE CHARGED STUDENTS LAST NIGHT *stop* BEAT THEM, TEAR GASSED, IN THEIR OWN HOSTELS *stop* ARRESTED MORE THAN 300 INCLUDING NEIGHBOR PK *stop* CAN YOU LET HIS PARENTS KNOW *stop* KEEP CHECKING FOR TELEGRAMS

PK WAS BEATEN *stop* TEAR GASSED *stop* ARE HIS PARENTS SENDING MONEY OR COMING HERE

PLEASE DON'T WORRY ABOUT ME *stop* WE ARE WORKING TO GET MEDICAL CARE AND RELEASE *stop* WHEN IS PK PARENTS TRAIN ARRIVAL

Every time Amla returns home with the yellow chit, Arni glues her eyes to Baba. He is dramatic: he pretends he doesn't see his wife; he turns his chin upward, looking at the wall behind her. Arni follows her mother wordlessly into the bedroom, where they read each telegram together. She hunches down to her mother's height and holds the paper with her left hand, her mother clutching it with her right. Twice, three times in one day—Anurag was right to warn ahead—and Amla packs a bag for PK's parents, two tiffins in case they are hopping on the overnight train. They don't talk about the telegrams otherwise, don't ask each other if they think Anurag should return home. They eat dinner in the kitchen while Baba takes his plate to the living room. They catch each other's eyes across the table, a knowing passing between them.

# FIFTEEN

On January 7, the colleges strike.

When Anurag hesitates to come home, Baba announces he himself will take the train to Ahmedabad. "Anurag doesn't think about how this looks for him," he grumbles as Ma hurriedly irons and folds a few shirt and trouser sets. "What will happen, with this being his final year? If the college strikes indefinitely, how can he graduate? Find work? Hm?"

Arni listens from the hallway, peeking through the open doorway at her mother's rushed ironing, one hand clutching the thin cloth she uses to keep fabric from burning. The doorway feels like a threshold, a line Arni can't uncross. She closes her eyes and forces her feet to carry her into her parents' bedroom.

Immediately, Baba stops speaking. He looks at her expectantly, and Arni takes a deep breath.

"I was thinking," she says, and then she pauses to rephrase. "I know it's been tense lately, with you and Anurag, Baba, and I mean no disrespect, but I . . . don't think he'll listen to you."

Baba raises one hand toward Arni and looks knowingly at his wife. "See what I'm saying? These children don't . . ."

"I think I have a solution," Arni continues, and she waits until both sets of eyes are on her. "I think I should go with you, since Anurag is more likely to listen to me."

"No, no." Baba stands up from his perch on the edge of the bed, as though walking Arni out of the room. "That wouldn't be right."

"He won't listen to you."

"It's a men's hostel, Arni, it's wholly inappropriate."

"I'll stay outside, or in the taxi," she offers hurriedly. "I'll talk to Anurag in the courtyard. I won't go up to his room."

The silence is encouraging. Arni adds, quickly, "Baba, he's stubborn. You can't—you can't convince him on your own. But I can, if I'm there with you."

Baba sighs. "And your schooling? You would miss days?"

"No, not really, Baba," she says. This is the one answer she is confident in giving him, the reason why she's even mustered the courage to say anything to him at all. "Sakshi's heard that the schoolteachers are also striking. They won't be open tomorrow."

When Arni glances at her mother, Ma radiates relief, nearly smiling as she says, "She has a point, Suresh. Take her with you. She'll bring Anurag home without a scene."

Baba nods slowly, and Arni imagines he is remembering the shouting match at the dinner table the week before, the possibility of that argument playing out publicly in the hallway of the men's hostel, an audience crowding around. "It's settled, then," he says. "We'll get you a ticket. Let's convince your brother not to throw his life away for this, shall we?"

**"This is what you want?"** Ma asks, sitting on the edge of Arni's mattress.

Arni nods slowly as she folds a kurti against her chest. She might not have realized it until this morning, but she feels certain now. "Yes," she says. "I think I know what I'm doing."

Ma smooths the bedsheet. "Thank you for doing this."

"Sure." Arni pauses. "Do you know where the navy leggings are? For this?"

The bed creaks as Ma gets up, and when Arni looks back at her, Ma has a stack of clothes in her hands. She begins distributing them—kurtis in one pile, leggings and dupattas in another—and Arni makes room. "Sorry," she mumbles. "I meant to put them away . . ."

"I like helping you," Ma says, and she places one hand lightly on Arni's shoulder blade. "Reminds me that you're still young."

Arni stops herself from saying anything. It's been better lately, the way she and her mother have been moving around each other. Ever since the night of Anurag and Baba's fight, they have eased into a quiet truce.

When Ma freezes beside her, her hand falling from Arni's back, Arni knows what her mother has found even before she says anything. "That's a clean pile of clothes," Arni says hurriedly. "I promise I didn't just—"

"I understand," Ma says. "It's hard to know where to place it." She pauses. "My mother kept it up in the house, and I didn't understand it, never really looked at it, until after . . ." She turns to Arni, hands outstretched. "You've got this, yes?"

Arni nods.

"I'll finish ironing your father's pants. I don't want him to decide last minute to take a pair that's still wrinkled."

"Ma," Arni says. That kernel of information, of Ma's history with the tapestry, is too tempting to give up. "Can I know more about it? Where did Nanima hang it up—did you, also? Put it up in your house?"

Ma looks down at her hands. "Arni." She hesitates. "Not now. As much as I want to, you need to be ready for—"

"Okay," Arni says abruptly, "forget it," because she can't hear it one more time, no—*You need to be ready for this responsibility* or *I need you to grow up*—no, she can't. And there are no other words to say. She turns, her cheeks burning, and then her mother is gone.

Their fragile détente breaks, just like that.

Arni is still fuming when they are ready to leave, Baba hunting for his glasses. She waits, one foot outside the apartment door and the other still inside, a tight coil of want and frustration spinning in her chest. She catches sight, then, of the mail pile on the floor. Leaning down to pick it up, she recognizes one envelope, its exterior dusty just like its sister had been months before. Fiza Qureshi's name in the upper-left corner.

*This is not yours to know,* the creature in Arni's gut tells her.

Still, Arni takes the envelope and crams it into her shoulder bag, leaving the rest of the mail on the kitchen counter. She doesn't know why; she can't even read it. But her mother's rejection is fresh, and before she can pause, before she can consider what she's doing, her father shoves their train tickets into her hand and Arni is staring at the closed apartment door.


**Arni sits in the women's carriage** on both trains—the first to Rajkot, the second to Ahmedabad—and as the train slows into the final station, she pulls at the worn-down edges of a thin pamphlet she brought with her.

Anurag had given her the pamphlet after his fight with Baba, later that night when Arni was hopeful he'd cooled his temper enough to tolerate her presence. Silent in the room, he'd handed her the folded paper. "Take a look," he'd said, and Arni watched him unpack ten, twenty, more pamphlets from his trunk.

She is enamored with the wealth of information presented on each thick sheet of paper. Arguments for dissolution of the Gujarat Legislative Assembly on one page, poems of the rising political consciousnesses on the next. Some of these are his, Anurag had said, though there's no name marking the authors. Other pages read like an almanac, listing black market vendors in Ahmedabad, and others still opt for flavor: "Assembly is a warehouse of the goons," reads one political cartoon.

Arni reads those words over and over. "Goons," she whispers to herself, and the woman next to her looks at her strangely. Arni shoots her a glare and they both return to pretending their bodies aren't pressed against each other on the train.

She's hidden the pamphlet within her maths book, unsure how others would interpret the explicit writing on its pages. She feels lucky that Anurag let her keep it at all; she feels like she tricked him, never handing it back, not even as he mentioned heading up to the roof to distribute them to the group of college students. The train whistle blows, and as the women around her begin moving toward the doors, the smell of perfumes mingling with sitting sweat, Arni turns the pamphlet to the pages with political cartoons, depicting a coed assortment of students protesting. They wear saris, jeans, baseball caps. Bubbles above their heads list out demands: employment guarantees, health care, education without discrimination. The wheels in her brain start turning, slowly at first, and then she is itching to grab her sketchbook, to imagine the scene at the political natak, to paint something that feels substantial. She tucks the pamphlet into her shoulder bag and meets Baba's eyes through the carriage window, from where he's waiting out on the station. She nods at him quickly, and he nods back, motioning for her to hurry. As she holds her bag against her chest, Arni can't help but feel warmth in her stomach, as though it is where she's holding a secret.

**Baba has Arni promise** to stay in the courtyard as he heads upstairs to Anurag's room. She nods dutifully; she isn't as interested in the hostel as she is in the campus, in the men and women milling about, leading lives she dreams of.

For a while, she is content to eavesdrop on the women students' conversations—exams that went well, dates that didn't—but then, slowly, a congregation of students and teachers begins gathering in the courtyard. If she leaves, Baba will be angry, she tells herself, so she must stay in the thick of this gathering. She measures what she's wearing, how she looks, against the other women present. Certainly younger—she takes her hair out of its plaits, runs her fingers through its tangles. More homely—she compares her dark churidar to the women students' jeans, high waisted and flaring at the ankles. Nothing to do about that now. She scoots closer to the small crowd.

"If you are planning to protest tomorrow, the police are still arresting those who block public transport," a younger teacher with circular glasses is saying. "There have been no hard actions from the Congress Party after our last march. We just have to keep pooling together."

"The unions are calling for a total strike on the tenth," a woman, likely a student, adds. "Everyone from government employees to Life Insurance Corporation."

"There is a chance the government will respond." Arni stands on tiptoes, eyes straining to make out this voice—another woman, but older. A teacher. "Focus on concrete demands if they ask for a conversation. They must be specific, clear. Time bound, if possible."

"Release of the students."

"Acknowledgment of police brutality."

"Is that all?"

"It's not just us," says the woman student. "We should move for more, for people to be able to live again. We should consider moving for the reappearance of essential commodities."

"We'll need to get numbers on that."

"Students at other universities would probably agitate with us."

"Are we in favor?"

Arni has integrated into the crowd at this point, and all around her, arms shoot upward. She looks left, then right, trying to find students without hands raised. She feels the excitement, the anger, the adrenaline. She hesitates and then she raises her hand, the energy coursing through her. She feels like one small body among a wave.

"Arni!"

She takes a step backward into the students behind her—"Sorry, sorry," she says quickly, "excuse me, pardon"—and finds herself face-to-face with Baba. He is red-faced, teeth grinding against one another. With her eyes, Arni traces the veins in his neck, his head held purposefully high. She wonders if his hand, curled loosely now, had been stretched into a forceful slap, moments ago.

Her voice catches in her throat as she prays he had not seen her raised hand.

"Come," Baba hisses, "we're leaving."

"I stayed in the courtyard like you asked," she blurts out. "Where's Anurag?"

Baba holds up a pamphlet exactly like the one Arni had pored over on the train. "He will have to come home eventually," Baba says.

"I can go upstairs?" She offers this weakly; if she were in her brother's shoes, she knows the decision she would make, too.

"We have caused enough of a scene here today, I think," Baba says quietly, and Arni focuses on keeping her eyebrows from rising. She understands what must have happened: Baba demanding in increasing volume that Anurag follow him downstairs, Anurag refusing and shoving the pamphlet in his hands, the eyes of countless boys watching them. Of course Baba left; there was no other way to save face. "Come. We'll stay overnight, and try again tomorrow."

**Baba demands that she stay back,** this morning. He wants to try again, does not want Arni anywhere near the students protesting, where he cannot watch her.

"If I can't convince him, you'll talk to Anurag this evening?"

She nods, and as Baba closes the door behind him she leans upright against her pillow. With the thin cotton sheet tucked up to her chest, she pulls the pamphlet and her sketchbook from her bag. In quick, decisive strokes, she traces the political cartoon exactly into her sketchbook—everything from the black-and-white shading to the word bubbles above the protesters' heads. She repeats the sketch once, twice; Arni goes slowly, her mind whirring with ideas.

If she can trace the cartoon people and the words, maybe she can absorb the meaning of these protests. She wants to learn; selfishly, she wants to be one of those women in high-waisted jeans. When her mind wanders, it's to the students on the Porbandar rooftop, wondering if any of them traveled to Ahmedabad to protest, if any were arrested.

In the afternoon, she tries sketching her own design. She glances back at the cartoon protesters; she places them in Porbandar, in the city square with the statue of Gandhi at one end of the scene and the raised stage opposite. She attempts to copy the cartoonish faces at first, but it feels wrong to her. Flipping to a new page in her sketchbook—more use than it's had in months, now—she draws each face in detail, entire busts. Here, her parents' faces: her father's thick eyebrows, his mustache, spectacles tucked into his breast pocket; her mother's sharp cheekbones, the curve of her nose, the sweeping hair curls. Anurag, Sakshi, Sakshi's parents. She inserts each figure into her imagined crowd, faces in profile, while others look onward to the stage.

Among them in the crowd: people with sheep masks on their heads, at various stages of removal. She sketches over Baba, has his hands postured as though wresting the mask from his face. Anurag's sheep mask is already in his hands. She hesitates on Ma, unsure, and then she pencils in the mask so that Ma is at the exact moment of removal, head leaning down and hands caressing the sheep's snout.

Arni holds the paper at arm's length, squinting at its flaws. The pencil is too dark in some spots, too light in others. She's better with paints, the way they force her to slow down. Arni curls the eraser in her fist as she gathers her next steps. This drawing has felt so much more calculated than anything she's done before; she wonders if this is the pressure of wanting to do this sketch right, to do the students— a movement—right.

The sun enters heavy, golden, into the rented room. She pretends she is not in the hotel but at home, that the desk she is working at is Ma's watercolor desk. She feels the warmth from the window on her back and begins again.

**In the solitude** of her bedroom, alone in their Porbandar flat, Amla is also taking pencil to paper. She is waiting for Fiza's next letter; it is taking longer than she expected. She is still processing the words she'd written on the page. *My queen*, she remembers, and her chest floods with warmth as she closes her eyes. If only she could be transported across time and space to Karachi, to evenings spent people watching outside Sind Club. If only she could do more than name the want to herself. To be able to imagine that future, to say it could be real one day, and not just to herself but aloud.

What was it she had written? *I go back to Karachi in my mind all the time*, she'd penned in her reply to Fiza.

> *Sometimes we are children. Sometimes we are as we are now. Each time, I am reminded what it means to be in your company—as a friend, as a confidant. The only person I would want to travel back and forth to Karachi with.*
> *The only.*

Now, at the desk, her fingers curl around the pencil. Something familiar and electric tickles her spine.

She opens unseeing eyes. The hand holding this pencil is not hers alone, not anymore. Her body moves of its own accord. The blood in her blood, the twitches and spasms of each muscle—not hers, no, but ancestral.

It's been so long since Amla has felt accompanied; so long since she has been prompted to paint without full control. She breathes deeply and slowly, a meditation settling into her spine; she allows it, reaching for a set of watercolors from the drawer beside the bed, tossing the pencil to the side. Taking the steel cup from the table, Suresh's water from the night before. Here, she feels guidance, draws perpendicular lines; here, have the sunlight hit just right. Here, the way the sky blends its colors together, azure and teal and at its brightest, nearly white as a bird's egg.

The pigment stains Amla's fingertips. As she brushes her hair from her cheeks, she leaves a stain on one side.

Later, she will look in the mirror, seeing evidence of her fugue state too plainly. She will want to vomit and also to sing, all emotions at once, at the idea of our lineage's return. When she walks to the window, where the page is drying in the sun, she will gasp quietly and take a small step back before picking it up and thinking that she will have to lock it away with the rest. She will wonder what it means. If it will come in this life.

Not yet, though, not now.

For now, her blood thinking of Fiza, she paints the palace.

In the evening, Arni corners Anurag in the hostel courtyard, jogging across its diagonal as soon as she sees him bike up to the building. She wasn't sure Baba would let her speak with Anurag alone; she doesn't trust his permission, half expecting him to get up from his bench to interrupt their conversation.

"I need to talk to you," she says, grabbing his wrist.

He shakes her hand off him, moving to unfold the cuffs of his trousers. "You're not going to convince me to come back to Porbandar."

She waves that away. "Yeah, I'm not trying. I need to ask you about"—she drops her voice to a whisper—"the protests."

Anurag eyes her cautiously and then beckons torward the opposite end of the courtyard from Baba. She wishes she'd brought her sketchbook down with her, or at least the pamphlet, to guide her thoughts. All she has is the final sketch, ripped out and tucked into her churidar. "I want to know how I can help with what you've been doing."

"Help with the protests?" Anurag raises an eyebrow. "I don't think that's a good idea."

She's been preparing her arguments all morning. "You said I had to think about the world I want to be a part of, and I want to get involved, and I know it's risky—"

"You don't know that, though." She has barely begun, and he is already frowning.

"—and I have something to offer with my painting. That pamphlet was designed by artists, poets, people bridging this political justice with—"

"Be quiet, Arni," Anurag snaps, and she is stunned into silence. "More than three hundred students from L.D. College were arrested, do you understand that?"

"I do, I get—"

"Do you even know three hundred people, Arni?" Anurag shakes his head. "They had tear gas and batons and shields, and they acted like every student was some goon out to get them. You can't be involved in that."

"But you get to be," Arni says, voice rising. She didn't think he would say no. She hadn't prepared for this part, has no rehearsed lines for this argument. And then she sees it, her opening—in the way her brother's eyes twitch, in the set of his jaw. Realization dawns. "Were you even there, the night PK and the others were arrested?"

He rolls his eyes at her, turning away, but Arni gapes at him. "You're not even out there," she says, and she wants to laugh, it's so preposterous, his condescension. "That's why you were sending us telegrams."

"That's not true," he says flatly. "But either way, girls—"

"Don't start," she says. "I saw the women out here yesterday, organizing. They're involved in the big decisions."

"Yes, there are women leading this, but it's not even . . ." He quiets as one of the first-floor doors opens, waving in greeting as a spectacled older man in a navy dhotiyu emerges. "It's not even that."

She scuffs at the dirt on the ground. "What next?" she asks. "My age?"

"Well, yes," Anurag says, his voice laced with exasperation, and she scowls as she hears it. "Look, you've been sheltered, Arni. You were babied; you didn't have the responsibilities Vibha and I had."

She winces. "I never asked for that."

"No, but you benefited from it." Anurag shrugs. "You don't know what it's like to fight for something."

Arni takes a deep breath, feels her fingers curl into fists. As if Anurag knows what it is like to fight for something. Slowly she releases her fingers, stretching her hands out. "I am learning to fight, Anurag, if someone in this family would give me some fucking space to breathe," she hisses, and the curse, the lowered tone, are just enough that he pauses. "I am going to help in a way that makes sense for me to."

She had pulled the folded sketch from inside her waistline, planning to hand it over to him, to ask him if it was helpful, if her drawing mattered, but now she asks nothing. She doesn't want to give him this power, not when he has so much that he doesn't recognize its value. Wordlessly, she tucks the paper back into her waistline.

"Arni," her brother starts.

"I'll tell Baba you have to see this through, that I couldn't convince you," she says. "You're welcome."

Anurag squints at her, eyes measured, but Arni doesn't wait. She turns, her strides long, and goes back to the bench where Baba has been waiting.

**Over breakfast on January 10,** the first day Baba and Arni are back in Porbandar, Ma announces that Meenafai will be coming to stay. She speaks to them as though she has always made the rules of their household, and Arni wonders where this version of her mother has come from.

Baba pauses mid-bite, pinching a mound of rice between fingers and thumb. "Your village aunt?"

"You mean the woman who raised me to adulthood and got us arranged? Yes," Ma says, passing a plate of thepla to Arni, "my village aunt."

"I can't remember the last time we went to the village," Arni says, and Ma nods, eyebrows raised, as though to say, *My point exactly.*

"I don't know," Baba continues. "Isn't it dangerous to travel, students rioting everywhere?"

He's anxious, Arni sees it.

This anxiety will only deepen, and in turn, his temper will only deepen, too. In a matter of days, he won't be able to leave the house for work. He'll spend all his time pacing their living room, sitting in silence while the uncles next door update one another on whom from the assembly has resigned. Sometimes he'll help Ma out with errands, eager for an excuse to leave the house, and Arni will watch Ma skeptically pile market trips onto him.

"The woman has been through worse," Ma says now, matter-of-factly. "And I could use the help since you're at home, too. What about you, Arni? Would you like a chance to see the woman who raised your mother, again?"

It's a trick to get Arni to tip the scales, recalling their old alliance against Baba. "Sure," Arni says, unable to muster more enthusiasm. She can't look at Ma without thinking of the last time they'd spoken, the burn of that rejection still fresh.

The entire walk to the school building, she thinks about the idea of a grandmother figure she barely remembers. Sakshi seems unbothered by her silence, even when they arrive to find the same sign on the front doors that has been up since before Arni left. *Bandh*, the handwritten note reads. *Stay home.* The picket line has been drawn.

They detour at Arni's insistence to the chowpatty, extending the walk back to the apartments. The streets are eerie, and she can feel Sakshi's tension seep into the once-comfortable silence. "Go on home without me, then," Arni replies, "I'm staying," but Sakshi looks at Arni with something between pity and exhaustion, and stays as long as Arni does. The sun is still rising into the sky, the market still setting up. Arni closes her eyes, feels her cheeks tingle with the ocean breeze. She licks the salt, both sea water and sweat, off her lips and leans back on her arms. Sakshi begins to hum one of those new George Harrison songs—"Be Here Now," Arni remembers—and then they are leaving and the moment feels gone before Arni can catch it.

Later, when night comes, Arni recognizes how close they were to getting caught up in a crowd marching to Kirti Mandir, the protesters mostly shouting but allegedly throwing stones, the police armed with tear gas. Her stubbornness, and how lucky they were, haunt her. Baba paces the length of the kitchen, the radio screeching away with news reports. Ma makes rounds to the other apartments, checking on the families with small children to see if there's anything she can do to help out. More than once, she volunteers Arni to bring one vegetable or another, often to trade, and Arni scowls as she is sent off with a tiffin of okra, of rice, of dry and unoiled rotli. She'd prefer to be standing at the apartment doorway, ears trained on the uncles next door. She doesn't want the political play-by-play of Baba's radio, only the words she picks up from the uncles' conversation: *Baroda riots. Total shutdown. Establishment of a coordinated committee.*

There is a quiet morning on the roof—the only reprieve in the days to follow—spent with the college students, smoking weed and flying a kite on Sankranti, as though the only priority that day is to fly their kite higher than the group on the opposite rooftop. Even then, the one woman student, Bhavna, hands Arni a pamphlet much like the one Anurag had given her except oriented toward Porbandar, and the day's reprieve is only that, a reprieve—and then for days the rhythm is constant. More students gassed in Ahmedabad; more parallel committees of students forming in other cities. Arni watches young men marching down the road, imagining she is one of them, itching to be.

When the citywide bandh with curfews is announced, Arni spends more time on the rooftop. She transfers the painting from her sketchbook onto the wall, Sakshi often beside her with her father's accounting books in hand. At first, each brushstroke reminds Arni of Anurag—of the possibility that he is present at every student clash the radio drones on about—even the possibility that he isn't, that he's sitting at home drinking and smoking and cheering the protesters on from afar as if this is the same. She is fueled by his dismissal. The Porbandar college students, still meeting on Arni's rooftop, crowd around her mural, and Bhavna always opens their circle to include Arni as they whisper of more concrete demands. Arni soaks in their words: A call for the PM's resignation. A call for the entire government's resignation. The entire assembly's.

Slowly, the labor of painting and the hours of insomnia take their toll. As she skips meals to finish the painting, as she watches Bhavna brainstorm slogans, she imagines she is the sibling who is at the clashes, that she is one of the women students at HK Arts who is arrested. That she is making her voice rise louder and louder, beckoning a new world.


***You don't have the responsibilities** we did*, Anurag had said before she left. *You never had to fight for something.*

She paces the meter outside her parents' bedroom door, Anurag's words filling her with the same fury as they did then. She carries the tapestry, and it weighs heavy on her forearms, the cloth warm, almost itchy.

Baba has stormed out again, after another argument with Ma about Anurag's refusal to return. For all the times she has been jealous of Anurag, of how beloved he is, now she is relieved not to be him. She is happy for her invisibility.

*This is the time*, Arni tells herself. *Now when it's just me and Ma.*

She raps her knuckles on the door twice, stepping purposefully into the bedroom when her mother beckons.

"I'm ready," she says, holding out the tapestry to her mother. "I know you didn't think I was before, but I am now."

"You're ready now?" Ma seems to be sizing her up, calculating. "How have you changed?"

"I can take on this responsibility," Arni says, not registering her mother's words. "I know who I am and what I can do. I can be a part of this lineage."

"You come back from Ahmedabad and just like that, you're different, is it?" Ma snaps her fingers. Her tone sharpens, even as she speaks more softly. "Tell me. What has changed?"

"Ma, you said—Vibha said—this can change the world." Arni is breathing heavily. She is certain, this is the right way to use this power. "People are fighting to be heard. Our lives—they're not our own. It would be selfish to have this power and not use it. I can use it; I can fix it."

"You want to change lives?"

"Yes. And you—you can teach me." Arni waits for her mother to smile. Isn't this what she had wanted Arni to say? She is being selfless.

"Even after everything I told you—" Ma is not smiling; her mouth is a hard line; she is fuming. "Everything I said about this power. And you want to go out there and change the world? You want to make life easy just like that?"

"Isn't that the point?" Arni can't help but blurt the words out.

What an opportunity, right? What a chance to make change? "I thought you'd be proud—I'm being brave. I'm taking a stance."

"I wanted a *careful* daughter," Ma hisses, and Arni hears what her mother isn't saying: *This is why I chose Vibha.* "Get out." Arni doesn't know what to say as her mother pushes her backward, toward the open door, into the hallway. When the door closes in front of her, Arni leans against it, scuffing the floor with her slippered foot. From the bedroom, she hears her mother mutter, "Not like this. Not like this."

# SIXTEEN

There is no time to wait for power, Arni decides.

This is how the first street mural is painted: she tells her parents she is going to Sakshi's after dinner, that they want to finish their science coursework and not be left behind by the school closures. Baba smiles proudly, pats her shoulder. "Good to have an educated girl," he says, and Arni brushes off the implication that she is to be had, that her education is geared toward someone else, and instead she focuses on stuffing her books into her bag, textbook after textbook; Ma eyes her as she leaves but doesn't say anything, and Arni just holds her mother's eye contact until she is at the door and then down the stairs.

She pulls a dark shawl over her head, unsure what the consequences are for breaking curfew. Bhavna, cigarette in hand, meets her in the alley with an address written on a piece of scrap paper. They make their way there together, where other collaborators have already hidden a box of paint canisters and brushes for them to use. Arni is amazed by the number of darkly dressed organizers who meet in the dark, who offer her a cigarette. She only refuses because she knows the scent will carry into her home later.

The shops have metal curtains that close vertically at night. The paint tins clang softly against one another as Arni takes them out, straining in the moonlight to make out the color names printed atop the lids. Bhavna glances around the storefront, like a spy out of an American movie, before beckoning the group to get started.

There are no real streetlights in front of the storefront, only the lights of apartments above it. They strain to listen for police or motors, remaining tense even when they hear none. Today, they are painting slogans from the pamphlets; Arni focuses, tries to mimic the style within the pages.

She lays out the cans in front of the metal curtain carefully and then takes her paintbrush in hand. She moves quickly, forcing her strokes to return to the impulsivity that guided her as a child—that instinct, that potential, that makes her a part of this lineage whether or not she is sewn onto the tapestry.

A dog barks; a motorbike two streets over belches. Someone whispers that they need to hurry up. Arni steadies the grates with one hand to stop them from creaking and keeps painting.

**When the news** of the murals along the shoreline stores is all the talk at the market, Amla knows immediately this is her daughter's doing.

At first, she'd tried to ignore it—the way Arni snuck out in the evenings, the badly made excuse about studying their textbooks downstairs with Sakshi. She hadn't wanted to say anything, knowing Suresh would be angry with this type of naive risk-taking, the dangers of a girl out at night alone. *I'll wait until we are alone,* she'd thought, and then of course they were never alone, not with the strikes and Suresh staying home, not with Arni avoiding her, with her daughter forfeiting the time she used to spend sitting paint-stained on the roof with Sakshi to instead go roaming for painting spots in the evening.

And maybe she let it happen because she remembered freely roam-ing the village where she grew up, all those endless early days with Bahaar and Padma when Bapu never restricted her, and even later, Meenafai trusted her to hold her own. The village where she painted those paintings—ones that mattered, even if she never loved the way in which they held meaning. Hadn't her skin thickened because of all that time, hadn't she created this armored shell from those first devastating mistakes? Hadn't they helped her survive?

For the first time, she wonders if this means Arni could survive, too.

She always forgets that Arni is the daughter most like herself—how much Arni might need to grow the way she had. She needs none of Amla's protection.

One morning after Meenafai has arrived—a tornado even in her old age, with her bags tossed about, her nicotine breath and loud belly laugh—and complained that Amla keeps her cooped up all day, Amla takes the older woman to the market, the long way. Then, with a canvas bag of market vegetables weighing down her right shoulder and Meenafai giddy to stretch her legs, Amla steers them toward the murals. Sometimes there are crowds nearby; today, only a pair of kids, a few police officers pacing anxiously. Amla keeps her distance, sunglasses over her eyes and a dupatta around her hair to keep out the breeze. She's not sure who she's hiding from; she only wants a chance to survey without having to answer any questions. She doesn't point them out to Meenafai but can feel the woman's eyes soaking them in.

There are three, each on adjacent metal curtains.

The first: a woman student with short hair and a bullhorn leading a crowd, calling for guarantees of employment, health care, education without discrimination.

The second: the same woman in profile, her bullhorn captioned with a speech bubble, demanding constructive reforms that the movement, the Navnirman Andolan, has been named after. Primary schools in every village, investments in public transportation, a police force that understands the meaning of protection. The hypocrisy of the Congress Party calling for these changes without placing their money or their hearts where their mouths are.

The third: a call for the resignation not only of Chimanbhai Patel but the entire assembly, the speech bubble owned by what seems like hundreds, thousands, of bright silhouettes, their figures painted in different variations of orange, and green, and white.

Amla should worry about Arni getting arrested. She should worry about her daughter's safety, with her sneaking around at night. She doesn't think about either of these concerns for longer than a moment. Instead she worries that if this girl can already contribute to this much change in the world, what will happen when Arni is given a power far beyond her knowledge?

This is good work; she believes it even as she fears for her daughter's safety. But she also believes, better this than abusing the tapestry. And yet—and yet, she cannot decide. Amla presses her eyes shut. Oh, this daughter—she makes Amla's heart break for the type of person Amla might have been if she'd never received this power. What to do with this power—what to do with this girl.


**At home,** Amla takes her aunt by the hand. She turns on the radio for Suresh and Arni as Meenafai announces "I guess we've got a lot of catching up to do!" and they careen straight from the front door to Amla's bedroom, where Amla closes the door with a huff.

"So eager to get me alone." Meenafai tsks. "What have I done?"

Amla feels like a child cusping on rowdy teenager. "It's nothing like that."

"Then?"

Amla exhales, her cheeks puffing out. "I told you something as a child and you didn't believe me," she says finally. "But I need you to, this time. I need you to tell me what to do." Amla listens against the door for a moment as the radio warbles Ravi Shankar. "Do you remember what I told you about the paintings?"

Meenafai stares at Amla before slowly sitting on the edge of the bed. "That wasn't anything, jaan. You can't blame yourself forever."

"I need you to believe me." Amla is pleading.

Meenafai watches her, considering. "Okay," she says calmly. "Let's say it's real. What's happened?"

"Arni has been leaving every night to go paint political murals. Those ones on the street." Amla rushes through her words. If she pauses, if she reflects on meanings, she won't say it at all. "Everything she demands, she wants, is *huge*. This great change. The resignation of Chimanbhai Patel, the overthrowing of the assembly. It's so much."

"This worries you?"

"She doesn't know how to handle responsibility. She's always jumping in, feet first. No caution." Amla wrings her hands, pacing. "How can I give this gift to her, when I don't know what she might do? When I could lose her, too? But now Vibha's gone, and"—she falters—"am I a bad mother if I deny my daughter this lineage?"

The older woman's face contorts as she chews on the inside of her bottom lip. "Remind me how you think this works."


**Arni knows every floorboard** that creaks, where to stand so that she doesn't interrupt the flow of light beneath her parents' bedroom door. She says something offhand about *how skilled this sitar is, isn't it, Baba?* and turns up the volume on the radio on her way past him. Baba grunts into his newspaper.

She lingers in the hallway outside of her father's line of sight, ear close to her parents' bedroom door hinge.

"I don't think what happened was coincidence, Meenafai."

"And I don't think you killed your father, Amu." A muffled shuffling of feet and bed creaks. "You are scared of your daughter's natural gift. She's not doing anything otherworldly, not now. You must leave room in the world for real people to make real change, jaan."

"But if this is what happens now, then what could she do when sewn onto the tapestry?"

"What could she do?" Meenafai's laugh rumbles. "She's not like your son, Amu. That boy is so prideful he'll do anything, so long as his name can appear in the papers about it. But your daughter—to care so much, at such a young age, when did we stop respecting that? Maybe you're right; she is an agitator. What is the harm in giving her more power in a world that is going to strip as much of it away from her as it can? Ha! That fight—it should give you life."

Arni leans closer, listening intently.

"And what if the entire world is controlled by some other force, yes? If you think god is watching us, like your husband thinks, hmm? If nothing matters, if it's all coincidence or fated, what does it hurt to try?"

Their footsteps come closer to the door, and Arni takes a half step back, her calves burning—but the bedroom doorknob is already turning and Arni panics; she won't make it to her room in time. She feels the brush of wood against her back and reaches an arm out and behind her, but before she can catch the frame, it's on the floor, the glass cracked but not shattered. She drops to her knees, the frame shaking between her unsteady hands.

"Arni!"

"I'm so sorry, Ma," she says, and when their eyes meet, Arni knows her mother has understood she'd been lurking at the door. Ma takes the frame from Arni's hands, cheeks white.

"You have to be careful, Arni," Ma says tightly. "You have to know where the line is."

Meenafai raps at the frame of Chandini Prakash with her knuckles. "This is a good likeness of your mother, though, Amu," she says, and Arni is relieved by the lightness in this auntie's voice, her easy forgiveness. "Aren't you looking for signs?" She swats Arni away. "I need jeera pani. Amu, you have jeera pani?"

Arni avoids eye contact with her mother, sidestepping her way to her room. She unearths the tapestry from the bottom of a clothes pile and sits back on her bed with the fabric in her lap.

Meenafai's muffled words echo in her imagination. *I don't think you killed your father*—isn't that what she had said? The words are a crack in Arni's pride. The implication is clear. Hadn't Arni begged for her mother's secrets without knowing what Ma carried? Here it was, the reason why Ma cared so much about caution.

Forget the power, Arni decides. She can be a part of this movement without the assistance of ancestry. But she is starting to see it in herself, that impulsivity that lured her to ask Ma for the gift without considering the consequences. Her arrogance, her belief that she would only ever do good things with the gift. The shame settles in Arni's stomach as she closes the bedroom door behind her, biting her knuckles.

**Forty-four towns face curfew,** Porbandar one of them.

Arni paints like she has nothing left to sacrifice. She nods politely while Baba shouts at no one in particular that Anurag is still in

Ahmedabad. She avoids Meenafai's probing eyes as she slinks to her room, readying her tote bag. She has started accepting beedis from Bhavna, and they end up in the bottom of the bag when she's too cowardly to smoke them—crumpled, a little tobacco smudging out, her canvas bag beginning to smell like the uncles next door. But she likes the reminder that there are women who are daring, who will hand a girl like her a beedi and a pamphlet, and then ask her, *What are you going to do to change our world?*

There are times when Arni is painting that she feels some heat coursing through her blood. She wonders if this is the lineage calling out to her. Sometimes she takes the tapestry from its place among her folded clothes, unwrapping it so it covers her bed like a new sheet. She places it face down, its dazzling side covered, and traces what must be tens, twenties, maybe hundreds of women—the tapestry denies her as she tries to count, makes her forget as soon as she's begun. She rests her index finger on the final stitched figure—Vibha. Arni wonders about her sister's changes, what they had been. What changes the other women on this tapestry had prompted. She thinks of her own murals and wonders if she is doing anything of importance. She tries to leave these thoughts with the tapestry, in her closet, but there are nights on the street when she worries with every brushstroke that her talent is only the result of this lineage—and in these moments, she falters a little, wonders what it means for anything to be innate. So Arni mostly tries to avoid the question, reminding herself that in the end there is no magic capable of saving anyone, just people marching and begging and organizing for change.

Still, it lingers, the question.

On one of the days the protests are distant enough that Baba doesn't stop Arni from leaving the house, she takes her mother's list of vegetables and agrees to return in an hour.

"No long detours," her mother warns. "Shouldn't take you long."

"I just need to move my legs," Arni says. "I might walk by the chow-patty. Only if it's quiet, no students."

Ma nods, handing Arni carefully counted paise. "Grab some extra fruit, if it looks ripe. The market bag is in the closet."

Arni leaves her slippers by the closet, taking soft barefooted steps to her parents' open bedroom door. Baba's wallet sits on the edge of the dresser, and Arni turns to ensure no one is watching. She has already made the decision. She pulls out the paise slowly, only three or four notes from what seems like ten or twenty, so few she's counting on him not noticing. These she tucks into the tight, high waist of her pants, under the cover of her kurti.

From her room she grabs an envelope with weathered edges—Fiza's letter. She tucks this, too, into the waist of her pants.

This isn't being a better daughter, she knows, but she needs this, needs to know. This is something she can figure out. If her mother won't tell her, she'll find out for herself.

"Okay, I'm going!" She lifts her hand to Baba on her way out, and he nods. As she swings open the apartment door, she hears him begin to lecture Ma.

"We need to stop treating her like a child who can roam about and more like a young lady with—"

But she doesn't stay to listen, shutting the door behind her, taking the steps down from their floor by twos. She presses her hand to the thick paper tucked against her stomach.

**Her father's money pays** for a rickshaw to the Sindhi neighborhood. She has the envelope with Fiza's letter in her hand, its lip sliced open, as she walks down the road of vegetable sellers. She taps on the shoulder of a girl maybe a few years older than her, and she asks if the girl speaks both Gujarati and Sindhi, and the girl nods, and Arni is relieved.

"I will pay you to read this to me," she says, and the girl takes the letter a little skeptically but still reads it to Arni, and Baba's money pays for this, too.

The thing about this moment, this memory, is that it feels invasive to focus on. The instinct to give this letter the privacy it deserves outweighs the urge to know all the information. I don't need to know the words Fiza has written to know that they were words of love, that some of the phrases hinted at escaping these lives together, that most of the ideas were dreams. Maybe Fiza had the luxury of knowing nothing she wrote would come true, so she wrote it all down—these wants, these desires. What is it like to declare your love when the only option is the status quo?

Arni listens, though. She's there for a reason. Maybe a part of her wants to cause harm, wants to unearth something that she knows her mother considers private, precious. But that spite begins to fizzle; as the letter is read aloud, she begins to understand the complexities of secrets, the kindness of a daughter who keeps them for her mother, as Vibha had.

Arni isn't appalled by the implications of Fiza's words to her mother, but instead by the largeness of this secret, which feels like it outweighs all the information she's ever known about Ma. This woman who raised her, who believes in a tapestry and ancestral memory, who calls Karachi her home more than Porbandar—who is in love with a woman nearly three hundred miles away. Arni doesn't know her at all.

**Meanwhile, the movement's hard work** is paying off—the protests, the murals. Over breakfast one day, Baba pinches his nose in thought. "I don't agree with how they're doing it," he says, unprompted, "but I'd be cruel to not see value in the things they are fighting for. I simply do not stand for the way they are doing it."

Arni nods. "Absolutely, the value," she repeats, and leaves the table quickly to avoid looking too proud in front of him.

Other members of the Congress Party begin asking for Chimanbhai Patel to step down. It has only been a few weeks since those riots in Ahmedabad and Baroda, the same day the school announced its strike. The nightly curfews have transformed Porbandar and so many other cities so quickly, and it will be a wonder to Arni, many years later, how much of a blip on the radar of history these sixty-three days of curfew will become.

Arni and Bhavna are long past painting slogans. As their group of collaborators switches streets and shop fronts, wary of police and curious residents, she edges into her own patterns. This is the first time her art has been for anyone besides the aunties on the rooftop, the college students escaping to the roof with their joints, Sakshi. She wants it—needs it—to feel like it's her own.

February 9, Baba wakes up in a bad mood. He lumbers around the apartment without speaking to Amla or Arni. He doesn't even turn on the radio, which last night had noted that Indira Gandhi herself had demanded Chimanbhai Patel's resignation. Now, he has handed it in. Crowds of people have emerged on the streets to celebrate. Baba doesn't have to forbid Arni from joining; it is clear in the way he closes the door and locks it, in the way he mutters, "We shall see what comes next."

"So you're a big dreamer, hmm?"

Meenafai's voice startles Arni, and she pulls her shawl tighter around her shoulders. Arni exhales slowly, is curt when she does speak. "Good morning, Meenafai."

"But you're an observer at home," the older woman continues quietly, voice raspy. Her fingers twitch, cigarette-less. "Always watching how the changes outside affect what's happening inside. Trying to fit the puzzle pieces together without getting involved. Your mother was the same when she was young."

"I'm not an observer," Arni says. "I *am* involved in the puzzle pieces outside."

"You tell your father that? He knows you disagree with him?"

Arni gapes, stunned.

"Same, same." Meenafai pinches Arni's shoulder. "What does it mean to you, to disagree with him in your head? Your brother disagrees loudly at home, and does very little outside. And you do a lot outside, but very little at home. So here"—and she twists her wrist, splayed fingers and cupped palm facing up, toward Arni—"you are an observer."

Arni pouts as Meenafai walks away in her hobbled gait. *You're wrong,* she wants to tell the old woman, even though she knows Ma would glare at her. *I'm nothing like my mother.*

At first, it insults her, this idea that she isn't doing enough. Meenafai is being willfully ignorant; the murals in the streets are evidence of her hard work, of her care and involvement. But as she takes laps around the flat, insult turns to shame. She has never stood up to Baba, not the way Anurag has. Meenafai sees through her—sees she is a coward. She feels suddenly that she cannot stay in the apartment for another moment. Agitated, she waits for Baba to retreat to his bedroom before beelining for Sakshi's front door.

She complains about Meenafai's words while Sakshi's mother places a plate of parathas in front of them, to eat with athanu. Through the open windows, Arni can hear the cheers from streets away.

"I think she's trying to connect with you," Sakshi says, mouth full. "She sees you, and she thinks of your mother, and she thinks that's common ground."

"It's just frustrating because . . ." Arni pauses. "This feels bad to say."

Sakshi motions for her to continue, ripping another handful of paratha.

"If Vibha were here, no one would say I'm like my mother." The tempo of Arni's words increases. "If Meenafai saw Vibha, she would never look at me twice."

Sakshi pauses mid-chew. "I don't think that's true. She loves you."

Arni shakes her head, takes a sip of her water. "I can't do anything right. Anurag gets to do whatever he wants, and Vibha was good at everything she did, and I'm just . . . I'm just trying to do one thing right, you know? And no one cares."

"Your murals are amazing." Sakshi wraps her hand around Arni's forearm and pulses it. "I see what you're doing. I'm telling you, you're doing it right. You're brilliant."

"I want to deserve it, you know?"

Sakshi nods. "You always deserve their love."

Arni forces a smile and nods back. *Love, yes*, she thinks, but mostly—mostly she wants to be chosen. For Ma to have chosen—to now choose—her.

**That week, two short chits** from Anurag arrive—one to their parents and one to Arni.

*I heard about the murals cropping up in Porbandar*, the letter to Arni reads. *The students said you've been a help. Glad to see you found a way in. We're not stopping here, so keep it up.*

Arni sits on the floor of her room, back leaning against the closet's wooden doors, and clenches the paper in her fist. Only a handful of words from her brother, and already she is angry. She grits her teeth and then, still sitting, reaches over to rummage through her backpack for a pencil.

*YOUR PAINTINGS ARE CHANGING THE WORLD*, she scrawls beneath Anurag's message. *I AM SORRY FOR NOT BELIEVING IN YOU. VIBHA WOULD BE SO PROUD. YOU DESERVE.*

She can hear her father's voice rising through the wall, and she takes two deep breaths as though she can distance her own temper from Baba's. She hasn't read the telegram addressed to her parents yet, but she gets the sense Anurag has refused, again, to come home. That he is possibly packing his bags to follow these movements in other cities, where they've begun to crop up like little, inextinguishable fires.

It does not help that the news will arrive that evening about the celebrations in Ahmedabad and Baroda gone askew, the police firing on crowds, killing some and injuring many more. Baba must feel this violence in the air, all this distance away. When he yells about it, Arni stays in her room. Soon after, announcing herself with two soft knocks on the door, Meenafai slips wordlessly into the room and onto the second cot.

Arni had thought the yelling would end soon, Baba's short fuse quickly extinguished, but she can hear her mother's voice interrupt his rambling. She scoots to the closed door, listening.

Ma's voice, firm but gentle, finds its way toward her. "They have to be their own people," she is saying, and Baba's voice responds louder, more forcefully, "What do you know about being your own person?"

"I am more my own person than some will ever be, Suresh."

The sound of a slap, of Arni's quick inhale caught in her throat. She and her mother haven't spoken in days, not since she left the letter from Fiza on Ma's pillow while Baba was out for a walk, then left the house herself, unable to face Ma. When Arni had returned to her mother cooking at the stovetop, Ma's tone was cold as she said, without once looking over, "Why would you do this again? What do you not understand?" Arni had reddened, feeling shame—but she couldn't undo what she'd already done. How could she explain to her mother that it had been necessary? She understood now. She was willing, now armed with knowledge, to play accomplice.

She imagines her mother in the hallway, cheeks stinging and red, eyes tearing up. Nothing out of character for her father, no, but she aches for her mother all the same. She scoots back to the wall by her closet, far enough away that her parents' voices disappear, and she closes her eyes and waits.

# SEVENTEEN

S tay for a moment, here with me.

I lie awake at night sometimes, thinking about what it means that Arni was not yet sewn onto the tapestry at this time. How the consequences of Arni's decisions, and lack thereof, surpass what she knows. Her world was once so small, in the way all of our worlds are when we are children. Now it has opened up; it threatens to swallow her whole.

At this moment, without any assistance from her lineage, her art is barreling a movement forward. An important movement, one of the only times a student movement has been so successful, so powerful, in this country. And sure, she makes mistakes; she reads those letters and fights with her mother. She is, after all, just a girl.

I am interested in Arni as she was then—when the life in front of her is more real than the potential of that life held in the tapestry, precisely because the two are divorced. Everything she does, everything she contributes to, comes from her and her alone. Does she make good decisions? Is the work she does without the tapestry important? Is the change she catalyzes without the tapestry's power better than what she would have done if she had been sewn upon it?

Nadya, this is the other possibility for our child: never being sewn upon the tapestry, even if the choice exists. Leading a fulfilling life without it. Is Arni better off because she knows the power of her work, without wielding that which her ancestry offers her? Or is she worse off because it is denied to her, because she cannot make the difference in the world that she yearns to, while she is young? If she were your daughter—if she were my daughter, our daughter—what would we do? Which path would we guide her toward?

**Each night, Arni sleeps fitfully;** she wakes cranky. She hasn't spoken to Meenafai, not since they both listened as her father yelled at her mother. As he slapped her. She wonders if that moment solidified her as an observer.

She has played witness to her sister's death, to her brother's role in a larger movement, to her father's rage. What would Meenafai think of Arni if she knew about her most recent transgression—listening while a stranger read her mother's secrets aloud?

The weather begins to turn in March. Arni notices how the breeze coming off the ocean feels warmer, even if only by a handful of degrees. She knows Meenafai feels it, too, spending each morning with the windows open, her cigarette held half-inside, half-out. Soon, Arni thinks, it will be sticky again, the scant rain cleansing her murals from the rooftop canvas. Come July, monsoon season will arrive, rainy season in a desert. The thought of it satiates her.

When she was younger, she'd beg her father to take them to the hill stations, to see the lush green burst around her. Or to Dandi Beach, to see where Gandhi made salt out of sand, a story that most of the neighbor uncles can recite not from textbook memorizations but from lived memories. There was a point, eventually, where Baba snapped at her for all her begging. She hasn't asked her Baba for monsoon travel in years now.

She is not the only one who has missed it. On the third day, Meenafai says to her, "You children loved taking the train rides from here to my home, during monsoon."

"I still would," Arni says.

"Yes"—and Meenafai drags slowly on her cigarette—"I guess it's still possible."

Arni watches the ashes spill onto the sill and wonders what it would be like for her to pull out one of Bhavna's crumpled beedis, to smoke a cigarette alongside Meenafai. "I dreamt of Vibha last night," she says without meaning to.

"The people we love often visit us in our dreams," Meenafai says, matter-of-fact.

"It felt real," Arni says. She takes two steps toward her great-aunt. "It was like she held my hand but also like she wanted to show me something."

"You know, your mother, it was the same for her. Always thinking your grandmother was showing her something."

"Was she?" Arni asks without thinking. Watches, to see how Meenafai will respond, if she will share her mother's stories with her.

Meenafai shrugs. "They're not my dreams," she says. She points her cigarette at Arni. "You could stand to talk to your mother a little more, though."

"Right." Arni backs away slowly, turning as she reaches the hallway. She closes the bedroom door behind her and grabs the folded tapestry from its corner in her closet. She spreads it out fully on the bed.

*Focus*, she commands, but she forgets what the tapestry looks like as soon as she sees any part of it. Her fingertips trace the final figure.

There is a vibration in her chest, she feels, or maybe it is only her heart pounding loudly in the silence. This is Vibha, this figure. This is her sister, beckoning to her from a dream Arni doesn't fully remember.

She hasn't cried for Vibha in months; she has not felt anything, numb to grief. Suddenly, she feels apologetic. Apologized to. Arni falls to her knees in front of the black fabric of the tapestry, in front of the low cot on which she used to curl next to her sister. The tears rush from within her.

**Arni's memory here grows fuzzy.** I turn to Amla for answers: Does the telegram from Anurag arrive in the morning or the afternoon? Does she take the chit of paper straight to Suresh, or does she read it first? What, exactly, are those words?

But these details, they don't feel like they matter. They're overshadowed by a more violent silhouette.

At first, a spattering of Congress Party assembly members resign, but the number quickly grows: ninety-five resign by March. National public figures begin speaking of the movement, and Arni soaks in the contrast between her family's flat and Sakshi's: where her father is tense and quiet as one national leader begins an indefinite fast in support of the call to dissolve the entire assembly, Sakshi's father whoops with joy. Here is support for the movement's demands. Here is support for a new, more equitable Gujarat—one where politicians have to answer to the masses for corruption, inflation, unemployment. For allowing a rampant black market.

On March 16, the assembly is finally dissolved. The students are victorious. Bhavna shares moonshine with Arni on the rooftop.

Anurag's subsequent telegram is direct: The work of the Navnirman Andolan is nearly done, but a similar fire in Bihar has now been lit. He'll come home, briefly, but he plans to follow this work where it takes him. He wants to follow one of the movement's leaders, JP Narayan, onto the next.

Baba throws a vase across the bedroom; Arni and Amla hear it shatter from the kitchen. Amla calls down the hall—"You okay, ji?"—but the bedroom door slams shut. Daughter looks at mother, and mother looks at daughter; Amla quietly returns to the vegetables she's chopping on the kitchen table and motions for Arni to do the same.

Their piles grow, red and green bell peppers julienned, zucchini and brinjal diced and piled onto plates. Arni isn't even sure what her mother is making, and the fact is that Amla has no idea either—she mainly knows to keep her hands busy when Suresh is angry; to avoid the urge to fix whatever it is that has been made wrong, an urge compounded by the possibility of ancestral solution.


**A few days later** and a few hours before Anurag arrives home, Meenafai asks Amla, softly, "You've stayed in touch with Fiza?" She stands at the flat's entryway. Her nails tap on the mail pile as she points to the topmost envelope.

Amla nods, sipping her jeera pani. The dishes in the sink are beginning to pile up; the fruit basket is near empty. She ignores them both. Through the kitchen doorway, she can see Suresh adjusting the radio dials, and she holds out her hand for the envelope. "With so many places closed and the curfew, it's nice to have someone to talk to."

"Mmm." Meenafai weighs the envelope in her left palm. "Lots to say."

Amla narrows her eyes. "You have an opinion you want to share?"

"No, no." Meenafai hands the envelope over. "You ever wonder what life would have been like if we'd all stayed in Karachi?" Her voice is weathered and shaky—more than Amla can chalk up to age.

"I imagine that life all the time."

"Me, too." Meenafai smiles at her—a toothless, gummy smile— and Amla thinks of all the years that have passed, all the stories they've shared. "If only."

"It was inevitable that it would end," Amla says. "I have to believe that."

"You would've left when my husband did in '48, if you hadn't already." Meenafai waves at the air, as though to brush away the tragedy of it. "Sometimes I think about what we all left behind. The furniture."

"The swing," Amla adds.

"The jewelry."

"So many of Ba's saris."

"The deeds to the mithai shops."

Amla pauses. "The friends, though," she says, even though she only ever misses the one.

Meenafai nods knowingly. "The family."

"I miss that feeling of being loved, of being surrounded by it," Amla says. "Ba's love, Bapu's love. Every day, I just went from one place to the next, wherever they would be."

"My love." Meenafai laughs.

"Yes, your love." Amla raises her glass to her aunt. "All of it."

Meenafai's face turns soft, gentle. She pauses before she says her next words. "Fiza's love."

Amla sips her water, her eyes closing. "Yes," she says. "I miss all of it."

**This is the mood** Amla is in when Anurag arrives home, when she lays the plates at each setting, all four of them, the empty fifth chair sitting ghostlike until she remembers Meenafai will take Vibha's seat. She adds the dishware: the steel plate of rotli, the large bowl of tur dal. Store-bought athanu.

She's thinking maybe she should have sent Arni to get Anurag today, maybe she shouldn't have sent Suresh, when the apartment door opens and the two men enter silently. They suck the air out of the space; she hates that they take up so much and give so little; it feels like the dal loses its steam and the kachumber wilts in their presence.

"Arni," she calls, and the girl enters the room, also quiet. Meenafai walks in behind her silently, and Amla is filled with the urge to bang her fist down on the table and demand attention. She feels like she is going mad, like no one has paid any attention to this meal she's setting before them; a meal she didn't even want to cook, but here it is, here is what it means to be in this family, to be this wife, this mother.

When they sit, Amla looks at them expectantly. Suresh bows his head to pray, and Amla meets Arni's eyes, neither of them interested in pretending. Paint sits crusty on the border of Arni's palms, and Amla resists the desire to ask her to wash up.

Instead she says, "Do you like the nutmeg in—"

"I don't understand why you think this country doesn't need a massive overhaul," Anurag bursts out, and Amla shakes her head because, of course, all possibility of a peaceful dinner is now lost.

"*I* don't understand why you think there is anything different between what Congress is offering and what your goddamn Andolan is peddling." Suresh's hands are out, his eyes widening.

"Men are not *gods*, and Gandhi was just one person who was flawed, like—"

"Like all of us, yes! But the best of—"

Amla feels herself shaking, seething, and she picks her rotli apart with both hands until it is a meal more suitable for a bird.

Her son carries the same energy forward. "You think so? You think the best thing for us was to be cut in half, our left and our right separated like—"

"You think you could manage an entire nation's shift away from imperialism better than—"

"Fuck, Baba," Anurag says. Amla anticipates the slam of the door before he even stands, gets to the knob, before the door is even open.

A stunned silence sits in the vacuum of Anurag's exit. When it breaks, the voice that cuts through is unexpected.

"Ma can't even go home, Baba."

Amla looks up, and there is her daughter—*Oh, don't make him angry with you, jaan, don't become his target*—and Arni repeats herself, slower and more directly toward her father: "Ma can't go home."

"Arni," Amla whispers.

"I'm tired of observing," Arni says, and Amla sees Meenafai's quiet nod, inconspicuous. "I'm tired of you not seeing the work that people are doing to be heard in this country, by this government."

"Quiet," Suresh says, but Arni cannot contain her momentum.

"Anurag was right"—and she gestures toward the door—"everyone is a politician, and no one is a god." She turns to her father. "But that doesn't mean that a system like this one, that keeps people from being able to survive, is . . . is right. Just because you're on top—head sheep, Baba," she says. "You can't see it, but no one deserves more or less than anyone else. Making it here, it's just luck and what someone powerful once decided you're born with: your money and your caste."

*I was wrong*, Amla thinks, *there was air left in this room*—and now it has truly been sucked out, and she refuses to look at anyone. Baba puts down his spoon; steel slides against steel, and Amla shivers at the sound. She wonders if Arni is proud of herself. Amla—Amla is.

"Who gave you permission to speak like that?" Suresh finally says, his voice quiet and seething. "Your husband? No, you seem to still be in my house. Your father?" His tone is biting. "I don't remember doing that."

"Suresh—"

"You, too," he says, vicious. "No more from you." He turns back to Arni. "You think you know everything, hm? Your college, your art. I am not *blind*. I indulged you—I took you to Ahmedabad when you asked, I let you traipse around with the manager's daughter like we are all the same—but no more."

The expression on Arni's face—she is terrified, Amla realizes. Arni has not had her father's anger targeted on her like this before, had not thought this far ahead when she spoke up.

"You are a disappointment," Suresh continues. "You and your brother—utter wastes. I will not spend a single paisa on tuition for college. We will have you married within the year. You will be out of this house, and I will be rid of you."

Amla stands with a start. "Suresh, no," she says, and then he is turning toward her, and she feels the sting of the slap on her cheek before she registers the sight of his arm moving. Even as her left hand touches her face, she repeats softly, "Suresh."

"And who are you?" he throws at her, blinking rapidly. "Talking to me like this? Disrespecting me, in my own house? My word is final. My word has always been final."

He shoves the table, the cups and bowls falling over, the plates rattling, and when he storms into the bedroom, Amla touches her hand quickly to Arni's shoulder. "I will not let this happen to you," she whispers, "I promise," and she scoots out of her chair quietly, relieved Arni is sitting at the table, yes, staying at the table, unharmed and safe, yes—this, it is all she asks for, all that she needs to be a good mother.

. . .

He tears through their bedroom, the sound of his anger reverberating through his rampage. Amla follows him into the room as the lamp hits the floor and shatters, asks him to stop as he sweeps an arm over the wardrobe and scatters the jewelry that had sat atop it. The teakwood box full of Fiza's letters had been sitting on Amla's side table, and she stares for a moment as those envelopes scatter. *Do not focus there*, she thinks. *Do not let him know.* So she makes herself ask what is happening, and then she asks again louder, and as she tries to grab his shoulder to make him pause, he shakes her off his arm like an insect. He pushes her away so hard she staggers back until her spine is against the wall.

Arni is at the open doorway. Amla shakes her head. *Leave.*

Arni can't imagine leaving. She stays.

"The reason our daughter has no shame," Baba says, his voice soft, dangerous, "is because you never taught her to have any. To know how to talk, when to talk."

Now Arni steps into the bedroom, into the space between her father and her mother. She cannot look at his face, focusing only on the faint lines of his gray button-up. The sweat stains at his chest, his armpits, his throat.

She is square between them. "Baba," she says.

"This is not your business," he hisses. "Get out."

"Baba, take a moment—"

"You have no place—"

"—calm down and have a civil—"

"—an embarrassment of a wife—"

"Baba!"

"I always knew you were the wrong decision," he says over Arni's shoulder. His spit lands on Amla's collarbone. "No family, no history, no home. A woman full of secrets." He looks at Arni, then. "Why are you not gone?"

Arni feels her mother's hand on her back, telling her it's okay to leave. She roots her heels into the floor instead. After everything, she must do this. "I am not letting you hurt my mother."

Baba laughs before he slaps her. "Your mother?" he says. "My wife, first." And then Arni's cheek is burning, her jaw swinging as though on a delay. He pushes her out of the way, and there is no one to protect Amla, not even Arni grasping desperately at her father's pants, his legs, his shoes. He is kicking, fists swinging, and Arni looks up at her mother just once, sees the blood at her lips, her father's hand at her mother's neck. And then she hears Meenafai at the apartment front door, calling out to the neighbor uncles, yelling for help. And when the uncles arrive, their wordless movements cut through the thick apartment air, their bodies a barrier between Baba's limbs and Amla's curled-up body.

They have to drag Baba away.

**Arni doesn't know** where they take Baba. She doesn't know where Anurag is, whether or not he's been filled in. She doesn't care. She sits on the couch where her mother lies, dozing in and out of sleep. Bruises are beginning to appear, splotchy, across her mother's body— the outsides of her arms gripped by an invisible hand; her throat, the dip in her collarbone, too, the pattern rising and falling as she breathes.

Meenafai checks in on them now and then, her head peeking in from the kitchen. "Chai?" she asks Arni, and it's not a question, and in minutes they are seated around Amla's sleeping body. Arni blows cool air onto her cup; the steam feels cleansing on her cheeks.

"He is always like this?" Meenafai asks. Her voice is low but not soft.

"Sometimes."

"She has put up with this?"

"It's not . . ." Arni falters. "I should have done something, sooner."

"You're just a child, jaan," Meenafai says, her eyes unfocused, staring at the opposite wall. "Just a child."

She is, Arni thinks, and she isn't.

In the silence that follows, she sees her world as a kaleidoscope, image after refracted image. What is she *doing*—what is she really doing, what doors is she knocking at, what marches are her feet joining like a metronome, left-right-left, sign in hand? Her excuse, Baba's rule, has staled. His words mean nothing.

She looks up at her great-aunt, who looks back at her without movement. All the words they haven't said hang, thick, in the air between them. "I'm gonna . . ." Arni says, and without explanation she goes back into her parents' room, untouched since Baba had been forced out, since she and Meenafai had coaxed her mother onto the sofa.

The jewelry is still scattered across the floor—an inheritance, once, broken petals now. The teakwood box, which had been sitting on her mother's side table—now in the corner, letters slipped out of chronology. Arni collects them carefully. She uses color, their age, to coax the letters back into order.

*I will not continue to be the type of daughter I have been*, she tells herself. *I will be better, for Ma.*

**Later, they clean the flat** as Ma sleeps, and the motions come back to Arni like muscle memory, from the days after Vibha's passing. Arni has to remind herself no one has died. The women dig the house slippers out from their hiding places beneath beds and under wardrobes. "I'll take this side"—she directs Meenafai leftward, now— "and you take this one."

They move systematically, mirror images. Every now and then, Arni asks Meenafai questions—*What was it like, being married to a priest? How often do your children come back from the city? Would I like Karachi?*—and she appreciates that Meenafai's answers seem thoughtful, even as she interrupts them to grunt when reaching for a higher shelf or squatting to sweep beneath the sofa.

Every now and then, Arni pauses her sweeping and watches her. She can see her mother in this woman; in the way they both move fluidly, in their composure. In the way their hair, long and thinning, wraps neatly into a braided bun at the nape of their necks.

"It is too easy to see life as before and after," Meenafai says when they are nearly three-quarters through their individual sides. "Sometimes I wish I could go back. Sometimes I wish I'd died with my brother, and then with my husband."

Arni resists the urge to argue it away, to say, *You don't mean that.* She reminds herself to be soft, to listen.

"No one knows more than your mother what it's like to live with regret," the old woman continues. "Not even me."

The two edge closer to each other, short brooms in hand. Arni is folded over herself, reaching wide for the dirty corners of the doorway, and Meenafai taps her spine. Arni stands up.

"We must take care of her," Meenafai says. She is so close that Arni can breathe in her smell—cigarettes, sweat, the minty balm she rubs into her joints. "She will give up everything for the people she loves."

"Like what?" Arni asks. She hesitates, and then she clutches at the opportunity. "Like this gift?"

"She kept it a secret from you, I get that."

Arni pauses. When the words come, they are quiet and heated. "Do you know what it's like to always be second choice?" she asks. Her voice catches. "To know you didn't deserve it at first? That it's only yours because someone you love died?"

Meenafai sighs. "Don't make the mistake your mother did."

"Which one is that?" Arni demands.

"Don't let one moment ruin your life." Meenafai rubs her eyes and forehead in large circular motions. "If you're going to base every decision on that single emotion, you're giving in to doubt and pain and everything that you don't deserve. You're letting it take your life. Don't do that."

Arni bites her knuckles, her hands formed into fists she hadn't noticed.

"You're enough, jaan. Nothing else matters."


**Ma awakes—Amla awakes**—out of a nightmare.

*Do you know what it's like to always be second choice?* Arni's words had slipped through her slumber. Her dreams were colored with these thoughts—she grasped for the hands of her mother over and again. Every time, she fell short. Her fingers curled around air.

It is dark. Amla removes the blanket that's been placed on her, folding it carefully. When she strains, she can make out the faint voices of Meenafai and Arni in another room—in her own, probably. What scene has been left behind, she wonders, what wounds does the room carry—but she has no desire to see those, not yet. She walks softly to the kitchen. On tiptoes and with splayed fingers, she feels around the top cabinets for a glass jar of dried leaves. Methi, so stale it barely smells anymore. She uncaps its lid and slowly pours the herb through her open fingers until a small brass key lands in her palm.

*Anything for the people you love*, she reminds herself. *This is who you are.*

She listens again for the sounds of the women who love her, and makes her way quietly to her daughter's room. She unlocks the drawer to those shameful paintings, the ones she won't share, and stares at them until the colors blur. Until she is crying, and she isn't sure if the tears are from not blinking or from somewhere else, deep in her memory. She takes the tapestry from its place in Arni's closet and holds it gently in her hands. All these collected items—the paintings, the tapestry, a scavenged needle and thread—help Amla's breathing slow. She sits on the bed and asks—Arni, Vibha, maybe, or Chandini, or even the first mother who she can barely remember, someone, anyone—for forgiveness.

Slowly, the weight of the lineage leaves her body.


**In the morning,** Amla waits for Arni at the kitchen table.

"You should still be sleeping," her daughter says when Amla places a pile of thepla in front of her. A cluster of sliced fruit already sits on a steel plate next to an assortment of store-bought athanu. Arni reaches for a ripe segment of sitaphal. "You don't have to do this today, Ma."

"I wanted to get some time with you, before Meenafai wakes up." Amla lowers herself slowly into the seat across from Arni, trying her hardest not to wince. Her joints feel as tender as the bruises. "I need to tell you something."

Arni waits, her face unreadable. Amla takes the tapestry from the seat next to her and places it on the clean edge of the table, the seats that Anurag and Suresh would have occupied had they been home. The silence of this moment is filled with the sound of the cars outside, the buzzing of a fly.

"I am sorry for denying you," Amla whispers. "I am sorry for never telling you, for choosing Vibha before you."

"Ma," Arni says, but she doesn't have the words to follow this.

"I thought I was right, to give this gift to Vibha, at that age. I thought I could teach her the way I'd want to have been taught." She shakes her head. "More than that, though, I was so focused on Vibha that I didn't see you. Your strength. Your core." She taps at her own heart. "I should have known you, and I didn't try."

Arni reaches her hand across the table, and Amla takes it. "I am the one," she says. "I am the one who is sorry."

"Arni," Amla says. "Listen to me. You deserve this. And I will teach you, and I will hold your hand if you want me to. I will share it with you, all of it."

Arni takes the tapestry and hugs its weight against her body. When they move to the living room and Arni unfolds it on the living room floor, just as they had done months ago, she can actually observe it. She sees Vibha in the figure before hers—a young girl of ten—understands the two of them together on the tapestry as two sisters in a row. She doesn't know where this understanding comes from, but when she looks at the other figures, she feels instinctively their relationships. Here are cousins; here are sisters. Here are rows of mothers and daughters. She lingers on the image of her mother, two figures before her own, also a child.

The bottom of the tapestry is empty. There is space for the generations yet to come.

Arni can feel the burden, the weight, descending upon her shoulders. She sees the empty rows in the black cloth after her own figure and understands that there is no fear of time running out. She understands that whatever this gift will mean for her has already begun to take root.

"I want to deserve this," Arni says, and when her mother hugs her, their tears mix on each other's cheeks.

"You do," Amla says, and she laughs into her daughter's hair. "Of course you do, my jaan. Thank you."

**Here, an afternoon spent** running through Amla's favorite memories gifted from each woman on the tapestry. Here, Amla recounting the years between her father's death and her marriage, her daughter's eyes revealing a new understanding of her. Here, the drawer of watercolors unlocked, paintings that show the sun peeking out after a length of monsoon; fields of bajri swaying, ready for harvest; Meenafai imagined one more time in the sitting room, both of them with silver hair, two old women holding each other's hands, foreheads close, secrets whispered. And eventually, not yet but one day soon, Amla will share the worst of the stories—of Bapu's death, Amla's only warning to her daughter.

There is one painting, her most recent, which Amla saves for herself. The first one in a long time that she has made, accompanied. She reminds herself that she does not have to share every secret.

One afternoon, soon after she is embroidered onto the tapestry, Arni returns to the roof. The sun is out, the ocean breeze beckons her up. Sakshi is there, and so are the college students, and Arni smiles but keeps going—her bag is heavy with new paints. She feels it in the tendons of her arm, the grip of her fingertips. She feels pulled to paint, and to paint now. She stretches her arms over her head, spine aligning.

Anurag had returned home the day after it all happened, fuming, and when he determined there was nothing he could do—no good at caretaking, or cooking, or listening to the women of the apartment share histories—he returned to the usual practice of the men in their apartment: smoking cigarettes and drinking Indian bourbon. He starts talking and talking, about the next train to Bihar.

Arni finds herself unbothered by him. He is not the center of her orbit; he wasn't there when Baba released his fury on their mother. He argued with Baba, sure, about politics and philosophy, but he hadn't been present when Ma needed him to stand up for her; and Arni understands now that this is something she can do. Something she has done.

And then there's this gift, this heat in her veins. Arni is separate from Anurag now in a way he will never understand. Her life is not just her own, but that of everyone who's come before her—she's listening to her mother, and those mothers before her—she sees this now.

She places the bag down with a clank and prepares a folded old towel for her legs. She starts at the lower-left corner of her favorite spot, that outer wall of the roof staircase. She starts with a mix of gray and white—a snowy mix, one she's only known in movies.

The mural takes hours, interrupted twice by Meenafai, who smokes a cigarette so close to fresh-drying laundry that some of the building women send over snarky looks. "Let them," she says, "I'm too old for nazar," and Arni laughs but barely listens. Something about this moment feels different from every other time she has painted.

She's led by her muscles more than her eyes, the familiar strain in them as she reaches over diagonally, her limbs like those of a dancer. She could close her eyes, she thinks; she could paint without ever knowing. Mentally, she feels drunk; physically, more coordinated than ever.

She is led.

When she opens her eyes, when her kurti is spotted with paint and her hair is oily with sweat, the mural isn't something she's ever seen before. A woman peeks out of an apartment window, the street gutters below packed with snow. A yellow taxi, not a rickshaw; the outline of twin skyscrapers in the distance. The woman is smiling, and Arni smiles back at her. For a moment, she thinks she can smell it, this future.

Her blood whispers to her from every vein in her body. *You can have this*, she thinks to herself, unable to decipher whether the motivation comes from within or from the lineage calling to her. *This, you get to have.*

# EIGHTEEN

I smile as I tell you this part.

"What's happening?" you ask. "What comes next?"

"This is it," I say. "This is how Arni grows into the woman I recognize. My mother." Her memories make it easy for me to be proud of her.

Baba would have returned—I'd put money on it—had Meenafai not stayed around. She guards the front door with a straw broom when she's suspicious; she befriends Sakshi's parents, asking them to let her know of the slightest possibility of Baba heaving up those stairs. She tells any neighbor who'll listen that she's *out to get him*, whatever that means. Arni finds out later that her father begins sleeping on the cot of one cousin or another, three blocks closer to the chowpatty. She doesn't mean to, but she still looks for him every time she takes the long way to the market. What he would look like in this crowd, what he would say to her if they happened to stand, toe-to-toe like adults, across from each other. Would he be able to tell that something about her has changed? Would he sense the power in her that he had been so frightened of in her mother?

The women's lives are immediately harder. Ma sells a considerable amount of their furniture, even as she takes up work, and Meenafai starts housekeeping, too.

"This might be the most we ever have," Ma says to Arni, gesturing around their empty apartment.

Arni looks around at all this space, all the memories she has built up here.

"This is the least we will ever have," Arni says, and she squeezes her mother's arm, "even if we move to a place where we have nothing."

At Sakshi's apartment, Arni tries to forget the wooden crate of paint cans and brushes that sits growing dust in the corner of her closet. She's already emptied the canvas tote bag she'd been lugging to the beachside storefronts, and even that had felt like mourning. Maybe she should pour the cans out, run the liquid down the rooftop and the sides of the building into the street below. But no, an animal might lap it up, a cat or a calf or a dog, like the one Vibha had brought home.

"Did you ever think of going to Bihar?" Sakshi asks as her mother puts two cups of dark chai in front of them. "Doing what your brother couldn't?"

This is also a fact of their lives now: Anurag moping around the apartment building. He didn't leave for Bihar, conviction eluding him; the movement continued without him. That realization is the hardest for him, that it could go on. Arni understood that Anurag had liked the idea of being a martyr, of propelling a cause. Maybe that was why he never pushed Arni more—he didn't like her eating up space that he thought was his.

And now he's at home, and Arni thinks he's withering somehow, growing smaller as Ma takes on more and more to ensure the continuation of their household. He spends his afternoons going from apartment to apartment, talking to different uncles about nothing. When Meenafai nudges him about getting a job, he daydreams aloud about being an academic, about the value of spurring some change or another by invigorating future students, but he doesn't make the move back to Ahmedabad to finish university.

"Sometimes I wish I were more impulsive," Sakshi continues. "Like you." She leans back and Arni traces her friend's eyes, the curls framing her face. "I know he didn't do it, but do you think you could?"

"Leave?"

"Move to a new city and fight for people you've never met before. Start your whole life all over again."

Arni picks at the stray threads of her shirt collar. She thinks of the tapestry, tucked among her pants in the closet. "I can't imagine it," she says, and she imagines the weight of her mother's every stitch.

Will her life be like this, divided in halves—before the tapestry, and after its integration into her life? Will it be the same halving forced by Vibha's death, is it inevitable that it must be; is that how all change works really, everything always interconnected—everything at once?

Arni wonders what more the universe will fold into this moment. She leaves Sakshi's flat deep in thought. When she's back in her own room, she examines the tapestry's figures, the colors unfaded despite time. The embroidery is perfect even as the edges of the cloth feel at risk of pulling themselves apart. She twists those soft edges between her index finger and thumb. She remembers how she once thought to burn the tapestry, before she ever understood what it was. She knows now there is little she can do to destroy this, even if she wanted to. No lineage can be so easily erased.

The second week of June 1975, they finally hold elections for the new state government, ending a year of President's Rule in Gujarat after all the resignations, and on June 12, the same day that the results are declared, Prime Minister Indira Gandhi is found guilty of tampering with machinery to win more votes in her election. She is allowed to continue to serve in her role while she launches an appeal, but this allowance is a mistake; two weeks later she has suspended civil liberties, granted herself extraordinary powers, and canceled statewide elections. The 1975 Emergency is declared.

JP Narayan, the man Anurag had wished to follow to Bihar, stands at a protest in Delhi and urges the people to reject the orders of government if they are unethical and immoral. Even Amla recognizes these words—this echo of the same statement made during the independence movement decades ago.

Arni will never know what all the movement's work would've led to. The new state government that she and Anurag and so many others hoped to create in the people's image is now considered dissident, anti-Indira: thousands of protesters will be arrested, including JP Narayan. The prime minister's extraordinary powers grant her the cover to detain, arrest—to torture. To destroy homes in the name of beautification. To censor the press and limit constitutional freedoms. Just like that, their dreams of a new, more equitable Gujarat dissolve.

Arni sits with her mother in their living room as the news comes in. This is a new balance for them, Arni holding power and being careful in its use, and Amla offering what guidance she has. What if Arni paints a peaceful street in Delhi?

"But you can't guarantee this timing," Amla points out.

What does peace look like, Arni wonders; what can she do to guarantee people's safety?

"Specific paintings of specific people at specific moments," Amla says. "Otherwise, nothing is bound in time."

Is Amla thinking of her own watercolors, the ones that haven't come to light yet? Her point is clear, but Arni still spends every Friday morning on that parlor seat with her mother, offering new suggestions for change and listening as her mother pokes a hole in each one. In the afternoons, she joins Sakshi and Bhavna and the other students on the rooftop, listening and waiting and trying to do whatever she can, even if it's only marking a single graffitied line on a metal door.

Meanwhile, Anurag fumes and stomps and declares softly that he isn't supposed to be in Porbandar. He wants to be elsewhere, and yet fear tinges his voice. Meenafai remarks quietly to Amla, "Don't worry about him. It's all talk," and it's true. There are reports of police and the government torturing political prisoners, of the prime minister's unelected son leading systematic forced sterilization of men, many of whom are Muslim, caste-oppressed, Adivasi. Anurag is nothing like those men, with his recognizable caste-privileged surname and no immediate need to be on the street protesting. He will stay safe, in the comfort of their slowly emptying flat.

Decades later, as Arni witnesses him age over a laptop screen, she'll wonder if she should have done more for him. Should she have painted a mural of her brother satisfied? Should she have given him a passion? Had she painted a mural of their intertwined lives, might he have found something brighter than reciting litanies to anyone who'll listen about what it was like to be part of the 1974 movement?

Nothing to be done about this now, no. Even if Arni had continued to paint all that time later, she would not have painted her brother with more power. She understands, now, the intoxication it had given him. She does not feel that would be safe.

**Arni dedicates herself** to her studies throughout the Emergency. She attends a women's college—Anurag finds sales work to support their mother and great-aunt—and then she receives a postgraduate fellowship in the United States. It is Vibha's wedding dowry, long stockpiled from years of Baba's government salary, an amount Amla has refused to pull from, that ensures those mornings of physics homework with Sakshi pay off, that she will be able to leave and forge her future.

The night before she leaves, her trunk already packed, Arni shifts her weight from one foot to the other in front of her empty valise. She packs her favorite long dresses first, the olive one with draping sleeves and the khaki one with buttons lined from breast to calf. The high-waisted jeans that remind her of Bhavna. Then she folds in the salwar kameezes she'd taken from her mother's closet when she was sixteen or seventeen, the ones thin enough to carry her through the monsoon season, and then her sandals, the dupattas she could throw on and match with anything, her favorite earrings, a single sari once intended for Vibha, and then the bag is nearly full—and she considers it: leaving the tapestry behind.

She doesn't hold the same anger she did when she was fifteen. Still quick to snap back in a debate with her friends, yes, but not the same creature. She doesn't know if she grew up because she was going to all along or because the tapestry forced her to.

*Let me leave this with you, Ma,* she imagines saying. *Take back this thing that is so important to you.*

She holds it in her hands, ready to stuff it into the cabinet with the other clothes she is leaving at home. Her thumbs make little circles on the rough fabric.

When Ma raps her knuckles on the door, Arni holds the tapestry up. "Another move," she says.

Ma looks like she wants to take the fabric from Arni, but settles instead for touching its top fold with one hand. "It's been through rougher ones than this."

*I'm sorry we didn't get to have it all earlier, Ma,* Arni imagines saying in that moment. *I'm sorry I was so stubborn.*

*We have the rest of our lives to make time, don't we?*

"You have to visit me," she says instead, and Ma nods, eyes brimming with tears. "You don't have to bring Anurag with you. I'll always meet you at the airport."

Her mother is weeping now. Arni kisses Ma's cheeks, and then she folds the tapestry into her valise so it is nestled at the very top edge. She leaves Ma outside the apartment, taking a taxi to the rail station to the airport to America. As she breathes in the bodies of the other women in that sweaty carriage, she keeps her hand firm on the suitcase. Maybe she's imagined it—she must have, she must have—but she could swear the tapestry grows warm against her palm.

**Oh, I should tell** you about that first winter, 1981, when my mother— when Arni—is in Brooklyn. You'd laugh if you could see how she tried to navigate it. She didn't know, you know? The way the air would be cold enough to scrape against the roof of her mouth as she breathes in. She'd never chapped her skin like this, and she watches with horror as it peels off her face, scratchy flakes on her cheeks and the tip of her nose. You and I sitting here, at this edge of Bed-Stuy— look at this cycle. How we return. So strange, this lineage.

That winter, Arni wonders how a place meant to be such an *answer,* such a *life,* can be so alien and dangerous. She wraps her scarf around her mouth; around her ears; around her neck and torso. She spends so much money that winter on things she doesn't know enough about to choose between. Like mittens and gloves—is there a warmth differential between the two? She buys a neck gaiter because the storekeeper promises its fleece won't rub her neck raw, but she can't manage to keep it tucked over her chin. It droops off her mouth the moment she's walked a few meters, and eventually it is tossed into a pile in the corner of her bedroom along with other now-unwearables: the thin cotton kurtis she brought from home, made of the most sweat-absorbent fabric; her mojari, which would be soiled if she wore them in the slushy streets and do nothing anyway to keep her feet warm; and her jewelry boxes, filled with dangling earrings that now get caught on her scarf, nearly ripping her ear off when she unwinds it from her neck.

She feels so alone, too. She wants to walk downstairs and talk to Sakshi. She wants to call her mother more often, but it's so expensive. She cooks in her apartment and pretends they're there—chats with them, has full conversations with no one.

When she sees the ad for an apartment in Jackson Heights, she jumps on it. For weeks now, at night, she has been dreaming of grocery stores with familiar vegetables, of store clerks who call eggplants brinjal. Here it is, her entrypoint to Queens, to a growing Little India. She actually squeals in the coffee shop—the barista sends her an alarmed look—and she tears a phone number slip off the corkboard, and then she tears off another just in case. She calls from the pay phone outside, stepping in place to keep her blood circulating in the cold.

"Please," she says in English, and then in Gujarati, in rougher Hindi, she says, "I need this."

The family renting to her has a small grocery near Seventy-Fourth Street. They have an extra room, they tell her, because their son is in graduate school. They'd be proud to have a university woman fill it in the meantime. Arni practices her Hindi to herself the entire subway ride, childishly wanting to impress them. This is the closest she's gotten to home in months.

But she doesn't need to: they're Gujarati, too, by way of Uganda and Tanzania. They have family in Surat, they say; has she been? They ask her about Porbandar and Ahmedabad, and she asks them about Dar, and they wonder if their nephews might have gone to school with Anurag ten years ago. Arni breathes a sigh of relief as the woman places a kettle of chai in the center of the table. She stretches in her rattan chair and feels her chest open.

That day, when she hands her envelope of cash over to these people she barely knows, who will be more important to her—to me—than she realizes, it is sunny. She is thankful for this, for the days it is so cold that there are no clouds. Wearing sunglasses feels like a blessing, like a way to pretend that this new climate isn't so bad. Sometimes she sits at her window and puts them on and watches the people outside, people who are so much more at ease in these surroundings than she is, and she pretends she is like them: in the sun, warm, comfortable. She pretends she belongs.

**In class and at coffee shops,** she is startled by reminders of a life left behind. Sometimes she sees Sakshi in the brown woman scurrying past her in the university hallway, books clutched to her chest. At first Arni had searched the woman's eyes for a glimmer of recognition, the desire for connection in this unrelenting city. Even later, when they pass each other with eyes glued to the tiled floors, Arni feels the air shift between them. The woman may not know it, might not acknowledge it, but Arni feels less alone knowing she is there.

She joins a collective in the city, mostly labor organizing. In the open room that constitutes their office and gathering space, Arni creates copies of prints made by another artist. She hasn't told anyone about those murals from when she was young; she feels more useful this way, learning and listening and contributing in small, considered ways. In each of the women at the collective who speak up, she sees Bhavna, even as she realizes she never knew enough about her.

She tries to describe Bhavna to the others, but always comes back to the small moments between the two of them: Bhavna handing her a beedi, meeting her after curfew, guiding her painting at the storefronts. She wants to follow Bhavna's example, the other women's examples. She understands the difference now, that there are times when observing is cowardice, yes, but that observing is also a form of action, of defiance—and the other side of this coin, as well: that taking action is sometimes arrogance, and other times absolutely necessary. The trick is in knowing which, when.

And so she does not bristle at small tasks; she savors every moment of printmaking, signmaking. When she looks back on being fifteen, when she remembers how Anurag looked down on their mother and how Arni herself had judged Amla, Arni has to remind herself that she was young. She did not understand then the strength her mother had. That not only visible things carry worth, carry importance.

Standing on that brown, flat carpet, with the hum of the copy machine filling the room, she imagines she has secret cousins, unknown ancestors on the other side of the world, who are more deserving of a gift like the one she's received. Who not only trust themselves to make the right choices, but actually do, over and again.

Maybe they are siblings to her in movement work, creating murals that facilitate change without invoking ancestral power. Maybe they are free from the trauma that haunted her mother, with paintings that never backfire so terribly. To Arni, it feels wrong for her to try to use the gift. All of her work reminds her that she does not know enough about the world to design it, alter it. She is grateful, simply, for the histories.

She wonders about the existence of sister-tapestries to this one. How they came to be. Maybe some have burn marks or peeling threads; maybe their colors glisten and dazzle just like this one. Hers sits in the trunk that used to belong to her mother, which she lugs through airports in London and New York. Once, a turbaned taxi driver sizes the trunk up and asks if she is Sindhi. She shakes her head no, and then regrets it, and she shrugs her shoulders as though to say maybe. "Mostly Gujarati," she says, and the Sikh man nods, and he helps her unload it from the cab with a little extra care.

Over her lifetime, she will feel alienated from this identity. She will wonder if anyone else remembers those student uprisings in 1974, if they will be anything but a blip on the next generation's understanding. Being a part of it made her feel Gujarati, she thinks, but everything that comes after lets her down. The vacuum after the 1975 Emergency lays the foundation for a political party rooted in Hindu nationalism. Anurag is upset about the student movements being undone, that no one will remember what they accomplished; Arni is upset about what this new foundation implies about her people, her community's values and beliefs—who they believe deserves to be considered *their people*. The gap between the two siblings grows into a gulf.

She thinks about how she is alive in New York City right now, how she is able to afford her life—her father's money, her surnames, her histories—and she wonders about those other women, the ones she imagines with tapestries of their own. The ones who may have more at stake than she does, who need their tapestry to survive.

*Not having to paint is a luxury*, she thinks, passing out printed pages to canvassers as they prepare for another local election. She will be up late that night, copying these same pages again for new volunteers tomorrow morning. *These are the worlds I create.*

**The next winter,** Ma sends Arni a trunk of items that she's held on to for too long. *My youth*, the note inside reads. *Yours, should you want it.*

Arni starts to wear her mother's jewelry around the house, placing rings on her fingers and tikas on her forehead, watching the way her hair bundles with the weight. A cotton robe hangs loosely on her thin frame. She tries rouge to imagine her mother's youth; she wishes she had her mother's eyes. When she stares at herself in the mirror, her face is nothing like her mother's.

This sadness only makes her want to wear her mother's shoes, clothes, even more. She tries on the blouses that barely stay on velvety hangers, the ones in the zipped bags beneath the bed. She feels the spaces of breast cups larger than hers sewn into the fabric. She knows the blouses will never look as good on her as they had, once, on her mother's body.

**Now Arni is a girl** in Queens.

Now she is in love with the boy who returns to his family from university, this once-unknown family that owns the grocery.

Now she is my mother.

When my father tells me stories of meeting my mother, he likes to linger on how passionate she was. It's more familiar to me than he realizes. I remember how much she was willing to do for the things she believed in, whether she was fifteen or fifty. She went from impulsive to steadfast, wise. It's how she grew up, the strength her mother had seen in her. The grocer's son, my-father-before-he-is-my-father, sees this in her, too.

And how lucky am I, to know what the memories look like on the other side. What it was like for Arni, this girl who felt such weight on her shoulders, who wanted to be deserving, to look at this man and see someone she can relax with. Someone with whom the weight doesn't even exist. Who likes it when she argues with uncles; who sneaks up to the building rooftop with her, where they sit under an industrial and starless sky of Queens. They clink imported bottles of Tusker together—and she wonders if this was all her sister had wanted, to feel so loved, so like Mumtaz—and she tells him the story of a dog that miraculously came back to life.

Sometimes she closes her eyes and sees through Vibha's, those evenings sitting in perfect and comfortable silence together. She feels Vibha paint, bestowing that love to her—understands what moved her, what Vibha had wanted for her. She aches at what her sister did not mean to sacrifice—looks around her, to this love and this life, and understands it for the gift it is.

Is this what it means for home to become a place she feels inside herself?

**And then Meenafai passes away.** "My last connection to everything I thought I was," Ma says over the phone. "I feel rootless."

Arni cries when she hears this, in the kitchen that sometimes feels claustrophobic, the way she turns around at the stove just to be face-to-face with the fridge. She twists the curly phone wire around her fingers, entangles her hands in the long-distance call. "Are you sure there is nowhere else you'd rather go?" she asks, hesitating before adding, "To London? Fiza?"

"I couldn't keep writing to her," Ma says. "I couldn't take care of Meenafai and your brother and the flat and the work and just . . . I couldn't spend my time wishing for something that wasn't going to come true."

Arni doesn't know what to say. Doesn't know how to fix the passage of time, the fear of never getting to love one person you have always loved.

"I painted it, too," Amla continues, her sobs echoing through the phone. "I painted one last good thing, and it never came true."

"I will apply for you today," Arni promises. "I will do everything I can to get you here and keep you happy."

"I'm not your responsibility. Anurag is here and he can take care of me. I know it's always tight for—"

"Family is all we have, Ma," she whispers, and it's the first time she voices this aloud, the removal of Anurag and Baba from her chosen history. Her alliance to the lineage, stated aloud. She'll keep repeating this phrase to her own daughter—to me—years and years later. "You are all I have."

Part Four

SPIRIT

I worried so much about making this history your burden to bear, too, that I tried to prepare for it. I rehearsed the thousands of ways I could try opening the conversation. I wanted to anticipate your responses—where you might doubt me. Where you might feel betrayed by me. Would you want more clarity here or specific details there? Some of this I got right; other questions I couldn't have imagined. Nothing is ever as simple in reality as it is in theory.

Back in the apartment, we both remove our shoes at the door. We move in parallel, our sweaters side by side on their hooks. The city lingers on me; I light one of our tabletop candles and breathe in its clean cotton scent.

"This is the last bit," I say, sitting down. I pat the seat next to me, and you follow suit.

"Where do we go, from your mother?" you ask.

"To me," I say, and I smile to make the moment feel lighter, but look how my eyes brim with tears. I cannot fool you.

"Hey," you say, and I shake my head.

"It's okay," I say. "I'm okay."

"I miss your mother, too," you say.

I know, Nadya. This type of grief, it was the reason for one of our first big fights—when your grandmother passed right after we got together. I knew mourning too well; I had experienced it in every possible variation in my memories. Your grief became a catalyst for my own—you hadn't known how I am constantly carrying grief in my memory—and I didn't know how to be there for you and still care for myself. I spent weeks on edge, unable to go to my studio, fearful of what I might do. When I meditated, I found myself returning over and again to wounds carried by others before me. You felt my agitation, chalked it up to the newness of the relationship, but the reality was I hadn't learned how to balance myself, and myself accompanied.

You asked me earlier if I would grieve these women once more if we had a child, if we sewed them onto the tapestry. Would I mourn as the lineage slipped from me, as I said goodbye to my mother for the last time?

I feel this loss prematurely. Even after my mother passed, I waited at the threshold, not yet ready to step through the door of my mother's memories. I grieved the version of her that I remembered, only wanting to visit her younger self.

But so recently, this changed. That's the last bit that you need to know.

"I know it was really sudden when I went home the other week," I say to you now.

"You never have to—"

"Still," I say. "There was something I needed to do. And I needed to be home to do it."

This is the part that makes the lineage a gift. Let me give these to you, the stories I've only just learned. It will make it easier, make it less impossible, for us to choose—together—where we go from here.

# NINETEEN

This is my share of the family history.

It was 2001, in the emergence of a Minneapolis summer, when my mother offered me a choice. "It is not a requirement," she said. "You are allowed to say no."

I was two months away from turning eighteen and going away to college. Dad was on a work trip, at a medical conference somewhere that is warm year-round, and Mom had asked for me to slow down this morning, to have chai and thepla with her before she went to the office for the afternoon. I remember trying to unscrew the lid of a glass athanu jar, handing it off to her when I couldn't.

"I want to give you time to think about it," she said. She wanted me to know, needed me to know, that I had a lifetime to say yes to a gift like this one.

I took those two months, and then I took more. I took the whole year—I left for college in St. Louis and watched the towers fall a month later, my parents sending me concise and detached email updates with the statuses of their New York friends, aunties and uncles

I'd met once or twice before. And then, at the end of winter, I watched the reports of pogroms in Gujarat on the common room television. For two months during the following summer, one other student and I returned to the country I had only visited twice before to help track the names of the living (thousands of Muslim Gujaratis, made homeless and dispossessed by Hindu Gujaratis) and the dead (hundreds of Muslim Gujaratis, massacred by Hindu Gujaratis) and the conditions of one of many makeshift camps, this one located in a graveyard outside of Ahmedabad. When I returned at the end of that summer, when my mother picked me up at the Minneapolis airport after twenty-eight hours of travel, I told her my answer was yes.

It was naive, the how and why of this decision. What did I know, what did I think I could do, by saying yes? Did I want a piece of this history or a chance at making the world a better place? The Jesuits at my university, they said things like *Ite inflammate omnia*. Go forth and set the world on fire. At nineteen it sounded powerful.

But after I understood what lived in the lineage's memory, I tempered those expectations. Understood the arrogance of that perspective—of thinking you always had the answer, were the right person to burn it all down.

Today—today, all I want is to live a contained and contented life. To reckon with myself first. If I play with heat, it will only be to build a world warm and filled with light. Not to salt any earth. Not to set everything ablaze.

**You know so much** of what came next: I moved to Brooklyn after college for a human resources job that left me enough time to work at a gallery on the weekends. I got to use the studio in the back after hours but still had to pay for my own materials. This meant I stuck with clay more often than not, the tools for welding out of my budget. The few friends who made the move from St. Louis to New York were all in investment banking, and I was reassured in my decision by their long hours, their booked weekends—a reminder that it was acceptable to pour my heart into a second job on the weekends because who else would I spend my time with, anyway?

I tried for years to establish a version of myself separate from the tapestry—I set up my boundaries: *I do not need to live in my mother's memories while I still have her in the present. I do not want to spend more time in the past than I spend living my own life. I do not want to be so brash as to think I can change what I see before my eyes.*

I told her these rules, and I think she might have felt relieved, knowing that her life wasn't going to be relived or questioned while she still had to answer for it.

My sheer luck to have met you then, Nadya, after I'd had time to settle into the city. Had time to understand the weight of this lineage.

Do you remember the first time I brought you home? December in New York was cold, but nowhere near as brutal as Minnesota. I warned you ahead of time—took you thrifting for a warmer coat than the sleek one you wore in all types of weather—and still, as we stood on my parents' doorstep, your fingers were numb. "How will I eat?" you asked me, laughing. "What if my hands don't work?"

I think I told you to worry more about shaking my father's hand, never mind eating, and you stuffed your hands so abruptly and deeply into your pockets that the threads threatened to rip. "I'm going to do this right," you insisted. "I'm going to impress your parents."

The night was perfect. Cozy and warm, the way Christmas Eve should feel. My mother asked you about law school, and my father made jokes about us reliving their young days in the city. You went to bed early, and Dad did, too. Mom and I sat in the kitchen after the dishes were done. The tapestry was never off-limits for us to talk about when we were alone, and sometimes I'd come home from college with a memory or two in a dream journal, memories that didn't belong to me but must've belonged to someone long ago. If Mom knew the same one, we'd talk about it, the way you might talk about a good book or a good wine—the different details you notice, your favorite moments.

I think Mom was waiting for me to bring up a memory that Christmas, but I didn't have one, and so we sat in the silence for a half hour. She finally broke, and asked, "Have you told Nadya anything? About the lineage?"

I shook my head no, and Mom nodded.

"Okay," she said. "If you—*when* you—want to, let's talk about it together."

"It feels a little bit like you asking me if we're going to get married," I said, laughing, and Mom smiled. "I'll let you know when— *if*—I start feeling that way. I think we have plenty of time."

"It's not a bad conversation." She laughed, too. "There are some histories I want to talk about with you."

I'd thought then that she was talking about stories where women confided their secrets only to have it blow up in their faces. Unforeseen retaliation. I don't think she meant this now.

Mom loved you. I think she knew that night that I loved you, too. She always had a way about these things—could predict which of my friends' relationships would last and which wouldn't. Which of mine would, too. I think she knew what two people who really, truly loved each other looked like, and she knew that they could look like us.

Maybe that's why I've been thinking so much about having this conversation with you, Nadya. I told her when I knew I wanted to marry you, winters later; I told her it was a while away but that it was there, in my clutches. It felt so nearly tangible. We should've talked about the tapestry then, she and I—we should've talked about whether she thought it would be a good idea to tell you or not—but

I had the impression that this was a good night, one she'd dreamt about as a mother, and that neither of us wanted to ruin it with something serious. We sat on the stools at the kitchen counter like we usually did, and Mom raised her glass of whiskey and I raised mine, and she called me jaan, and we smiled giddily into our drinks.

And so we never talked about it. Whatever Mom had wanted to say, she didn't. And then she was in the accident, and she never said anything to me again.

Now here we are, years after that night at the kitchen counter, one year after she passed.

For so long, I hadn't been sure of what to do. But after dinner with your parents, I was certain: I needed to tell you about this lineage and its weight. I just couldn't do it without my mother. I wanted to smell her perfume and peek inside the drawers of that old art desk; I wanted to lay claim to her paints and her brushes even if I'd never use them. I needed to open that door to my mother's memories that I had long kept closed, to be knee-deep in her life before I told you this history.

Which meant I had to go home. I told you a truth, but not the whole one—that Dad had gathered Mom's things into boxes for me, and if I didn't go through them now I never would. You understood: I'd been frozen in grief for a year; of course I hadn't mustered the courage to return after the funeral.

But the whole truth was that I was finally ready to close my eyes and find her in my memory. To hold her close and know, truly, that she believed I would do my best with the weight she'd given me.

**When I got there last week,** I was startled by how large the house felt. My body, acclimated to our Brooklyn apartment, had to recalibrate to Midwestern suburbia. I walked around the house's perimeter, the iced-over dirt beds where Dad plants in the springtime. I savored the space, the quiet. The memories.

A note inside the screen door from Dad: *In Cleveland for a conference. I stocked the fridge. See you on Tuesday!*

The mail had started to pile up on itself inside the sunroom door, the garden rendered ugly by weeds and frozen sunflower stalks. Even when the taxi sidled up to the curb, the driver turned to me sympathetically. "That snow'll get you," he said before remote-opening the hatchback. "Gotta take care of it."

I wanted to snap at him, something about insensitivity and a situation he could hardly understand—how my father barely managed to hold himself together, how I had avoided returning for months, scared of confronting my mom's life and my dad's sadness alone—but I didn't. I didn't. Instead I smiled and the driver waved goodbye, and I lugged my suitcase up the icy walkway and unlocked the door.

Inside, surrounded by a dozen boxes in the living room, I saw the consequences of my delay. Each box was stuffed with items I might find meaningful, might want to take with me back to New York. My one local cousin, who'd help out Dad, had held on to these even when I told her that I didn't need most of my mother's things.

"You'll want these," she'd promised, the sounds of duct tape and folding cardboard fuzzing her words. "I would want—"

"I have a lot of memories of my mother," I'd said, twisting the ring on my index finger—a gift from my mother, that ring—and the other two on my right hand and the two pairs of earrings I was wearing, all from my mother. The only thing on me that wasn't hers is our wedding ring.

"I know you said I should just ship you her saris and jewelry and . . . But, Ayukta, there's a lot of stuff she held on to. Your old schoolwork, her old blueprints. All these photo albums. I'm not sure I should do anything before you go through them."

336

"Only a few, then, okay? One or two."

"Sure, of course," she'd said, and I thought I could hear her start counting. "Not a lot—"

"Three maximum, okay?"

"—enough to be certain you won't have regrets. Great. I'll pack them up tight so you can take your time. I'll let you go so I can get back to this, then, okay? Talk soon, Ayukta."

And so there were a dozen boxes, each slightly larger than I'd imagined. I angled the house key against the first box's taped edges and ripped it along its length.

Those first days passed all the same: I borrowed an air mattress from the neighbor and placed it in my childhood bedroom because I couldn't imagine sleeping anywhere else. I tried to stay up until fatigue set in, but each night I ended up taking half an edible, sleeping only once the stress left my neck and shoulders. In the mornings, I procrastinated by walking over to the corner coffee shop and slowly sipping my latte by the hearth, students already gabbing at one another over textbooks and novels. Only after a few laps around the neighborhood would I resign myself to that day's box.

A box a day is not grueling, not really, except that I could feel my chest caving in long before the sun set. When I stretched, I could feel my ribs expand, heart opening after a day of holding and hunching.

I found the letter from Rohini Thakur on my third day at the house.

The box that day seemed, at first, to be only my mother's architecture textbooks, with her familiar handwriting in the margins. I flipped through them lightly, touching the pages where she'd clearly answered one of the problem sets incorrectly and had to redo her answers. I don't remember my mother as someone frustrated or fazed in my own life, but the rigor of those scratch-outs made her feel familiar in a different way. The Arni I knew from memories.

The yellowing envelope fell out of one of the textbooks, or perhaps it was pressed between two books and I hadn't noticed. Maybe it was a bookmark. For a while I placed it to the side, recognizing its foreign return address as something distinctly nonacademic, nonarchitectural. I waited to open it, assuming there might be another box filled with other yellowing envelopes from Rohini Thakur, that this one had accidentally ended up among notebooks and protractors.

But there were no other envelopes—not like this one—in the rest of the box, nor in the next one, nor the one after that. The fifth day came to an end and I poured the bottom third of a bottle of wine into a mug. I closed my eyes; I took a sip. I slid the letter out of the envelope.

*22 August 1982*

*Dearest Arni:*

*When my mother passed, I'd written a lot of her community to let them know. One of them was a friend of your mother's—Fiza. When she wrote back, I found that her visa to the US was approved.*

*Amla is in the US with you now, correct? This is why I write.*

*Fiza is going to New York to live with her brother. (How small is the world, to be reduced to so many people we love in one space?) He's her only family. She has no one in London holding her down, so she's leaving. Simple choices.*

*I wrote the address down on a clean chit you can hand to a driver. Would you make sure she is really there? Would you find out if it makes any sense at all for them to meet? Amu should know, if the answer is yes.*

> *Much love, my child. Visit soon.*
> *Rohini masi*

Fiza. Fiza.

I knew this name—*why did I know this name*—and as I closed my eyes, tapping my nail in a quick staccato against the tabletop, I reached out to the lineage. Tendrils of memory:

—here, my grandmother Amla as a child, Fiza her best friend;

—here, the night that Amla's father is killed, the company of Meenafai and her eldest daughter, Rohini;

—here, Amla and Fiza, that stolen moment in the London Airport bathroom;

—here, my aunt Vibha looking up at the portraits her mother hung along the hallway of their flat, Fiza Qureshi's face in watercolor;

—here, Amla writing to Fiza about the death of her daughter;

—here, the letterbox: the beauty of an object like that, a box my grandmother received from her mother, a box that used to hold watercolors;

—and the moment where all the memories I have watched throughout my life end, the moment when my mother becomes my mother and the rest of what I know is only what she has told me.

But then, didn't the name feel familiar in my own skin, too? Memory like a haze. There was a way to find out if—how Fiza mattered, after the year I was born. The door, the threshold, was right there.

I snapped open my eyes, breath fast, palms sweaty. While my mother had been alive, I had drawn a line there; since her passing, I'd been too overwhelmed to cross it. Here it was, finally—the right time, and that door, ready to open beyond me.

# TWENTY

And still I couldn't. Not yet.

I waited, wanting to talk to Dad when he returned last Tuesday but waffling over how much to ask. Did he know Fiza? Was hers simply one of a thousand names that had echoed through the house during my mother's life—a casual reference to an ancestor, an auntie, a family friend—an insignificant, likely faceless name? And if so, would he wonder why it mattered so much to me if he knew her?

"Sleep okay?" he asked, pouring chai. He scooted the sugar bowl toward me cautiously. "I've been working on it, but it's not that great still."

"It smells wonderful." I heaped sugar into the cup, the chai's darker color betraying how overboiled it was. "Like Mom made it."

He scoffed. "Don't lie. She's laughing at it right now, I'm sure." He poured the tea into a saucer, and I shook my head in refusal when he offered one to me. "You haven't been back since . . ."

I nodded. "I'm sorry it took so long."

"Don't be." I watched him balance the chai-filled saucer, remembered being awed by this as a child. "There's no right way."

I cleared my throat. "I've been going through the boxes."

"Find anything you want to keep?"

"Actually, yes," I said, taking the creased envelope from my back pocket. "I found this letter."

Dad smiled. "She used birthday cards like bookmarks, your mother."

"It mentions someone named Fiza. Do you know who that is?" I watched his eyes carefully, to see if this was a person he knew himself or if he had heard my mother's stories. If my mother had ever shared my grandmother's love with him.

His eyes lit, recognition clear in his expression. "You don't remember Fiza?"

There it was again, that feeling in my gut that I couldn't only know Fiza from my grandmother's memories. Where did my ancestors' knowledge end, and mine begin?

I paused, tried to remember all of the older aunties who had rotated through our doors during my childhood, but their names and faces had blended together long ago. Fiza could have been any of them.

I went with the safest answer, the one that would protect this inheritance of mine. "Should I?"

Dad crossed the kitchen to the living room, and I heard the sound of books thudding on the floor. When he returned, he had three photo albums in his arms.

"Were these in the boxes?" I recognized them, worn navy cloth on their covers, labeled in my mother's neat handwriting on the back.

"No, these have always been for keeping." He checked the dates on their back covers, flipping open the most recent album. It begins in 1982—the year of the letter, and the year before I was born.

I'd seen this album tens of times at least, always during the holidays when family friends visited. When you visited, Nadya, I'm certain Dad pulled out this same album and had you cooing over my baby photos. We don't have a lot of stamina for home videos, the shaky cameras and strange audio, but we love a photo of a baby in this family.

He flipped through the pages, scouring for some photo in particular, mumbling to himself. Finally, he stopped. "There," he says. "Fiza."

I'd seen this photo before, all those tens of times: a much older woman, a grandmother, holding my toddler self in her lap. It's from a few years after the ones with my own grandmother holding me have stopped—that is, a few years after Amla passed. This woman is dressed smartly, her hair pulled back into a bun, her wrinkled face grinning at the camera. She looks fragile.

"I always thought this was a random auntie," I said softly, more to myself than to Dad. "I don't even think I ever asked."

"Your mother never talked to you about this?" He looked confused. "I would've thought when you—"

"I think she was saving some talks," I said, and I wonder about that moment when she asked me to tell her if I was going to share the lineage with you. Maybe she thought I already knew her memories, believed that I'd already visited them—that I'd broken that rule, of not visiting her life after my birth.

Dad moved to one of the other albums, this one dated five years earlier. I've seen it: my parents taking silly photos at Coney Island during their early dating years. He flipped to the final third of the book, after some blank pages. "There's more?"

He nodded and turned the album so that it faced me. "I don't know very much about what it was like," he said, "but you could go through these."

I stuck Rohini's letter into the album to mark the page and closed

343

it. "Soon," I told him. I couldn't put the puzzle pieces together while he was watching. "I think I'm going to shower before I go through this and those boxes."

"On your time," he said, shrugging. "I'll be in and out, visiting listings."

I nodded, and when I was upstairs with the water running, the bathroom turning into a sauna from the heat, I knew I could wait no longer. I felt the weight of my mother's life, her secrets, pressing against that door I never opened. I closed my eyes and gave in.

**If you were to ask me** to describe how it feels, I would only be able to describe beach waves. Think of the moment your feet make contact with water, the way the sand gives beneath your soles, coaxing you in further. The repetitive nature of this, of sinking into sand because of rushing water—and then, suddenly, you're farther into the water than you'd thought you were, partially because you've been sinking and partially because of desire. I want to know more, and suddenly I'm bouncing off the beach floor. The water is rushing over me, embraces me. It is not just that I want it—it wants me, too.

Maybe the right description is in the word *drown*, or *devour*. Maybe, *release*.

I reached one hand out to my mother's memories. I asked; I desired. The lineage took my arms, leading me farther into the water.

It is 1982, the year before I am born. The year of Rohini's letter. I see my mother—I am my mother—looking down at that chit of paper outside of a gray New York apartment. She buzzes up, asking for a name and giving her own. One steel door, and then the wooden one, and then up those winding and endless walk-up stairs.

The door is open when she gets to apartment 422. It is Fiza's brother who meets her at the door; I know this because my mother knows this, because she has heard his name before, in a memory or a childhood story. She tries to explain who she is, but before she can spit out a sentence that does any real explaining, Fiza comes through the bedroom doorway in a rush and just takes my mother's face in her palms—cupping her cheeks and surveying her features.

"You really are your mother's daughter," she says.

"How did you know to come here?" Fiza's brother asks, and it only makes sense for him to be suspicious. My mother feels this, the weight of having to explain this exactly right.

"I got a letter from Meenafai's daughter Rohini," my mother says. "I heard your visa was approved. I wanted—I wanted to check. To make sure." My mother, my age at this time, falters. She inhales slowly. When she speaks, the words tumble out. "My mother, Amla, is here in the city with me. I'd applied for her while I was studying. We left my father in Gujarat. She is alone here, too."

Now I watch Fiza, the way she freezes, and then it's like her body collapses on itself. "Oh," she says. "*Oh.*" And her brother holds her up, and my mother hugs her, and I marvel at the significance of this day I never knew existed—this memory so long before me.


In Dad's office, where he's already packed most of his things into boxes, is a map I've always loved. You've seen it. It fills the majority of the wall, at least six feet wide, thumbtacked into the plaster because he never cared to pay for a nice frame. I traced the journeys my blood has carried with my fingernail: Gujarat to Sindh, Sindh back to Gujarat. To New York, to Minnesota, to New York again. Sometimes I ask myself what the cyclical nature is supposed to signify, if anything. When I combine it with the ancestry, with the art, am I supposed to unearth some particular meaning?

The stairs creaked and Dad lumbered into the room. "I found

a decent one," he said, holding up his phone. "You want to take a look?"

I scrolled through the page absently. "Are you sure you want to leave this house?"

"We got bills to pay, jaan," he said, sitting heavily in the swivel chair. "I don't need this much space on my own. I don't want to *heat* this much space, you know?"

I handed the phone back. "It looks fine," I said. "Buy a futon so I can visit."

"Did you go through the album?"

"A little bit." My eyes focused on the italicized Arabian Sea label on the map. "When did Fiza die?"

"A few years after your grandmother." He cleared his throat. "She was a part of our family, too, you know?"

"I guess I don't," I said.

"It's hard when all you have are childhood memories," he said, patting me on the shoulder. "You were so young you'd hardly remember, but seeing you with the two of them when you were born—your mother was so happy."

I watched his back retreat out the office door and around the corner. I wondered, what would my mother have told me, if only she'd had the time?

**The next morning,** I trimmed the evergreen shrubs that line our front porch. My shoulders, my neck, ached as I cleared the snow from every paved surface outside the house. I even salted down the sidewalk and the stairs leading up to the deck, my arms heaving. The bag was heavier than I thought it would be, but I refused to use the dolly Dad pointed me toward. I had been away for so long; had left him here, alone with his grief. I wanted to punish myself, the way my sculptures feel punishing, made with the physical labor it takes to bend and heat and twist metal.

Dad made me chai twice before he left the house for another condo viewing. I sipped from the cup he'd left on the sunroom ledge as the car backed out of the driveway, one hand raised in a goodbye. What would it be like for him to be alone? Maybe he'd call me all the time. Maybe he'd get a dog.

I soaked my body in a bath filled with Mom's fragrant Epsom salts—eucalyptus, jasmine, and rose. The water was scalding, and also slowly draining; every few minutes I turned the water back on with a push of my big toe to refill what had disappeared. I kept my eyes closed and slowed my breath, resting one hand on my stomach and the other on my heart.

I was carried.

The water lapped at the tub's edges. When I listened to it, I wondered if I was imagining something else—being a child, bathing in this same tub. My grandmother would visit us, flying in from New York for a week or two at a time. She insisted that her life in the city was good, that she wasn't ready to move somewhere even colder. She was happy we had a place in a suburb, yes, but moving from New York to Minneapolis reminded her of what it had been like to leave Karachi—and now Karachi was nothing like she remembered, no, a whole different place that felt foreign when Fiza described it. She wouldn't do this transition until she was old, she said. Until she planned to never return to New York, so she knew she'd never see it changed. She wasn't ready to leave until really called, as though to a grave.

She must have mentioned Fiza in front of me, and sometimes Fiza must have been there, too. They lived together, they flew together, they spent so much of their time in our house together, even. They told me tales, together, building fictions by trading who had control over the story's next sentence.

Do I remember this, or does it come from my mother? I think of what you and I have, Nadya, and I think of my mother protecting Amla's memories—why? Because she knew I'd inherit them one day, or because there's something so amazing in a love like this that it can't be told, only lived?

My mother—this gift—shows me the answer. Keeping this secret is the only way she can think of to make up for reading Amla's and Fiza's letters all those years ago in Porbandar. This is the regret she has, not giving her own mother some privacy. It's only when I am grown that she realizes her mistake, that she's kept something I've longed for, this queer ancestor, from me.

I wonder how my mother might have described their story to me. How do you do this love justice, how do you protect and also share something that's not yours to describe? Fiza, whose love connected my mother to her mother, who connected Amla to Karachi. Fiza, whose love collapses time.

I wrapped myself in a towel and headed straight to the albums then, all still stacked neatly next to the air mattress. My hair was damp—the water uncomfortable on my back—but I didn't pause to tie it up. I needed to know.

I flipped through the album Dad had pointed at, past the photos of his and Mom's early dating and even past their wedding. When I saw the blank pages, I thought, *There is no turning back from here.* I took a deep breath, and then I turned the page.

*Amla and Fiza, mid-embrace, in Fiza's brother's apartment.*

I hear their laughter and close my eyes. When they see each other, the sounds are guttural, instinctual. Amla stands in the doorway, unable to walk farther in. Fiza has had all the time since Arni was there to prepare for this moment, and she walks directly toward Amla. She takes Amla's hands in hers. "Jaan," she says, laughing, "you are here." She touches Amla's hair. "Fully silver."

"You are real?" Amla asks, throat catching. She lifts a finger and touches Fiza's cheeks, the mole she has known since they were just girls. She looks at Arni. "This is real?"

Arni nods, and Amla looks back at Fiza, and they embrace, so comfortable in each other's arms it is impossible to know how much time passes in that clutched hold. "You are exactly as I imagined," Amla whispers to Fiza. "I do not know that I deserve this." Arni pretends she doesn't hear her mother say this, doesn't hear the loss in those words.

"I had never imagined," Fiza says, and she holds Amla at arm's length and looks at her brother and Arni. "I had never thought this could happen."

*Amla and Fiza, holding the keys to their apartment.*

They stand on either side of the door, Arni behind the camera. "Say cheese!" she directs, and they do.

The apartment is nothing fancy, nothing more than a kitchen and a bathroom and a living room that doubles as the bedroom. They are renting this apartment as roommates. It smells a little like nicotine.

"Personality," Amla calls it. "Like Meenafai's around."

Fiza points along the walls, naming where they could put the sofa, the dining table, the desk for Amla to paint at. "I don't do that much anymore," Amla says at first, but Fiza shushes her.

"I would never say never," Fiza says.

Whenever Arni visits, the apartment seems to bloom with more foliage: a pothos plant here, its vines extending across the room; the curry plant's aroma lingering in the air even when Amla isn't using it to cook. Arni and her husband send them money, and the two of them find work that sustains them. Arni takes photos of them lounging and living in their tiny apartment: Amla painting a commissioned piece for someone in the community, Fiza coming home with halal leftovers from leading a women's group in a basement prayer space. The two of them in their castle.

*These are lives*, I thought, *full lives.*

*Amla and Fiza at Disney World, soft-serve ice cream cones in their hands.*

They travel more than I could have imagined; Arni gifts them her camera. They rent a car and drive to Florida from New York—Arni has been teaching them, through day trips out to New Jersey—and show her the photos they took along the way. The monuments from a distance in DC, an avenue of oak trees in Georgia. The two of them with Mickey Mouse hats and silly grins on their faces.

"Where next?" Arni asks, and Fiza and Amla look at each other for the answer.

"Maybe San Francisco," Amla offers, and Fiza laughs. "For *Full House.*"

The photos always make it into the album. Through Arni, I can sit with them and see how they smile after a trip, sitting down at the coffee table to go through the photos systematically, a story for each one. It is good for them that the memory is no longer with Amla, that they get to have their secrets.

*Amla and Fiza in San Francisco.*

*Amla and Fiza in Santa Barbara.*

*Amla and Fiza in Boulder.*

*Amla and Fiza in Sedona.*

*Amla and Fiza, visiting Minneapolis after my parents move there, every chance they can get.*

**The rest is a story** I've told you before, Nadya, because I knew it from family facts. Amla's heart attack when I was barely a toddler.

Fiza must have visited my family for a few more years—the photos show it—but then she was gone, too. I was young enough that I don't remember it very well at all. Today, more than thirty years later, I have barely anything from those years in my own memory to hold on to—just an undirected grief, the feeling of some inevitable loss I can't pin to one person.

You know how I am about mortality. I fear losing my dad, more than I feared losing my mother. And I am always fearing the day you and I are old, when we might lose each other. I won't be able to visit you in my memory, the way I can with Chandini, with Amla, with my mother. I understand the desperation Amla felt when she tried as a child to sew Fiza onto the tapestry; the devastation when she failed.

I will lose you when I lose you. It terrifies me.

"What were they like?" I asked Dad, placing the album in front of him.

"You ever seen two people who deserve so much to be together?"

"You and Mom," I said, and he smiled.

"Thank you." The chair creaked as he adjusted his weight. "And still, nothing like that, though."

I felt the tears behind my eyes, and Dad must have seen them because he opened his arms to me and I crumpled in them. "I miss them," I said, and maybe he understood and maybe he didn't. "I miss Mom."

"Me, too," he said, taking me by the shoulders. "But in your heart, always."

I inhaled slowly. "I wish I could know I'm doing right by her. By them."

"You are, you are. How could you not be?" he said, and when I hugged him again, I pretended it was Mom in my arms, that it was my grandmother and Fiza and Chandini and every mother I have ever wished for.

. . .

When I landed in New York yesterday, the boxes already shipped and en route here, I detoured before I came home. I stopped by my studio. You weren't home yet, and I knew you wouldn't be for a few more hours. I needed some time alone; there was a sketch I needed to get out of my head.

Do you remember my last show, at that small Bushwick gallery? It was right after Mom passed. I was obsessed with her hands, the way mine were starting to look like hers. I tried to get the bulge of her veins just right, tried to remember the length of her nails. I modeled so many hands in clay, avoiding colored glazes, but ended up carving most out of wood. I think I was convinced that pulling from nature could somehow breathe my mother's hands back to life.

The final products always seemed off.

During that phase (*the hands phase*, you called it), there were times when I looked in the mirror and wasn't sure I looked like myself anymore. I told you this once, Nadya, when we were on the fire escape with wine-filled ceramic mugs, those ones I'd made while teaching a university class, and you looked at me sort of oddly. You said, "Who do you think you're becoming?" I shrugged and looked up at that starless sky and wondered the same thing.

I could've told you everything that night. I should have. I kept choosing to keep you out.

But yesterday, time blended into itself. I sketched page after page at my table, taping some together so I could imagine the size of the final sculpture. How to get Amla's cheek perfectly, Fiza's clavicle and neck. Here, my mother's fingers curling over a Polaroid camera's metal edges, witnessing. I drew each detail over and over. I wanted them done right.

I don't know how to measure my mother's life, or her mother's—I don't know how to measure my own—but I know I've been scared for so long of the memories and the power and the art. How do *you* measure our life together, Nadya? I thought I was uncertain about a child, but I think what I was worried about was something completely different. *Legacy.* Something about seeing the conclusion to my grandmother's story—something about seeing the healing in those memories—helped me understand how we've survived for so long. How we've been carried.

I think I knew then what I'd say to you. How I imagined saying it to you, in bed, in our home.

Here we are, all caught up in time. Back in our bed. I am gripping your hands, the veins in my arms ridging up with tension.

You lean over and you kiss my nose. "Ayukta," you say, and then you kiss my forehead, my closed eyes. "Ayukta."

I didn't know I was crying, but look, here are my tears on your shirt. My breath, stuck in my throat. You press me to your chest and I feel my cheeks, your cotton tank top, dampen.

"I didn't know how much it would mean," I say, muffled, and I can feel you nod in my hair. "I think that's what my mom wanted to tell me."

"I wish I could've known them," you whisper.

"I wish you could have, too."

My whole body rises and falls with your every inhale and exhale, and gradually my breath slows to match yours. I hold your ribs beneath my fingers as I settle back to equilibrium.

Outside, it is quieter than Bed-Stuy normally feels, but here we are enveloped in golden light. I feel certain that I am just me in this moment, here with you.

"What are you thinking?" you ask.

Oh, Nadya. I take a moment to think before I answer. "Does it scare you?" I ask, leaning up with my elbows on either side of your body so that I can see your eyes when you answer.

This decision is yours, where we go from here. I don't trust myself to have that power, Nadya. There is an ancestral call to continue this lineage, to keep the memories of all these women alive. How would I ever know, whether it was my decision or that of those who accompany me? The weight of this explanation must sit with you.

We lie like this for ten, fifteen seconds under the comforter. I try to stay still. I need you to tell me, after all these hours of confession, of outpouring. It is your turn now.

You finally speak. "I do not need you to be small," you say. "Whether it is you, or you accompanied, I choose this every time."

You intertwine our fingers slowly and I cradle against your body. This is the gift you give me: to never wonder where home is.


**At the studio,** I begin a new project.

My day starts with wedging clay, still moist within its plastic. I build my rhythm slowly, rocking forward and backward between my feet, my right placed ahead of my left. The heaving push-pull of flattening the clay beneath my lower palms, and then folding it back down over itself. I don't have to glance away when I reach for the bench scraper, repositioning the clay. My vision goes soft. I listen only for the popping of air bubbles and the floor groaning beneath my shifting weight.

Inhale, push-fold. Exhale, push-fold. Over and over again, this motion my muscles find deeply familiar.

The new sketches line the wooden table I use for planning, but I don't study them as I turn to a block of perfect earthenware clay sitting on my turntable. Here, I roughly carve out the shape of a face. It will take me hours, days, and I don't know if I'll be happy with it at the first go. But I close my eyes and keep breathing in that slow, consistent tempo.

I address the lineage in my bones: *I want to make art that is true but doesn't change anything. Nothing new—just history.*

No words appear in that blankness that feels outside of myself, but a calm settles. I cannot change anything if I sculpt women who are long dead. In that quiet, the lineage offers me memories of touch, of fingers mapping hills and valleys of bodies. There are ancestors who know these faces intimately, who have memorized gauntness and puffiness and softness and lines with the eyes of artists. I do not have to see them to be able to sculpt Amla and Fiza, Chandini and Anurag, a hundred prior ancestors and the people they loved, perfectly.

In time, I will adjust the plastic cover over this clay until it becomes less moist but still malleable, the face roughly sculpted but not yet refined. I will begin to hollow this first sculpture out from the bottom, and then ensure every detail on the face feels right. Will I make one of these, or two, or ten?

The evening sun casts shadows along the studio floor and I imagine hopping over and darting around them like a child in the morning in Porbandar. I feel them in the room with me, my ghosts. My many mothers.

Will I sculpt your face, Nadya? I know its every contour beneath my hands. I would recognize you without needing to study you.

I promise myself that I will wait until we are past all this decision-making. I want to sculpt your face without changing a single part of our lives. I want to look back on our life one day and say, *This was all inevitable*, and know it was never forced.

You knock at the open studio door. "Still on for dinner at home?" you ask, leaning against the frame.

I nod at you, wiping my hands on my apron. "I'll get cleaned up."

You wander over to the table of sketches, your hands hovering above them, tracing silhouettes in the air. You don't say anything, and I don't either. I repack the clay, sealing it; I wash with steaming, soapy water up to my elbows. You hand me the lotion, and even though we are quiet until the studio door locks behind us, it feels comfortable.

"I love it," you finally say as we emerge into the golden hour.

I pull my beanie and mittens on before glancing at you. "You do?"

When you smile, I do, too. "I'm excited to meet them," you say, and we turn the corner toward home.

# ACKNOWLEDGMENTS

How strange to write these notes. How easy to be grateful.

Thank you, Stephanie Delman and Danya Kukafka, for your care and belief in this story, in Ayukta and Nadya, in Amla and Fiza. I am so lucky to have champions like you. Thank you to Khalid McCalla, Allison Malecha, and the incredible people who make Trellis Literary Management what it is.

Thank you, Nidhi Pugalia, for seeing the possibilities and falling as deeply into this world as anyone could. I am so thankful for what we have done, here, together. This love extends to Kristina Fazzalaro and Magdalena Deniz, Raven Ross, Ryan Boyle and Sara Carminati, Dave Litman, Meighan Cavanaugh, and Kathryn Ricigliano. Thank you as well to the larger Viking team: Brian Tart, Andrea Schulz, Kate Stark, Rebecca Marsh, Lindsay Prevette, and Tricia Conley and Diandra Alvarado.

Thank you to the advisers and mentors who helped me become a writer who could tell this story in the way I hoped to. Sugi Ganeshananthan, you've shaped me into a better writer, student, teacher, reader, organizer; sharing space with you has been a gift. Richa Nagar, thank you for your close reads and thoughtful questions, and especially your insight into the dynamics of this history and these politics. Thank you, Julie Schumacher and Megan Giddings, for workshopping versions of this novel with so much care. Thank you, Douglas Kearney, for your endless advice and your reminders to write what I felt compelled to.

Thank you to my fiction cohort—Sruthi Narayanan, Tim Reynolds, Julian Robles—and the MFA community at Minnesota.

Thank you, David Ebenbach and Norma Tilden, for giving me reasons to believe in my own writing and letting me into workshops I had no business being in.

Thank you to my family, for letting me mine their brains and our stories as I built this world. Your love and support has always meant the world to me. Thank you, ancestors. Thank you, all who came before me.

To Maya, the type of first reader I don't know I deserve: Thank you for your dining table and endless coffee, for knowing when I need my hand held and when I need a deadline. I am forever grateful for your collaboration and love.

To Kabir: it is a strange thing to be witnessed in this practice; thank you for never making me feel the pressure of this process, for the details of shared life that sustained days of writing, and especially for the happy hour where I found this book's final chapter.

To my friends, my community, my loves: How could I have done this without you? Thank you. Thank you. Thank you.